A Long and Lonely Road

KATIE FLYNN

arrow books

Published by Arrow Books in 2004

17

First published in the United Kingdom in 2004 by William Heinemann

Arrow Books

The Random House Group Limited
20 Vauxhall Bridge Road, London, SW1V 2SA

www.randomhouse.co.uk

Addresses for companies within The Random House Group Limited can be found at: www.randomhouse.co.uk/offices.htm

The Random House Group Limited Reg. No. 954009

A CIP catalogue record for this book is available from the British Library

Typeset by Palimpsest Book Production Limited, Polmont, Stirlingshire

Penguin Random House is committed to a sustainable future for our business, our readers and our planet. This book is made from Forest Stewardship Council® certified paper.

Printed and bound in Great Britain by Clays Ltd, Elcograf S.p.A.

For Dorothy Nelson, of Appley Bridge, whose story of the bombing of Liverpool on the worst night of the Blitz I have shamelessly borrowed. Thank you Dorothy!

Acknowledgements

Grateful thanks go, as they have gone so many times, to Alan Hague, a stalwart supporter of the Flixton Aviation Museum, whose knowledge of Norfolk and Suffolk airfields, and the planes that flew from them, is truly unparalleled.

Thanks go also to Graham Jones of Rhosddu, Wrexham, who shared his knowledge of life – and death – in submarines and to Flt Lt John Taylor of Rhuddlan, who lent me a rare book on Liverpool during the war which had not previously come my way.

And then there is Gwyn Thomas of the Suffolk Records Office, who set us on the track of a hurricane which caused extensive damage in 1943. And thank you Gwilym Williams of Wrexham, for straightening me out on the Welsh language and correcting my spelling.

And last but not least, grateful thanks to Joy Thomas of The Heritage Museum in Wrexham, who worked extremely hard to track down the evacuation of Liverpool children to the small town of Ruthin during the war.

Chapter One
1938

'Petal! What the devil are you doing? Oh, if our mam saw you now, she'd give you such a wallop! Come on out of it this minute, d'you hear me?'

Four-year-old Petal twisted round to look up into her elder sister's face. She tried to move and when this proved impossible, she gave Daisy a sweet smile but remained where she was, crouched on the dirty paving stones with one arm thrust as far as she could get it between the iron bars of the drainage grating. 'I'm stuck,' she said. 'Me cherry wob bounced out of the downpipe and went straight into the drain. I could see it so I put me hand in to gerrit back, only – only it were further off than I thought an' now I can't pull me arm out, though I've tried ever so hard, honest to God I have.'

Daisy gazed despairingly down at her small sister. Petal had soft fair curls, big blue eyes and an enchanting smile, yet she was always in trouble. Often she got away with it because grown-ups could not believe that such an angelic-looking child could be as naughty as Petal was. They thought it far likelier that Daisy, who had straight brown hair and a thin, intelligent face, would be the one who thought up all the mischief. But now Petal's enormous blue eyes were beginning to brim with tears; it was clear that in her imagination she was never going to escape and would be in the most awful trouble.

Daisy sighed, and had crouched on the paving stones

to examine her sister's plight more closely when a shadow loomed over her and a voice spoke in her ear.

'What's the little tyke done this time, then? Gawd, Daisy, when I thinks how your mam sends you out each mornin', clean as a whistle an' fine as fivepence, then how your kid ends up the way she does . . . well, it's downright strange, that's wharrit is.'

Daisy turned round and eyed the speaker indignantly. It was Nicky Bostock, who lived two doors away at No. 11, Bernard Terrace, and how he dared criticise anyone else for being dirty she could not imagine, for Nicky was filthy, from the top of his dusty head to the soles of his bare and blackened feet. Daisy knew he was not altogether to blame for this because he was what her mother called 'a passed-down child'. This apparently meant that his own parents had disappeared long ago and he had lived, for as long as he could remember, with a foster mother and father, neither of whom was related to him by blood. In fact, Mam said she thought Nicky coped very well, maintaining as much independence as possible and steering clear of the Ryans whenever Mr Ryan was drunk, or Mrs Ryan wanted a scapegoat.

Right now, however, Nicky was grinning down at her and Daisy felt she should support her small sister. 'It isn't her fault this time,' she said defensively. 'She must have fallen over and her arm's got jammed down the bleedin' drain. Anyway, what business is it of yours, Nicky nosy Bostock?'

Nicky grinned, clearly not at all insulted. 'Fell over!' he said derisively. 'Who d'you think you're kiddin', Daisy McAllister? I seen her playin' cherry wobs wi' young Jacky; she were fishin' out one what went down the drain, that's what she were doin', dirty little bugger.'

Daisy's eyes widened. She sometimes swore herself when in company with her peers, but the word 'bugger' was strictly forbidden to her and Petal, though they heard it often enough on their father's lips. She was about to reply indignantly that he should mind what he said and stop cussing, when Petal piped up.

'I isn't a dirty little bugger,' she said tearfully, if untruthfully. 'Oh, Daisy, do stop arguing and help me! I'm stuck, I tell you!'

'Let me have a look,' Nicky said gruffly, kneeling down next to Daisy. The child had rolled up the sleeve of her ragged cardigan to well above the elbow and had jammed her arm in so hard that two purplish marks showed where the bars had caught it. But surely, if her hand had gone in, then it should have come out, Daisy thought confusedly. She was still trying to work out what best to do when Nicky spoke. 'Aw, Gawd, trust a bleedin' girl,' he said, leaning over and seizing Petal's arm, none too gently. 'She put her hand in to fetch out the cherry wob flat like, but now she's gorrit in her fist. So, a' course, she can't gerrit out again.' He shook Petal's arm impatiently. 'Lerrit go, you little thickhead, or you're there for life, I'm tellin' you.'

Petal gave a wail of protest, so Daisy said reassuringly: 'Nicky's right, Petal. If you flatten your hand out, it'll come out easy peasy. After all, it's only a cherry wob, when all's said and done.'

'It ain't, it's three,' Petal wailed, her fist still obstinately closed. 'I found two others in the mud when I were diggin' for mine, an' if I flatten me hand out I'll lose 'em all. It took me ages to reach them an' I got ever so mucky. I *can't* leggo of them now.'

'Then you're there for life, kiddo,' Daisy said grimly. She knew better than to try to reason with Petal;

threats might work, diplomacy never would. 'Well, I'm off home, it's dinner time. Are you coming, Nick?'

Petal's face grew pink and she tugged fruitlessly, then turned to her sister once more, a smile curving those angelic lips. 'Oh, Daisy, I've had an idea, a real good 'un! We can do it if you'll help me and it won't take more'n a few seconds. If I open me hand, you can put two fingers through the bars – they'll fit easy – an' take the cherry wobs off of me. I can't do it meself 'cos me other hand's proppin' me up. Oh come on, Daisy, be me pal.'

Daisy could not help smiling to herself. When it came to getting what she wanted, Petal could outsmart most. She was about to agree to have a go when Nick intervened. 'You're that sticky wi' mud, I reckon that the cherry wobs will come up with you if you goes through the bars slow an' careful, like,' he said. 'As soon as your palm's clear of the grating, I'll pick 'em off.'

The manoeuvre was completed successfully and Petal stood up, rubbing her cramped knees and grinning happily as Nick handed over the precious cherry wobs. Her face was dirt- and tear-streaked but her smile was so sunny that both the older children found themselves smiling in return. 'Thanks, Nicky,' Petal said gratefully. She turned to her sister. 'Is it really dinner time, Daisy, only I'm starving.'

'Me, too,' Nicky said. 'I'd best go in an' see if I can talk old Ma Ryan into givin' me some bread an' a cut o' cheese.' As the girls headed for their door, he strolled alongside them, suddenly remarking: 'You doin' anythin' after dinner, Daisy? Fancy a stroll down to the river? Or we could go to the gardens?'

Daisy looked doubtful. She had suspected for some time that Nicky rather liked her; he tended to hang about in her vicinity, and often walked home from school with her, though he seldom attended himself. The trouble was, he was generally known to be what her mam called 'a bit on the sharp side'. Daisy knew he stole, nicking fruit off the stalls, rooting through the bins at the back of Taylor's bakery shop in Stitt Street for stale buns, or broken sausage rolls. She knew he had to do this – food was always short in the Ryan household – but knew, also, that adults did not condone such behaviour and would blame her equally if he stole whilst in her company. So she said that she and Petal were going out with their mam and gave Petal a glare when the younger girl opened her mouth to argue. She looked a trifle apprehensively at Nicky because she did not want to hurt his feelings – he had rescued her little sister after all – but he appeared to have taken the remark at its face value.

'Okay,' he said cheerfully. 'I'll mebbe walk you home from school on Monday, then,' and with a casual wave of one hand, he was gone.

Daisy turned to Petal as they went down the jigger, heading for their back door. 'Honest to God, Petal, the scrapes you get in!' she said. 'And where was your pal Jacky, anyway? If he were a real pal, he'd have helped you to get out, not just run off.'

'He were losin' . . . well, until my cherry stone went down the drain, he were,' Petal said sunnily. 'He ran off with all the cherry wobs except the one down the grating, so I'm going to kill him after I've had me dinner.'

Daisy laughed. 'If Mam hasn't killed you first,' she observed. 'She sent you out clean, if not tidy, and Nicky was right, now you look a real little scruff bag.' She bent over her sister to straighten her stained and spattered cardigan, then reeled back, a hand flying to her nose. 'Petal, you stink! You smell worse'n the privy on a summer's day. It's a good job our dad ain't due back in port till tomorrow or he'd have had your hide – and mine, and Mam's as well – if he got one whiff.'

'I can't help it, Daisy. Drains is smelly things an' I were stuck in that one for hours and hours,' Petal said. 'Anyway, it weren't *my* idea to try to get the cherry wob back, it were horrible Jacky's. He tried with a stick but that weren't no good, so he said since I had the skinniest arms and it were my stone, I'd better have a go meself. It were him rolled up me cardy sleeve,' she added, with a touch of resentment, 'and when I first put my hand through the grid and the pong came up, he said I were a ninny and bet me two liquorice sticks that I'd never reach it. He dared me, Daisy, and no one can refuse a dare, can they?'

'No, I suppose you had to have a try, though I wouldn't have,' Daisy said. 'It's too bad of Jacky to put a dare on a kid of four – why, he's seven, isn't he?'

'Six or seven,' Petal admitted. 'But it's no use saying I'm only four, because if I do that he won't let me play with his gang, an' I like boys' games better'n girls', so I do.'

'Oh, come on, Petal,' Daisy said reproachfully. 'You and Fanny play at shop and tea parties and all sorts when she's around. I bet you were only playing with Jacky because Mrs Hanson had taken Fanny to do the messages.'

'Ye-es, Fanny weren't there. But I *do* like playing with Jacky's gang,' Petal said obstinately. 'And he owes me two liquorice sticks because I got the cherry wob back, didn't I, Daisy? So it's ya boo and sucks to him, isn't it?'

Daisy laughed; she couldn't help it. Jacky was a

right little bruiser but Petal wasn't afraid of him, not she. 'All right, have it your own way,' she said, as she opened the back door. 'But I wouldn't be too keen to tackle Jacky meself.'

'Yes, but Jacky says his teacher telled them that boys were never to hit girls, so that's all right.' She turned large blue eyes up to her sister's face. 'Only if boys shouldn't hit girls, then why is it all right for dads to hit mams?' she enquired, as they entered the kitchen. Daisy felt her face warm as the blood rushed to her cheeks and she looked guiltily across to her mother frying potatoes in a large blackened pan on the stove, but Rose McAllister did not appear to have heard. She turned as the two children entered, and Daisy thought how pretty her mother was with her dark hair tied back from her face with a piece of twine, her cheeks flushed from the heat of cooking and her big, dark eyes with their curling lashes seeming to smile at them both. My mam's always smart, though her clothes are old, Daisy thought with pride. Why, even with the big calico apron wrapped round her, you can see how small her waist is and how clean and neat she is.

'Oh, Mam, Petal's got herself mucky. I'll give her hands and face a bit of a wipe at the sink, but her cardy's covered in mud; can I take her upstairs to find a clean one?'

Daisy did not want to tell her mother that her little sister stank like a midden but soon realised it would not be necessary. Rose glanced down at Petal and gasped as the smell hit her. 'Cripes, Petal, whatever have you been doing? If that pong is coming from your woolly, you'd best dump it in the sink and I'll deal with it later,' she said, as Daisy picked up the dishcloth and began vigorously rubbing at her sister's face and hands. 'I'd ask what you've been up to only I bet I'd rather not know.' She watched as the filthy cardigan was dropped into the sink and said, as her children trotted past her, heading for the stairs, 'Don't be long now, these spuds are almost ready; I give you two minutes at the outside.'

'Awright, Mam, we'll be back before the cat can lick her ear,' Daisy said cheerfully, shepherding her little sister out of the room. 'We love fried spuds, don't us, Petal?'

Rose turned the fried potatoes gently in the pan, smiling to herself at her daughter's ingenuous remark. Not that it was ingenuous really; it was a fair enough question. Why was it that boys were taught not to hit girls, yet when they became adults a great many men thought nothing of battering their wives or giving their kids a good hiding for the most trivial offence?

Steve McAllister was a case in point. He was a stoker aboard the SS *Millie May*, a coaster plying between the small ports of South America, so his times at home in Liverpool were blessedly infrequent. When he came ashore drunk, Rose could understand his truculence, even his violence, but the truth was, like his father before him, he was a man of vicious and capricious temper. After nine years of marriage, she knew how suddenly he could change from a relatively good mood to a foul one, and until a couple of years previously she had feared and dreaded his homecomings.

Not any more, though. On that winter's day, two years ago, she had been frying liver and onions on the stove when the back door crashed open. Steve had lurched into the room, eyes bloodshot, and had stood swaying in the doorway for a moment. 'Wharra you cookin'?' he had demanded, his voice slurred from the drink. 'Whassin that bleedin' fry pan?'

'It's liver and onions,' Rose had replied levelly, though with a wild and thumping heart. 'It's your favourite dinner, Steve.'

He had scowled and taken a couple of shambling steps towards her. 'Not today, it ain't,' he had said thickly. 'Today, I fancy fish 'n' chips an' a bottle o' porter. Put that bleedin' pan down an' go an' buy some, quick.'

'I've no money,' Rose had said truthfully. 'An' I'm not going anywhere. You'll have to make do with liver and onions.'

He had taken two more steps towards her and Rose had known what was coming. Once, she would have let go the pan and tried to run round the table, slipping out of the door before he had turned back towards it, but now, suddenly, she was filled with defiance. She took the big iron pan in both hands and swung it in a wide arc. Liver, onions and hot fat flew across the short distance which separated them, splattering Steve's face and hands. For a moment he stopped short, then, with a howl of rage, he grabbed for the frying pan, clearly meaning to turn her weapon upon herself. But the pan was almost red hot from the heat of the fire, and for a sickening moment Steve was unable to let go of it, though his roars of pain and rage reverberated around the small room, which was filled with the smell of sizzling Steve.

Rose had given a short, harsh laugh. 'I warned you,' she had said, in the most threatening tone she could produce. 'I've had enough of it, Steve. The kids are in bed, thank God, but I'll not let you touch me again in one of your moods, so be warned.'

But he hadn't been listening. The moment he had

torn himself free of the pan, he had rushed across the kitchen to bend over the pail of water under the sink and plunge both hands in it, whilst uttering a stream of abuse and sobbing with the pain of his burns.

Rose had eyed his rear thoughtfully, still swinging the frying pan. One good whack on that tempting, trouser-clad target, and Steve would end up with his head in the pail of water as well as his hands. But she had felt that such a move might be carrying the war one step too far and, still holding the frying pan, had begun to clear up the liver and onions.

Presently, Steve had stood up. She had glanced across at him. His face had been red and blubbered and tears were running down his cheeks. He had glared at her but to her secret astonishment – and great delight – she had read something very like respect in his glance. Oh, there had been hatred there and a desire for revenge, but it had been clear that her action had surprised him. She had thought he would think twice before attacking her again.

And so it had proved. She had made a point of letting him see that she would no longer allow herself to be a victim, that she would hit back with any weapon to hand if he threatened her again. Of course, there had been other times when he had hit out at her and she had had no chance to defend herself, but she always made sure that afterwards he suffered in some way, and gradually he had learned to keep his distance.

Sometimes, she thought back down the long years to their courtship and wondered how on earth she had been so blind. She told herself that a girl of seventeen, kept too close by strict and elderly parents, had had no idea what marriage and a family involved. But the truth was partly that she had been swept off her feet by the handsome, swaggering young seaman, who had brought her presents from faraway places and taken her dancing and to the theatre and the cinema – three things of which her parents disapproved – and partly that to go out with Steve had shown her parents that she was no longer a child who could be told what she might and might not do.

So they had married in the teeth of deep parental opposition, though her parents had not withheld their consent, and moved into the little house in Bernard Terrace. Her parents had kept a small shop on Stanley Road, but after her marriage they had sold up and moved out to Great Sutton, on the Wirral, where a newspaper and tobacconist's shop, with a flat above it, had provided them with a decent living. As her own marriage degenerated, Rose had been less and less anxious to take Steve to visit her parents because her pride could not let her admit how right they had been. However, she had taken the girls to see their grandparents as often as she could, and both her mother and her father had adored the little girls, softening towards them in a way they had never done towards Rose. Sadly, when Petal had been two and Daisy six, first her father, then her mother, had succumbed to influenza, which they had neglected in order to keep the shop open. They had sent for Rose, asking her to take over the shop for a few days, but it had been too late.

Rose had always had to save hard and plan well ahead for her visits to Great Sutton, but when they came to an end she found she missed both the trips away from the city and her parents. Mrs Darlington had been well past forty when Rose was born, and now that she was a mother herself Rose realised how difficult it must have been for the couple to find themselves parents at such an advanced age. Both only children, they had not understood Rose's need for the companionship of young people like herself, or her yearnings for independence from the narrow and rigid lives they led. And truth to tell, having grandchildren had mellowed them beyond belief.

Now, Rose turned the potatoes in the pan and glanced, anxiously, towards the kitchen door. The *Millie May* came into port tomorrow so she and the children would make do with fried potatoes for their dinner today. She would save the liver and onions for the following day, as she always did. Petal had asked her, when Steve was last in port, why they always had liver and onions on her daddy's first day home and Rose had smiled grimly at Steve, over the child's blonde head, and said sweetly that it was Daddy's favourite dish. Steve had glanced quickly away, refusing to meet her eyes, but Petal had been quite satisfied with the answer, especially as she was fond of liver and onions herself.

Rose fished out the tin plates and began to serve the potatoes, just as the kitchen door burst open and the children ran into the room. Petal was wearing a fawn-coloured cardigan which had once been Daisy's, and looked considerably better than when she had entered the kitchen earlier. When Petal was born, Rose had breathed a sigh of relief because she would not have to buy much in the way of clothing, though Steve had been bitterly disappointed, or so he had claimed. Now, Rose thought that Daisy was a motherly little soul and took as much pride in Petal's appearance as she would have done had she been the child's mother. She had brushed out Petal's soft curls and straightened the child's long grey stockings. She had even rubbed most of the mud off Petal's worn black plimsolls, and done her best to brush the child's short grey skirt. Rose wished she could have afforded decent boots for the children to play out in at this time of year, but it took her all her ingenuity to have them properly shod for school. Petal had started in the infants' class the previous September so now, Rose thought ruefully, she had two decent sets of clothes to keep clean. It was not that Steve was ungenerous; because of his long absences, the shipping company who owned the *Millie May* paid her an allotment every month, but it was not really sufficient for all the expenses of home and family. Rose had to work, but since the majority of women living in the terrace were in the same position, she thought nothing of it. The only real problem was that work was so hard to find and so poorly paid. 'Haven't you heard about the Depression?' employers would say, grimly, when offering one a tiny wage for work that would mean many hours of slavery each week. 'You're lucky I'm offering you work at all, so if you ain't content with the money I pay, you'd best go elsewhere.'

Only there wasn't an elsewhere, Rose thought now. She put the crockery on the table and went to the cupboard to fetch the sauce bottle. Doling a meagre amount on to each plate, she smiled approvingly as Petal ran to fetch the cutlery and Daisy filled a jug of water at the sink. Then she took her own place, poured water into their enamel mugs, and picked up her knife and fork.

'I do love fried potatoes,' Petal said earnestly, carefully dipping a piece into the puddle of sauce. 'But it ain't as good as liver and onions . . . I wonder what Daddy will have brung us back?'

Rose sighed. Steve was so unreliable, that was the trouble. Christmas was not far off, but even so, you could never tell. He might come home laden with presents for his small daughters – he never brought Rose anything – or he might come in empty-handed, then hand the girls half a crown apiece. Or, of course, he might come in roaring drunk, having spent his wages at some dockside pub or other, and try to persuade her to fork out her hard-earned money so that he could start another pub crawl as soon as possible.

Sometimes, when he was drunk, he would tell the girls in a self-pitying voice that he had brought them a grosh of presents – beautifully dressed dolls, a parrot in a cage, even a puppy – but that these objects had been stolen from him as he left the ship. With tears in his eyes, he would explain that, because of his loss, he had taken 'a l'il drink or two' to cheer him up, which was why he now felt so ill that he would have to go straight upstairs and lie down.

Rose could never tell whether there was any truth in these stories because there were occasions when Steve did bring the girls presents. Of course, she knew they had not been stolen, thinking it likelier that he had simply put them down somewhere, or even shed them on his passage home. What she did know, for sure, was that the gifts would not reappear and that Steve would spend the rest of his time ashore drinking with his mates, only returning to Bernard Terrace for food or a night's sleep.

Still, there were worse fates than Steve, Rose told herself, eating her fried potatoes and wishing she had been able to afford a bit of meat or fish to go with them. Charlie Briggs, young Jacky's father, was a docker and usually out of work. When he was in work he drank and when he wasn't he stole, either from his wife or from his old mother, who lived three streets away. Poor Nellie Briggs had to put up with his constant presence, often sporting black eyes or a limp, for her husband was even more violent than Steve. The kids avoided him whenever they could, but it wasn't always possible and they, too, were often marked.

'Mammy? It isn't long to Christmas, is it? *Will* Daddy bring us presents, d'you think?'

'I don't know, queen; if he can, he will, I suppose,' Rose said, coming abruptly back to earth. 'But isn't it Santa Claus who brings presents at Christmastime? Remember the poem Daisy's been telling you?'

Petal nodded eagerly. 'Oh yes, I 'member.' She closed her eyes and rocked herself gently backwards and forwards. '*'Twas the night before Christmas and all through the house, Not a creature was stirring, not even a mouse . . .*'

'That's right, so you hang up your stocking on the end of your bed, and you never know . . .'

Regardless of whether Steve remembered Christmas or not, Rose was determined that this year the children should have something in their stockings. Last year had been a really bad one. She had been employed as a waitress, earning reasonable money and determined that they should have a good Christmas. She had meant to order a piece of pork from Mr Pollard on the corner of William Henry and Salisbury streets and had planned various little treats to be bought on Christmas Eve, when shopkeepers, fearing to leave goods unsold over the holiday, would drastically reduce their prices. Then Daisy had come out in spots. It was chickenpox, and seven days later Petal had followed suit. Rose had begged her employer for a few days off – just a few days – whilst the infection was at its height, but Mr Grundy had told her, sadly, that this was his busiest time of year and unless she could find a babysitter, he would have to replace her. She had found a woman willing to brave the chickenpox, but she had only lasted a day. Rose had come home at seven that evening, exhausted after a ten-hour shift on her feet, to find the fire out, Petal burning up with fever and crying dolorously, and Daisy trying to fill a stone hot water bottle from the kettle, because she was so cold. The old woman was fast asleep and snoring on Rosie's own bed and had been most indignant to be turned off without pay, swearing that she would have the scuffers round next morning and take Rose to court, if need be, to get her money.

Of course it had been an empty threat, but it had meant that Rose had had to give up her job. Steve had not come home – which was a blessing – but nor had he sent any money to ease matters, though Rose had written to him explaining that she was out of work through his daughters' illnesses, and could do with some financial help. So they had had an absolutely awful Christmas. Stockings had not even been hung up because Rose needed all the money she had left to pay the doctor; indeed, Christmas Day had passed like any other day, with the children still in bed, though their temperatures were beginning to ease. None of them had referred to the holiday until long afterwards, when it occurred to Petal that she had been cheated.

'Didn't Santa even *try* to come down our chimney?' she had asked plaintively. 'Didn't he leave even an orange? Or a few sweeties?'

Rose had answered, diplomatically, that of course he had visited them. 'Only I used the orange to make you a nice hot drink and you sucked the sweeties when your throat was so sore,' she had said.

Now, Petal's knife and fork clattered on to her plate and she glanced hopefully up at Rose. 'Them spuds was lovely but I've still got a little chink in me belly what needs filling,' she said plaintively. 'Is there any pudding, Mammy?'

'You should say tummy, not belly,' Daisy interposed. 'Or I suppose you could say stomach; that's what the teacher says in school. And I don't see how you can still be hungry. You're littler than me, but you ate just as many spuds.'

'Smaller than me, not littler,' Rose said absently. She liked the children to speak nicely. 'Daisy, fetch the loaf from the bread crock, and Petal, you can see if there's any jam left in the big jar on the bottom shelf of the pantry. I'll have to get some more tomorrow, with your dad coming home, because he likes a jam butty to round off a meal.'

Petal slipped off her stool and went over to the pantry, closely followed by Daisy, and presently the children returned with their spoils. Rose cut a thick slice, halved it, and eyed the jam in the jar. She doubted if there was sufficient even to cover the one slice, then remembered a trick her mother had often used and, fetching the blackened kettle from its place on the hob, poured half a teaspoon of boiling water into the jar and began to swill it around. Then she tipped the jar on to the bread, spread the thin jam carefully, cut the slice of bread in half, and handed a piece to each child. 'There you are, something to fill the chink,' she said cheerfully. 'And when you've eaten that and I've washed up and cleared away, we'll go up to the shops and buy something nice for tomorrow's dinner.'

'Liver and onions,' Petal said gleefully, through a mouthful of bread and jam. 'Will Daddy be at home for Christmas, Mammy, or will he have gone back to the *Millie May* by then?'

'It's only three days to Christmas, so I suppose

they'll probably remain in port over the holiday,' Rose said, trying to keep gloom and foreboding out of her voice, though feeling both. Steve was bound to get drunk over Christmas and it troubled her that he might spoil things for the kids if he ran out of money and could not go out on a pub crawl every night. So far, Steve had never laid a finger on the children, though since hearing Petal's remark as she had entered the kitchen earlier Rose had been aware that her girls must know full well that Steve could be violent. However, there was no point in meeting trouble halfway; she would simply have to hope that the spirit of Christmas would triumph over the spirit of Guinness and that he would leave the three females to enjoy their holiday whilst he went off to the pub to drink with his cronies.

Presently, the meal washed up and cleared away and the fire banked down, the three of them donned their coats and hats, picked up Rose's marketing bags and headed for the shops. Once, Rose would have pushed the big old pram, but a year ago it had mysteriously disappeared. Since it was during one of Steve's periods at home, and since he had been unusually short of money, she imagined that he had sold it. It was annoying, of course, and she felt that if anyone had had the money it should have been she, since it was her parents who had presented her with the pram when Daisy was born. Naturally, she had said nothing to Steve about it; she had merely served up a dinner of blind scouse and dumplings, and when Steve had poked, disparagingly, at the vegetables, demanding to know where the meat had gone, she had said simply: 'To the same place as the pram, I dare say,' and had noticed with satisfaction that he had avoided her eyes, though he had eaten the rest of his stew without complaint.

'Mam, where's we goin' first?' Daisy asked, as they descended from the terrace into Salisbury Street. 'If we've got ever so many messages, we ought to gerron a tram and go up to St John's market. Stuff's cheaper there, everyone says so.'

'That's just what we're going to do,' Rose said, taking Petal's small hand in her own and setting off along Salisbury Street in the direction of Islington. 'Petal's little legs aren't up to walking all that way and coming back, and when we're laden with heavy bags, our little arms aren't up to it either.'

That made Daisy laugh, though she said wistfully: 'If we still had the pram, Petal could have had a lift among the messages, coming home, which would have saved a penny or two. I wonder what happened to that pram?'

'Oh, Daisy, me darlin', you sound like a little old woman sometimes,' Rose said. Daisy's old-fashioned ways amused her but they also made her sad. Because of their circumstances, Daisy had had to grow up and take responsibility for her little sister in a way which Rose thought unfair. However, she knew that most of the children of Daisy's age who lived in the poorer districts of the city were in the same boat and, like Daisy, none of them seemed to resent it.

They emerged on to Islington, crossed the busy road and joined the queue at the tram stop. Rose had never told Daisy what she thought had happened to the pram and did not intend to do so now but said, instead: 'Never mind the pram, queen. You like a tram ride, don't you? And if we'd had the pram, we couldn't possibly have got it aboard! Ah, here comes one now!'

Steve came home, announcing that he would be with them until after the New Year, but his mood was far more sober – in every sense of the word – than usual. Rose had bought some chestnuts from a street vendor and Steve had made a punch, using liquor which he had brought back with him, and some of the fruit which Rose had purchased earlier in the evening from the stalls on Scotland Road. She had been astonished when Steve had suggested that they all go and do the messages together, and downright flabbergasted when he had said he wanted a quiet evening at home. She had asked him, solicitously, if he were feeling well, and he had given her a strange look. For the first time, he had actually seemed interested in the children's activities, had carried Petal in his arms when she got tired, and had persuaded Daisy to sing the carol which she had sung as a solo in the school concert.

So now the two of them settled down in front of the fire and Steve arranged the chestnuts on a shovel which he pushed beneath the hot coals. Then he poured a small quantity of hot punch into two mugs, and handed one to Rose. 'There you are,' he said gruffly. 'I've put the stuff I brought back in the cupboard under the stairs. It ain't a lot, but it'll be more'n they got last Christmas.' He lowered his head, then looked up at her, his expression still one that she had never seen on his face before and found difficult to read. 'I got you something an' all,' he added. He sounded almost ashamed, Rose thought with amusement, and once more she wondered what had happened, why he was not off drinking with his pals, or trying to pick a fight with her.

'I've not got you anything because we don't exchange presents, do we?' she said, after the pause had begun to lengthen. 'I told you I'd had some pre-Christmas work in the bakery, but I spent all the money I earned on grub and a few bits for the kids. I – I'm sorry, but you know how it is.'

'Aye, I know how it is,' Steve mumbled. 'But me and the fellers was talkin' after old Chamberlain came back from Munich, waving his bit of paper an' sayin' "Peace for our time" and that. I ain't much interested in politics, nor what they call world affairs neither. But there's a feller what slings his hammock next to mine, called Alby Cohen. He's from Liverpool, like what I am, an' he's a Jew. He telled us about that there Crystal Night, where them Nazis dragged women an' children out of their beds, an' killed 'em, just for bein' Jewish. He said Chamberlain were a fool if he thought he could stop that there madman . . . what's 'is name, oh aye, Adolf Hitler . . . from swallering up as much of Europe as he could gerr'is hands on. He said he reckoned this 'ud be our last Christmas before old Hitler sent his Nazis across the Channel, our last Christmas without – without wonderin' if there'd be a knock on the door, if some storm trooper were goin' to come in an' drag our kids out on to the street.' He swallowed. 'It made me think, like; seamen don't get to see their kids at Christmas all that often, and . . .' His voice petered out. Then he cleared his throat and started again. 'Alby's clever, not like the rest of us. He knows a thing or two, does Alby. I reckon if he says there's goin' to be a war, then he's right an' Chamberlain's wrong. So Alby's signed off from the old *Millie May*, so's he can join the Royal Navy, and – and I'm goin' to do the same. I reckon they'll be needin' men when war comes an' Alby says if we gerrin first we'll likely get the better jobs, bein' more experienced, like.'

Rose stared at him. She had always thought him a man of few words and had never before heard him talk for so long. This Alby, she reflected, must be a pretty strong character to have made such an impression upon her usually unimaginative husband. But he was looking at her, clearly expecting a reaction. 'But suppose Alby's wrong, Steve?' she said slowly. 'You've never said much, but I've always thought you were happy enough aboard the *Millie*. If there isn't a war . . .'

He interrupted her at once, shaking his head almost reprovingly at her. 'No, no, you don't *understand*. Alby's been there, he knows all about it. He's got relatives living in Germany; some of 'em's already in these here camp things, what the Nazis have set up, but others are trying to go on with their lives, an' they've talked to him, told him things. There *will* be a war, Rosie, you've gorra believe me.'

'I – I think I do believe you,' Rose said hesitantly. He had not called her Rosie since Daisy was born, and though she could never forget how badly he had treated her in recent years, it was wonderful to think that his attitude might change, that he might become a softer, pleasanter person. 'I've not thought much about Hitler, or what's going to happen – I've been too busy seeing the kids get fed and the rent gets paid – but I know the newspapers think there's trouble coming, and if it does, we're all going to have to pull together.'

'That's it,' Steve said eagerly. 'And there's somethin' else, Rosie, something I've not told anyone, 'cept for Alby. A couple o' times, when I've been on the booze, I've – I've seen things.' He shuddered. 'Horrible things – hands chopped off at the wrist an' oozing blood, creepin' across me blanket, headin' for me throat. Giant crabs and great, slimy crocodile things, slitherin' down the bulkhead . . . Once, I got fightin' mad wi' the things an' started attacking them; I thought a great old snake was curlin' round me, tryin' to squash me ribs, but it were Alby, tryin' to stop me goin' mad. He said it were the drink; well, I knew it were. He said if I didn't ease off, I'd end up mad or dead.' He grinned, suddenly, and for a moment Rose saw the swaggering young seaman for whom she had abandoned her home, broken her parents' hearts and almost ruined her own life.

'So I'm off the drink, 'cept for the odd glass now and then,' Steve said. 'Hey, them nuts is done to a turn; I'll peel you a couple. They reckon stokers have asbestos fingers. Now we'll see if they're right.'

For the rest of the evening, the two of them examined the presents they had bought for the girls. There were two real dolls, proper ones with eyes that opened and shut, curly hair and soft, huggable bodies. Rose knew the girls would be absolutely delighted, though in her heart she doubted that these grand babies would ever replace the home-made rag dolls which Daisy and Petal cherished. Then Steve had bought each girl a rubber ball – one red, one blue – and pretty little jackets made of what he told her proudly was angora wool. 'They'll love everything,' Rose told him warmly. She had bought them the new plimsolls they so desperately needed, and a skipping rope each, as well as some hard-boiled sweets and two small bars of Nestlé chocolate. 'They're going to have a wonderful Christmas, Steve,' Rose said, as the two of them made their way up to bed. 'A lot better than last year, I can tell you.'

And sure enough, Christmas Day was celebrated to the full. Steve's gift to Rose was a necklace of crystal beads, and though she had had no present for him, she had made sure that his day was a happy one. Towards evening, though, he grew restless, and when the children were in bed he slipped on his coat and announced that he needed some fresh air.

Telling herself, grimly, that he would doubtless return in a drunken rage, Rose went early to bed and fell asleep almost at once. She did not wake until eight o'clock next morning and realised, when she did so, that he could not have been on the drink, since he had managed to slip into bed beside her so quietly.

This happy state of affairs lasted until New Year's Eve. Steve left the house as soon as the girls were in bed, and had not returned by closing time. Rose went to bed, armed with the coal shovel, and heard her husband crashing into the house in the small hours. He was swearing and shouting at her to come down and pull his bleedin' boots off, and twice she heard him come stumbling up half a dozen stairs and then fall heavily down them. The last time he did this, he shrieked to her to come down at once. 'Gi' me a hand up, you snooty bitch, 'cos I'm thinking I've broke both me bleedin' legs, an' it's a wife's duty to gerra feller into his own bed,' he bawled. 'Aw, c'mon, Rosie, or it ain't only my bleedin' legs that'll be broke come mornin'.'

Rose sat up in bed. It had been so nice having him home sober that she felt almost tempted to go downstairs, but past sad experience told her that this would be a mistake. He would hit out at her, or grab her; might injure her so that she could not return to work, and the money she earned was a necessity. Besides, even if she had wanted to, she was not strong enough to propel him up the stairs, and anyway by morning he would have forgotten everything, have a horrible hangover and probably want to spend the rest of the day either on the sofa or in bed.

Slowly, Rose slid under the covers again, pulling the blankets up over her shoulders. Steve's voice had sunk to a mumble; probably he was more asleep than awake. She was beginning to drowse herself when a small voice spoke, almost in her ear, causing her to give a convulsive leap. 'Didn't you hear Daddy call you, Mammy? He were hollerin' pretty loud. He woke me up. Daisy woke up and started to cry, but she's gone back to sleep now. I took a peep down the stairs, but I can't see him. Are you going down, or shall I?'

Rose sat up in bed once more and put her arms round her little daughter; Petal was shivering. 'Yes, I heard him, queen, but I didn't go down because I don't think Daddy is quite himself.'

'Oh, you mean he's drunk,' Petal said matter-of-factly. 'And when daddies is drunk, they sometimes hit mammies, don't they? If I go, will Daddy try to hit me? I know Mr Briggs hits Jacky, but Daddy's never hit me, has he?'

'No, darling,' Rose said, trying not to remember the number of times she had had to get between Daisy and Steve. He had threatened the child in the past but, she was bound to admit, had never actually struck either of his daughters. Only his wife. 'Look, Petal, you slip into Mammy's nice warm bed and I'll go very quietly down the stairs and make sure he's all right.' She slid out of bed on the words and tried to pick Petal up and pop her between the covers, but Petal resisted.

'No Mammy; if you're going down, then I'm coming with you,' she said, and set off for the stairs at a brisk trot. It was a cold night. Rose whipped a blanket off her bed and wrapped it round her shoulders, then followed her daughter's small, determined figure. Petal pattered ahead of her, and presently the two of them stood in the empty hall. Steve was nowhere to be seen, but through the open kitchen door Rose could hear rich, vibrating snores. She and Petal tiptoed into the room and there was Steve. Since he had managed to heave himself on to the sofa he was obviously not suffering from broken legs, and although his snores were not musical, at least they seemed to indicate that he was well enough. Mother and daughter exchanged relieved looks and then Rose removed the blanket from her shoulders and placed it, tenderly, across Steve's slumbering body, tucking it in so firmly that he would have a job to escape from it. She wondered whether to place a large jug of water conveniently to hand since she knew he would wake with a raging thirst, but decided against it. On a previous occasion she had done so, and Steve had drunk the water and then piddled all over the sofa. If, on the other hand, he had to get up to reach the water, he would use one of the buckets, might even stagger to the outside lavatory if he was sober enough.

'Poor Daddy,' Petal whispered as they retraced their steps. 'He'll have a rotten headache in the morning, won't he, Mammy?'

Agreeing, Rose accompanied Petal back to her bed and tucked her in, glancing across at Daisy as she did so. Poor little soul! She must have been woken by her father's shouts, but her memories of him were clearer – and more unpleasant – than Petal's. His bubbly, blonde little daughter had always been his favourite, though Rose had to admit that he treated them fairly so far as presents and so on were concerned. But he could be harsh and sometimes quite spiteful towards Daisy, whilst treating Petal with obvious affection. Of course, Petal found it easy to show her own affection, having no bad history with her father. She would climb on to his knee, throw her arms round his neck, even play that she was a dog, pretending to bite his outstretched fingers and crowing with amusement when he acted as if he had been hurt. He would suck in his breath and roll his eyes, exclaiming that she was a real little devil, so she was.

He never played like that with Daisy, never had, probably never would. So of course the child was afraid of him. Rose had seen her elder daughter looking wistfully on when Steve and Petal played together, or when Steve read to Petal from a book, but Rose knew there was nothing she could do about it. If Steve really kept off the drink, if he could show some sort of warmth towards Daisy, then there might be hope of closeness in the future. But Steve would have to earn Daisy's trust, and for the moment at least he seemed pretty well indifferent towards his elder daughter.

Rose tucked Petal in, turned to leave the room, then turned back. 'Where's Millie? Come to that, where's Maudie?' she asked, a sudden suspicion entering her head. 'When I put you to bed the night before last you were both cuddling your new dollies, but now I can't see either of 'em.'

'No. That's why poor Daisy were crying,' Petal said. 'When we come up to bed tonight, they was gone, and Daisy said Dad had took 'em. I don't mind much – I loves Josie Ragget best – but poor Daisy were real upset.' Petal sat up on one elbow, gazing across at her mother in the flickering candlelight. 'I say, Mam, if he's took 'em to Uncle's, then you could gerr'em back when it's safe, couldn't you?'

Despite herself, Rose gave a little choke of laughter. Petal was that knowing! Once or twice, when times were hard and extra expenses cropped up, Rose had had to go to the pawnbroker's on the corner of Islington with some article or other. Mr Parr or Mr Mordaunt would hold the object until she could redeem it, but she did not think she had ever explained any of this to Petal. However, the child clearly understood the intricacies of pawnbroking, so she might as well use the knowledge to comfort her girls.

'Yes, if your dad has taken them to the pawnshop we'll redeem them as soon as his ship sails,' she said comfortingly. 'Petal, who told you about – about Parr and Mordaunt's?'

'Jacky, of course. His mam pops his Sunday kecks on a Monday morning and gets 'em out again the followin' Saturday,' Petal said sleepily. 'I do like Mrs Briggs, Mam, she's ever so kind. If you can't get our new dollies back, I could ask—'

'No!' Rose said with rather more force than she had intended. 'Don't say a word to anyone else about your dollies, please, queen. I'll get them back as – as soon as I possibly can. Will you promise me you won't say a word to Mrs Briggs?'

'Awright,' Petal mumbled. 'Night night, Mammy.'

'Night night, chuck. And don't forget: not a word to anyone about your dollies.'

'I promise,' Petal said, yawning. 'I do love you, Mammy!'

Daisy lay curled up, with her old rag doll clasped firmly against her chest, and listened to Mam and Petal talking. She did not wish to admit that she was awake because she knew it should have been she who had accompanied her mother downstairs; she who understood very well how dangerous it could be for Mam to venture anywhere near Dad when he was drunk.

The trouble was, she had been so upset at the loss of her brand new doll that she had sobbed herself into quite a state and it had simply not occurred to her that she should go and wake her mother when her father had fallen down the stairs. Indeed, she had felt downright relieved at the crash because it meant that he was unlikely to come up and start trouble when he reached his bedroom.

But Petal had not hesitated. Daisy had heard her get up and trot through to Mam's room, had even heard the slight creaks as they descended the stairs. She had sat up in bed, thinking guiltily that she should really go down and lend her support, but before she had even poked a toe out from beneath her blankets she had heard her sister and mother returning. Quick as a flash, she had cuddled down again and was glad she had done so. She gathered that her father had been asleep and had given them no trouble, and when Petal had explained about their loss of the dolls she had been delighted to hear Mam say that she would get them back as soon as Dad had left for sea once more. Until Petal had talked of Uncle, it had not occurred to her that the dolls might have been pawned. She had imagined that Dad would have taken them to the pub and sold them to someone there, but if they'd really been pawned, and Mam seemed to think it likely, then they could be redeemed as Mam had suggested.

Now, Daisy turned over and put her warm arms round her sister's solid little back. Petal was so brave, but then she had never known what it was like to be in Dad's bad books, to be growled at and cursed, and, if Mam was in the other room, to receive a stinging slap round the legs, merely for the crime of walking past his chair and getting between him and the warmth of the fire for half a second.

Still, I'm brave in some ways, Daisy told herself defiantly. I never let anyone bully Petal and I help Mam all I can. And tomorrow morning, I'll go down early and help her with the breakfast, even if Dad's awake and shouting. And as soon as he's gone, we'll get our beautiful dolls back from Mr Parr's shop.

On that happy thought, Daisy slept.

Chapter Two
1939

It was a beautiful, sunny Whit Monday, and since the children had a day off school Rose had decided to take them to New Brighton. They had caught the tram down to the Pier Head, crossed the floating bridge, in company with a great many other people also intent on a day out, and were now aboard the ferry. The two little girls were hanging over the rail and chattering excitedly to one another, but Rose had read the headlines on the fly sheets that morning, and her pleasure in the day out was tinged with apprehension. The news was so bad! Ever since Steve had joined the Royal Navy, she had been conscious that, despite Mr Chamberlain's 'peace for our time', the rumbling of war in Europe had not gone away. In fact, it had got worse. It was impossible not to worry when you had small children in your care and a husband at sea, though Steve's desire to stay on the wagon had not proved very long lasting. He had been home twice since Christmas and on each occasion had come back full of good resolutions, only to fall by the wayside the first time he walked through the door of the nearest pub. Rose had remonstrated with him, reminded him of Alby Cohen's words, and when he was sober he always assured her that his drinking bouts were at an end, but this had not, again, proved to be the case.

However, he no longer attempted to use physical violence against either her or the children, because Rose had made it plain that such behaviour would be met with all the force she could muster. Fortunately, drink made him noisy as well as abusive, and she usually heard him coming as he tumbled across the threshold, cursing as he mounted the steps and blaming everyone else if he slipped and fell.

Rose sighed to herself. What was she doing, ruining a beautiful day by thinking about Steve? She had acknowledged to herself long ago that she had been a fool to marry him, but at least now she was in a much better position, financially, than she had ever been in her life before, and she had rumours of war to thank for that. Conscription had come in in April, though so far only for men aged twenty, and she had managed to get a job making uniforms, in a large factory on Long Lane. The pay was excellent, the other girls were friendly and the work itself was well within her capabilities. Rose paid Mrs Briggs to give an eye to the children when they came out of school, and a slightly larger sum to take care of them during the holidays. She had worried at first, knowing that Mr Briggs was a violent man, but she soon realised that Mrs Briggs was quite capable of controlling her husband when money was involved. After all, the girls played out with the other children when the weather allowed, only going into the Briggses' house when a meal was forthcoming, and during the Easter holidays Mrs Briggs's eldest, a strapping fourteen-year-old called Dulcie, had kept the girls happy and amused, even on wet days.

'Mammy.' Petal's shrill voice cut across Rose's thoughts. 'We're moving! We're at sea, like Dad is. There's lots of ships in the docks – one of 'em might be his!'

Rose shook her head, smiling at her little daughter. Because she was now earning regular wages, she had not brought a carry-out with them, but had promised them that they should have their dinner in a real café.

Because of this, both girls had insisted upon wearing the pink gingham dresses which Rose had been fortunate enough to spot on a stall in Paddy's market, and had immediately snapped up. She had had to let the hem right down on Daisy's dress, and had taken out the darts on Petal's, but thought that her daughters looked both sweet and smart, and was proud of them.

'Mammy, might one of the ships be Daddy's?'

'No, queen, I don't think so. If Daddy was in port, he would have either let us know or come home himself. But his ship has gone up to Scotland for manoeuvres, whatever that may mean. In his last letter, he said it might be two or three months before he was back in Liverpool, so we don't have to worry – I mean . . . oh, well, his ship can't possibly be one of the ones you can see,' she finished lamely.

'Good,' Daisy said roundly. She caught her sister's reproachful eye and gave Petal a little push. 'Oh, I know you're Daddy's favourite, but even you can't have forgotten what happened last time he was at home.'

'I try to forget,' Petal said, rather wistfully. 'After all, it were my best coat as well as yours that he took.'

'It weren't the coats I were thinking about,' Daisy said, with dignity. 'I were thinking about the row when Mam found out they'd gone and told him off. And don't pretend you weren't scared, Petal, because you were shaking like a leaf. I had my arms round you and I felt you trembling like anything.'

'Well, it was all right; when your dad saw I was really angry – and I'd picked up the poker – he simply walked out of the room,' Rose said, smiling to herself. If Steve had had a tail, it would have been clamped between his legs, she thought now, remembering how his self-righteous fury had oozed away into mumbles when she had raised the poker. She wondered how he could believe that she would ever dare to actually hit him, but supposed that a violent man expected violence from others. Whatever the reason, he must have acquired some money from somewhere – she did not like to imagine where or how – because he had turned up several hours later, no longer drunk, and with the missing coats over his arm. Now she assumed that he must have pawned the coats, but had been saving the money for a binge, which, if she had not intervened, would have started as soon as his favourite pub opened its doors.

'Well, I were a bit afraid,' Petal admitted. 'But it was all right, wasn't it? Dad takes things because I suppose he needs some money, but we get 'em back. We got our dollies back as well as our coats, didn't we?'

Daisy heaved an exaggerated sigh. 'Mam got the dolls back, not Dad,' she said severely. 'An' tell the truth now, isn't it nicer at home when Dad's at sea? No rows, no fights, no swears . . .'

But Petal had tired of the whole conversation, it seemed. She swung round and headed for the bows of the ship. 'C'mon, Daisy. If we're right in the front, we might see a mermaid or – or a penguin, or even a whale,' she shouted excitedly. 'First one to see a mermaid gets to choose which café we has our dinners in.'

Rose, following her daughters more slowly, thought what an odd mixture Petal was. Did she truly believe she might see a penguin or a whale? Petal was nearer babyhood than her sister, could still half believe in such things as mermaids and fairies. Rose had noticed that if they had cake for tea, Petal invariably thrust a few crumbs of it into her pocket, and could be seen, later, spreading such crumbs out on a nearby wall. When questioned, she had said that it was for the fairies, though Jacky Briggs had scoffed at the idea.

'It were mice, more'n likely, or mebbe bleedin' rats,'

he had said scornfully. 'You'd believe anything, you!'

'It weren't mice, it were sparrows, 'cos I've watched 'em come down and peck away. But it might be fairies, don't you see?'

Jacky had not seen, but Rose, overhearing the conversation, thought she had. Petal knew, with the practical side of her mind, that sparrows ate the cake crumbs, but according to the dreamy, imaginative side, it could have been fairies.

'She'll go far, that 'un,' April, the girl at the next machine, had said comfortably, when Rose had told her of the conversation. 'She'll be a perishin' lawyer, or the Prime Minister one of these days, tek my word for it!'

So now Rose watched indulgently as her daughters scanned the foaming bow wave, hoping for goodness knows what weird or magical creatures in the water below. And presently, when the ferry was alongside the dock and beginning to disgorge her passengers, she took Petal's hand in hers and bade Daisy catch hold of her small sister. Rose's other hand was encumbered by what the children called the outings bag, for though she had not brought food with them, she carried some bottles of lemonade, a couple of towels and the brief bathing suits she had made for them out of remnants bought on Paddy's market.

As the three of them began to walk up New Brighton Promenade, Petal burst into song. '*Here we go gathering nuts in May, nuts in May, nuts in May,*' she carolled, breaking off to remark, 'Oh, that's the wrong song 'cos it's not a cold and frost morning, is it, Mammy?'

Daisy laughed and swung her sister's hand vigorously. '*Oh I do like to be beside the seaside,*' she sang. '*Oh I do like to be beside the sea, Oh I do like to stroll along the prom, prom, prom, Where the bands all play tiddly om pom pom . . .*'

Singing lustily, the McAllisters continued to head for the beach.

Steve and Alby came off watch together and went down to the seamen's mess. Despite the fact that it was almost June there was a heavy swell running and it was too cold to spend more time than you had to out on the deck. Steve looked at Alby as the two of them settled on one of the long benches. He was a small man, a good six inches shorter than Steve himself, with curly black hair, sallow skin and very dark eyes, fringed with thick stubby lashes. He was also very much more intelligent than Steve knew himself to be, though Alby never shoved it down your throat that you weren't brainy, as some of the others did. Sometimes, Steve wondered why they were friends, because they were so different. Alby's locker was packed with books, some of which were novels, though many were impressive tomes on politics, international affairs and history. He had offered to lend them to Steve, who had given him a pitying glance. 'I ain't goin' to waste my time readin' a lot of stuff I wouldn't even begin to understand,' he had said honestly. 'Readin' is hard work for me, not enjoyment. Why, even when I'm listenin' to the wireless and the news comes on, me mind goes wanderin' off an' I come back to reality to find the bloody news bulletin's over. Why don't you play cards or do crosswords, or have a go at shove ha'penny, like the rest of us?'

Alby had laughed; one of the things Steve liked about him was that although he was clever, he never tried to influence other people, never made you feel small. 'I don't mind the odd game of cards from time to time because I reckon you're right: everyone needs to relax now and then. But you need other people to play cards with – unless it's patience – and when we come off watch, it's sometimes hard to get a card school going.'

Now, the cook leaned through the hatch and grinned at them as other men came trooping down the companionway and into the mess. 'Come and gerrit,' he bawled. 'It's bacon chops, boiled spuds an' cabbage wi' a currant duff for afters.'

There was an immediate jostling rush to grab tin plates from the pile and to get into a queue, and very soon both Alby and Steve were digging into their food. 'I know the cabbage is only dried, same as the mashed spuds is, but it's good grub, ain't it?' Steve said, through his mouthful. 'Is your old woman a good cook, Alby? Mine has her faults, but she turns out a grand meal when the dibs is in tune.'

'Aye, Rachel's a grand cook an' all,' Alby said dreamily, pausing with a fork full of meat halfway to his mouth. 'Her suet dumplings are the nicest I've ever tasted. Her mam's a good cook, too, only she's more for foreign food, having been brought up in Lithuania. She didn't come to England till she were in her twenties and of course she brought her cookin' with her, so to speak.'

'Aye, like the Chinese,' Steve said knowledgeably. 'They're good cooks, though when I were a kid me brothers an' meself used to believe they ate dogs an' rats an' that.' He grinned at his friend. 'I dare say your Rachel can turn a couple o' rats into a tasty dinner, if she's a mind.'

'You cheeky bugger,' Alby said. He punched Steve's shoulder, then stood up to carry his empty plate back to the hatch and fetch his currant duff. 'Mind you, if she were pressed, I reckon Rachel could make something tasty out of three old cabbage leaves and a sole of a boot.'

Laughing, the two men joined the queue at the hatch for their duff.

* * *

As soon as the meal was over, Alby went and fetched one of his books from his locker and settled down into a corner to read. He had said nothing to Steve, as yet, but the first officer had told him he had put Alby's name down to take the examination next time they went ashore which, if he passed, would set him on the road to promotion in the Royal Navy. So now, though he seldom mentioned books to Steve, Alby studied in every spare moment. He was not aiming to run the Navy exactly, but he was very attracted by signals and thought that that would be a career which would satisfy him, particularly once the war he was expecting started. The Yeoman of Signals would be either on deck or on the bridge with the captain, and he would be using both manual skills and the knowledge which he was even now acquiring. Oh yes, if he could start on the ladder which would lead to his becoming a signaller, he would, he thought, get a good deal of satisfaction from the job. Of course, the extra pay would be very welcome too, now that he and Rachel meant to set up home together, for though they had married the previous year, they were still living with Rachel's parents and saving up for a place of their own.

He was immersed in his book when someone tapped him on the shoulder. Glancing up, he saw Steve looming above him, looking excited. For a moment, Alby felt annoyed at the interruption, then grinned up at his friend. Steve did not realise he was studying, he remembered. 'Yes, old feller, what's biting you?' he enquired, closing his book but keeping his finger inside to mark his place. 'I thought you'd joined the card school; don't say the game's over already?'

'No, no, nothing like that. But, Alby, the fellers were talking and Dan Williams has brought down a notice off of the board. It says the Navy is looking for submariners

– fellers to man submarines – and the pay is grand, better'n we're ever likely to get aboard HMS *Jericho*.'

Alby took the notice and read it, frowning slightly as he did so. He had never actually been aboard a submarine but could guess from the pay alone that it must be pretty grim. 'How are you in confined spaces, Steve?' he asked shrewdly. 'Ever been shut in a broom cupboard by your dad, or an angry teacher? I reckon a submarine's a bit like that, only one hell of a lot worse. Money ain't everything, old feller.'

Steve scowled down at the notice, clearly thinking it over, and Alby felt guilty because, though money was *most* certainly not everything, he was studying in order to get better pay himself. Poor old Steve never even thought of promotion and would not, Alby knew, be happy in a higher position. He was definitely not born to command, and though he could be both arrogant and overbearing towards those younger and less important than he conceived himself to be, he had never shown the slightest desire to rise from his present lowly rank.

On the other hand, Steve had a wife and two kids. He had told Alby that Rose was now earning good money, making uniforms for the forces, and Alby guessed that a man like Steve, who considered all males superior to all females, would secretly resent being out-earned by a woman.

But Steve was still thinking and it was several moments before he answered. 'Well, I dare say you're right and a sub would be a bit cramped like. But, Alby, you've always said we've gorra fight this 'ere war with everything we've got, else the bloody Huns will overrun us, murder our kids and tek our wives off to Germany for slave labour. And the money's good, ain't it?'

This was the moment, Alby realised, to tell Steve

of his own plans. It would not be fair to discourage Steve from applying to join a submarine by allowing him to believe that he and Alby would remain shipmates. Alby knew it was not naval policy to put a man who had gained promotion on the same ship in which he had served as a rating; discipline was easier to maintain when you were amongst strangers. Accordingly, he cleared his throat and began. 'Steve, old feller, you'll have to make up your own mind on this one, because – because I've been meaning to tell you I've decided to try for a job in signalling. Mr Jenkins told me what exams I'd have to take and how to prepare myself for them, so I've been doing a lot of studying and next time we're in port I'm going to sit the prelims . . . they're the first exams you have to pass to get a foot on the ladder. So you see, there's no point in my signing up for submarines because I doubt they'll need signallers and anyway, I don't like enclosed spaces.'

Steve frowned. 'You're real clever, Alby. You'll pass them exams all right, never you fret. But I don't see why it should matter that you want to go for a signaller. You'll still be me bezzie, won't you?'

Alby was touched by Steve's remark and tempted to let it go at that. After all, Steve would find out, in the fullness of time, that he, Alby, would almost certainly be moved to another ship upon his promotion. But one look at Steve's anxious face decided him that it would be wrong to take the coward's way out. He must explain to Steve that his promotion would probably mean his departure to another ship.

He did so, making sure that Steve understood, seeing the disappointment dawning in the other man's eyes as he took it in. It was obvious that Steve had never considered that they might be parted and was taking it hard, but even as Alby tried to think of some words of comfort, Steve's face cleared. 'Suppose you do get shifted, like you think, what's to stop me requestin' a move as well?' he asked eagerly. 'Oh, I know fellers mostly stay with the same ship, but when the war starts things will be different, won't they? Come to that, I might go for a submarine and then say I didn't like it an' get meself moved back to whichever ship you're on.'

Alby grinned; he couldn't help it. He and Steve had only been in the Royal Navy for a few months, but they had both noticed the difference between naval and merchant shipping. Discipline in the Navy – which was the Senior Service after all – was far more rigid than in the merchant fleet. With the best will in the world, Alby could not imagine the Service letting Steve flit from ship to ship as the fancy took him. But he knew his friend too well to try to make the point now. The best way of getting unpleasant facts into Steve's mind was to imitate the Chinese water torture: drip, drip, drip. You had to keep plopping the same idea over and over into Steve's apparently indifferent ear, and, eventually, he would assimilate what you were saying. But Steve was talking; he had better listen in case a reply was needed.

'. . . so you see, if our Rose finds out that she's earning more'n me, she'll put on even more airs,' Steve was saying earnestly. 'She were an only child, so her mam and dad spoiled her rotten, and I know she's cleverer than me, though only in a bookish sort of way, of course. She weren't so bad a few years back; she minded what I said, did what I telled her, but now, because she's gorra good job . . . well, life ain't that easy when I go home, to tell the truth.'

'Oh, I'm sure you're wrong and she still respects you as much as ever,' Alby said tactfully. 'Tell you what, Steve, next time we dock in Liverpool, I'll take you home to meet my Rachel, and then I'll come round to your place an' meet your Rose. How about that?'

Steve brightened. 'You might tell her she's wrong, once or twice, put her in her place,' he said eagerly. 'She'd tek it from a clever feller like you.'

Alby laughed. 'I shouldn't think that would make me exactly popular with your wife,' he pointed out. 'Specially if she came in and said, "Dinner's ready!" and I said, "No, it ain't!" I should think she'd give me a thick ear, and it 'ud be well deserved.'

Steve laughed too. 'Right then. And next time we're in Liverpool, I'll enquire about submarines.'

Alby was worried by the thought of Steve, who was six foot two, getting inside a submarine and then discovering that he, too, suffered from claustrophobia, but he very soon stopped worrying on that score, at any rate. When they went ashore in Kirkwall, in early June, the first thing they heard, when folk realised they were from Liverpool, was the word *Thetis*. Eyes rounding with horror, Steve listened to the dreadful details of how the *Thetis* had sunk in Liverpool Bay when undergoing sea trials. He heard how, for three terrible days, the men inside had tapped out Morse messages of despair on the hull, which had reared for a quarter of its length out of the sea. The Admiralty had eventually winched the submarine from its watery grave by looping chains around its body, but by then only four men had escaped and over seventy had either drowned or died from carbon dioxide poisoning.

'Well, the *Thetis* has made me mind up for me,' Steve said to Alby, as they climbed into the liberty boat to return to their ship. 'Why, only a madman would volunteer after that, and though I'm none too bright, I don't mean to lose me life for a few extra bob in me pay packet.'

'I think you're very sensible,' Alby said gravely. 'No

point in putting yourself in more danger than you need, old feller.'

'No, and you might not pass the exams after all,' Steve said brightly, and looked puzzled when Alby laughed.

'Mammy, if there isn't going to be a war, why do we have to have gas masks? I hate mine, I does. It smells of poo an' I won't wear it.' Petal looked with distaste at the small black-snouted gas mask with which she had been issued. 'I shall throw it away when I get home.'

Rose and the two children were walking back to Bernard Terrace. It was a fine summer afternoon and Rose sighed despairingly as she looked down into her small daughter's defiant face. 'No, Petal, you can't throw it away because if there is a gas attack, it could save your life,' she explained patiently. 'I know it smells funny – that's because it's made of rubber – but it's better to be alive than dead, wouldn't you say?'

Daisy, viewing her own gas mask with equal distaste, reached round her mother to rumple her little sister's fair curls. 'Don't be daft, Petal,' she said briskly. 'Mine smells horrible, too, but I bet gas would smell worse. Anyway, it's just a pre— pre— oh well, it's just in case there's a war. An' those Nazis are so horrible they might easily cheat an' send gas over without lettin' on a war had started, so just you keep your gas mask ready, like it says on the posters.'

Petal stuck out her lower lip. 'But it makes a roarin' sound when I breathe,' she objected. 'And it pinches me round my face an' that horrible rubber thing pulls my hair.'

Daisy sighed dramatically. 'Yes, it pulls my hair, too,' she agreed. 'But when we get home, Mam'll fix it so it's comfortable. And anyway, if there isn't going to be a war, they'll expect you to hand it back in, I suppose, for the next war, you know,' she ended, with the practicality of childhood.

'You're probably right, Daisy,' Rose said with a chuckle, 'but actually, everyone seems to think it's only a matter of time before the war starts. Still, no need to spoil a nice summer day by talking about it.'

Daisy agreed and when they reached home, Rose took their gas masks in their small cardboard cases and hung them, with the coats, on the back door. She devoutly hoped that all the talk of war would come to nothing, but she did not believe that the government would be placing huge orders for uniforms if they did not consider war was imminent.

Life, however, had to go on. She and her friend Maisie, who lived next door, often talked over what they would do if – when – war started. Both young women were aware of the air power which Germany had used in support of the rebels in the Spanish civil war, and everyone assumed that they would start air raids over Britain the moment war was declared. Liverpool, with its busy docks, was bound to be a target and Maisie had talked about evacuation of children, half fascinated, half repelled by the idea. Like Rose, she only had two children, a girl of fourteen and a boy of six. 'They're sayin' some mams can go along wi' their kids but, for one thing, I'd die o' boredom, stuck in the bleedin' country,' she had said frankly. 'And for another, I'm in the best paid job I've ever had an' I don't mean to give it up wi'out a struggle.'

'I can't afford to give mine up,' Rose had replied. 'But perhaps the kids won't have to go, perhaps it won't come to that. It's all right for you, Maisie, you've got Dick workin' on the docks, so that'll be a reserved occupation, and your Trixie's selling china in Bunney's, so she won't be evacuated, 'cos it's just school kids. I know your Freddie would have to go, but you'll still have some company. But I'd be all on me lonesome, and I don't fancy that, I'm telling you.'

But that conversation had taken place several weeks before. Now it was the last day of August, the school holidays were drawing to a close, and somehow war no longer seemed something which might or might not happen, something which could be pushed to the back of one's mind as a problem for tomorrow. The last time he had been home, Steve had bought her a wireless set and commanded her, brusquely, to listen to the news bulletins. 'If there's anything important in 'em, mind you tell me in your letters,' he had said. 'Alby's Rachel is goin' to do the same, but of course letters foller us for weeks sometimes, afore they gets delivered.' He had looked at her keenly. 'What did you think of my pal Alby, then?'

Alby had come round to Bernard Terrace on Steve's last leave and Rose had taken to him at once. He was short and swarthy, with a large Roman nose, and he was one of those men who even grew hair on the back of their hands, something Rose usually abhorred. But somehow, within a few minutes of meeting Alby, one forgot his looks and was only aware of a strong and delightful personality. However, Rose had looked at Steve cautiously, because she never knew how her husband would take even the most ordinary remark. 'Alby? Well, he's no oil painting, is he? But he seemed really nice,' she had said, trying not to sound either insincere or too impressed. Before they were married, a friend of Steve's had asked her to dance. Naturally, she had done so and had been astonished at the depth of Steve's fury. She knew now that, had they been married then, he would probably have become violent as soon as they were alone, but at the time, though she had felt a little uneasy, she had not read the signs aright.

Now, however, caution was second nature in her dealings with Steve. Besides, much though she had liked Alby, she knew Steve would never have cause to be jealous in that direction. Alby adored his Rachel, was proud of her, brought her name into every conversation and generally made it clear that he was a man deeply in love.

'Can we play out now, Mam?' Daisy's voice brought Rose's thoughts abruptly back to the present. 'After all, we'll be in school again in a few days' time.'

'Yes, all right, only your tea will be on the table in half an hour, so don't go too far,' Rose warned. 'Petal, stay with Daisy, there's a good girl.'

She wondered whether she ought to make them take their gas masks then prudently decided against it. She could just imagine Petal carefully placing hers in the path of one of the big shire horses who pulled the brewery carts, or balancing it on a tram line, or getting rid of it in some other fashion.

'Right you are, Mammy,' Petal said briskly, heading for the back door. 'If me pals are playin' out, then—'

The back door opened so abruptly that Petal gave a squeal of alarm and jumped back, then leaped forward and cast herself at the intruder. 'Daddy, Daddy, Daddy!'

Steve swung her into his arms and gave her a hug, then put his arm round Daisy's small shoulders; an action unusual enough to make Rose stare.

She smiled at her husband, though a trifle cautiously. What on earth was he doing here? He usually tried to let her know when he would be in port but, of course, letters went astray or were posted too late to arrive before ships docked, and this must be a case in point. 'Hello, Steve. Fancy seeing you,' she said, reaching for the big iron ladle which hung on a hook beside the stove.

Steve saw the movement and gave an exasperated sigh before standing Petal carefully down on the kitchen floor. 'I aren't drunk, if that's why you're grabbing for the ladle,' he said gruffly. 'We're mobilising down south, but we needed some new parts in the engine room, so we're here till tomorrow noon. Looks like we won't back down over Poland, so war's a certainty.'

Rose had been doing her best to follow the complicated manoeuvres which were going on in Europe, but had more or less given up. She knew that there was a pact between Britain and Poland – each one promising to defend the other – and knew that Germany was threatening to attack that country in order to gain access to the Baltic Sea. But of the diplomatic moves which were being made, she knew nothing. Mr Chamberlain's 'peace for our time' had become meaningless and she realised that Steve, as a member of the armed forces, was far more likely to know what was going on than a mere machine worker in a uniforms factory. Quietly, she turned away from the ladle and went across to the pantry. 'I didn't know you were coming but if bacon and egg and a pile of fried potatoes will do you, I can have it ready in five or ten minutes,' she said. 'If there's going to be a war, I s'pose I'd best spend me savings on any food which is likely to be rationed. What do you think?'

'Good idea,' Steve said. He turned to the children who were standing, staring open-mouthed. 'Go on, you two, gerroff an' play wi' your pals while you've got the chance.'

As soon as the girls had banged the door shut behind them, Rose began to pile bacon, eggs and cold potatoes up on a plate and heat a knob of lard in the big black frying pan. As she had said, it was no more than ten minutes before she was able to place a plate of cooked food before Steve and hurry over to the pantry to fetch a bottle of his favourite HP Sauce. Only when he was tucking in did she venture another question. 'When do you think it'll start then, Steve? Only they're saying in the factory that this war will be an air war and Liverpool will be a prime target. I know you said, ages ago, that if war came you wanted the kids out of it, away from here, but I can't go with them. My war work isn't as important as yours, but as they conscript more and more fellers – and girls – for the armed forces, they'll all need uniforms. And anyway, the money really is a help. Only – only I feel it's a bit hard on the kids, sending them off alone.'

'You send them,' Steve said, shovelling in the food. 'They'll be a deal safer away from the city. But they ain't goin' to send 'em far, just into North Wales, I dare say, or the Wirral. You'll be able to visit 'em. As for when it'll start, weren't there some sort of ulti— ultimatum? I reckon it'll start when that runs out.'

All through the evening, Steve was good with the children and behaved reasonably towards Rose. Next day, she went with him to see him off, a thing she hadn't done since the early days of her marriage. Her feelings towards him were still ambivalent, but he was going into danger, there could be no doubt of that, and the least she could do was wave him off and wish him well.

On the dockside, she saw Alby and his wife. They were clinging unashamedly, and tears were running down the woman's pale cheeks. Rachel was small and plump, with very large dark eyes, thickly curling black hair, and skin as pale as milk. When Steve called out to Alby, she hastily wiped away her tears and turned towards them, revealing a smile of great sweetness. 'I'm being awful silly, because I know they'll come home safe,' she said in a small voice, addressing Rose. 'Only it's so hateful seeing them go off after only a few hours ashore.' She turned back to her husband. 'Now mind you take care of yourself and write me lots of letters,' she said, in a voice that she strove to make practical. 'And if you're right, and the war really does start quite soon, then I'm going to leave me Auntie Leila's shop and take up some war work, like what Rose here has done.' She turned back to Rose. 'I'm real good wi' me needle,' she confided. 'D'you think they'd take me on?'

'I'm sure they would, because most of us are just machinists and they always need workers in the finishing department,' Rose said encouragingly. She was guiltily aware that her own lack of emotion over Steve's departure must be putting her in a bad light with the younger woman, but she could not help it. For many years, Steve had beaten and bullied her and she had dreaded his homecomings; the fact that he now seemed to treat her better could not make up for the bad times. She knew that, for some time at least, the mere sight of his tall figure would be enough to start the cold trickle of fear down her back and the churning of apprehension in her stomach. But now Alby was wrapping his arms round Rachel, stroking her hair and kissing her with a degree of tenderness which made Rose's stomach lurch, this time with envy. How wonderful it must be to be loved like that! All around them, other men were saying goodbye to their womenfolk, mostly showing little emotion, though several of the women had tears on their cheeks. Alby released Rachel and turned towards the gangway and Steve grabbed Rose's shoulders – she could not help a quick wince – and kissed her briefly on the forehead. 'Mind you take care o' them girls o' mine and see they're sent off somewhere safe,' he said. And before she could reply, he was mounting the gangway, leaving her without so much as a backward glance.

Rose and Rachel stood and waved until their men had disappeared into the bowels of the ship, then Rachel wiped away the tears, blew her nose and smiled up at the other woman. 'You're so sensible, Rose,' she said in a small voice. 'But you an' Steve have had years together; Alby an' me's only been wed a twelvemonth. I expect I'll get used to sayin' goodbye to him, given time.'

The two women turned away from the quayside, heading back towards the city. Rose did not want to tell Rachel how she felt about Steve, yet it seemed like cheating to pretend that she was hiding deep emotion, able to conquer her sadness by strength of character. Hesitantly, she remarked that her married life had not been all plain sailing. 'Steve wouldn't think much of it if I wept all over him. And besides, I've been seeing him off for the best part of ten years now,' she confided. 'To tell you the truth, Rachel, there have been times when I were downright glad to see him go. He – he's not so good when he's downed a few pints, if you see what I mean.'

Rachel looked up at her, her big dark eyes full of understanding. 'I did wonder, from something Alby let fall once . . . but he said all that was a thing of the past. He said Steve's been off the drink . . . oh, for ages.'

'He's been much better,' Rose acknowledged, as they crossed Islington. She paused on the far pavement. 'Want to come back wi' me for a cuppa and a scone? You could meet Daisy and Petal; they're good kids but if Steve's right, and war really does break out, I'm goin' to send them to the country, so you may not meet them again till the war's over.'

'I'd like that,' Rachel said gratefully, falling into

step beside her. 'When d'you think I could call round to your factory, ask them if there's any jobs goin'?'

'Come on Monday morning, around nine o'clock; Mr Mellors's assistant will be in then and she'll tell you when to come for an interview,' Rose said.

The two young women chatted amicably as they made their way back to Bernard Terrace. Rose had left Daisy and Petal in the charge of Dulcie Briggs, knowing she could be relied upon to keep the children out of mischief and to organise them into games which would not lead to fights or damage to property. As they entered the terrace, Rose saw that today it was skipping. Two big girls turned a rope while at least a dozen smaller ones dashed in and out, chanting the strange, sometimes meaningless catches and songs which accompanied jumping rope. Daisy, her pony tail bobbing as she jumped and her face pink with exertion, saw her mother and ran out and Petal, who had seemed absorbed in a game with a number of other small girls, came flying over as well.

'Why didn't they come to see their daddy off?' Rachel enquired. 'Surely they would have enjoyed that?'

'I'm afraid it's rather old hat for them,' Rose said. 'They're back to school on Monday so they want to play with their friends whilst the holiday lasts.' She shot a quick sideways glance at Rachel. 'To tell you the truth . . .'

'Mam doesn't usually go down to the docks to see Dad off,' Daisy interrupted. 'Usually, Dad goes down earlier to have a jar or two with the fellers. Only today, he asked Mam to go since she weren't working. We could have gone, me and Petal, only the dock's always so crowded when a ship's leaving and we get shoved and pushed around, you know, being small.'

Rachel laughed. 'I'm small meself, so I know what you mean,' she said cheerfully. 'D'you know who I am?' She pointed a finger at Daisy. 'I know you must be Daisy . . .' she transferred the pointing finger at the younger girl, 'and you must be Petal; but do you know who *I* am?'

Petal said nothing. She put her index finger in her mouth and regarded Rachel solemnly before suddenly remarking: 'It's rude to point, missus; my mammy says so and so does our teacher.'

Rachel laughed again. 'You're right,' she acknowledged. 'But aren't you even going to have a guess?'

Petal did not reply, but Daisy said thoughtfully: 'You might be a pal of me mam's, someone what works in her factory, but I don't think you are. I think you must be the lady what's married to Dad's friend Alby. I think you're Mrs Cohen.'

'Clever girl,' Rachel said approvingly. She fished a small purse out of her handbag, flipped it open, and handed each child a round, brown penny. 'There you are, a prize for being so clever. Now don't go spending it all in one shop.'

'Thank you *very* much,' Daisy said fervently. 'Can we go and spend it now, Mam?'

Rose agreed that they could go to the corner shop, but Petal hung back, gazing from the penny in her fist to Rachel's face. 'Only – only I didn't guess, so I shouldn't have the penny,' she pointed out. 'It isn't fair that I should have a penny when I couldn't think who you were.'

'Ah, but you reminded me that it's rude to point,' Rachel said, virtuously, but with a twinkle. 'So you see, you are just as entitled to your penny as Daisy is.'

Petal thought this over for a moment, then nodded vigorously. 'Okay,' she said, joyously. 'Come on, Daisy, I'll race you to the corner shop.'

Chapter Three

The first Sunday in September was warm and sunny, and when Rose looked out of her bedroom window her first thought was how nice it would be to take the children to the beach. Next day they would be back in school and who knew what the weather might do in the days ahead. But then she remembered that they were to spend today with Aunt Selina and Uncle Frank, which was an even nicer prospect than a day on the beach would have been. No sand in the sandwiches, no long journey, and no fretfulness towards the end of the afternoon because Aunt Selina and Uncle Frank would make sure that the day was as perfect as possible.

Selina was not, in fact, Rose's aunt but first cousin to her mother, though Rose had always called her Auntie since Selina was a good twenty-five years her senior, and it had seemed more natural, somehow. Selina and Frank lived in a neat house in Penny Lane. Frank ran the corner shop, helped out by his wife, whilst his elderly sister Ethel, who lived with them, saw to the house when her sister-in-law was working.

The children always enjoyed their visits to Penny Lane for they were much indulged, since Aunt Selina and Uncle Frank, childless themselves, adored children. There was always a delicious roast dinner with a special pudding for dessert, a high tea containing all the children's favourite food and, in between the two meals, a walk in nearby Prince's Park, with a bag of bread to feed to the ducks. If the weather was too wet to make outdoor pursuits possible there were various board games – old-fashioned, but none the worse for that – and usually some small gift to take home: a couple of brilliantly coloured gobstoppers, one of Ethel's home-made finger puppets, or a large and juicy orange. In short, the children always looked forward to a day spent in Penny Lane and Rose shared their feelings. Telling Aunt Selina and Ethel all about factory life, repeating the funny things the children had said or done, and hearing, in return, stories of life in the corner shop, was soothing, relaxing. The fact that the McAllisters were given delicious food which appeared on the table as if by magic helped to make each visit a memorable one, though Rose knew that they would have enjoyed their visits to Penny Lane even if they had only been given bread and margarine to eat and water to drink.

Having checked on the weather, Rose washed and dressed quickly, then popped her head round the girls' door, not at all surprised to find them already prepared for the day ahead. As the door opened Daisy, engaged in buttoning her small sister's cardigan, beamed across at her mother. 'We are almost ready,' she said proudly, 'because Aunt Selina said, last time we saw her, that if today was sunny, we could have an early dinner and take a picnic in the park. Oh, Mam, Aunt Selina's picnics are the best in the world and there'll be bread for the ducks, and perhaps some cake crumbs for the little birds. And Uncle Frank said he'd take us out in a boat on the lake if we were really good. I do *love* Uncle Frank!'

'Then we'd better have jam butties for breakfast so we can eat them as we walk down to the tram stop,' Rose said practically. 'I'll nip down and put the kettle on so we can have a cup of tea before we leave, though.'

'I'd rather have milk,' Petal observed. 'Or lemonade . . . could me and Daisy have lemonade, Mam?'

Luckily, Rose had made lemonade the day before, and presently the three of them set out for the tram stop. It was early, not yet nine o'clock, and the streets were quiet, the heat of the day already bringing with it a certain lassitude, though the children ran along in front of their mother, calling to one another and carefully avoiding the cracks in the paving stones.

They reached the house in Penny Lane and were warmly welcomed by Selina, Frank and Ethel, Selina telling them that despite the warmth she had prepared a roast dinner. 'Frank wants to listen to the Prime Minister's speech on the wireless, otherwise we might have had a cold dinner in the park,' she told them. 'But we'll eat early – I reckon we can leave the house soon after noon – and take a picnic tea out with us. I dare say there'll be a stop-me-and-buy-one in the park, so if you get too hot on the boating lake we can have a round of ice creams to cool us down.'

The children were delighted at the prospect of an early dinner and a long afternoon spent in the park, and very soon they were gathered round the dining table, watching eagerly as Uncle Frank began to carve the joint, which was beef today. It was flanked by a great many golden brown potatoes, whilst a dish piled with teacup-sized Yorkshire puddings stood in front of Aunt Selina and a tureen containing cabbage and cauliflower awaited Ethel's attention. Rose was in charge of the gravy jug, golden-bubbled and smelling delicious, and Uncle Frank had just dug his carving fork into the joint when he glanced at the clock on the mantelpiece and seemed to remember something.

'Best switch on the wireless set for a moment, Selina,' he said, pointing to the brown, box-like structure which stood right in the middle of the sideboard. 'Unless I'm much mistaken, Neville Chamberlain is going to tell us what's happened with that German feller. I can't believe they'll march into Poland, but we'd best listen to what the Prime Minister's got to say.'

Aunt Selina stood up and went over to the sideboard. For some moments, strange sounds issued from the large brown box. Then there was music, faint but recognisable. Aunt Selina twiddled the knobs and a voice, speaking harshly in some foreign language, boomed out.

Uncle Frank gave an exclamation of impatience and laid the carving knife down on the dish. 'Sit down, Selina,' he commanded, though not unkindly. 'You never will leave well alone. It were tuned into the Home Service earlier; all you had to do was turn the bloody thing on.'

Rose stared. Frank was seventy years old and had never previously used strong language in her presence, but before she could comment, another voice came from the radio. '. . . no such undertaking has been received and that consequently this country is at war with Germany.'

For a moment there was a stricken silence, then Frank began to carve the beef. 'Well, it were only what we must have expected,' he said heavily. 'We gave 'em chance after chance, but in the end the chances run out and it's war.'

Rose looked round the table. Her daughters seemed both solemn and puzzled, and Aunt Selina and Ethel had tears in their eyes, though neither let them fall. Rose herself felt a great many emotions, but realised that the chief one was relief. Whatever lay ahead, at least they now knew where they stood; they were at war and because they were an island, they could start pulling up the drawbridge, so to speak. It had been different for Poland; there had been no declaration of war, no warning of intent. Germany had simply invaded, aware of her immense military superiority, heedless of the rights and wrongs of the case. Rose's worst nightmare – that they might wake up one morning to find storm troopers at their door – no longer seemed a possibility. Forewarned was forearmed, and Mr Chamberlain's words – 'we are ready' – must mean something, after all.

Uncle Frank, at the head of the table, continued to carve, laying the big slices of beef tenderly on a plate which he then passed to his wife, who added roast potatoes and Yorkshire puddings before handing the plate to Ethel for vegetables. Rose, last in the line, poured gravy and passed the plate to Daisy, who regarded it with satisfaction, though the manners dinned into her by her mother prevented her from so much as touching her knife and fork. Uncle Frank was cutting Petal's meat into smaller pieces, and as he did so he glanced across at Rose. 'I saw in the *Echo* that plans for the evacuation of schoolchildren are already made,' he observed. 'You'll send these two? Only we all saw pictures of what happened in Poland. I know they can't march across the Channel – France is in the way for a start – but them Heinkels and Dorniers don't take no heed of such things. The only safe place will be deep in the country where there's nothing worth bombing.'

'Steve and I talked it over and agreed they'd have to go,' Rose said uneasily. She had tried to prepare the children, making evacuation to the country sound like a huge adventure, but it was one thing to talk about the possibility of parting and quite another to realise that it was actually upon them. When they turned up at school next day, Daisy and Petal would be labelled and led off to Lime Street station. Parents would not know their ultimate destination until they received the postcards which the children had been given to send, and Rose dreaded the moment when she would see them off on the first journey they would ever have taken without her.

Everyone now had a laden plate before them and Uncle Frank took the remains of the joint over to the sideboard, then returned to the table and sat down again. He picked up his knife and fork, the signal the children had been waiting for, and they all began to eat, though Rose felt that the food on her plate could have been sawdust, for all the attention she gave it.

Selina, however, was made of sterner stuff. 'I've made a steamed apple pudding with custard for dessert, but no one won't get any if they don't finish up every mouthful of their first course,' she announced. 'This here war is bound to mean shortages, rationing and that. So we'd best make the most of this grand dinner. I want to see clean plates and big smiles from everyone, because war or no war we're taking that picnic to the park and having a grand old day of it.'

'I'm sure we'll all eat up,' Rose said gaily. 'And tomorrow, you two girls will be starting the biggest adventure of your lives. I expect you'll be living on a farm, with animals all around you, and they'll let you help with feeding the little lambs and milking the cows . . . oh, you'll be doing all sorts! Don't I wish I could go with you, but now we're at war uniforms will be needed even more urgently, so I can't just abandon my job.'

'We'll all be doing something towards the war,' Aunt Selina said approvingly. 'Well done, Petal, well done,

Daisy, those plates are so clean I'll scarcely need to wash 'em up. Now come along, Frank, you're going to be last again.'

'When I were young, my gran told me to chew each mouthful a hundred times,' Frank observed, grinning at the children. 'I doubt if this pair so much as tasted their grub, let alone chewed it a hundred times. Still, they look pretty well on it.' He finished his last potato and heaved a satisfied sigh. 'Now who's going to help Aunt Selina to clear these plates and bring on the pudding?'

'Mammy, I know I'm not in Daisy's class at school, but – but I can stay with her on the train, can't I? And what about when we get to – to wherever we're going? Only I'd rather be with Daisy, even than with the other kids in my year, and – and who'll help me dress in the mornings and tell me to change my socks if I aren't with Daisy?'

Petal's small face, looking anxiously up at her, wrung Rosie's heart. Petal had put into words what had been worrying Rose herself, for though the teachers had assured parents at a meeting some time earlier that every effort would be made to keep families together, they had admitted that this might not always be possible. But Rose smiled reassuringly down at her little daughter, determined not to let her own fears show. 'I've told Miss Adams, and Miss French, that you must be kept together so I'm sure they will see that you aren't parted.'

As she spoke, the untidy group of children and mothers entered Lime Street station and Rose, glancing up at the clock, realised that she must begin to make her way to the factory, for lateness would not be tolerated. The teachers were rounding the children up, trying to get them back into line, and Rose bent over Daisy and gave her a hug. 'Take care of your little sister, queen,' she said quietly. 'You've got your postcard? You won't forget to write it as soon as you arrive, letting me know your new address? I'll do my very best to come and see you at the weekend, but if I can't make it I'll write back to let you know your postcard has arrived safely. Have you got your carry-out? Your gas mask? Your toothbrush and your little suitcase? Yes, I see you've got everything; you're a good girl.'

Tears trembled on Daisy's long lashes but she caught hold of Petal's hand and smiled bravely up at her mother. 'Yes, we've got everything, Mam; you've checked us at least six times this morning already, and we've not had a chance to put anything down,' she said. 'I'll do everything you told me and I won't let them separate me and Petal, no matter what.' She glanced round her rather wildly. 'But – but I haven't seen Nicky, Mam. He'll be coming with us, won't he? I know he's not often in school, but he won't stay in Bernard Terrace when all the other children have gone, will he?'

'No, no, he'll be here somewhere, along with the Ryan kids,' Rose said, rather absently. She felt tempted to add that they might not recognise Nicky with his layers of dirt washed off and his best clothes on, for everyone had been warned that the children must look respectable. At that moment, however, she caught sight of him. His hair had been cut cruelly short and he wore a shirt and trousers, both far too large for him. Rather to her surprise, his gas mask case was slung over one shoulder and one pocket of his shabby jacket bulged with what was, presumably, his carry-out. He saw her watching him and came over to them, grinning cheerfully.

'Mornin', missus; wotcher, girls,' he said. 'You awright, Daisy? I'm lookin' forward to it, me. Be a change from Ma Ryan's awful cookin', any road.' He turned to Rose. 'And don't you go worryin', missus, I'll keep an eye on these two for you.'

'You won't be able to; you're eleven an' Daisy an' me's younger,' Petal pointed out dolefully. 'Oh, here comes Miss French; she's shouting at you, Nicky.'

Miss French bustled up to them, telling Nicky crossly to get back to his own age group, waiting until he did so before patting Rose's arm and assuring her that she would take care of Daisy and Petal. 'And I don't mean to have my girls mixing with toughs like that young fellow,' she said decisively. She turned to the children. 'Say goodbye to your mother, my dears, our train has arrived.'

Rose turned to the girls and kissed them, lifting Petal up in her arms first and then doing the same to Daisy. 'My darlings, take care of yourselves and each other,' she said urgently. 'And – and have fun and be good.'

'We will be good, Mam,' Daisy said. 'Now you go off 'cos you mustn't be late for work. We'll be all right, see if we ain't!'

It had been a long and tiring day and the children's carry-out was nothing more than a memory before they arrived at their destination, the small town of Ruthin, set deep in the Welsh countryside. The children were ushered off the train and lined up in a long crocodile on the platform. The teachers were reinforced here by half a dozen friendly and efficient-looking country women who were to show them the way to the Town Hall, the temporary reception centre where they would meet the people who would take them in.

As they left the station, Daisy looked around her. Ahead of her, rearing above the slate roofs of the little town, she saw a church steeple and the face of a gold-figured clock; saw too that though the town itself was in a hollow with hills all around, it was also built on a hill so that the road up which the ladies were leading them was a steep one. Daisy looked round her with pleasure; in the warm September sunshine she thought it a fairytale town, a far cry from the huge imposing buildings and crowded streets of Liverpool but none the worse for that. She took Petal's hand, for her little sister had begun to lag. 'Not far now,' she said encouragingly. 'And when we get there the lady said we'd get give a nice tea. You'll like that, won't you?'

'Yes, I'd like to have me tea,' Petal admitted. 'I shouldn't have ate me carry-out so quickly – you did say I shouldn't – but I was so excited that I couldn't wait.' She heaved a deep sigh, dragging on Daisy's hand. 'Is it much further? Only me little legs is achin' like billy-o.'

Daisy was about to reply when she saw the children at the head of the crocodile turning into a large stone-built building. It had narrow windows, above which were pointed, almost churchlike, arches and over the double oak doors there was a carving of an ancient castle. Daisy and Petal, still holding hands tightly, went through the doors into a milling crowd of children and adults, feeling somewhat at a loss. Their teachers could not be immediately identified in the throng, but before Daisy could begin to panic someone grabbed her elbow and she turned to see Nicky Bostock grinning down at her. He had a plate in one hand piled with sandwiches, biscuits and buns, and a mug of tea in the other. 'Ain't this just prime?' he said, pushing the plate into Daisy's hands. 'Go on, gerroutside o' that lot, the pair of you. Us fellers were sent ahead and I'm already full to burstin'. Here, Petal, hang on to me mug o' tea and I'll fetch you an' Daisy one – or would you rather have milk? There is milk – I see'd a big jug of it.'

Both girls opted for milk and Nicky disappeared into the crowd once more, so Daisy steered her little sister to a vacant chair and they sat down with the plate of food in Daisy's lap and began to eat. A big, commanding-looking woman with cropped grey hair and a weather-beaten face saw them and came over. 'You've not lost much time,' she observed. 'Well, I just hope you can eat all that food since you've helped yourselves to such a quantity. You should never forget there's others just as hungry as yourselves, you know.'

Daisy was so humiliated at this suggestion of greed that she only stared, open-mouthed, but Petal was made of sterner stuff. 'We was give it, we didn't ask for it,' she said, her voice shrill with indignation. 'We's too little and weak to push through that great crowd round the food tables, so don't you say we took more'n our share, 'cos we never did. Our mam's brung us up not to grab, missus!'

The woman's face grew so red that Daisy thought she was about to burst but, apparently, she was not angry, only amused, for she gave a great bark of laughter and ruffled Petal's long fair locks. 'I apologise unreservedly . . . that means I'm sorry I misjudged you,' she said, still smiling. 'And anyway, the ladies' committee have been truly generous and provided enough food for double the number of children who have arrived here today, so you tuck in and enjoy it. Want a drink?'

Once more, Daisy opened her mouth to reply but was forestalled by the arrival of Nicky carrying two

Bakelite mugs of milk. He handed them over and took his own mug of tea back from Petal, then dragged over another vacant chair and sat down on it, grinning up at the large lady. 'The bossy woman in the blue check dress telled me to give her a hand and take some drinks round,' he informed her. 'Them what's supposed to be servin' is stuck behind the trestle tables and the crowd's so thick that little kids can't get through; or the mugs get knocked out of their hands, which is worse. I'll just down me own tea and then I'll gerrin the scrum again, see if they need any more help.'

Daisy watched with awe as Nicky drank his tea in one long swallow and then disappeared into the crowd once more. She glanced across to where the elderly woman had stood, but she had disappeared so Daisy sipped her milk and ate the food, and told herself that she was lucky to have a friend like Nicky who would look out for her and Petal, in this land which was as strange to him as it was to herself.

They had just finished their food, and Daisy had placed the plate and the empty mugs neatly beneath the wooden chair she and Petal were sharing, when a large man in a tweed suit got up on a chair, clapped his hands loudly and asked for silence. 'Now you've had your teas, children, we're going to start moving you out of here,' he said briskly. 'The folk who will take you in will come to *you*, so if you could all sit down quietly, on the floor, you'll either hear your names called or someone will come over and introduce themselves. In the meantime, stay where you are unless you hear your name. Is that clear?'

All round the hall heads were nodded, and now that everyone was seated Daisy saw, for the first time, that there were a great many grown-ups in the doorway, some of them pushing and jostling and all of them scanning the children's faces eagerly, and giving little smiles and nods of encouragement whenever they met a child's eye. On either side of the doorway there were middle-aged men holding lists and talking to the waiting women and then some of the women were handed sheets of paper and waved into the room. The first women called out names, children raised their hands and at long last Daisy could see that things were beginning to move. She and Petal sat cross-legged, gazing with interest at the faces of the women as they advanced into the room. Most looked kind and interesting, but there were one or two, Daisy thought apprehensively, who had mean, pinched faces or tight little mouths, which she thought augured ill for the children they were given.

Presently, however, the hall began to empty, though the press of women in the doorway did not seem to have decreased by very much. Nicky, sitting beside her, leaned over. 'I heared someone say that a good few of the kids what was expected haven't arrived,' he whispered hoarsely. 'I wish we could choose the women, 'stead of them choosin' us, specially now there's so few kids left.'

'So do I,' Daisy murmured in heartfelt tones. She looked at Petal, whose fair curls were rumpled and whose eyelids were beginning to droop, then down at her own neat person. She had seen Fanny Hanson and her sister Esme go off with a fat and comfortable-looking woman, and wondered why two girls renowned for being both untidy and dirty had been chosen in preference to Petal and herself. She voiced the thought to Nicky, who said reassuringly that this was not the case. 'Them women gets give name by the fellers – someone said they're council officials –

standin' each side of the doorway,' he explained. 'You'll get took by someone nice, don't you worrit. And so will I, of course,' he finished, his tone of bright optimism contrasting oddly with the worried look in his eyes.

And presently, there were only six children left, and Daisy saw Petal's eyes filling with tears and felt angry enough to jump to her feet, even though she was immediately told to sit herself down again by one of the ladies' committee. 'I shan't,' Daisy said, defiant for the first time in her life. 'We – we don't care if no one wants us, my sister and me, 'cos we've got a good mammy back in Liverpool and if none of these ladies wants us we'll go back to her right now, even if we have to bleedin' well walk every inch of the way.'

There was an indignant murmur from the waiting women and one of them surged forward and took both Daisy's hands in a warm and comforting clasp. 'It's a scandal the way they've arranged things, my little love,' she said warmly. 'There's a dozen women here what 'ud be happy as larks to have you live with them, but we aren't allowed to choose else a nice little couple like you and your sister would have been took among the first.' She reached out to pat Petal's cheek. 'What's your names, loves?'

'We're Daisy and Petal McAllister,' Daisy said, rubbing her eyes with the backs of both hands, 'and – and the boy what's with us is Nicky Bostock. He lives near us only he's got no mam and dad, so he lives with the Ryans, and – and they went ages ago.'

'McAllister and Bostock, McAllister and Bostock,' the woman murmured. 'I guess there's someone at the back of this lot . . .' she indicated the women in the doorway, 'who can't get through to you, but I'll soon put that right. You wait on a moment.'

She turned and pushed her way through the crowd and presently reappeared with a broad beam almost splitting her face in two. 'They are for Mrs Blodwen Williams of Ty Siriol,' she said breathlessly to the nearest council official. 'She came in the pony and trap and meant to leave the pony in front of the station where there's tethering posts and that. But someone has left a couple of wild sheepdogs tied up there, and Myfanwy – that's the pony – wouldn't settle, so Mrs Williams had to wait until the dogs' owner turned up. She's down there now, doesn't like to leave the pony, so if you'll tick them off I'll take them out to the trap.'

The man to whom she had been speaking consulted his list, marked it, and then nodded, and the woman took Daisy and Petal by the hand and would have led them out, but Daisy hung back. 'Wharrabout Nicky?' she asked wildly. 'He's the only one left now and I telled you, the Ryans went ages ago!'

The men consulted their lists with worried frowns, shaking their heads, but the woman who held the girls' hands was of a more practical turn of mind. 'Count up the Ryans,' she said suddenly. 'If this lad lives with the Ryan family, I guess someone simply didn't realise he wasn't a Ryan too. Go on, count the Ryans.'

There was an anxious moment whilst the men scanned their lists, then one of them said, slowly: 'There's more'n one family of Ryans, you know, but I've got a group here, eldest Nicky, then four others, the youngest Tommy.'

Daisy gave a crow of triumph. 'Nicky's a Bostock . . . I *telled* you so,' she said. 'Is he to go with 'em, after all? Can someone show him the way?' She looked back. Nicky was standing in the hall with both hands shoved deep into the pockets of his trousers. His lips were pursed as though he was whistling, but no sound emerged, and though he had ducked his chin and was staring down at his feet, Daisy thought there were tears on his stubby black lashes. She did not wonder at it, for the tiny taste she had had of being unwanted still hurt her with an almost physical pain.

'He can't go to Mrs Hepzibah Evans; she was grumbling she hadn't got room for the children she did take, so she won't thank you for an extra one . . .' one of the men was beginning, when the woman who was holding Petal and Daisy let them go and surged back towards Nick. 'Get your stuff, young man, you're coming with me,' she said briskly, ignoring the murmurs from the women in the doorway and the council officials. 'I'm Mrs Foley and my husband and me have got a flat over our butcher's shop in Clwyd Street. You look a likely lad to me and the child I was expecting hasn't turned up yet . . . besides, I can always squeeze in an extra one.'

Nicky looked up at her. 'Thanks, missus,' he said gruffly. 'I – I won't be no trouble.' As the woman and the three children pushed through the crowd in the doorway, he gave Daisy's shoulder a poke. 'Thanks, Daisy, but I knew it would be all right, really,' he muttered. 'See you in school tomorrer, I reckon.'

They emerged into a cool dusk with a sliver of moon already showing as the daylight faded. Mrs Foley handed the girls over to another woman before bustling Nicky away in what Daisy guessed to be the direction of Clwyd Street, and the girls were led back down the hill to the station where they saw a pony and trap from which a large woman was descending. She had bright red cheeks, thick grey hair plaited into a coronet around her head, small twinkling brown eyes, and an expression of great friendliness; Daisy liked her on sight and knew, from one glance at Petal's face, that her sister felt the same. Their companion led the girls up to the trap, saying as she did so: 'Here's Daisy and Petal McAllister, Mrs Williams, come all the way from Liverpool to stay with you until it's safe for them to return to their own home.'

Mrs Williams held out two arms like bolsters, and gathered the girls into a warm embrace. 'Sorry I am that I couldn't come into the hall after you, fynwy fechan i, but Myfanwy has a mind of her own and there was nowhere to tether her where she wouldn't be in the way,' she said. She produced, from her pocket, a couple of lumps of sugar and handed one to each child. 'Want to get on her good side? Know how to feed a horse?'

'You must keep your hands flat or they'll nibble your fingers,' the girls replied in a chorus, for Mammy often gave them a piece of carrot or perhaps even a bit of bread to give to the milkman's old dappled mare. We may not be country children but we do know something about horses, Daisy thought proudly, as she felt the pony's soft lips twitching across her palm.

With the pony satisfied, Mrs Williams helped the two children into the trap. Before climbing up herself she checked that nothing obscured the white painted bands across the back of the trap, though there seemed to be very little traffic around at this time in the evening.

As soon as she had taken her seat, she clicked to the pony and the equipage moved forward. Daisy looked around her as the pony began to trot along a curved road and across a bridge over what Mrs Williams told her was the river Clwyd. Then they turned right into the road which led, their companion said, to Ty Siriol, which was the name of her farm. On the left hand side Daisy saw a stone-built school with gabled windows and a sizeable playground, and when she remarked on it Mrs Williams told her that it was Borthyn School, where she and Petal and their schoolfellows would be attending classes.

She began to ask Mrs Williams about the farm but had scarcely got out more than a few words when Petal spoke in an urgent undertone. 'Daisy, is we going far? Only I need the lavvy ever so bad.'

Despite the fact that she had almost whispered, it was Mrs Williams who replied. 'You poor little thing. I'll draw up just as soon as we're clear of the houses and I dare say you can use the ditch, for we've had nigh on two weeks of dry weather and the farm's still some way from here. Dilys – she's my daughter – will have supper on the table for when we get home.' As she spoke, she drew the trap into a gateway and indicated that the girls should get down. Petal leaped out with such alacrity that she almost fell and Daisy, following more slowly, realised that she, too, needed to spend a penny, and the sooner the better. She steered Petal towards the gate, unlatched it and swung it partly open, then looked into the meadow beyond and changed her mind, shutting the gate before Petal could venture through it. 'There's huge cows in there; we'll do what Mrs Williams says and go in the ditch,' she announced. 'No one will see us 'cos of all that tall grass and wild flowers . . . oh, Petal, I said in the ditch, not on the bank! You can be seen for miles, I should think.'

'I don't care,' Petal panted. 'I'm in a *hurry*, Daisy, and that means I can't wait. But you can go in the ditch if you like. Can I get back in the trap when I've finished?'

'No you can't, you can jolly well wait for me,' Daisy said crossly, bobbing down. 'I shan't be a minute . . .

oh, Petal, your skirt's got tucked into your knickers. Wait a minute and I'll straighten you out.'

'I want to get back in the cart,' Petal whined. 'I stung me bum on a stinging nettle and I want to sit on it and squash the sting out of it else I shan't be able to sleep tonight. Come *on*, Daisy!'

Presently, the children got back in the trap and the pony set off once more, trotting briskly along the road, though Mrs Williams kept well to the side.

During the drive, Daisy suddenly knew that she would remember this journey all her life. As they had left the town behind she had seen the great humped shoulders of a mountain range on her right, and she could even make out the dim shapes of sheep and cows in the meadows. In places, the road was tree-lined, in others, pasture. The breeze which blew into her face smelt of sweet country things, without a hint of smoke from factory chimneys or Mersey mud. Above her, stars swam in the dark blue of the sky, and the silver eye of the moon lit up the road ahead so clearly that it could almost have been day. The quiet was only broken by the creaking of the pony's harness and the tappety-tap of its hooves on the tarmacked road, and Daisy thought these sounds were far more beautiful than the sounds of home: the clank and clatter of trams, the hooting of ships on the Mersey, and the constant hum of traffic and shouts of noisy, exuberant people going about their daily business.

Mrs Williams began to talk, telling the children that her name was Blodwen and that they should call her 'Auntie Blod'. 'You'll meet my daughter, Dilys, and Mr Williams – you must call him Uncle Gwil – when we reach Ty Siriol,' she told them. 'I have a son as well as a daughter; his name is Gareth, but he's in the Rifle Brigade and abroad at present, so you aren't likely to meet him. We've farmhands who work for us, of course, and neighbours who come and go, but a farm in the Welsh countryside is probably very different from your own home.' The children were seated one each side of her and now she looked a trifle anxiously first at Daisy, then at Petal. 'I guess you'll be homesick at first, but we'll do our best to see that you're happy and I'm sure you'll soon settle in,' she told them. 'Someone will drive you into Ruthin to school each day – it'll probably be Dilys or myself – so you won't lack for friends, and your mam can come and stay whenever she's able, though I believe she has a job?'

'Yes, she does; she makes uniforms for soldiers and sailors and airmen,' Daisy said eagerly. 'It's very important work; she's helping with the war effort. But she'll come and visit us just as soon as she has some time off, she promised.'

'Well, isn't that grand?' Mrs Williams said heartily. 'I understand from your teachers that none of you will be expected in school tomorrow, and maybe not the day after either, so you'll have time to get to know the farm before your mam arrives. Dilys will take you round tomorrow, and show you where everything is – hens, pigs, sheep, barns and stables, cowshed and byres – and you'll find you soon grow accustomed.'

'Will we be able to help on the farm?' Petal squeaked. 'Our mammy said there were all sorts of jobs what needed doin' on a farm. Feedin' animals and c'llectin' eggs and cuttin' corn . . .'

Mrs Williams laughed. 'We'll teach you to do all of it in time,' she said reassuringly. 'And we've a quiet old pony which Dilys used when she was a girl; you can learn to ride on Feathers if you like.'

'We'd love that, wouldn't we, Petal?' Daisy said

eagerly. 'Do you have dogs and cats? Petal and me's always wanted a dog or a cat, but Mam said it were just another mouth to feed, and besides – besides, our dad doesn't like cats or dogs. I see him kick a cat right across Bernard Terrace once, when he thought no one were lookin'. The poor thing were only walkin' along, mindin' its own business, when it found itself flyin' through the air on the toe of Dad's sea boot.'

Mrs Williams said something under her breath, in a language which Daisy guessed must be Welsh, then smiled apologetically. 'Sorry, I was forgetting. As you say, a good reason for not keeping a cat, but to answer your question, we've three sheepdogs and probably half a dozen cats. So your dad's a seaman, is he? Then I dare say he won't be home all that often.'

Daisy agreed, thinking that Mrs Williams sounded as though she had no wish to be visited by a man who kicked cats. She wondered, rather doubtfully, if she should not have told this lovely, comfortable woman about that particular incident, but then the trap turned right, into a wonderful leafy lane which wound between high banks. Trees grew on either side, sometimes leaning over the lane so that their mingling branches turned it into a mysterious tunnel, and Daisy sat forward on her seat, gazing ahead with all her might, spellbound by the beauty and strangeness of it.

'Not far now, chicks,' Mrs Williams said, as though guessing how tired they both were. 'Now don't forget, you may call me Auntie Blod and Mr Williams will be Uncle Gwil, because there's no sense in formality when you're all sharing a house. Here we are then, home at last!' As she spoke, she turned the pony into a large, paved yard, surrounded on three sides by what Daisy imagined must be farm buildings. Ahead of them was the farmhouse. It was a low, whitewashed building, slate-roofed and somehow reliable-looking, as though it had been there for many hundreds of years and would still be there in the hundreds of years to come. There were no lights showing, but as Mrs Williams drew the trap to a halt someone opened the door and a great rush of golden light spilled out. The room thus exposed by the open door was warm and homely, with a big table covered by a red and white gingham cloth, upon which stood a large pot of something which steamed.

But before she could begin to wonder what was in the pot, a figure emerged and came towards the cart. Mrs Williams began to speak in Welsh, then stopped abruptly, heaving herself out of the trap and holding her arms out to Daisy. 'Got to remember to speak English, I have,' she said, in self-reproof. 'Dilys fach, this is Daisy and the littl'un's Petal.' She stood Daisy down on the cobbles, lifted up the drowsy Petal, and handed her to the girl called Dilys. 'You take the children inside while I deal with the trap and Myfanwy here.'

Daisy saw, as soon as they entered the lamplit kitchen, that Dilys and her mother resembled each other closely. Dilys was a tall, sturdily built girl, with rich golden hair and rosy red cheeks, very like her mother's. But Daisy found herself concentrating on the contents of that steaming pot and was grateful when Dilys, following the direction of her gaze, said with a laugh: 'We cooked a mutton stew because Mam thought there might be some delay on the road – and how right she was!' She had carried Petal into the kitchen with as little effort as her mother had shown, and now she put the child down in a comfortable ladder-backed chair, well supplied with cushions, and indicated that Daisy should sit on the one next to it.

'In the normal way we'd wait for my mam, we would, but I reckon the sooner you get fed and into bed the better.' She began to ladle a generous portion of stew and potatoes on to two dishes which she put down in front of the children. 'Eat up, my little ones, and tomorrow I'll take you round the farm and show you what sort of place it is.'

Next day, Daisy woke to find sunshine streaming through a crack in the window curtains. For a moment, she lay there, wondering where on earth she was and why she appeared to be sunk in some delicious warm softness which cradled her like a mother's arms. She remembered being told that this was a beautiful goose feather bed. Petal, no doubt, was still sound asleep beside her, and this was Ty Siriol . . . and today, the beautiful, golden-haired Dilys was to show them round the farm.

She sat up and immediately realised why the shaft of sunlight had only now struck her face. Petal was not in bed, but at the window, spread-elbowed on the broad sill with her nose pressed to the glass. The window, a sash one, was open at top and bottom, and now that she was properly awake Daisy could hear a number of fascinating sounds: buckets clanking, boots clumping across the yard, a cockerel crowing somewhere in the distance, and a cow – perhaps several cows – making the low contented sound which Daisy had always been told was mooing.

'I say, Petal, what's out there?' she said eagerly, jumping out of bed and hopping across to the window.

Petal turned and beamed at her. 'It's cows, and two black and white dogs, and heaps and heaps of chickens,' she said excitedly. 'Let's go downstairs, Daisy. I wants me breakfast but I wants to go out into all that lovely sunshine more than anything else. Oh, Daisy, ain't we lucky? The lady with the golden hair what helped me undress last night just came out of that shed with two buckets full of milk. I bet I can have some for breakfast if I ask nicely.'

She headed for her clothes but Daisy grabbed her shoulder and jerked her to a halt. 'Washing first,' she said firmly. 'A nice strip-down wash first thing, Mam said, *and* we're to clean our teeth. Is there water in that tall jug or do we have to go down and fetch it?'

'There's water,' Petal said. 'It were too heavy for me to lift but I dabbled me hands in it, honest to God I did, Daisy. Won't that do, just for today?'

'No, it will not,' Daisy said firmly. She found that Petal was not the only one who could not lift the jug but she managed to tilt it so that water ran into the round basin. She helped Petal to wash first, then washed herself, shivering as the cold water touched her warm skin, but determined to have what her mother would have called 'a proper wash'. Once they were both clean, she helped Petal to put on her underwear, cotton dress, socks and sandals, then dressed herself and brushed her hair. Petal's long wavy hair had already had the brush dragged through it. Daisy would have liked to plait her own hair or make a pony tail, but could not manage it, so left it loose. Then she and Petal plumped up the pillows and pulled the blanket across the feather bed. As they left the room, Daisy glanced round it. Whitewashed walls, a wooden floor, black with age and as uneven as the surface of the sea; a wide window with a broad sill overlooking the farmyard and framed with yellow curtains, and a roller blind which Petal must have let up in order to watch the activity below; the wash stand with its jug and basin and an enamel bucket beneath . . . aha, that would be for the slops. It was too late to call Petal back – she was already halfway down the stairs – but Daisy retraced her steps, emptied their washing water into the bucket, and peered under the bed. She remembered Dilys telling them there was a chamber pot stowed away there, for their use, but doubted whether Petal had woken for long enough to take advantage of it. However, she heaved it out and examined it critically, glad to find it empty but awed by its proportions. It was a giant pot, fit only for a giant bottom; Daisy knew she would never dare perch on it in case she fell backwards and got wedged. She wondered if they could ask for a smaller one, then dismissed the matter and, hefting the slop bucket in both hands, made for the stairs.

Their first day on the farm was a wonderful one for both children. They met Mr Williams, a small, wiry man whose checked cap seemed to be a permanent fixture, since he did not even take it off when he sat down to dinner. Because his wife and daughter talked all the time, Daisy thought he seemed a very quiet man. He ate enormously, answered any question put to him in monosyllables, had a mug so huge to hold his tea that Daisy thought a mouse could have enjoyed a good swim in it, and smoked a pipe which Auntie Blod told them smelled so terrible that he was never allowed to use it in the house. The only time he volunteered any information was when Petal asked the identity of the young man in the photograph on the parlour mantelpiece. It happened that Dilys and her mother were engaged in noisy conversation at the time, so Mr Williams was the only person to whom Petal could address her question. He grinned at her, revealing surprisingly white and perfect teeth. 'That's Gareth, our eldest,' he said briefly. 'Joined up. Rifle Brigade.

Won prizes for his shooting . . . competitions and that . . . has our Gareth.'

At this point, Auntie Blod and Dilys began to dish up and the conversation turned to what task the farmhands would undertake that afternoon.

As soon as the children had got up, Auntie Blod had taken them round the farmhouse. It was a large, rambling building, built on several different levels, so that there were steps up and down all over the place. Daisy was intrigued by what Auntie Blod called her stillroom, a sort of walk-in pantry or larder, lined with shelves upon which stood rows and rows of jams, bottled fruit and pickles of every description. The children gazed with awe at such a quantity of food, for though their mother fed them as well as she could, she did not store food in the house and had never made jam, or preserved fruit, in her life. 'Why aren't there apples or pears? Don't you grow them?' Petal had asked, having scanned the shelves. 'There must be everything else in here, except for apples and pears.'

Auntie Blod had given her an indulgent look. 'These here are all soft fruits . . . soft vegetables too,' she had explained. 'You don't see no 'taties, nor turnips or swedes either, because, although we keep 'em, we keep 'em raw, not cooked. Presently, we'll go outside and take a look at the dairy, and then I'll show you the apple loft and the potato clamp.' She chuckled richly. 'Farmers don't waste nothing; we grow too much to eat it all while it's in season, so we store the surplus.'

True to her word, when breakfast was over, she escorted them round the farm buildings. Daisy was very impressed with the dairy which had recently been built, where Auntie Blod spent several hours a day. There was a butter churn, huge marble slabs upon which containers of milk stood to cool, and a great many gleaming pans, ladles and other instruments for the making of butter, cheese and cream. Tentatively, she had asked if she might help next time Auntie Blod made butter or cheese, and was delighted to be told that, when they were not in school, they might help in all sorts of ways.

Auntie Blod had then returned to the house to prepare the dinner and Dilys had taken them all round the farm. They had seen enormous pigs – which Dilys called sows – surrounded by little pink babies. They had seen the great lumbering cows and their wet-nosed, long-legged calves. They had been introduced to the great Clydesdales who worked as hard as any man on the farm, Dilys had told them, and she had given the children carrots to feed to Myfanwy and Feathers, the ponies who pulled the trap and had once been ridden by Dilys and her brother, Gareth, when they had been younger – and a good deal lighter – and needed to get about without constantly begging lifts from their parents.

When dinner was finished, they were told they might feed the hens and were given a small scoop of corn each. Normally the hens were fed morning and evening, and not in the middle of the day, but Dilys said they must grow used to the way the poultry mobbed anyone leaving the farmhouse – she had clearly noticed that both Petal and Daisy had clung very close to her when the hens had appeared to be about to attack.

Daisy and Petal set off across the yard feeling a considerable degree of trepidation when the hens rushed towards them, flat-footed and splay-legged, making the most unholy din. Some of them actually took to the air in order to see what was in the metal scoops the children held, but as soon as Daisy, gritting her teeth, hurled a handful of grain on to the cobbles, they abandoned their attempts and began eagerly pecking, shouldering each other aside, stamping on each other's feet, and generally behaving like the undisciplined, greedy louts Daisy had thought them.

'I shan't mind the hens any more,' Petal confided, when the last of the grain had gone. 'You know that big shed on wheels, in the next field? Auntie Blod said she shuts the hens in there at night, because of foxes. She said they lay their eggs in there as well – did you peep inside when Dilys took us past it? I'd like to collect the eggs but I don't want to have to fight a great heap of chickens – hens, I mean – if they'd rather keep them.'

'The way you said it, it sounded as though foxes laid their eggs in the hen house,' Daisy said, with a giggle. 'I know the hens are all right, really – Auntie Blod said so – but I'm not going into that old shed when they are in there, not for a fortune. I did peep inside and the smell made me eyes water. There are lots of smells on a farm, aren't there? I thought the pigs would pong most of all, though I like their smell, but hens really stink.'

By this time, the hens, having eaten all the grain, had wandered off, so the children turned their steps back towards the farmhouse. They had reached the kitchen and were about to ask Auntie Blod what they should do next when Daisy clapped a hand to her mouth, giving a muffled scream. 'Oh, Petal, the postcard! We promised Mam we'd send a postcard just as soon as we knew our address! Oh lummy, she'll be so worried . . . she thought we'd arrive yesterday afternoon, not late at night, and I don't suppose there's a post box for miles!'

Overhearing, Auntie Blod turned towards them.

'It's my fault, so it is,' she said guiltily. 'Promised, I did, that you'd write as soon as you were settled, but it doesn't matter; fetch that postcard, cariad, and you can take it to the box at the end of the lane.'

Daisy ran up to her bedroom and fished the card – already stamped – out of the string bag which Rose had given her to carry their small, personal possessions in. Then she thundered down the stairs again and shot into the kitchen. Petal was eating a hot buttered scone and drinking a mug of milk, and Daisy settled herself at the table beside her with her postcard and a pencil. Starting was easy . . . 'Dear Mum . . .' but with so much to say and so little space, Daisy wondered what first to choose. Thinking it over, she realised that a lyrical description of the farm might make her mother feel that her daughters were not missing her at all, yet if she started off by saying they were homesick, her mother would be very distressed. In the end, she asked Auntie Blod what she should best do.

Auntie Blod considered. 'Just say you've arrived safely, that Ty Siriol is a farm and that Mrs Williams will be pleased to see her – and put her up for the night – just as soon as she can spare time to come,' she instructed. 'I'll write the address for you, so there's no mistake, and tell her what bus to catch.'

Petal lifted her face from her mug and stared at Auntie Blod. 'Does a bus come past here?' she asked incredulously. 'We haven't seen one all day, have we, Daisy?'

Auntie Blod laughed. 'They doesn't come all the way up here, cariad, but they stops at the end of the lane, like. Only two buses a day, there are. They leave Ruthin at eleven in the mornin' and five in the evenin', so if she drops us a line and tells us which one she'll be on, you girls can go over and meet her – give her a hand with her bag.'

'That will be lovely; but our mam works shifts at her factory and she doesn't seem to get much time off,' Daisy observed. 'But I'm sure she'll come just as soon as ever she can.' She held up the postcard. 'Have I left you enough room for what you want to write, Auntie Blod?'

Auntie Blod sighed. 'Better drop her a line myself, this evening, when I have a bit more time,' she decided. 'I can't cram all I want to say on no postcard, and I need to think before setting things down in writing.'

The farmer's wife picked up the card and scrutinised it, then took it from Daisy's hand and sat heavily down at the table. Painstakingly, she wrote the address, the tip of her tongue emerging between her lips, very much as Petal's did when she was trying to write neatly, and Daisy saw that Auntie Blod's writing was large and round; very similar to her own, in fact.

'There you are!' Auntie Blod said presently. 'I'll give Shanna a shout – she's the oldest sheepdog. She'll go down the lane with you and make sure you get there safely.' Chuckling, she added, 'Dilys would tell you Shanna's so clever she could post the card herself, and she's not far wrong at that. Now eat up your scones and drink your milk and when you come back, we'll walk down to the birch pasture and you can watch Bess and Becky – they're Gwil's two younger dogs – workin' with the sheep. You'll like that.'

Returning from her shift at the factory, Rose pounced on the postcard, realising at once that it had come from Daisy. Although the children had only been gone a couple of days, she was already missing them dreadfully. The house seemed to echo with the ghosts of their childish voices, and because she was now alone, she did not bother with cooking or a fire. She was buying a gas cooker, paying for it in weekly instalments, so she always made herself tea and toast, but it wasn't like a proper meal, and oddly enough she went to bed early because there seemed nothing worth staying up for.

She carried the card over to the kitchen table, lit the gas under the kettle, and then sat down to read the very first communication she had ever received from her elder daughter, for they had never been parted before. Daisy had not written much, merely said they had arrived safely and were living on a farm and liked it very much, but there was something reassuring in the fact that the children's foster mother – if you could call her that – had added a line of her own. *Your girls is grand*, she had written. *You are lucky! Letter follows. Yours faithfully, Blodwen Williams.*

The kettle boiled and Rose made herself a cup of tea, then went over to the bread crock for a loaf. She cut a thick slice, then hesitated. To be sure, there was a good canteen at the factory and she had had sausage-meat pie and chips there, earlier in the day, but now she realised she was hungry, no doubt because she was no longer anxious about the children. Deciding to have something more substantial than tea and toast, she went to the cupboard and scanned the shelves, pulling a face as she did so. She had been too busy to go shopping on the two previous days, although Rachel had warned her that she really ought to get in some groceries since folk were buying up everything they considered might be rationed – or unavailable – as the weeks went on. Her pantry shelves contained a tin of baked beans, a bag of rice, two tins of condensed milk and a tin of carrots. The meat safe was empty and there was, she knew, only half a loaf of bread in the bread crock. I'll have to pull myself together, Rose thought, because I don't intend to sit here and starve! Goodness, there's no more than a pinch of tea in the caddy – I really must get to the shops before they close, or I'll see nothing but empty shelves.

Having decided to eat a proper meal, she realised that beans on toast would not be sufficient, but there was always Wilson's fish and chip shop on the corner of Mary Terrace; it was only five minutes' walk away. I'll nip down there and buy myself some . . . and perhaps I'll pop in on Rachel and find out how she got on at the factory because she'll have had her interview by now . . . she's lucky really to be living at home, because I'm sure her mum cooks her a hot meal every night of the week.

Rose glanced at the clock above the mantel. Yes, the chip shop would be open; probably there was already a queue, but that didn't matter. With the children gone, one thing she did have was time.

Rose bought her fish and chips and carried the newspaper parcel round to Mrs Edelmann's house. If her friend was successful, Rose remembered, she and Rachel had planned to walk to and from work together when they were on the same shift, for since Rachel had applied for a job in the finishing department, and Rose was a machinist, they would be in different parts of the building, so though they might meet each other in the canteen from time to time they would have little contact during their actual working day.

Reaching Rachel's home on Langsdale Street, Rose tapped on the door and then stood back, suddenly realising that she could scarcely march into someone else's house carrying fish and chips which would undoubtedly make their presence felt, for she had sprinkled them with salt and vinegar in the shop, and the smell of hot vinegar was already making her eyes water.

She was just considering whether it might be better to walk swiftly away, hoping that her gentle knock had not been heard, when the door swung inward and a small woman in a pink wraparound apron, stood looking enquiringly up at her. She had black hair, parted in the middle and pulled back into a bun on the nape of her neck, and large, doe-like dark eyes. She was not pretty, being strong-featured with rather sallow skin, but there was still a degree of similarity between herself and the much prettier Rachel. Rose thought that she would have known this was Rachel's mother even if they had not met on the Edelmanns' doorstep.

'Yes?' Mrs Edelmann said.

'Is Rachel in?' Rose asked hesitantly. 'I'm – I'm a sort of friend . . . we don't know each other very well, but our husbands are aboard the same ship, and . . .'

Mrs Edelmann's face cleared, her big, dark eyes becoming soft and friendly. Then she smiled and stood back, gesturing for Rose to pass her. 'You must be Mrs McAllister,' she said, and Rose noticed that she had a slight foreign accent. 'Go through, Rachel is in the kitchen.'

Rose began to protest, to explain that she did not wish to fill their house with the smell of fish and chips, but this only made Mrs Edelmann laugh. 'My house is full of the smells of cooking; your fish and chips are nothing,' she said. 'Go through, go through. Rachel will be delighted that you have come calling. She has been lonely since Alby sailed.'

She shepherded Rose through an open doorway into a large kitchen. It was growing dusk outside and the room was lamplit, whilst a bright fire burned in the open-fronted stove. Rachel was standing by a pan of fast-bubbling water, dropping shaped pieces of what looked like pastry into it, but she looked round and beamed a welcome as Rose entered.

'Mrs McAllister, how nice of you to call! I expect you've come to ask how I got on with Mr Mellors this afternoon. But I'm forgetting my manners – would you like a cup of tea? Some cake, perhaps?'

'I'd love a cup of tea,' Rose said, suddenly aware that she was thirsty. 'But I've just bought fish and chips for supper because, to tell the truth, I've no food in; it doesn't seem important to get the messages now I've only myself to feed.'

Rachel smiled, swung open an oven door set in the wall beside the fire, and, taking the parcel from Rose, tucked it into the oven and slammed the door. 'It'll stay hot whilst you drink a cup of tea,' she said comfortably. 'Now sit down, do. Have you heard from the children yet?' she added, turning back to Rose.

'Yes, there was a postcard when I got back from work,' Rose said. 'They're on a farm and seem really happy, though it's early days yet, of course. But their foster mother is writing me a letter, so obviously she's a nice person.'

Rose settled herself in the chair and presently the two young women, both with a cup of tea before them, were seated on opposite sides of the table whilst Mrs Edelmann took Rachel's place at the stove.

Rose sipped her tea, then glanced questioningly across at Rachel. The younger girl smiled. 'I'm to start tomorrow morning, in the finishing department,' she said, jubilantly. 'I'm to have a month's trial but Mr Mellors gave me some work to do and left me for half an hour; when he came back I'd finished and he seemed really pleased with the result, so it looks as though you and I will be working together, Mrs McAllister.'

'I'm Rose and you're Rachel,' Rose said, smiling. 'Our husbands call each other by their first names so it would seem very odd if you and I did not follow suit. I've only been in the finishing department once, when I was sent to take a pile of uniforms through, and to tell you the truth, I can't remember a thing about it. Will you be working with a lot of other girls? Did you know any of them? Did they seem a friendly crowd?'

Rachel gave a trill of laughter. 'What a lot of questions! I think there are four other girls and one man doing the finishing,' she said. 'Mr Mellors took me through and introduced me but didn't leave me with them. One girl – she told me to call her Liz – will show me the ropes when I start and check that I'm doing as I ought. I don't know whether you know her – she's a tall girl with gingery hair and freckles and a mole on her cheek, just below her left eye. She seemed friendly enough so I hope we'll get on.'

'Oh, Rachel, I *am* glad,' Rose said warmly, reaching across the table to give the other girl's hand a congratulatory pat. 'What shift are you on tomorrow? I'm on days this week, which is eight in the morning till four in the afternoon.'

'I'm on days for the first month, I think,' Rachel said. 'And it would be lovely to go together, but there's no need for you to come out of your way. I'll walk up to the main road and wait on the corner. What time would be best?'

'We'd better say half past seven, since the buses are pretty crowded with folk going to work in the early mornings,' Rose said. 'We can go to the canteen together as well, as we're both on days, and I can introduce you to my friend April. She's really nice, you'll like her.'

As she spoke, Rose began to get to her feet. She realised that she wanted to get home so that she could eat her fish and chips and have a read of the new Denise Robins romance before going to bed. For the first time since the children had left, she believed she would be able to concentrate on the book, and not find her mind wandering. 'Thank you very much for the tea, Rachel, Mrs Edelmann,' she said politely, going across to the oven and taking out her parcel of fish and chips with some care, since the newspaper was now very hot. 'I'll see you tomorrow, Rachel, at half past seven prompt.'

Mrs Edelmann nodded but Rachel accompanied Rose to the front door and let her out. She said wistfully: 'I do not ask if you've heard from Steve because I'm sure you have not, but I expect, like me, you watch for the postman every day in the hope that a letter will arrive. And now you'll be waiting for the children's letters as well. If – if you hear before me – for letters can go astray – you will tell me, won't you?'

'Of course I will,' Rose said warmly, then gave a little wave and set off along the pavement. For the first time it occurred to her that being in love with your husband had some very real disadvantages. Rachel worried about Alby, wondered how he was getting on, longed for a letter from him as much as she herself had longed for her children's postcard. I wish Steve no harm, she told herself as she hurried along in the deepening dusk, but with the best will in the world, I can't put the clock back and feel about him the way I did in the early days of our marriage. Come to that, the early days of our marriage weren't all that rosy either. His bullying had begun the first time he had returned from sea and, until the incident of the frying pan, had continued relentlessly ever since. Things were better now – the frying pan and Alby had seen to that – but with Steve, you simply never knew.

Rose turned into Bernard Terrace and headed for her own front door, feeling a glow of contentment at the prospect ahead of her. A fish and chip supper, a big pot of tea and then an early night, curled up alone in her double bed with a good book: a far better and less dangerous companion than Steve would have been.

Rose fished the key out from round her neck – no need to leave it dangling through the letter box now that she was the only occupant of the house – and let herself in. She went through to the kitchen and lit the gas under the kettle, but did not take off her coat for the empty house felt chilly. She bustled about, getting a plate from the dresser and a bottle of tomato sauce from the pantry, and, when the kettle boiled, made herself a cup of tea and tipped the fish and chips on to her plate. By now she was extremely hungry and she ate quickly, drinking the scalding tea as soon as it was safe to do so. Then she washed up her plate and mug and headed for the stairs. If the children had still been living at home, she would have prepared breakfast and laid the table, but for herself, bread and jam and a cup of tea would be quite sufficient.

Presently, she climbed into bed and opened her book, telling herself that now she knew the children were safe and well, she could enjoy her solitariness without feeling guilty. Even so, she was conscious of the quiet of the house around her. If Petal lay on her back, she snored, just a gentle little rumble, and Daisy sometimes talked in her sleep, and Rose found herself missing such small sounds. At the end of the first chapter, she put the book down and blew out her candle, nipped out of bed to let up the blackout blind and open the casement, then got back into bed and gazed, a little resentfully, at the bland face of her alarm clock, set to go off at half past six. It should have comforted her to remember that, had the children been at home, the alarm would have sounded at six, for she would have needed the extra half-hour to get them ready for school, but somehow it did not. What was an extra half an hour when compared with the pleasure of her children's company?

Telling herself brusquely not to be such a fool, Rose pulled the blankets up round her ears and settled herself for sleep. No doubt the morning would bring a letter from Mrs Williams, and anyway, she meant to visit this Ty Siriol just as soon as she had a day off. Despite the war, trains and buses were still running, though the government had cancelled all public assemblies such as cinema and theatre shows. Yes, she would visit the children just as soon as she could. On that thought, Rose fell asleep.

Chapter Four

By December, Daisy felt as though she had lived on the farm all her life. Naturally, she and Petal attended the local school but only on a part-time basis. One week they had lessons from half past eight to half past twelve, the next from one o'clock to four. Their classes were somewhat disorganised by the fact that whereas at home boys and girls had followed a different curriculum, here boys and girls shared the lessons as well as the classrooms. It was soon seen that in some subjects the girls were well ahead of the boys whilst in others the boys did best, but no one seemed particularly bothered by this. Daisy noticed that even the teachers were more relaxed, seldom punishing anyone for lateness or inattention and being particularly careful to see that no child felt left out or ill done by.

The school was a low, old-fashioned one-storey building, with a slate roof and tortoise stoves in every classroom, though these had only recently been lit for the weather had continued mild right up to early December. Now, however, when Daisy and Petal left the farm, sitting behind Myfanwy in the trap, they passed through a veritable fairyland, for the trees were rimed with frost as was every twig in the hedge, every blade of grass on the verges. Daisy had never seen anything so beautiful, and loved to walk across the frosted grass when she crossed the pasture, hearing it softly crackle beneath her stout wellingtons.

On this particular morning, they left the farmhouse

just as the sun came up over the eastern hills. It was round and red and so brilliant that it took Daisy's breath away. She clutched Petal's hand and pointed and saw that Petal, too, was dazzled by it. Even Auntie Blod, who must have see the sun rise a thousand times, stood for a moment, staring, before leading them over to the stable where Dilys was just finishing tacking Myfanwy up and strapping her into the shafts of the trap.

'Mornin', girls; *bore da*,' she said cheerfully. She led the pony out into the yard as she spoke. 'I'll be meeting you myself when school's finished, to give Mam a chance to do her dairy work.' The two children scrambled into the trap and settled themselves on the leather seat, pulling up the horse blanket, which was always kept on the bottom boards, to cover their legs, for their socks ended at the knee and their skirts began six inches higher, leaving an area much prone to chilblains. Dilys glanced reproachfully up at Daisy. 'I thought you were going to get up early so that you could come with me when I took the churns down to the main road for the milk lorry to pick up.'

'I did mean to,' Daisy said remorsefully. 'But we don't have an alarm clock and Auntie Blod didn't wake me early . . . well, I forgot to ask her to,' she added honestly. 'Couldn't you wake me yourself, Dilys? Only I would love to come with you.'

'Maybe I'll wake you tomorrow,' Dilys conceded. Auntie Blod picked up the reins and Dilys stepped away from the pony's head, giving Myfanwy an encouraging slap on the rump as the pony began to move. 'See you at half past twelve, girls, and don't you be late,' she added, raising her voice. 'You must love your school, 'cos you're always last out!'

Daisy and Petal waved and shouted until Dilys was

out of sight, then they settled back to enjoy the journey. Daisy, who felt the cold, was careful to keep her hands under the horse blanket, though she was wearing the thick mittens which her mother had knitted for her and brought to the farm last time she visited. Both girls had a pair and pronounced them lovely and warm, but once the trap was moving the wind nipped at their noses and pinched their cheeks to scarlet, and a hand left outside the horse blanket, even when warmly mittened, would soon have frozen fingers. And frozen fingers mean chilblains, Daisy reminded herself. She had suffered from chilblains ever since she could remember and dreaded the itching which was worse even than the flea bites that had tormented them when they first came to the farm, though now the cold weather seemed to have sent the fleas into temporary hibernation. Auntie Blod had explained that you could not wash feather beds, but she hung them across the washing line from time to time, beating them vigorously with an instrument shaped like a three-leafed clover on a long handle, and this seemed to do the trick.

'I wonder what your mam will do for Christmas?' Auntie Blod said idly now, turning the pony and trap into the main road. 'Likely she'll come to us, do you think? We'll have one of them gobblecocks for our dinner and I've already made a big ol' puddin' and a Christmas cake what'll scarce fit into my largest tin, so there'll be food to spare.'

'It'd be lovely if she could come,' Daisy said wistfully, 'but it all depends on the factory, you know.'

'Well, hope for the best, we must,' Auntie Blod said philosophically. 'I 'spect you're doin' all sorts of Christmas things at school, aren't you? I remember, years ago, Dilys were the Angel Gabriel in one of them nativity plays which Miss Bronwen Jones organised; comes of having a yaller head, she said. An' the next year, she were the Virgin Mary. Are you doin' a nativity play this year?'

Despite the difference in their ages, Daisy and Petal were now in the same class, though the teachers gave them different work. Because numbers were falling there was a mix of country children and evacuees in each class, and the girls were learning to get on well with the local children. One of the teachers, Miss Dodd, had returned to Liverpool, but the remaining staff managed well with their dwindling classes. After Christmas, the rumour went, everyone would be having full-time school again; not something to be relished, exactly. But Auntie Blod had asked a question; Daisy shook her head. 'No, not this year; this year we're giving a concert,' she said. 'Some of us are going to sing carols and do dances; the boys are going to recite a poem, verse and verse about, you know, and the really tiny ones – that means you, Petal – are going to do a nativity *scene*; there's a cardboard donkey and a cardboard ox and we're all to bring a shoe bag full of straw or hay for the stable and Miss Bronwen Jones is going to get costumes from the dressing-up cupboard. Petal's the Virgin Mary and Sandra is lending her new doll for the baby Jesus. Its eyes open and close and when you tip it back it goes waa-aa, waa-aa, like a real baby,' she ended, rather wistfully, though when she thought about it, what was a doll compared with the charms of a kitten or a puppy, or a little new, milky lamb?

'And how do you like being the Virgin Mary?' Auntie Blod asked, turning to smile at Petal. 'An important part, it is, cariad.'

'Ye-es, but I'm not allowed to say anything,' Petal

said aggrievedly. 'I wanted to say "No room at the inn" and I wanted to look at the baby and say "It's a boy!" but Miss wouldn't let me. She was really mean. She said I was rude and I'm not rude, am I, Daisy?'

Daisy considered this as the pony clip-clopped along, its ears pricking forward and the breath rising from its nostrils in a cloud of steam. 'We-ell, I think you were a bit rude,' she observed. 'You shouldn't have pulled up the dolly's skirt before you said, "It's a boy!" That's what Miss Bronwen Jones thought was rude.'

'Yes, but how could I tell if it was a boy or a girl when it has almost no hair and only a long nightie thing?' Petal asked. 'I didn't know about boys having that little tassel until I saw Danny Spellman in the school toilets, but I knew that cows are different from bulls and boy dogs from lady dogs, so what's wrong with looking at a dolly?'

Daisy would have answered her sister sharply, but Auntie Blodwen tactfully changed the subject. 'Well, well, never mind,' she said. 'Are you making Christmas cards and paper chains and that? Out here in the country, there's holly and ivy for the asking – mistletoe too – and I dare say you'll be decorating your classrooms. Is it very different at this school from your old one?'

Daisy considered. She had been happy enough at St Ambrose Council School in Prince Edwin Street, but nowhere near as happy as she was now. For a start, her school day was very much shorter, but it was not only that. In this school, everything was geared to the countryside which surrounded them. There was a big nature table in each classroom and the pictures on the walls were all of country things. The children were expected to know the names of the trees even when they could not be identified by their burden of leaves, and pictures of field mice, shrews, stoats and weasels, rabbits and hares were pinned up all over the place.

Having considered the matter, Daisy said: 'I like this school ever so much better than the old one. It's – it's slower, somehow. Quieter. The teachers don't get as cross as they did at home, and they teach nicer things, stuff that's easier to understand. Things about animals, and plants. And Mel – he's a boy in our class – told us that in summer we'll go for nature walks, and be allowed to help on the farm during school time, if there's haymaking, or harvesting.'

Auntie Blod nodded, then drew the trap into the side of the road, for they had reached the school and could see children streaming across the asphalt playground, calling out to one another and greeting Daisy and Petal.

'Right you are. Dilys will be fetching you at dinnertime, so don't dawdle coming out. See you later.'

Blodwen sat in the trap and watched the children joining up in small groups in the playground, waiting until the bell rang and the pupils began to line up. She saw the young lad, Nicky Bostock, who lived with the Foleys on Clwyd Street engage Daisy in earnest conversation and smiled to herself. Nicky had been to the farm twice for tea and she had liked him; guessed she would see a good deal of him over the coming weeks. Only when the children had disappeared into the building did she click to the pony and set off on her journey back to Ty Siriol. Although she had said nothing to either Daisy or Petal, she had been anxious for some time about the number of children who were returning to the city. She supposed it was natural enough for parents to miss their offspring, and many of them found the long journey to visit both expensive and time-consuming. Others, of course, did not bother to visit, but wanted any child who could be useful back with them once the first fear of an immediate air attack had worn off.

For it was clear that such fears were needless. The war had been a fact for more than three months, but there had been no sign of the invasion which the government had feared, let alone attacks from the air. Once or twice enemy aircraft had been reported approaching the coast, but all they had done was drop leaflets, which had seemed to make the whole idea of evacuation pretty pointless. For her own part, Blodwen thought the parents should leave their kids where they were, for the time being at least. Why take a child back into danger? Oh, the danger might not be immediate, but it could surely not be discounted so early in the game? At the time of the Spanish Civil War, Blodwen had been to the cinema and seen the newsreel pictures of what the German air force had done to the great cities of Spain; could such scenes be forgotten so easily? But she had realised, as soon as the children began to get into lines, that the evacuees were very much thinner on the ground than they had been. She thought that of the hundred or so evacuees who had become pupils at this particular school only fifty-odd still remained. The children had told her that one of the teachers had gone back to Liverpool, and she had heard from another farmer's wife that at least one more would not be coming back to the school when term started again in the New Year, but surely Mrs McAllister, a sensible woman, would not try to take her children home? She had a full-time job, was sufficiently well paid not to grudge the cost of the journey to Ty Siriol, and was obviously very attached to Daisy and Petal. Surely she would leave them where they were so happy, at least until they were certain that there would be no bombing, no invasion?

So far, Mrs McAllister had shown no signs of wanting to take the children home, but the truth is, Blodwen Williams, that you've grown so fond of them that parting would be a real blow, the farmer's wife told herself severely. She had liked them from the first, and the more she got to know them the fonder she grew. At fifty-five, she was hoping for grandchildren, she supposed, but there was little chance of that. With Gareth in the forces and Dilys stuck out here on the farm, she might have to wait as much as five or ten years, she thought, and in the meantime Daisy and Petal were with her, making her laugh, curling up beside her on the couch of an evening to learn a poem or practise writing or even just listen to a story on Children's Hour. Losing them would be unbelievably painful. She had always liked children, especially small girls, but these two, she had long decided, were thoroughly delightful. Bright, intelligent and loving, they were a credit to Mrs McAllister's upbringing, which could not have been easy since Blodwen did not think that the girls' father had been much help.

Reading between the lines, she had gathered that Mr McAllister was not a good father, though because he was at sea a great deal she supposed that his relationship with his children would naturally be a good deal less close than that which existed between Gwil, Gareth and Dilys. But Daisy was afraid of Mr McAllister, and that was all wrong; children should love their parents, even if they regarded them with some awe. Blodwen had not sensed that either Daisy or Petal was in awe of their father, and she knew very well that both Dilys and Gareth thought of Gwil as a friend, someone to be admired and imitated, but never, in any circumstances, to be feared. No. There was no escaping the fact that Daisy feared Mr McAllister, and even Petal thought of him as unpredictable, though it was clear she was her daddy's favourite. As for Mrs McAllister, she never referred to him if she could help it, except in the vaguest and most general of terms.

The trap rattled along, and as Blodwen turned the pony into the rutted lane she made a mental note of a huge holly tree, heavily laden with scarlet berries. She would get Elias to come down later with a pair of shears and a basket, to cut holly for the house. Perhaps the children would like to accompany him and, if so, he could take them along to the orchard too, for there was an ancient apple tree there upon which mistletoe grew in round, circular clumps. It was too high for Elias to reach but if he lifted Daisy into the lower branches she would be able to climb up and break off some mistletoe twigs. Yes, the children would enjoy that, and Blodwen thought it was good for Daisy to climb trees and behave like a tomboy occasionally. Petal was the bolder of the two in a good many ways, but lately Blodwen had been encouraging Daisy to enjoy pursuits such as tree climbing and swinging from the knotted rope which, long ago, Gareth had attached to one of the lower branches of the great beech tree at the back of the stables, and Daisy had proved to be just as athletic as her sister.

And when I finish my dairy work, I'll write to Mrs McAllister and suggest that she comes for Christmas and spends a day or two with us, Blodwen decided, as the trap emerged from the lane into the farmyard. We're awful lucky that she's such a nice woman and so easy to get along with. Some of the mothers . . .

dear heaven, that woman whose boys stayed with Mrs Evan Williams, she were really rough. The language! And the dirt! They never washed properly, if at all, and their clothes were mostly rags. And Mrs Evan Williams said the mother's table manners – and the boys' – simply didn't exist. They all crammed their mouths with food, talked while they ate, jumped up from the table in the middle of a meal without so much as a by your leave, and didn't know the meaning of please and thank you. Oh aye, Gwil and I were real lucky we were given the McAllisters.

Blodwen climbed down from the trap, led the pony into the stable and left old Ben to deal with Myfanwy. Yes, there was no doubt about it, she was lucky with her evacuees and would write and invite Mrs McAllister to stay for the Christmas holiday this very day.

Rose saw Rachel waiting for her at the bus stop as she hurried along Shaw Street, and quickened her pace. The letter from Mrs Williams had arrived just as she was leaving the house and reading it, as she walked along, had obviously slowed her down, since a glance over her shoulder revealed that the bus she wanted to catch was only yards behind her. Panicking, she broke into a trot and reached Rachel, halfway down the queue, breathless but triumphant. Fortunately, the bus drew up almost as she arrived and those people behind Rachel were too eager to get aboard themselves to point out that she had jumped the queue. It was, of course, perfectly legitimate for a friend to save you a place but there were people who simply barged in and they were becoming increasingly unpopular as queues grew longer.

Petrol had been rationed since mid-September but it was food shortages which were hitting city dwellers hardest. In the last year of the previous war there had been rationing of foodstuffs, and Rose was beginning to think that even rationing would be better than traipsing from shop to shop in a vain effort to buy something perfectly ordinary, like a bag of sugar or sultanas, in order to make some sort of cake for the festive season.

She said as much to Rachel as they boarded the bus but her friend only laughed at her, shaking her head. 'You should see my mam's larder; the shelves are so laden I'm surprised they don't collapse,' she said. 'The older folk remember the last war, when you couldn't buy so much as a loaf of bread without queuing for half an hour, and things like sugar, bacon and butter were all rationed. I told her she was a wicked old hoarder, reminded her that the government had said hoarding was unfair, but she just stuck her nose in the air and said I'd be glad enough of her larder when Alby comes home wanting a decent meal. I'd offer to let you have some sultanas and that, but why don't you come round to us for Christmas? You can be sure of a good feed and a warm welcome – Mam and Dad thoroughly approve of you, Rosie!'

The two young women were sitting side by side, having been lucky enough to get aboard just as a couple of elderly men were alighting. Rose gave Rachel's hand a squeeze. 'You and your mam are so kind, I don't know what I'd do without you. But I had a letter this morning from the girls' foster mum; she's invited me to join them for the holiday and to stay overnight, if I can, and I really would love to be with the children, see their faces on Christmas morning. But I'll have to ask Miss Marriott if I can be off for four days in a row and then work straight through for eight days, say. She's norra bad old stick; I'm sure she'll let me have the time off if it's possible.'

Rachel smiled at her. 'Well, you certainly won't be short of food if you're going to that farm. Why, she sent you home with eggs and butter and home-made bread last time you visited, and the time before, you had so many apples and pears in your bag that you could hardly walk. Mam was most impressed; she just wished I were young enough to be an evacuee so she could stock up her larder all over again.'

'I gave you half of everything,' Rose reminded her. 'Since the stuff was perishable, it was the sensible thing to do. Why, I had omelettes for four days in a row; I felt quite egg-bound.'

'Don't think I'm not grateful,' Rachel said hastily. 'Mam were made up with all that fresh country food.'

'And I took Mrs Williams's advice and laid the apples and pears out on newspaper in the children's room,' Rose continued. 'I have a look at them every now and then – and eat one or two – and they're keeping really well, just like she said they would.'

'Tell you what, Rose, if Miss Marriott can't spare you, you come to us. No need to let us know until nearer the time because, as I said, Mam's catering for a dozen, by the looks of it.'

The bus came to a juddering halt and both young women got to their feet and headed for the exit. 'Thanks, Rachel,' Rose said, as they jumped down on to the pavement and began to make their way towards their workplace. 'It'll be a real treat to have four whole days off at once.'

'Ye-es, I know what you mean,' Rachel said. 'But suppose something happens and the fellers come back? You'd – you'd want to be at home then, surely?'

'Yes, of course, only we've not heard that there's any chance of them being back in the 'Pool for some time,' Rose pointed out. 'And anyway, Ty Siriol isn't that far away, and Steve knows how to get there. The girls write regularly – and so do I, of course – so he'd just have to hop on to a train and then get the bus . . . or I suppose he could hitch-hike.' She looked almost appealingly at her friend. 'I can't let the children down on the off chance that Steve's ship might come in, can I? I think Christmas is more important for children than for the rest of us and I'm sure Steve would agree. He – he's quite fond of the children in a way, especially Petal.'

If Rachel noticed anything strange about Rose's last remark, she did not comment, and the girls joined the short queue to clock on. They always tried to arrive early, so the fact that they had to queue to clock on did not bother them. Rose took her card from the rack on the left, pushed it down into the machine and pulled the lever, then checked that the time had registered before sticking it into the rack on the right, and Rachel followed suit. Then the two girls went their separate ways, Rose calling out as she did so: 'See you in the canteen at half twelve; save me a place in the queue if you're first and I'll do the same if I am.'

When Rose had left Liverpool on that Saturday morning it had been cold but clear, with no sign of snow, but by the time the train chugged into the small Ruthin station snow was falling gently from a lowering sky and the wind seemed to have dropped completely. Rose got down from the train and thanked a burly young farm worker for lifting down her case, then looked hopefully around her. Schools had broken up two days before and Mrs Williams had written that someone would meet her, since the arrival of the train did not coincide with one of the twice daily bus departures. The platform looked bare, and though the flakes fell softly, they were sufficiently frequent to make it difficult to see more than a few yards. Sighing, Rose bent to pick up her suitcase and even as she did so heard rushing footsteps and was nearly knocked backwards by her daughters' enthusiastic welcome.

'Mammy, Mammy, Mammy! Oh, it's so lovely to see you! Auntie Blod's waiting in the road because Myfanwy doesn't like being tied up and left when the snow covers all the grass and she's got nothing to chew on.' That was Petal, her eyes bright, her cheeks rosy as apples.

Daisy, hanging on to her mother's arm and jigging with excitement, said importantly: 'Poor Mammy, I bet you're cold and tired from the long journey. Was it cold in the train? Auntie Blod's brought a stone hot water bottle for you to put your feet on and she says the kettle's on the hob so there'll be a nice hot *panod*.'

'Yes, it was freezing on the train,' Rose said with a reminiscent shudder. 'A hot water bottle sounds lovely, darling; but what's a *panod* when it's at home?' she asked, imagining a small pancake of some description. 'No, don't try to carry my case, it's far too heavy for you. Daisy, you can take my handbag and Petal can carry my umbrella. There's not much point in putting it up because umbrellas are only good for rain, not for snow.'

'A *panod* is a cup of tea, I think,' Daisy said, as they reached the pony and trap. Mrs Williams climbed ponderously down, seized Rose's heavy case and tossed it into the bottom of the trap as though it weighed no more than a feather. Then she kissed Rose on the cheek, told her she was as welcome as flowers in spring, and boosted her into the trap with such force that Rose was quite surprised not to clear it all together and find herself standing on the further side. However, she sat down, with a child on either side, thanked Mrs Williams fervently for meeting her in such dreadful weather, and settled down as her hostess clicked to the pony and the small party headed for the hills.

'Was it snowing in Liverpool, Mammy, when you left?' Petal asked eagerly, once they were on the move. 'Auntie Blod says it nearly always snows at Ty Siriol but they never get thick yellow fog like we do at home. And usually the snow comes after Christmas, not before, so Auntie Blod says it won't lay. That is what you said, isn't it, Auntie Blod?' she added anxiously.

'That's right, cariad,' Mrs Williams said cheerfully, but she did not take her eyes off the road ahead and kept the pony to a walking pace. Even so, Myfanwy stumbled a couple of times and when they reached the lane Mrs Williams climbed down, announcing that she would lead the pony because the surface of the lane was so rutted and uneven Myfanwy could easily take a wrong step and end up with a broken leg.

Eager to seize what they clearly saw as a great advantage, the children scrambled out of the trap and ran ahead, Daisy leaping up to grab at branches and tip their light powdering of snow down into the lane. For her part, Petal walked just ahead of the pony, turning back to warn the sturdy, rough-coated creature of potholes and other hazards as she went.

Rose, too, had climbed down from the trap, though she regretted her decent leather shoes. Wellington boots would have been practical but she had not even considered the possibility of snow when she had set out, and although her case contained a great many things, it held no boots. However, if Mrs Williams was right and the snow did not continue for long, she supposed that boots would not be necessary. She said as much to her hostess, who laughed, but shook her head. 'The snow won't last but it'll leave a deal of mud behind it,' she observed. 'Farmyards is mucky places and knowing your daughters as I do, I guess they'll want you to go with them to feed the poultry, take fodder out to the ponies, watch the milking and so on. You'll need boots all right, but we've plenty to spare. You can use a pair of Dilys's; better that than ruining good leather.'

'I feel ashamed,' Rose said ruefully, as they entered the yard. 'But on both my previous visits the weather was dry and I wore sensible brogues.' She wrinkled her nose at the black court shoes, now mud-spattered, which had been her Christmas present to herself. Still, they would clean up and could be worn whenever there was no possibility of having to leave the farmhouse.

'Come on in, Mam. You can pull the kettle over the fire and make the tea while Auntie Blod sees to the pony and trap,' Petal said, running to open the kitchen door.

'Indeed she cannot,' Mrs Williams said roundly, smiling at her guest. 'You go up to your room and make yourself at home, unpack and so on, and by the time you come down I'll have a nice cup of tea and a piece of Victoria sponge all ready for you.'

Christmas Day dawned clear and bright, though with a sharp frost. The hours at the factory were long and the work quite hard, needing a good deal of concentration, so Rose was happy to agree not to try to get up when the children did, but to have a bit of a lie-in. She suspected that she would wake at six anyway, but slept deeply and was awoken by the children giggling as they opened her door.

Rose shot up in bed just as Mrs Williams entered

flanked by Daisy and Petal, with a tray in her hands. Rose began to apologise for her tardiness, but was assured that her daughters had hoped she would not wake early, since the surprise they had arranged for her depended upon her remaining in bed a little later than usual. 'We made your breakfast ourselves, tea, toast, and bacon and egg,' Daisy said proudly. 'Only the tray is so heavy we couldn't carry it, norreven between us. Put your knees down, Mam, then Auntie Blod can stand it down.'

Mrs Williams, smiling broadly, settled the tray comfortably in front of Rose. 'The girls is saving opening their presents until you come down,' she said. 'And I'd be much obliged if you'd use me given name – Blodwen – because having you call me Mrs Williams all the time seems a bit formal, like.' She pointed to the tray. 'There's marmalade in the jar with bluebells on and a nice pat of our own farm butter in the little glass dish. Now we'll leave you to have your breakfast in peace, or at least I will. I expect Daisy and Petal will watch every mouthful; they've had their own, by the way.'

'Oh, Mrs Will— I mean Blodwen, you really are too good,' Rose said, looking hungrily at the bacon, eggs and mushrooms which filled the plate. 'I hadn't realised how hungry I was.' She began to eat as the older woman left the room and beamed at the children as they climbed on to the bed. 'What a wonderful Christmas present! You couldn't have given me anything nicer than a proper cooked breakfast, on a tray.'

'We thought you'd like it,' Petal said, clearly gratified by this enthusiastic response. 'Daisy and I made the toast and filled the milk jug, and Daisy curled the butter with Auntie Blod's little butter-curler. But of course, norreven Daisy were allowed to fry the stuff, 'cos fry pans is dangerous, Auntie Blod says so.'

Involuntarily, a picture of herself in her kitchen at

home, swinging the heavy frying pan in order to keep Steve at bay, appeared before Rose's eyes and she choked back a giggle. It wasn't really funny, she knew, but it was better to laugh than to cry, and Petal was clearly unaware that her remark about the danger inherent in a frying pan could be taken two ways. And now Daisy was chattering, full of plans which she was anxious to share with her mother, so Rose brought her mind back to the present.

'. . . and after dinner, there's to be a party – they have one every year – with Auntie Blod's sisters, and their husbands, and all their children coming here,' she said excitedly. 'Some of the kids is our age – a couple of them are in our class – and Auntie Blod says there will be all sorts of games and fun, as well as a lovely tea. But of course, the animals have to be fed and the cows have to be milked, so we'll be able to help, just as we usually do.'

Rose began to spread butter on to her toast, looking thoughtfully at her daughters as she did so. When she had left Liverpool, it had been on her mind that she might bring the children back to the city when she returned there on Wednesday. It would make her life a great deal more complicated but she had noticed that most of the children who had left on 4th September were already back in Liverpool. Schools which had been closed were reopening, teachers were returning, and despite such things as the blackout, conscription of men between 19 and 41 save for those in essential employment, and shortages of most basic foodstuffs, life was returning to normal. The panic which had caused the mass evacuation of children was subsiding and though there had been no official admission that this exercise had not been necessary, the streets of Liverpool teemed with children once more.

The trouble was, Rose could see how happy Daisy and Petal were and knew, in her heart, that they were far better off on the farm than they would have been in Bernard Terrace. The Williams family were almost self-sufficient and although Mr Williams grumbled that no doubt laws would be brought in which would interfere with his farming practices, as had happened in the last war, Rose was certain that the sturdy independence of the family would make sure that they were not unduly interfered with.

So what to do? She missed their companionship horribly but was not selfish enough to think that more important than their happiness. But perhaps the children should be consulted over such an important matter. Rose took a sip of tea, then put her cup down and cleared her throat. 'You like it here, don't you, darlings? I know you're a big help to Auntie Blodwen and Dilys, but what about school? At first, you were with your friends, but a good many of them have come home. Do you miss them?'

Petal began to say that she would quite miss Fanny, who had gone home for Christmas and did not mean to come back, but Daisy, shrewder than her sister, interrupted. 'Oh, but we've made new friends, haven't we, Petal? And when we start school full time in the new year, we'll soon get to know the rest of the children. And in the spring, your friend Maldwyn Griffiths is going to take you birdnesting and fishing for tiddlers in the brook and if Nicky is still here he and me will come along as well. And there'll be little lambs, some of 'em orphans; they're the ones Auntie Blod feeds with a real baby's bottle. And there's primroses and violets – not to buy, to pick – all over the banks . . . oh, spring is going to be wonderful this year.'

Rose smiled lovingly at her daughters, reflecting

that Petal's genius for friendship was a truly enviable attribute. Petal made friends easily and could pick and choose her companions, whereas poor little Daisy, she knew, would have missed Nicky Bostock fearfully had he gone back to the 'Pool and would have found it hard to replace her old friend with a new one.

'So you don't miss Bernard Terrace too much? Or me, or your daddy, either?' Rose asked, rather wistfully. She wanted the children to be happy, of course she did, but she wanted them to miss her, too. At these words, however, both small girls hurled themselves at her, hugging and kissing her and assuring her that they missed her very much and only wished she could be with them at the farm, and not stuck, all by herself, in Bernard Terrace.

'But you come and visit whenever you can, don't you, Mammy?' Petal said, as Rose carefully stood her tray on the bedside table. 'And Daddy might come when he's next on leave, I suppose.'

She did not sound unduly thrilled by this last suggestion, but Rose was comforted. Her daughters truly loved her, truly missed her, but living on the farm was like a wonderful holiday, the sort of holiday they would never have enjoyed but for the war. She crossed the room and began to pour water from ewer to basin, then turned to shoo the girls out of the room whilst she washed and dressed. 'Don't worry about the tray, I'll bring it down when I'm ready,' she said briskly. 'Now, off with you, and help your Auntie Blodwen.'

She would have closed the door on them, but Petal turned a beseeching face towards her. 'You will hurry, won't you, Mammy?' the child asked anxiously. 'We haven't opened a single one of our presents yet, but

Auntie Blod let us have a feel of what she's bought us, and oh, oh, I *do* want to see if I've guessed right!'

It was hard to wake up on Wednesday morning, very, very early, before the sky had even begun to lighten, for Mr Williams was going to drive Rose to the station to catch the milk train, which would get her back to Liverpool in time to catch her usual bus to work. Rose had borrowed Dilys's alarm clock and when it shrilled, she wished, passionately, that she could hurl it through the window and go back to sleep. However, she got groggily out of bed, dabbed shrinkingly at her warm flesh with a wet flannel, dressed hastily, and headed for the stairs. Duty called and though Mr Williams had assured her that he was often up at this hour, she felt it was an imposition for him to get out their old Austin to take her to the station.

Downstairs in the kitchen, she was surprised to find Dilys, very bright-eyed and cheerful, frying sausages and cold cooked potatoes in the big, black pan. Rose stopped short, staring across at the younger woman. 'Oh, Dilys, don't say you've got up specially to make breakfast! I could have managed perfectly well with a slice of bread and jam; that's all I ever have at home.'

Dilys tutted, much as her mother would have done, Rose thought. 'That's no way to start the day,' she said severely. 'Besides, I'm on early milking this morning and either Mam or meself always gets up to feed whoever is on earlies. 'Da' will be in any moment, so you and I aren't the only ones looking for a cooked breakfast.'

Secretly, Rose wondered whether she would be able to eat a cooked breakfast at such an early hour, but somehow, when the food was dished up on to the plates and Dilys, Mr Williams and herself were seated at the table, her appetite returned with a rush. She finished off her meal with toast and marmalade and two large mugs of tea, and then Dilys picked up a stout brown paper parcel which had been standing on the dresser and handed it to her. 'Mam has put you up a piece of cheese, some cold fowl and half a dozen eggs, as well as some links of our home-made sausages,' she said rather shyly. 'It's been grand having you, Mrs McAllister, and I hope it won't be too long before you're back again.'

Dilys then picked up her suitcase and carried it out to the car, while Rose, cradling the parcel, tried to express her gratitude to these two hard-working people who had found room for her children in their lives and in their hearts.

It seemed strange to be driving along the lane with glass separating her from the frosted beauty of the trees and hedges, for she had grown used to going on foot, or perhaps in the pony trap, during her stay with the Williamses, but it was a good deal warmer and also quite a lot faster than the other methods of transport, and it seemed no time at all before Mr Williams was drawing up outside the station and hopping out to carry her suitcase.

'Thank you so much, Mr Williams,' Rose said, trying to take the case from him. 'I can manage this, honestly I can, and I know you'll want to be off back to the farm to get on with the work. I keep trying to tell you how grateful I am to all of you . . .'

But she was speaking to empty air. Mr Williams had stridden ahead of her on to the platform and placed her suitcase a foot from the line, and even as he did so she saw the train approaching, the steam from its smokestack rising white against the black and frosty sky. It drew to a halt alongside the platform and immediately the station, which had seemed to be deserted, sprang into life. Milk churns rattled as they were heaved up into the guard's van, a man with a large flag came running out of the ticket office to have a word with the engine driver, and a couple of passengers appeared and climbed aboard.

In the dim blue light which was all the illumination allowed, Rose selected a corner seat and tried to thank Mr Williams again, but he was having none of it. 'A pleasure it is,' he said gruffly, and shot a surprisingly large, calloused hand. Rose put hers into it and they shook briefly. Mr Williams stepped back as the guard came along the train, slamming doors, and Rose let down the window on its leather strap and leaned out.

'Please thank Mrs Williams for the parcel of food,' she called, as the train began to chug out of the station. 'And thank you again, Mr Williams.'

He grinned; she could see the flash of those incredibly white teeth, even in the dark, then she pulled the window up and sank into her corner seat. She told herself that she was lucky to have had such a wonderful break and be going back to work with many happy memories, but all she could think about was how cold and lonely the house would seem, and how much she would miss Daisy and Petal.

By the end of January the snow, which had begun to fall in earnest on the hills of North Wales some time earlier, reached Liverpool for the first time. Rose got letters from Daisy extolling the marvels of sledging, for Maldwyn Griffiths and a group of other children had accompanied Daisy, Petal and Nicky up to the long, sloping pasture behind Ty Siriol armed with rough wooden sledges, and had instructed them in the art of choosing a smooth pathway and descending on the sledge – or indeed, on a sturdy tray – at incredible speed.

Daisy's letter had been almost incoherent as she struggled to get her feelings into words; the wind in her face, the enormous cold, the thrill as one steered one's vehicle round a bump and the astonishing way one took to the air and soared into a snow bank when one's conveyance hit an obstacle. Then there was the return to the farmhouse, cold but elated, to drink tea and eat hot Welsh cakes and boast of their prowess.

Rose envied the children but hated city snow. Pavements became treacherous in the extreme and Bernard Terrace had to be negotiated with considerable care, since the children made slides which were occasionally hidden and could cause a most unpleasant fall. Of course, all the houses were cold, but because Rose was alone and often did not bother to light the fire, her house felt like an icebox. Draughts she had scarcely noticed before seemed to stab at her through every available crack around windows and doors, and because she had no time for shopping – working girls could not join long queues – her meals became little more than hasty snacks. She told herself that she had a good hot meal in the canteen every working day and usually either cooked something or went round to Rachel's house on her day off, but even so, she dreaded another fall of snow and longed for spring.

Oddly enough, she soon realised that many of her neighbours thought her a strange parent to have left her children in their foster home when so many others had brought their families back to Liverpool.

On this particular day, as Rose hurried across to her house, Maisie, her next door neighbour, laden with marketing bags, stopped her. She was an old friend and had clearly decided to give Rose a bit of a talking to, for she began the conversation by saying, bluntly, that she thought Rose was foolish to leave the children in North Wales. 'They'll be more that Blodwen's kids than yourn, by the time this bleeding war's over,' she commented. 'I wouldn't be without my Freddie for longer than I had to; that's why I brung him back at the beginning of December. Besides, he'd started bed-wetting so he couldn't have been happy.'

'Well, Daisy and Petal are extremely happy,' Rose said, rather defensively. 'But it was different for your Freddie; he didn't like his foster mother, did he? And you said he were with a big family and felt left out. Of course it makes it easier for my Daisy and Petal, because they're together. The Williamses have taken the girls to their heart, I'm telling you.'

Maisie nodded. 'Aye, you did tell me, and that's why I say them girls won't want to come back, ever, if you don't shift 'em soon,' she said, almost aggressively. 'And if they were home, you'd have to keep the house warm and cook yourself decent meals once in a while. You're beginning to look right peaky,' she finished.

Rose sighed but did not attempt to defend herself further. 'I may bring them back in the spring,' she said reluctantly. 'I'm only trying to do what's best for them, Maisie.'

'I know that,' Maisie said, standing her marketing bag down and giving Rose's shoulder a reassuring pat. 'But there's others as don't, and of course, you leavin' the girls in a safe place gets up some folks' noses, 'cos they feel guilty about bringin' their young 'uns home. I do meself,' she added, with a burst of honesty. 'Tell you what, queen, I know you're havin' a job to get your messages, what with workin' every hour God sends, so why don't you pop an envelope through me front door with a list of what you need and a few bob to cover the cost? It'll be no skin off me nose to buy a bit extra as I go round the shops.'

Rose thanked her and promised to leave a list the very next day, and went indoors, heartened by the conversation in one way, though also a little cast down. She was trying so hard to do the best for her children! It seemed unfair that she should be criticised, particularly as she would much rather have had the girls at home. But being a parent was never easy, she concluded. She went into the kitchen and lit the gas under the kettle. Then, because of the conversation with Maisie, she got together paper kindling and some small pieces of coal, and laid and lit the fire. Maisie was right about one thing: she really must make more of an effort to eat properly, so she would start by cooking some of her bacon ration and putting it between two thick slices of bread. She got up and fetched pan and bacon, and as soon as the rashers started to sizzle the delicious smell sent her back to the pantry; she would fry a couple of rounds of bread as well, and heat up a tin of beans, and when she had eaten she would write a letter to Steve, telling him all about the fearful weather and the children's ecstasy over the snow. After that, she would write to Daisy and Petal. Then she would tune in her small wireless set to keep abreast of current affairs, and when the nine o'clock news was finished she would go up to bed, snuggle down under the great mound of blankets – for she had put the children's bedding on top of her own – and forget her troubles till morning.

Once this plan had been followed, however, and she was tucked up in bed, she found herself mulling over Maisie's words. She did not really think that the children would grow fonder of Blodwen than they were of herself, nor did she think they would resent coming back to Bernard Terrace when the time was ripe. Naturally, they would miss the country, but she supposed that, when the war was over, she, Steve and the girls could visit the Williamses from time to time, keeping the friendship green. If only Steve did not return to his pre-war drinking habits, then perhaps life could be pleasant for all of them, though she supposed, sadly, that when hostilities ended her lovely well-paid job would go too, and she would be forced to work very hard indeed, for long hours, in order to earn half her present salary.

Next door, the sound of feet thundering up the stairs came clearly through the thin wall and Rose sighed. Because she was alone in the house, she had become much more aware of the sounds from neighbouring properties. It was odd, because it had never occurred to her before that Maisie McBride and her family were noisy, but they certainly seemed so now. Dick shouted at the children, and Trixie shrieked with laughter, banged her bedroom door, and turned the wireless up so loud that Rose sometimes thought Steve need not have bothered to buy her a set.

On the other side, the Gray family were even worse. Maud Gray had six boys still living at home, the eldest sixteen and the youngest four. When they fought, which was often, they thumped into the wall with such force that Rose's pictures jumped, and Maud's strident voice could surely be heard all the way down to the Mersey as she bawled imprecations and poured curses down on the heads of her rumbustious young.

It isn't as if my children were ever particularly noisy, Rose told herself now, so why I should be so aware of my neighbours, I really don't know. But I am, and that's all there is to it. Of course, when Steve was home and started a row, I suppose the neighbours pricked up their ears and thought us as rowdy as themselves, so I really shouldn't grumble. Oh, but how I wish the girls were curled up in the next room right now!

Next door, Trixie's door slammed, and after perhaps ten minutes of comparative quiet, the Gray brothers came thundering up the stairs on the other side. Most of them were already in bed, Rose judged, so this would be the two eldest, and to give them credit, once they got into their room, they were careful not to make a noise which would wake the younger ones.

Nevertheless, Rose continued to listen to the boys as they got ready for bed until, at last, she fell asleep.

Chapter Five
April 1940

'Use your eyes, girl!' Maldwyn's voice was low but Petal could hear the touch of impatience, nevertheless. 'Look for a thickening in the hedge, move your head slowly from left to right, then up and down. The leaves on the hawthorns are so tiny still that almost anywhere where there's a thicker bit could mean a nest. Now come along, I've showed you half a dozen, so you must find the next one.'

Petal and Maldwyn were in the Three Acre Wood, or rather they were skirting it, looking for birds' nests in the hawthorn hedge which surrounded it. The wood itself was mixed, with some mature trees, some saplings and good thick undergrowth. There would be many nests within it, but Maldwyn was a practical boy and believed in covering as much ground as possible in a workmanlike fashion. When they had found all the nests in the hawthorn hedge, he explained, they would pick out the ones they wanted, taking one egg only from the nests of their choice.

Petal agreed to this because she agreed with everything Maldwyn said. Over their time at Ty Siriol, he had become her best friend; he had taken her sledging, taught her how to sail a home-made boat on the pond at the back of the farm, gone with her to the picture house in Ruthin for the Saturday morning show, even helped her to understand the Welsh which most of the local children spoke when out of school. He was the third and youngest son of the Griffiths family, who farmed half a mile up the road from Ty Siriol. A thin, dark-eyed, dark-haired boy, only a little older than Petal herself, he had taken her under his protection when the children returned to school in early January, translating remarks made in the playground until, almost without realising it, Petal began to understand well over half of whatever was being said in Welsh.

But right now, birdnesting was important because it would be her mother's birthday in another five weeks and Maldwyn was going to show her how to make a beautiful – and free – present, for which birds' eggs were an absolute essential. So she scanned the next section of hedge eagerly, spotted a nest and was rewarded by Maldwyn's quick, shy smile and by an emphatic nod of his head.

'You done well,' he whispered. 'It's a blackbird's nest and their eggs are greeny-blue; real pretty.'

Having peered into the nest to verify the truth of this statement and to count the eggs, the two children moved on, discovering another four nests – robin, blackcap, song thrush and blue tit – before Maldwyn decreed that they should now retrace their steps. 'We need, say, half a dozen blackbird eggs, three thrushes and one or two each of the smaller birds,' he said instructively. 'We'll have to blow them really carefully . . . but it's easier to show than tell, and don't forget, only one egg from each nest.'

By dinnertime, the soft collecting bag which Maldwyn carried with such care contained the right number of eggs and the children turned their steps towards Ty Siriol once more. Normally Nicky and Daisy would have accompanied them but today they had gone to a picture show in Ruthin so the two young ones had gone collecting on their own.

I must be the luckiest person in the world, and the happiest, Petal thought, as they headed for the back door. When Auntie Blod and Uncle Gwil listen to the news I know war is horrid, but I do so love the farm, it's perfectly splendid, and oh, how I wish Mam could come and live with us, too, so that we could stay here for always.

She and Maldwyn entered the kitchen. Maldwyn had been invited to have his dinner with them when he had called for Petal earlier in the day and now he went across to the sink, as of right, to wash his hands and face before the meal, greeting his hostess cheerfully as he did so. 'We've got the eggs, one from each nest, like I said, and after dinner I'm going to show Petal how to blow them without making cracks or spoiling them in any way,' he said proudly. 'What's in the pot?'

Auntie Blodwen turned from the range and smiled at them. 'It's lambs' tail stew, and I'm saving Daisy's share for suppertime.'

Petal winced and saw Maldwyn do the same. Uncle Gwil had told her that lambs' tails had to be docked because otherwise they were a prey to infection, getting caught in the undergrowth and trailing on the muddy ground in wintertime, but even so, she hated the thought of eating a tail whose owner was even now gambolling in the fields. However, Auntie Blod thought this reaction was ridiculous. 'You eat mutton, which is a dead sheep when all's said and done, and you eat eggs, which would turn into hens if we left 'em under the broody,' she said. 'Besides, there's a war on and it's wicked to waste food, Mr Churchill said so.'

But settling down at the table, Petal decided to feed Uncle Gwil's sheepdogs with the meat in her portion, whenever no one was looking.

* * *

Steve McAllister arrived back in Liverpool late one afternoon in May, just a couple of days before his wife's birthday. Not that he remembered that, he just thought the date vaguely familiar. He and Alby hefted their ditty bags and walked together up the sloping road from the docks, Steve at least feeling both exhausted and angry, for their ship, HMS *Jericho*, had been involved in enemy action out in the Atlantic, where she had been accompanying a convoy from the United States, and Steve had actually felt a shot pass within inches of his head, and had known sickening fear when a torpedo had struck somewhere below the water line. But they had been lucky; the torpedo had done minimal damage, and though water had been coming in and the pumps were in constant use, they had got home safely. And now the *Jericho* would be in dry dock for at least five days or possibly six, whilst the damage was properly repaired and the ship revictualled.

Part of Steve's bad temper had been caused by his friend, who had refused to nip into a dockside pub for a few bevvies before returning home.

'It's all right for you,' Steve had growled, slowing to a snail's pace and gazing longingly at the Goree Vaults. 'Your missus will give you a grand welcome and there'll be a hot meal set on the table in a trice. All I'll get will be a cold look and a bit of bread and scrape.'

'If you go home drunk, then it's all you'll deserve,' Alby pointed out. 'For the Lord's sake, why anticipate trouble? Very likely, she'll rush down to the chip shop as soon as you enter the house . . . unless she's already got something hot on the stove, that is.'

'How can she, when she don't know I'm in port?' Steve groaned. 'And I'm that hungry, me belly thinks me throat's been cut. I'd like to get hold of whoever buys supplies for the *Jericho* and ring his bloody neck.'

Alby sighed. 'Yes, something definitely went wrong,' he agreed. 'No ship with a full complement should run short of food two days before docking. But I suppose it were a longer journey than they'd anticipated, keeping out of the way of the wolf packs and so on.'

'Well they ought to have antic— anticipated it,' Steve grumbled. He heaved a sigh and straightened his shoulders. 'Still, you're right; no point in looking on the black side. Rose ain't a bad wife; she's a grand little cook, so she is. It's just that if the kids is still in North Wales, she don't bother all that much wi' makin' meals. She said so the last time she wrote.'

'Aye, I dare say we'll both notice some changes,' Alby admitted. 'My Rachel's never worked before so she won't be at home all the time. It'll seem strange when she goes off in the mornings, the way I used to do.'

'Yeah, but it's worse for me,' Steve said, unwilling to admit that anyone could suffer as he was suffering. 'You've got your ma-in-law to cook meals an' clean the house an' that; she'll darn your socks and front-to-back your collars and sew buttons back on. I bet Rose won't even offer to get me a hot meal, not when she's got a good excuse to come home and sit on her bum after work.'

Alby stopped dead and grabbed Steve's arm, swinging him round so that they were facing one another. 'You've got a right nasty chip on your shoulder, you have,' he said accusingly. 'I thought your wife were a real nice woman; I only saw your girls once, but Mrs McAllister had made sure they wore pretty clothes and were clean as a couple of little whistles. She put a good tea on the table for all of us – I reckon her home-made bread takes some beating – and now that she's not got the kids to look out for, the place will be like a new pin and there's bound to be nice food in the house. So stop expectin' the worst and start deciding to enjoy your leave, hear me? And if things does go wrong, come round to our place and we'll see you're fed and watered, old feller.'

Steve could not help laughing and reluctantly agreed to do as Alby said and give Rose a chance. Then they climbed up Everton Brow and Steve turned right into Salisbury Street, leaving Alby to continue on his way. Presently, Steve turned into Bernard Terrace and headed for his own front door.

It was locked. Steve groaned but put his hand through the letter box, fumbling around for the string. It was not there. He stood back, asking himself what the devil his wife was playing at, feeling the anger rise and a tide of heat stain his cheeks. She had no right to lock him out. The key should have been there; suppose the kids came back early from school.

He remembered then. The bloody kids were in Wales, his bloody wife was working at the uniform factory on Long Lane and he was bloody well locked out of his own home. For a moment, he was so furious that he stepped back a pace, preparing to attack the door like a human battering ram. Dammit, was he no longer master in his own house? He had been locked out like a naughty child; it would teach her a lesson if she came home to find he had broken the door down.

Luckily, however, common sense prevailed. The door was old but both sturdy and solid. There was a back door, which led straight into the kitchen, but for all he knew she might have bolted that before leaving.

She could not lock it since there was no lock, but the bolts top and bottom rendered it even more impregnable than the front one. Restlessly, he went back along the terrace and turned down the jigger and into his tiny backyard. There was a lean-to scullery or washhouse at the back, with a sloping tiled roof, and, to his joy, he saw that the back bedroom window was slightly ajar, no doubt because it was a warm day. Steve glanced around him. If he put his foot on the kitchen window sill, he should be able to scramble up on to the scullery roof and thence to the bedroom window. The trouble was, it was bloody undignified and anyone passing by might see him and realise he was locked out of his own home. Still. It was either go in by the bedroom window or stay outside, and it pleased him to think how shocked Rose would be when she returned from work to find someone in the house. He told himself that if there was no food in the place, he would hide behind the kitchen door when he heard her coming, and give her a good buffet round the ear to show her who was boss.

Despite the fact that he had long legs and strong arms, he found it extremely difficult to get from the yard to the roof. He made it in the end though, clutching so desperately at the slates that he brought two of them crashing into the yard. Unfortunately, this drew the attention of a couple of urchins passing along the jigger. The first one nudged his companion and said, in ringing tones: 'There's a bleedin' burglar climbin' on the McAllisters' roof! Ooh, he looks a real bad 'un; he's got one o' them faces burglars have in the Beano. C'mon, Charlie, let's run for the scuffers.'

Charlie, however, demurred. 'They'd never believe us, norrunless we take the feller captive ourselves,' he said. He bent and picked up a stone which he hurled, with great accuracy, at Steve's head. Steve's roar of mingled pain and wrath seemed to egg the boys on, for a positive rain of missiles followed. Bits of rotting vegetable matter, stones and even lumps of coal bounced off his head and shoulders, whilst the boys screamed at him to get bleedin' out of it and come down afore he were knocked off of his perch.

'When I get down, I'm gonna bleedin' kill you,' Steve howled and was almost glad when the noise brought Rose's friend Maisie out of her back door.

'What the devil . . .? Oh, it's you, Steve,' she said. 'Why on earth . . . oh, I reckon you're locked out, is that it?' She did not wait for an answer but turned to the two boys, who had ceased raining missiles upon the enemy now that an adult had hove into view. 'Off with you, kids,' Maisie said. 'You done right to try an' discourage a burglar, only he ain't one. He's been an' gone an' locked himself out, that's all. Go on, get home, before he comes down and clocks you one.'

'Are you sure he ain't a burglar, missus?' the younger boy said plaintively. 'He looks like a burglar, he's got a right nasty face on him. And he's broke the slates on the roof and he throwed bits o' stuff at us.'

'You threw first . . .' Steve started, then realised that it was beginning to sound like a kids' quarrel, and shut his mouth firmly. Ignoring the watchers below, he scrambled on to the ridge of the roof and began humping himself towards the window. He could hear the boys' muffled giggles and a quick glance showed him Maisie grinning like a Cheshire cat, but by now he was past caring. All he wanted was to get into the house and plan a revenge upon Rose.

Once down in the kitchen, he searched for food and found only bread and margarine and half a jar of rhubarb and ginger jam: a concoction which he hated. He was quite glad the fire was not lit since it was a warm day, but he lit the gas under the kettle and made himself a pot of tea, tipping the last of the sugar into his cup out of sheer spite. It made it far too sweet, but when Rose came home she would have to drink her tea without any sugar at all.

Having eaten two thick slices of bread and margarine, he decided to go out, using the back door and leaving it unbolted, of course. He had no idea what time she would be home but thought he would go to the pub and have a couple of bevvies; then he would take his friend Alby up on his offer.

Acting upon this resolve, he left the house and was soon ensconced in the Salisbury Arms, tipping back a pint of porter and trying to remember the way to Langsdale Street.

Rose was on a late shift, which had meant starting work at two in the afternoon and not finishing until ten. It wasn't a bad shift – in some ways she quite enjoyed it – since the bosses usually worked during the day and so things were a little more relaxed on both the two until ten and the ten until six shifts, though she had never got used to sleeping in the daytime and was glad that the late shifts only came round about once a month.

As a finisher, what was more, Rachel, like the bosses, only worked days, and Rose missed her company dreadfully. This afternoon she had set off for the bus alone and presently reached the factory, taking her place on the bench alongside April, and beginning to assemble the various parts to be fed into the maw of her commercial sewing machine.

She had been doing the work for a year now and it had become almost automatic, which was a blessing, since it allowed her to let her mind wander. With only a couple of days before her birthday, she was thinking of her two days off, which she would spend at Ty Siriol, and of seeing the children again. She was more delighted with them every time she visited, she told herself now. Daisy was sensible, nowhere near as nervous as she had been, far more self-confident; Nicky was still billeted in Ruthin, though Mrs Ryan was always threatening to get him back since he was useful and kept an eye on her younger children, and Daisy spent a good deal of time with her old friend. The two of them took excellent care of Petal and her friend Maldwyn, seeing that the younger ones were never bullied and did not get into too much trouble.

'Penny for your thoughts,' April said suddenly, when they had been working more or less in silence for a couple of hours. 'I reckon it's time for a break. That last seam I done weren't as straight as it might have been, but five minutes of movin' around and a nice cuppa would do us both a power of good.'

Rose glanced up at the round face of the clock on the wall. 'She won't blow the whistle for the best part of an hour,' she pointed out sadly, 'but there's always the lavvies . . . you go first, since it was your idea.'

April waited her moment, then hurried from the room. When the supervisor passed behind April's chair and gave Rose an enquiring look, she pretended to be surprised but said that April must have been caught short. The supervisor accepted this, though she frowned and pursed her lips, and when she was once more at the other end of the long room Rose also abandoned her work and hurried off to the toilet block.

When she returned, Rose joined in the general chatter which was going on. The girls discussed the rises in the price of a stamp, the Prime Minister, Winston Churchill, the new film at the Rialto and the chances of their going off on a firm's outing when August arrived, despite the war. Then it was time to go to the canteen for a hot meal – bangers and mash with baked beans on the side, followed by apple pie and custard – and before she knew it, a whistle shrilled and the girls began to tidy their places, leaving for the cloakroom just as the new intake hurried in to take over their machines.

It was a mild night, with a gentle wind blowing, and as she climbed off the bus in Shaw Street and headed for home, Rose's thoughts reverted to her days off once more. She loved her visits to the farm and congratulated herself that her girls were getting the sort of childhood she herself would have loved. They knew so many things that had completely passed the young Rose by! She had watched Daisy carefully measuring boiled potato peelings and other vegetable leftovers into a bucket, adding hot water, and then staggering out to the grain store where a vast bin contained large quantities of meal. Her daughter used a tin scoop to measure meal into the bucket, stirring it vigorously with a long metal spoon until it was apparently of just the right consistency, before adding a few handfuls of corn, stirring the mixture once more and hefting the bucket out to the yard.

The hens, alerted by heaven knew what sounds, flocked to her side, some making a spirited endeavour to leap into the bucket, but Daisy fended them off with the metal spoon, laughing as they flapped eagerly around her. Then she began to dole out the mixture, throwing it as far as she could so that all the poultry got a share, and when she could get no more out of the bucket she laid it on the ground for a moment, so that the greedier hens could peck out any last scraps of food still adhering to its galvanised sides.

Rose knew that Daisy had been frightened of the chickens when she first went to the farm. She had been nervous of horses, would not have dreamed of feeding the pigs in case they decided that she herself would make a tasty morsel, and went out of her way to avoid the great grey and white geese, with their big orange bills, their venomous hissing, and their huge, splayed feet. Rose herself was not fond of the geese but now Daisy – and Petal – knew just how to deal with the aggressive birds. They would kick and clout their way through the creatures, though they were careful never to turn their backs, for an angry gander, especially one who had been kicked, would think nothing of nipping at bare legs or arms, provided the owner was not actually looking at him at the time.

Blodwen has been so generous to me and so good to the children that I really ought to take her a little present, Rose was telling herself as she put her key into the front door. It was half past ten and the houses were quiet, not even the Grays creating the usual din they made when Mrs Gray began to hustle the younger boys off to their beds. Rose locked the door behind her and headed for the kitchen. She would make herself a cup of tea but she would not eat anything since she had had a meal not much more than three hours ago. She went into the kitchen and across to the stove, then something made her pause. She glanced round her, frowning slightly. Something was . . . different, though right now, she could not say exactly what. She went across to the window and pulled down the blackout blind, then reached up and lit the gas lamp. Then she turned back to the stove, carefully shielding the match she had used, hoping to be able to light the gas under the kettle with the same flame.

Afterwards, she wondered what had made her pick up the kettle, for normally she put enough water in it to make a cup of tea before she left the house, but now, to her surprise, the kettle was empty.

Frowning, Rose considered, glanced at the stove top to see if the kettle had suddenly sprung a leak and examined the floor. No dribble of water from sink to stove to indicate that the kettle had leaked on its journey earlier that day. Shrugging, she carried the kettle to the sink and half filled it, carried it back to the stove, lit the gas and perched it on the ring. Then, waiting for it to boil, she looked around her once more. What *was* different about the room? It was warm, a bit stuffy, but then the day had been warm, and the house did tend to get stuffy with all the downstairs windows shut. Another glance round convinced her that the only real difference was that the pantry door was not quite shut and investigation quickly eased her mind. Earlier that day she had asked Maisie to buy her a small loaf of bread, a packet of teacakes and some fruit, whatever was available. Strawberries were coming into the shops soon; she would have liked some strawberries.

Rose went over to the pantry and checked and sure enough there was a small loaf and a packet of teacakes. The fruit looked like apples, though – but it was still a bit early for strawberries, she supposed, and apples would be just as good.

The kettle hissed and began to whistle and Rose grabbed it off the stove before it screamed like a soul in torment, the way whistling kettles will if only half filled and left over the flame. She made herself a pot of tea, waited for it to brew for five minutes whilst she ate a teacake, then drank the tea. She always cleared up before going to bed because she hated facing a dirty kitchen and a piled-up sink next morning. She began to tidy up now, humming to herself as she worked. Next day she would be on the two until ten shift again, and the following day as well, but then there would be two wonderful days off to spend with her children, two dreamy country days.

Because she was happy she cleared the kitchen in record time, refilled the kettle, then headed for the stairs. She was halfway up them before another thought occurred to her; a thought which stopped her in her tracks, brought a cold sweat breaking out on her forehead, neck, breasts.

Maisie did not have a key to Rose's house, so how had the messages managed to get into the pantry? Rose had often toyed with the idea of having another key cut, but somehow she was always too busy, and anyway, Maisie never minded hanging on to a few groceries until Rose was able to go next door to pick them up. It was not as though Maisie had to wait for the money, because Rose always paid in advance.

Puzzled, Rose remained where she was for several moments, halfway up the stairs, staring before her, trying to work it out. Then, with another shrug, she began to climb the stairs once more. Fool that she was, she must have forgotten to lock the front door . . . no, that couldn't be the answer because she had just unlocked it, hadn't she? On the other hand she had not checked the back door . . . yes, that must be it. She had been in a hurry to leave earlier in the day, must have forgotten to bolt the back door, and Maisie had let herself in, dumped the messages and gone out again.

But that would mean the back door would still be

unbolted, and if it was, Rose should really retrace her steps and shoot the bolts before going up to bed. She half turned, then weariness attacked her again. Why should she bother with the back door if it had been unbolted all afternoon and evening? She had nothing worth stealing, so there was no need for her to go downstairs again tonight.

With a light step and a lighter heart, Rose climbed the rest of the stairs and crossed the narrow landing towards her bedroom door. She opened it and went straight across to pull down the blackout blind. She had her arm up to the cord when some small sound – the creak of a board, an intake of breath – told her that there was someone, or something, else in the room. She gave a gasp of sheer terror and half turned, even as something hit her a heavy blow between the shoulder blades and she fell forward, striking her head against something hard and cold. For one moment longer, she was conscious of a voice, a presence. Then she plunged into blackness.

Rose came to herself aware only that she was lying on something soft and in pretty complete darkness, though when she moved her head slightly she became aware of a lighter square and realised that this must be a window. But her wits were still addled by what had happened and terror still blurred her thought processes, making it difficult to concentrate. She tried to move her head again and moaned as pain stabbed at her brow, then opened her eyes to find a dark figure bending over her. Immediately, fear told her to pretend she was still unconscious and she closed her eyes quickly.

'Rose? Rose, wharrever's the matter? It were a joke, for God's sake! I come home soon after two o'clock to find meself locked out, and when I did manage to gerrin, there weren't no food, norreven a bottle of ale. I were that disappointed; I've been dreamin' about gerrin' home ever since the ship were damaged and the officers telled us she'd be in dry dock for a week.' Somebody was chafing her hands; rough fingers pushed the hair back from her damp forehead. 'Rosie, for God's sake, speak to me! I didn't mean no harm, I just thought I'd surprise you. Only that bleedin' blind got wrapped round your hand somehow and it brought the whole lot down and your forehead hit the window pane. Rose? Rose?'

Rose opened her eyes. She looked up at her husband's bulk and thought, bitterly, that she should have guessed he had come home. And hiding away in order to terrify the life out of her was just the sort of thing he would do, though on this occasion his 'joke' had gone a little too far, even for him.

'Rose? Oh, thank Gawd, you ain't dead.' His voice, which had been uncertain, almost pleading, suddenly became aggressive. 'Trust you to give me the fright of me life, you perishin' little bitch. Why, I go to tap you on the shoulder and next thing I know you're flat on the floor an' out cold, an' I s'pose you'll blame me for it. Well, blame away, I can't stop you, but I'm tellin' you, that great lump on your forehead ain't nothin' to do wi' me. *And* I'm sober as a judge, wharrever you may like to think.'

He had been bending over her and Rose, groggily beginning to sit up, realised that his breath did not smell of drink, and his speech was not slurred. She put a hand to her sore and aching forehead and felt a warm wetness, saying as she did so: 'I don't understand. If you didn't go to the pub and you docked at two, where have you been?'

'Are you all right now? Here, I'll give you a hand to get down to the kitchen because I daren't show a light, not now you've dragged the blind down. But I can still see there's a nasty cut on your forehead – I can see it in the moonlight – an' I just hope you ain't goin' to blame me for that an' all!'

Rose was tempted to reply acidly that, since he and she were alone in the house, she could scarcely blame anyone else, but bit her tongue. It would not help to antagonise him further, and right now it seemed that guilt and remorse were fighting for supremacy. She would try to give him the benefit of the doubt, for the time being at least. Perhaps it had just been a joke, though she thought it likelier that he had meant to give her an awful fright to pay her back for being out when he had come home. Still, no point in giving him an excuse to be even nastier to her.

'Rose? Can you hear me? Lemme give you a hand to stand up.'

He pulled her up and Rose stood, swaying for a moment, trying to collect her thoughts. By his own admission, he had been ashore since two o'clock, and it was now getting on for eleven at night. If he had not been boozing, and she was pretty sure he hadn't, where had he been?

She did not ask the question at once, however, but waited until they were safely downstairs in the kitchen. Then she watched whilst he drew down the blinds, lit the lamp and set a match to the ring beneath the kettle. Still feeling weak and with her heart banging unevenly, she settled herself in an armchair, sipped the hot cup of tea he handed her, and decided she must sort this matter out. 'I'm sorry, Steve, but I'm still very confused. If you've been home all day . . . oh, I don't understand! There was something –

something in the pantry, something that shouldn't have been there. Oh, it was the groceries I'd asked Maisie to buy. If you were here when she delivered 'em, you could've ate the lot, I wouldn't have grudged you, and Maisie would have told you I was on the evening shift. If you knew I'd be home by half past ten, why didn't you wait up for me? You could have given me a fright just as well in the kitchen as in the bedroom.'

Steve shrugged; he had the grace to look more than a little ashamed. 'Oh, I dunno . . . it just seemed . . . the fact is, I took meself round to Alby's place. I couldn't go out of the front door, because you'd locked it, so I went out the back and left it unbolted. That inteferin' cow next door saw me comin' in an' knew I was home, so after I'd gone she nipped in with wharrever she'd bought for you an' stuck 'em in the pantry.'

'Oh, I see,' Rose said wearily. 'Well, I suppose the same applies; Rachel must have told you my shift ended at ten.'

Steve heaved an enormous sigh. 'She did. And since you're bound to find out anyway, they gave me a grand supper – that woman's a prime cook – and then we played cards until nine o'clock or so. Here, the cut on your forehead has stopped bleeding. So if you've got a bit o' plaster, I'll stick it on. And if the cross-questioning and blaming has finished, then I reckon we ought to forget about it an' go up to bed.'

Once more, Rose was filled with an overwhelming desire to be truthful, to tell him that she did not wish to share a bed with someone who had played such a mean trick on her, but again she held her peace. To be fair to Steve, though his advances in bed were often rough, he had never deliberately caused her pain when they were making love and though tenderness was unknown to him, his satisfaction afterwards usually meant that he rolled away from her and slept at once, freeing her to go to sleep herself, secure in the knowledge that he would snore until the alarm clock went off.

So she accompanied him meekly up to their bedroom and climbed into bed, though when he flung a rough arm across her body and tried to pull her against him she feigned sleep and presently, muttering beneath his breath, he turned away from her and was soon snoring.

Rose, however, lay awake for some time. The sticking plaster made her forehead prick and burn and various bruises from her fall were beginning to make themselves felt, but worst of all was the recollection of her two days off, which she had meant to spend at Ty Siriol. She supposed she could suggest that Steve accompanied her – Petal would be pleased – but because of her husband's unpredictable behaviour, her little holiday would be fraught with worry instead of the relaxing time she had anticipated.

Rose sighed, lying very stiff and quiet between the sheets. How nice it had been to be able to sleep alone in this bed, without fear. But presently, despite her anxiety, the rigours of a long and eventful day took their toll; Rose slept.

That night, curled up close in their bed, Rachel burrowed her head into the soft spot of Alby's shoulder, so that his chin rested on her hair, and said, sleepily: 'Well, I'm glad I've got to know Rose's husband at last. He's awfully nice, isn't he, Alby? And how he loves his little daughter. I wonder if he'll go down to the farm when Rose does? When I told him she meant to go for her birthday, he looked a bit cast down, said he'd been planning a surprise for her, wondered whether he might bring the kids home, just for a few days, you know. He seemed to think they'd be safe enough and I know Rose misses them dreadfully. I agree with her that the countryside is safest, but just for a few days . . .'

Alby pulled his wife's soft and yielding body even closer and turned his head to plant a kiss on her temple, feeling the flutter of the pulse which beat there against his lips and aware of a rush of tenderness, mingling with desire. He was so lucky! He and Rachel had met at a dance and from the moment he had taken her in his arms, he had known with absolute certainty that she was the girl for him.

'Alby? I was just saying . . .'

Alby chuckled. 'You always are – just saying, I mean. The thing is, sweetheart, that I'm not at all sure how Steve would enjoy a stay in the countryside. He likes pubs and dances and snooker halls and, above all, the company of other men. It's odd because, personally, I enjoy the company of men or women, but there are some fellers who literally dislike the opposite sex and I believe Steve is one of them.'

'Dislike? But how can you say that, my dearest? Steve was very sweet to me, and to Mother as well. He praised her cooking, asked her about her Wednesday Sewing Circle, complimented her on her choice of paintings for the sitting room wall . . . and when I talked about work, he seemed truly interested.'

'Yes, but I suspect he was being polite. It's difficult to explain, love, but whereas I talk about you a great deal, aboard ship, he scarcely ever mentions Rose. He seems to think that simply being a male of the species confers wit and intelligence, two things a woman cannot possibly possess. Didn't you notice that some of his remarks – even the complimentary ones – were . . . condescending, as though he were doing your mam a favour by praising her choice of pictures?'

There was a pause whilst Rachel appeared to mull over his remark, and when she did speak, it was slowly and more thoughtfully. 'Ye-es, I know what you mean,' she said at last. 'But how can he believe Rose isn't intelligent? She's ever so quick and clever and – I don't want to insult your friend, Alby, but he's really not at all quick on the uptake, is he? Not clever, either. Well, Rose showed me one or two of his letters and he doesn't write as well as Daisy does, and his sentences are all short and sort of chopped up.'

Alby laughed. 'Yes, and that's one of the reasons why he and Rose don't hit it off the way you and I do,' he explained. 'Steve bitterly resents having a wife who he secretly knows is cleverer than he is, so he spends a lot of time plotting to take her down a peg, if you know what I mean.'

'That's horrid!' Rachel said indignantly. 'Why doesn't he try to get cleverer himself, though? I mean he could read books, study, like you have. I expect he'd feel much better if he got made a Leading Seaman, or whatever it's called.'

'It's hard to explain,' Alby said. 'But I think the reason is that while he believes himself to be superior to all women – not just Rose – he still has a sneaking suspicion that he'll never really get much further, either in the Royal Navy or in the merchant fleet. And now just you stop talking for one minute, or it'll be time for breakfast and we shan't have slept a wink.'

A week later, Rose locked her front door carefully behind her and hurried along the terrace in the pearly, early morning light, turning into Salisbury Street and hoping that she was not going to spoil her first day of freedom by missing the bus. It was odd to think of it as her first day of freedom because she had been back at work for two days, but in the early hours of this morning the *Jericho* had sailed on the tide. With her husband aboard her, and not liable to return to the city for several weeks, Rose had been aware of a strong feeling of relief as soon as she awoke and now she found herself eager to get to work, knowing that the next time she came home again her stomach would not clench with dread at whatever might await her.

In actual fact, however, Steve had been perfectly reasonable, for once. Embarrassed by the cut on her forehead, the black eye which had appeared next day, and the many bruises on her arms and knees, he had been quick to explain his wife's appearance as being the result of an unfortunate accident. She had been pulling down the blackout blind when the whole thing had collapsed and she had fallen against the sash window, cutting her brow, blacking her eye and bruising herself considerably in the fall. Most neighbours had appeared to accept this explanation without question, but Maisie had lived next door for too long. She had raised sceptical eyebrows and had actually snorted when Steve had said that the trip to the farm had had to be cancelled because of his wife's injuries. 'Anyone who believes that, would believe anything,' she had said to Rose when Steve had wandered back indoors. 'If he gives you more stick, queen, you want to go to the scuffers. They'd mebbe give him a taste of his own medicine which might make him think twice before doing it again.'

But, for a variety of reasons, Rose had decided to go along with Steve's story. After all, he was hardly ever home. In future, she must be more careful. She had allowed him to take her front door key and have another one cut, but she had decided that she would never again leave the house without first smearing the hall floor with a light dusting of either flour or cocoa powder. Then she would be able to see immediately if someone had come in, and could act accordingly.

Despite her resolve, however, she had taken no precautions before leaving the house that day. He had only just sailed, and anyway she meant to go down to the farm as soon as she had finished work, even though she would have to return by the milk train the following morning. The children had made her a surprise birthday present, and their disappointment when she had written to say she would be unable to visit them had been severe. Daisy, aided and abetted by Blodwen Williams, had telephoned the factory during Rose's dinner hour and had begged her mother to come to Ty Siriol, if only for a few hours.

'It took ages and ages to make your present,' she had said plaintively, her voice very tiny and strange in Rose's ear, for this was the first time she had spoken to her daughter on the telephone. 'And it's ever so delicate, Mam, not the sort of thing you could send through the post. It – it would end up in a thousand pieces, Auntie Blod says.'

So Rose had promised and Daisy had put Auntie Blodwen on the line. 'Just tell us the time of the train you'll be arriving on, cariad,' she had said briskly. 'Someone will be there waiting. And we'll deliver you with the milk churns, first thing the following day.'

It had taken some arranging, nevertheless. Rose had changed shifts so that today she was on mornings and tomorrow she would be on afternoons, which should give her time enough to get to the farm and back. Fortunately, by now, Rose was a quick and experienced worker, so her supervisor had agreed to her swapping shifts, anxious to keep her staff happy.

Now Rose turned into Shaw Street and headed for the bus stop, then waved as she saw Rachel hurrying along the pavement towards her. This was the first time she and Rachel had met since Steve's return and Rose beamed at the younger girl, suddenly realising that Rachel's feelings over the departure of the *Jericho* would be the exact opposite of her own. She wiped the smile off her face and was about to say something sympathetic when Rachel spoke. 'Rose, whatever's happened? You look as if you've been in a road accident! Steve never said you'd been hurt when I saw them off last night.'

'Oh, that,' Rose said airily, indicating her still puffy eye and the sticking plaster across her forehead. 'It were the stupidest thing, Rachel, but it happened almost a week ago, so I'd all but forgotten about it. I was in my bedroom, pulling down the blackout blind . . .'

By now, Rose had told the story so often that she was almost word perfect, and had no difficulty in sounding as though it were no more than the truth; in fact, she almost believed it herself. Watching Rachel's face, as they joined the bus queue, she was pretty sure that Rachel had believed it too.

'I bet the children got a surprise when they saw their darling mam looking like a prize fighter,' she remarked with a chuckle, as the bus came to a halt beside them and the queue began to inch forward. 'It must have been lovely for them to see both of you, though. It'll be the first time for ages that they've had their mam and their dad together . . . and it was your birthday, too.'

'Oh, Rachel, thank you so much for the birthday card,' Rose said belatedly. The children had made her cards, but Rachel's had been the only shop bought one, since Steve did not believe in marking such occasions and always left the buying and sending of cards to her, birthdays being women's work. But she must answer Rachel's questions, or her friend would get a totally distorted view of recent events. 'But I didn't get to see the children, unfortunately. I was knocked unconscious when I hit the window pane and Steve thought I'd best not go off into the country. Besides, he wanted to arrange a little party . . . just family, I mean,' she added hastily, seeing the trap yawning before her. 'Only I wasn't quite well enough to do any catering, so we went to the Derby cinema on the Scotland Road, instead. We had a meal first. The following night, we went to relatives and had a pretty good time.'

'I see,' Rachel said slowly, as they climbed aboard the bus and moved up the central aisle. 'Steve did say something about a surprise when he came round to our place that first afternoon.' She looked, shrewdly, at her friend. 'Rose, are you sure you only banged your head on the window pane? Only, I know how keen you were to go down to the farm and see the kids and I wouldn't have thought . . .'

Rose laughed, trying to make it sound as though the suggestion were genuinely amusing. 'What else did you think I'd done? And of course I was disappointed over not seeing the children, bitterly disappointed, in fact. But in wartime, we wives have to put our husbands first, don't you think? And anyway, I'm catching the first train to Ruthin this afternoon when my shift finishes, so I shall see the kids all right. They've made me a birthday present which is too fragile to post so I couldn't let them down.'

She was watching Rachel's face as she spoke, and saw her relax, begin to smile. It was annoying that she had to lie to her best friend, but better in the long run. Steve had been much easier to live with since he had palled up with Alby, and Rose did not intend to do anything to spoil such a useful friendship.

By the time they reached the factory, Rose had told Rachel all about the film she and Steve had seen, the dance they had attended, the evening they had spent with Aunt Selina and Uncle Frank in Penny Lane, and Rachel had reciprocated with her own news, for she and Alby had gone house-hunting, or rather flat-hunting, and had seen a couple of places which they both liked and could afford.

'Only they aren't so near the docks; they're even further out than the factory,' she disclosed as they approached the time clock. 'It would be nice for me in one way . . . there are gardens and things . . . but you and I wouldn't be able to travel to work together. Still, we could meet in the canteen as usual.'

Rose tried not to look dismayed, but realised that she felt it. The journey to work was long and dull, only made bearable by Rachel's company, but she could scarcely say so. Instead, she wished Rachel luck with her house-hunting, but could not forbear reminding her friend that she would miss having someone waiting at home for her each evening, would miss her mother's cooking, too. 'And she does your messages for you as well,' she pointed out, a trifle reproachfully. 'Believe me, being all on your own is no picnic, queen.'

'Oh well, it will probably come to nothing.' Rachel said equably. 'But it was fun looking.' They punched their cards and set off for their places of work.

* * *

Daisy and Petal were waiting on the platform when Rose's train drew in, for though they now attended school for a full day since so many of the evacuees had returned to their own homes, the routine was less strict than it had been before the war. Children, especially the older ones, were allowed off school as a matter of course if they were needed on the farms, and for an event as important as meeting a parent who had rushed over just to be able to spend a few hours with her small daughters there had been no question of denial.

'Come in early tomorrow,' the teacher had instructed them. 'And Petal, you can show your mam how nicely you read; she'll be pleased, I'm sure.'

Now, as Rose stepped down from her carriage, Daisy and Petal flew forward, immediately asking her what she had done to her face and Rose explaining that she had fallen over when pulling down the blackout blind. Then they were hugging, kissing and chattering. Rose kissed them both, lifting them into the air to do so and noticing how much heavier they had both grown, then they set off across the station and into the road where Blodwen Williams awaited them, sitting in the pony trap and beaming all over her face.

'Hop in, Rose,' the older woman said briskly, as soon as Rose was near enough to hear her. 'Walked into a door, did you?'

Rose explained, as she climbed into the trap, closely followed by her daughters.

'Come along, girls . . . and don't go sitting on that parcel, Petal, or you might just as well have sent it through the post!'

'Oh, Mammy, do open it,' Petal cried as soon as they were all packed comfortably into the trap. 'Maldwyn helped – he's awful good – but me and

Daisy did all the threading. It took ages . . . oh, it's the prettiest thing!'

The 'prettiest thing' was revealed as a long piece of fine waxed thread, upon which were strung the most beautiful birds' eggs, each one selected for colour and size. Rose marvelled over it, touched that the children should have made her something which had cost them a great deal of effort, whilst Daisy assured her that they had taken no more than one egg from each nest, because otherwise it would not be fair on the little mother and father birds. 'And we blew them by making a teeny hole in each end of the egg and puffing air until all the egg white and yolk had come out; then we washed them ever so carefully in warm water – Petal did that – and then, when they were dry, we strung them. And Maldwyn says you can loop them across the mantelpiece in your parlour, or across a picture rail, if we've got one,' she continued. 'Do you like them, Mam? Do you really and honestly like them?'

Rose assured her daughters that it was the loveliest present she had ever received, and after that the hours seemed to fly by. She and Blodwen talked about the possibility of the children's returning to Liverpool and Rose admitted that she felt they would be safer at Ty Siriol than they could possibly be in Bernard Terrace.

'So for the time being at least we'd like to leave them here,' she said. 'Why, they're even learning Welsh – it would be a sad thing, to my mind, to drag them back to the city when they're so happy.'

Blodwen had nodded vigorously. 'Aye, you're right, and we love having them,' she assured her guest. 'They're a help already in a great many ways, and will get even more useful as they grow older. And next time your husband's home on leave perhaps the two of you could come over for a couple of days? I'd be – interested to meet him.'

So now Rose, making her way home on the milk train, told herself that she was very lucky indeed. The Williams family loved her children and would take every care of them. If she took them home they would have to go to a child-minder, and though there were excellent women minding children in the neighbourhood they could not hope to compete with the Williamses. Steve had asked, a trifle wistfully, if she would not do better to bring the children back now that the danger seemed fairly remote, but Rose thought this would be downright selfish. If Steve had been prepared to put himself out he could have gone down to the farm with her and seen his children for himself. But the thought of being a long way away from the docks, his pals and even the pubs he frequented, though he had drunk only the odd pint now and then, had been enough to push the thought of seeing his children into the background.

She decided that, if he could give her advance warning of his next leave, she would have Daisy and Petal back in Bernard Terrace for a few days. And then she leaned her head back and went gently to sleep, only waking when the train pulled into the next station and people began to come aboard.

Chapter Six
September 1940

'Do you know, Petal, that we've been here a whole year? Isn't that amazing? When we get home I'm going to write to Dad and tell him we can both speak Welsh pretty well, because he's going to come to Ty Siriol on his next leave, and it would be nice if he knew about us speaking Welsh.'

Petal sniffed and gave her elder sister a chilly look. Did Daisy think she was daft or something? She was doing well at school, had headed her age group in the last end of term exams, so naturally she was well aware that they had been in Wales for a whole year. The two children were no longer picked up from school in the pony trap, because the Williamses were too busy most of the time, but they had arranged a sort of rota with other local farmers who had either children of their own or evacuees, and today it had been the turn of Mary Jones, whose family lived another two miles away from Ruthin. She was a pretty, lively girl who had recently volunteered for the WRNS and had told the children that this would be her last trip into town since she had been accepted and would leave for London early the following week.

Because the lane which led from the main road to the farm was just over a mile in length, the children were always dropped off at the corner, which was wonderful in warm summer weather – like today – but not so good when it was raining cats and dogs or blowing a hurricane. Petal, who had no objection to walking when the weather was clement, idled along, thumb in mouth, admiring the first flush of autumn colour in the hips and haws beginning to brighten the hedgerows and wondering what was for tea today, whilst her sister rehearsed what she would say when she wrote to her parents later on.

'Only Auntie Blod said not to say she'd been rather poorly,' Daisy reminded her sister. 'You'll be writing as well, Petal, so you must say we're all pretty stout. That's what Dilys calls it, anyway. And that's rather annoying, because Aunty Blod's better now, but if we can't say she was poorly last week then we can't say she's better, either. Shall we write separate letters this time, or will you add a bit to the bottom of mine?'

'Separate to Daddy, the other to Mammy,' Petal said quickly. She was well aware that Daisy did not love Steve as she did, though she had no very clear idea why. It was true that Daddy spoiled her and sometimes did not seem to notice Daisy, but she thought this was because Daisy jumped and went pale when Daddy tried to pull her on to his knee or talk to her about his ship, or her school, as he had done when they had gone home to see him while he was on leave last month. The trouble is, you've got to have a good memory to remember your daddy when he's been at sea for . . . well, for a long time, and perhaps Daisy's memory isn't as good as mine, so she treats him a bit like a stranger, and daddies don't like that.

'Righty-ho,' Daisy said now, and began to skip. It wasn't far to the turn in the lane which then widened out into the farmyard. Petal began to skip as well. Soon be home! Soon be having a nice big slice of apple cake – she did love apple cake! Auntie Blod had announced her intention of having a baking day since she had missed it last week, being poorly, so there would be other good things as well as apple cake. Meat and potato turnovers, delicious little round cakes with their initials marked on each one, shortbread to take to school for elevenses, and lots more, including the big cottage loaves for eating at home and the tin-loaves for taking as carry-out.

As the farmhouse came into view, Daisy began to run; for all she was so much older, Petal guessed that her sister was just as eager to reach the kitchen and be invited to 'try one of me special jam tarts' by dear, kind Auntie Blod as Petal was herself. The two of them entered the kitchen at a gallop, only to stop short, staring. The kitchen table was laden with good things, steam was rising gently from the oven in the range, but Auntie Blod was sitting slumped in a chair, her face grey, her lovely hair tumbling out of its coronet of plaits. Her eyes had been closed, but they opened as the two girls erupted into the room and, after a shocked moment, her pale lips moved.

'Daisy? Is that you, cariad? I – I'm glad you've come home because I – I'm not feeling so good. There's such a bad feeling in my innards . . . need help I do, more than I ever dreamed I would. D'you think you could run out to the field by the wild rose copse and fetch Dilys, or Uncle Gwil?' She put out a hand to them and, to Petal's horror, it was trembling. Auntie Blodwen, the best person in the world after her mother, was frightened! Petal took the hand in her own small, warm ones, and was frightened herself; it was so cold, and wet, too, despite the warmth of the kitchen.

'Daisy will go,' she said quickly. 'But I'll stay here with you, Auntie Blod. I – I'll make you a nice *panod* and you'll better in a trice, see if you aren't!'

Daisy glanced from one to the other, showing relief when Auntie Blod shook her head. 'No, ducky, I don't fancy nothing, to tell you the truth. Sick to my stomach I am, and right strange I do feel. But if you'll stay with me, cariad . . . I own I'd feel better.' She turned her eyes to Daisy, without moving her head, and Petal saw that her skin was saggy and grey and looked as wet as her hand felt. 'You'll hurry? Tell Dilys . . . and her dad . . .'

But Daisy was already out of the kitchen. Petal watched her cross the yard at a fast run and disappear in the direction of the wild rose copse. Then she pulled up a chair so that she might continue to hold Auntie Blod's hand but could do so sitting down, for she now had to acknowledge to herself that she was very badly scared. Auntie Blod had always seemed young and strong and wonderfully capable, but now one glance at that grey face and sagging body made Petal realise that her foster mother was old . . . old as the great, hump-backed hills of the Clwydian range which formed a backdrop to Ty Siriol. Old as the ex-headmaster, Skinny Skelton, who lived in a house in the square and sometimes came tottering into school to present a prize, or take an ill teacher's place.

'Auntie Blod? Are you *sure* you wouldn't like a cup of tea? I can make you one, honest I can.'

Petal's voice sounded very small and scared in her own ears, and she was just hoping that Auntie Blod had not noticed when she felt the hand, which had been lightly gripping her own, slide out of her grasp, felt it slump back on to the older woman's lap . . . and thought, for one horrified moment, that Auntie Blod had . . . had . . .

Petal gave a small gasp, said in a tiny voice: 'Auntie Blod, you mustn't die, please don't die! Petal's here, I'll look after you!'

And even as she spoke the words the kitchen door

crashed open and Dilys entered the room, closely followed by Daisy and Uncle Gwil. 'Mam, oh, Mam!' Dilys said, falling on her knees in front of her mother, whose eyes remained closed and whose head drooped in a terrifying fashion. 'Oh, Mam, and you kept saying you were better . . . Da, fetch a blanket. She's cold as . . . as charity!'

'In a moment,' Uncle Gwil said, his voice surprisingly steady. He bent over his wife. 'Blod, my dear one, can you hear me? I'll get Elias to fetch the car round and we'll take you to see Dr Evans; just you hang on there and we'll see you right.'

Petal did not expect Auntie Blod to answer, but after a moment she said, her voice slurred and slow: 'I hear you, Gwil. Hang on I will, boyo!'

Uncle Gwil actually chuckled before straightening up and heading for the stairs. 'I'll fetch that blanket,' he said briskly, then turned back to address his daughter. 'The doctor will likely want her in hospital. I shan't be two ticks.'

Daisy crossed the room to Petal's side and took her hand. 'Auntie Blod will be all right,' she whispered comfortingly. 'Don't worry, queen. Once the doctor sees her he'll make her better in no time.'

Petal mumbled an agreement, but privately, eyeing Auntie Blodwen's crumpled face and sagging body, she was not so sure.

Rose was shopping, something she scarcely ever did now because Maisie, only working three days a week, usually did it for her. But today she was on the night shift, which meant she had time to herself, and fairness dictated that being free for once, she should do the messages for Maisie as well as for herself. She had called round at her friend's house earlier, to pick up the ration books, and now she was queuing at Annie Baker's greengrocery in William Henry Street. She had done the grocery shopping, keeping an eye on the list Maisie had given her in the pious hope of finding some of the unrationed, but also unobtainable, goods for sale, and now she was queuing for early apples which were beginning to appear in the shops, for potatoes, carrots and, hopefully, for oranges.

'Hey, Rosie! Get some for me, will you, then I won't have to join the bleedin' queue, which already goes halfway round the block!'

Rose glanced behind her and grinned at the speaker. It was one of the girls from her bench at the factory, Helen Foster. Helen had recently moved into Bernard Terrace to live with her mother. She had four small children, ranging in age from eighteen months to seven years, and had been openly critical of Rose's keeping her children on in the country when she could have had them home. Rose had pointed out that Helen's mother looked after her four while she was at work, whereas she herself had lost her mother some years earlier and would have had to find a child-minder for Daisy and Petal, but Helen had been a bit dismissive . . . until last month, that was. The bombing of London and other British towns, as well as the dog-fights which were taking place daily over the south of England, had made people realise that the cities were not safe places for either adults or kids, though so far Liverpool, which should have been a prime target with the route across the Atlantic from the United States ending there, and the docks busier than they had ever been, was comparatively unscathed.

So now Rose smiled back at Helen and said she was queuing for apples, carrots, spuds and oranges, if they had any. Helen came over, ignoring the fact that half the queue were glaring at her, and pressed some money into Rose's hand.

'Fetch us a stone o' spuds and a couple o' pounds o' them apples then,' she wheedled. 'Oh, by the way, what's up at your place, eh?'

'Up? Nothing, so far as I know,' Rose said, staring, 'an' I can't carry a stone o' spuds, even if Mrs Baker would let me have 'em, which she won't.' Was Helen trying to tell her that Steve was home? But when she asked if Helen had seen her husband around, Helen shook her head.

'No, or I'd of said. But the telegraph boy was knockin' as though he were a-goin' to have the door down as I came past. You expectin' a telegram? Anyroad, he went next door, to old Maisie's – I saw him knocking.'

Rose's hand flew to her mouth and she pushed her purse and her shopping list into Helen's hand. 'A telegram? My God, I must get home at once! Be a dear, Helen, and finish my messages for me. You can take my place in the queue – no one will mind.'

Helen agreed and Rose hurried home. As she turned into Bernard Terrace she saw a telegraph boy pedalling his bicycle along in the gutter, and waved him down. 'I'm Mrs McAllister; I live at number seven. I believe you were trying to deliver a telegram earlier, when I was out doing my messages . . .'

Even as she spoke, the boy was fumbling in his bag and held out a small, yellow envelope. 'Any reply, missus?' he asked cheerfully, as Rose spread out the small sheet of paper and began to read. 'A reply's sixpence – if it's short, that is.'

Rose's heart, which had begun to beat overtime, steadied to a more normal pace as she read the words. *Mrs Williams took ill stop Going to hospital in Wrexham stop Please come urgent stop Williams.* For a moment, she could not think straight, then she made up her mind. She had given her purse to Helen but she ferreted around in her handbag and found two threepenny bits. The boy had his notebook out and was looking at her expectantly. 'Just say, *Will be with you soonest possible, McAllister*,' she said, and watched the boy's pencil take down her words. She knew she ought to tip him and rooted round in her bag once more, finding a couple of pennies and pressing them into the boy's hopefully extended palm. 'Thanks very much. How soon will it reach the Williamses, do you suppose?'

The boy shrugged, glancing at the address. 'It'll take me ten or fifteen minutes to get back to the post office, so it should be there in the time it takes the young feller in Ruthin to cycle to . . .' he looked at the address, 'to the sender,' he finished, obviously not wanting to try to pronounce the Welsh words. 'Don't worry, missus, it'll be there before you are, even if you was to fly.'

'But Mammy, *why* did we have to leave? Auntie Blod was always telling us what a help we were and anyway, you keep saying she'll be right as rain in no time, now she's in hospital. And there's school, all our friends . . . how long will we be away for?'

Petal's small voice was beginning to hold a distinct whine and Rose sighed to herself as she answered the question which had already been asked and answered a dozen times. 'Darling, Dilys will be far too busy to look after you properly, just think about it. There will be all the farm work, all the housework, all the dairy work, to say nothing of baking, doing the washing and ironing, feeding the stock . . . oh, a hundred different things, and only poor Dilys and Uncle Gwil to tackle the lot. Because of the war, farmers have to produce as much food as they possibly can and, of course, all the younger men have been conscripted into the forces. The ones who are left, Elias, and old Dewi, aren't as strong, can't do as much in a day as the younger fellers did. That will put a heavy burden on Dilys, but as soon as Auntie Blodwen's well again, I'm sure they'll want you back.'

The three of them were sitting in the train heading for Liverpool. Daisy, who had let Petal do all the complaining, wondered whether it was time to speak up, but decided against it. Last night, she had been so worried about Auntie Blod that she had been unable to sleep, so had stolen downstairs. Reaching the kitchen, she had found Uncle Gwil and Dilys still up and had climbed, miserably, on to Dilys's large and comfortable lap. The two were talking in Welsh and after a moment, during which Dilys soothed Daisy as though she had been a baby, clucking and patting, father and daughter continued their conversation, clearly believing that Daisy could not understand a word.

'It's a big operation, Da, but Mam will come through it all right. She's ever so strong, the surgeon said. But she won't be no manner of good so far as the farm's concerned for at least six months, maybe longer. When she's recovered from the operation, they'll be sending her to Rhyl to convalesce, so it could be as long as ten weeks before she's even back with us.'

'Aye; it'll be the first time we've spent so much as a night apart since we were wed,' Uncle Gwil said glumly. 'If only our Gareth were home, we'd manage somehow. But without him, I tell you, my love, I don't know which way to turn.'

'Well I do,' Dilys said, with a briskness Daisy had never heard in her voice before. 'We must apply for a Land Girl – more than one – and tell the Ministry it's urgent. Other folk have Land Girls and reckon they're a real boon.' She lowered her voice. 'The only thing is, we shan't be able to keep the children because Mam won't be well enough to cope and the Land Girls can't be expected to do anything in the house – they're farm workers, really.'

Uncle Gwil digested this for what seemed like an age to Daisy, but when he spoke, it was decisively. 'Aye, you're right. We've been managing somehow, with the older fellers and me – and you, girl – working every hour God sends, and more, but harvest time made me realise that we'd do a good deal better if we had more pairs of hands at our disposal. Your mam's a wonderful woman; she thinks nothing of starting her work at five in the morning and not stopping till ten at night. Mebbe it's that which has brought her so low. But the truth is that when she comes back she'll need more time to herself, because no matter how she sees it, she's not a young woman any more. Yes, we'll apply for a couple of Land Girls next time we go into town. I don't suppose we'll get anyone for a while, but I'll explain to the Ministry chap and I'm sure they'll do their best.'

Daisy had listened to this conversation with only half her attention and presently Dilys had carried her up to bed and popped her in beside the still slumbering Petal. Warmed and comforted by Dilys's cuddles, and by the fact that both father and daughter had seemed certain Auntie Blod was going to get better, Daisy had not allowed the significance of their words to worry her until she awoke next morning and began to think. If the Williamses were going to have Land Girls – and many of the farmers in the area already employed such young women – and Auntie Blod would not be well enough to look after them for many weeks to come, then she and Petal would have to go back to Liverpool whether they liked it or not and a return to the farm in the near future was unlikely, to say the least. The two of them would have done everything they could to help, but in her heart Daisy knew that the reliance which they all placed on Auntie Blod could not be fulfilled by two children.

So now, sitting in the railway carriage whilst her mother tried to calm Petal's fears, she wondered whether Rose had been told about the Land Girls and the impossibility of the children's returning to the farm until Auntie Blod was completely better, or whether she believed that they would soon go back to Ty Siriol. And another point: if Auntie Blodwen was going to be in hospital for a long time, could the McAllisters visit her there? Wrexham was a bit nearer Liverpool than Ruthin was, so perhaps they could all go – armed with a bunch of chrysanthemums – and see for themselves that their dear Auntie Blodwen was actually getting better. Daisy thought she'd never forget that fearful grey and sagging face, the slurred and cracking voice. If only she could see Auntie Blod looking more like herself, then she knew the nightmare – that Auntie Blod might die – would begin to recede.

Daisy waited until her mother had stopped speaking and then put forward the suggestion that they should visit Auntie Blod in the Wrexham hospital, just as soon as they could. 'Because Dilys said they'll send her to Rhyl to con— conva something or other, and Rhyl is a long way off,' she observed. 'What do you think, Mam? We could go on your next day off and take her some flowers.'

'That's a very good idea,' Rose said approvingly,

smiling brightly at her daughter. 'You're a good girl, Daisy, thoughtful and kind. Yes, as soon as she's allowed visitors, we'll make our way to the hospital in Wrexham; that's a promise.'

In the event, it was almost the end of November before the children actually got to see Auntie Blodwen again, and then it was only because the staff agreed that, for once, they would waive their 'no children on the ward' rules since Mrs Williams was to depart in another few days to Rhyl, where she would convalesce.

They arrived at the small station at noon so Rose, who knew Wrexham quite well from previous visits to Auntie Blod, took them to Steven's Café in Hope Street, where they had a first rate meal, Petal announcing that the sausagemeat pie with mashed potato on top was almost as good as Auntie Blod's.

After that, they walked through the narrow streets to the War Memorial Hospital, an imposing modern building, built of red brick and sandstone, with elegant balconies overlooking a small side street. The children had grown accustomed, if not reconciled, to the idea that they would probably not return to live at Ty Siriol for a long, long time. *If ever*, Daisy said mournfully inside her head, but that was one idea she did not share with Petal, for her small sister had whined and wept and even wet the bed upon first returning to Bernard Terrace. Daisy knew that in her heart of hearts Petal still believed in a happy return to the farm, and she did not intend to be the person who disillusioned her little sister.

But now, standing outside the building, staring upwards, Petal seemed surprised that the balconies were not crowded with eager patients – Auntie Blod well to the fore, obviously – waiting to greet the visitors. She held a tiny bottle of lavender water in one hot hand whilst Daisy grasped a bunch of shaggy tawny chrysanthemums, and both children were eager to hand their gifts over and be extravagantly thanked, for they had saved their weekly pennies up and bought both perfume and flowers out of their own money, with only a little assistance from Rose.

'Come along, children,' Rose said briskly, taking a hand of each, for suddenly they had both hung back, overawed by the size of the place and by the strangeness of it, neither having even visited a hospital before, far less been a patient in one. Rose, who had visited Auntie Blodwen twice already, led the way in as though she owned the place, and Daisy was glad they had someone with them who knew the ropes, for the hospital's steady refusal, until today, to allow them to visit had made her imagine the whole place as a sort of prison and the nursing staff and doctors as warders, and not always well-disposed ones either.

'Up here, along here, round this next bend,' their mother was saying, and as they reached the entrance to the ward a nurse came towards them. She recognised Rose, and greeted her as Mrs McAllister.

She was an elderly woman, whose collar and cuffs were so rigidly starched that she had pink marks at neck and wrists, and she told them they must not stay too long. 'Mrs Williams has had a very serious operation and must not become too tired,' she said gravely. 'Very fond of children, she is, which is why I agreed to this visit, but it must be a short one; do you understand?'

Considerably awed by this little speech, the children nodded, round-eyed. But then Rose was ushering them through the doors on to the ward. It was a long room with tall windows, though no balcony that Daisy could see, and someone was waving to them, smiling, gesturing to them to come closer . . .

Daisy hung back for a moment, unsure. To tell the truth, she had been secretly dreading that the Auntie Blod in the hospital bed might look like that other Auntie Blod, the incredibly old, grey-faced one who had collapsed in the kitchen on that memorable, dreadful, afternoon. But to her infinite relief, the Auntie Blod in the hospital bed was the real one, the one who had taken them in, loved them, spoiled them. To be sure, her hair seemed to have rather more white in it than Daisy remembered, and her rosy apple cheeks were pink rather than red, but the blue eyes twinkled and the mouth was curved into a real, unaffected and happy smile and the arms she held out were strong-looking . . . young-looking, even.

Still Daisy held back, embarrassed by the number of nightgowned women in the beds on either side of the central aisle, not wanting to make a fool of herself – was that really Auntie Blod looking so well and fit or was she just imagining it? – but as usual, Petal had no such scruples. She dashed forward and flung herself into Auntie Blod's arms with such force that that stout person reeled for a moment. But then she laughed and heaved Petal on to the bed and held out her arms to Daisy, and Daisy gave a strangled sob which she tried to turn into a laugh, and the next moment she was being hugged too, and her chrysanthemums were being declared the most beautiful flowers ever to be brought into the hospital, just as the lavender water was the very thing for which Auntie Blod had longed, particularly since she would soon be going away to the convalescent home in Rhyl, and would want to impress all the nurses and doctors and other patients she would meet there.

'And are you settled, glad to be back with your mam again?' she asked presently when the first ecstasy of greeting was over. 'Hard it is on children to be carted from pillar to post, I always think. But if there's no danger, the place for a child is with its mother, that's what I say. And the child-minder? Mrs – Mrs Briggs, is it? She's kind to you? A good woman who is fond of the little ones?'

'She's all right,' Daisy acknowledged. She knew it would be tactless, unkind almost, to say that Mrs Briggs's idea of tea was bread and jam. Daisy understood, now that she had actually suffered from the rationing, that they had been tremendously lucky at the farm. Because they grew, or reared, so much of their own food, the shortages really hadn't affected them at all, but now . . . well, Mrs Briggs's teas were a case in point. Also, because she looked after other children as well as Daisy and Petal, they had to put up with a certain amount of competition at the tea table. Amos and Andy, eleven-year-olds, could eat twice as quickly as anyone else and had often cleared a plate of bread and margarine and eaten half the horrid seed cake Mrs Briggs provided before Daisy and Petal had done more than take a couple of tentative bites of their own portions.

However, they could scarcely tell Auntie Blod what they had not brought themselves to tell Rose, so Daisy said sedately that Mrs Briggs was very kind and her daughter, Dulcie, great fun. When questioned, she admitted that it was nice to be with all her old school friends again . . . though she missed the farm and the Williamses. Nicky had returned to Liverpool within days of their own homecoming, which was blessing for Daisy as there was no one at her present school who was half as nice and kind as he.

Petal opened her mouth to say something and Daisy shot her a warning glance. Petal shut her mouth again. They had both been reminded by Rose that they must not upset their kind foster mother by admitting how much they missed Ty Siriol, and Daisy, at least, was determined not to say how horribly unhappy they had been at first. Often, she thought of their time on the farm as a sort of lovely dream which had happened in another life, and when she had told Rose this, her mother had smiled sadly and said that they were very lucky kids to have a time like that to look back on.

'When I'm grown up I shall marry a farmer,' Daisy had said, and Petal, always keen to go one better, said scornfully: 'Oh, Daisy, don't *marry* anyone. I shan't. I shall *be* a farmer, just like Uncle Gwil.'

It had made her mother laugh, Daisy remembered, and she was just about to tell Auntie Blodwen how funny Petal had been when she happened to notice that the lovely pink colour which had come into Auntie Blodwen's cheeks as they talked seemed to have disappeared; and even as she noticed this, she saw her mother move, make a tiny gesture with one hand. *It's time we left*, the gesture said. *Auntie Blod's getting tired.*

Immediately reading the message correctly, Daisy got to her feet and kissed Auntie Blod and bade Petal follow suit since she had just noticed the time, and they really must not miss their train. Auntie Blod kissed and hugged them, kissed Rose, said goodbye, reminded them that they would always be welcome on the farm, though until she got home again things might be a trifle awkward, and though she was feeling ever so much better she didn't think she'd be much use as a worker for a while . . . the stitches caught at her when she tried to walk . . . oh, but they were not to forget her, she would never forget them, would expect them to write regularly, as indeed they had done throughout her stay in hospital . . . She was still waving as they left the ward, and as they retraced their steps along the corridor her mother gave Daisy's shoulder a squeeze. 'You are a kind little girl to make it easy for us to leave without upsetting Auntie Blod,' she said. 'Actually, we'll have an hour to kill before the next train, so we'll take a look at the shops. There's a Woolworth's here, I seem to remember; we might buy a little toy, or some sweets perhaps – I've still got some coupons left.'

'I don't see why you say Daisy's so good,' Petal said, much aggrieved. 'I'm every bit as kind as old Daisy, and a lot littler. Why don't you say *I'm* a kind little girl? And if she's the only one getting sweets, or a toy, it ain't bleedin' well fair!'

'You won't get anything at all if you swear, young lady,' Rose said severely, though Daisy noticed she was trying to hide a smile. 'And you're a good girl, too, mostly, so you shall have a toy, or some sweets, when we reach Woolworth's. Wasn't it nice to see Auntie Blod looking so much better? And wasn't she pleased to see you both? As for writing letters, you've both been very good about doing so whilst she was in hospital, so I'm sure you'll write just as much when she's in Rhyl.'

The children agreed that they would do so and it was not until they were in the main shopping street that Petal began to cry. 'I want Auntie Blod to be back at the farm so we can visit her there,' she wept. 'I love her so much, Mammy, and I like people to be in their own places; Ty Siriol is her place, not horrible hospitals, or that other place in Rhyl. Oh, Mammy, I miss Auntie Blod so much.'

'So do I, Petal, but at least we're with our own mam, and not with someone else,' Daisy said, whilst Rose tried to distract her little daughter by pointing out that Woolworth's was only a few yards up the road. 'Think of Jenny Platt, living with that horrible old grandmother because her mam has been and gone and joined the ATS. And Bernard Terrace is nice, isn't it? We've got lots of friends there, and – and Dulcie Briggs lets us play really good games . . . oh, *do* stop crying, Petal, everyone's staring!'

Petal gave a deep sigh, and allowed her mother to blow her nose and wipe the tears from her cheeks, then she smiled bravely up at her sister. 'I'm all right now,' she said huskily. 'I hope they sell little Dinky cars in Woolworth's because I don't see why boys always have to have the best things, and I'd like one of my own.'

'Only another five days before Christmas,' Rose said, as she and Rachel met on Shaw Street and turned their steps towards the nearest bus stop. 'I'm off for three whole days because I've got the children; are you working over the holiday, Rachel?'

'Yes, but I've got the twenty-eighth, twenty-ninth and thirtieth off,' Rachel said. 'It's different for us . . . we don't much mind when our holiday comes so long as we have one. And Alby may suddenly arrive home, which would make my Christmas, even if it was a bit later than yours.'

'Yes, it would be lovely if the *Jericho* came into port, though I don't suppose Steve will have had a chance to get the children presents,' Rose said. 'But still, I've managed to fill a stocking for each of them. And we'll have a Christmas dinner, though it may not be all that lavish.' She looked curiously at her friend, noticing the pink flush on Rachel's cheeks and the brightness of her eyes. 'What's up, Rachel? I do believe you've heard from Alby . . . are they coming home?'

'I wish they were, because I've got some news for Alby and I'd dearly love to see his face when I tell him,' Rachel confided. 'Oh, Rosie, I've got to tell someone or I'll burst! I'm going to have a baby in the spring . . . well, in May. I've told my parents, of course, but Alby will be absolutely delighted; if only he were coming home!'

By now, the two young women were standing at the bus stop and Rose turned to give her friend an exuberant hug and a kiss on the cheek. 'That's wonderful news, the best news I've heard in weeks,' she said joyfully. 'Just think, Rachel, this time next year we'll both be scouring the shops for toys, or games, or children's books. Can I tell the kids? Petal won't mind one way or the other, but Daisy is always nagging me to give her a baby brother or sister.' She laughed, a trifle self-consciously. 'I did try to explain, but despite knowing all about sheep and cows I don't think she understands the . . . facts of life yet.'

'At ten years old I should hope she doesn't,' Rachel said virtuously. 'And yes, you can tell them, if you make them promise not to say anything to Steve when they write. I'm going to write to Alby with the news, of course, because who knows when the *Jericho* will come back to Liverpool? Why, the last time they were in port, it was in Southampton, I think, and they weren't there for long enough to get home, even for a few hours.'

'Perhaps I won't say anything just yet then,' Rose decided, as they climbed aboard the bus. 'Did I tell you that Maisie next door has an aunt in the country, who makes her own mincemeat, the sweet sort? She's given Maisie a couple of jars of it and Maisie is giving me one of them, so this afternoon when I get home, I'll be baking mince pies. Fortunately, I've been saving my flour and marge ration for weeks and weeks, so I could do a big bake for Christmas.'

'My mam does all of that, bless her,' Rachel said smugly as they squeezed along the aisle, past passengers already standing. 'Don't forget, Mam's invited you and the kids to tea on Boxing Day. My father has been keeping a bottle of sherry to toast the baby's health when he's born, but he said we would all have a tiny glass to celebrate when you come round.'

'Lovely,' Rose said, trying to sound enthusiastic, though she disliked the taste of all alcohol and much preferred a nice cup of tea. 'And don't worry, I wouldn't miss one of your mam's high teas for all the world.'

'Mammy, when the mince pies is done, can me and Daisy share one? I know they're really for Christmas Day, but it's *nearly* that, only another five days to go and I'm hungry *now*. Me and Daisy ate up all our sausage and mash but we've still got a little gap, just about the size of a mince pie. Oh, Mammy, do say we can.'

Rose was about to reply when the sirens started to wail. She glanced towards her oven, which already contained a tray of mince pies, and at the table, where another trayful had just been completed. There had been raids, on and off, ever since the children had returned home, but none of a particularly serious nature – not if you lived some distance from the docks, at any rate. The McAllisters were used to them, took them in their stride, though Rose resented the broken nights which made work next day seem so hard. But whenever the siren sounded she popped the children into the Morrison shelter, where they slept soundly enough, whilst she herself curled up alongside them and usually managed at least some sleep. There had been several such alarms in November, culminating in a raid on the 28th during which almost two hundred people had been killed and many homes destroyed. This had almost frightened Rose into sending the children away once more, though heaven knew who would take them since the Williamses could not do so, but the attack had been followed by a quiet period when no enemy aircraft had even been seen in the skies, and this had made it seem unnecessary to split the family up once more. Now, despite a most unpleasant sensation in the pit of her stomach at the sound of the sirens' wail, she decided she could not possibly go to the public shelter immediately or the mince pies would be ruined, and it was infuriating to think of spoiling good food for what might very likely turn out to be a false alarm. And of course the sirens sounded just the same, even if the enemy aircraft were heading for Wallasey, or Birkenhead, or perhaps further up the coast, at somewhere like Barrow-in-Furness. She decided that the children must squeeze into the Morrison shelter, which took up a good deal of room under the big kitchen table, just until the mince pies were cooked. After that, if it seemed that the raid might be a bad one and provided it was safe to do so, she would take them, and all their impedimenta, along to the shelter; hopefully, they would not be there long. She glanced up at the clock above the mantel; it was half past six. In normal circumstances, the children would begin their bedtime preparations in half an hour anyway, so they might as well do so now, in case later they were in the shelter and unable to clean teeth, brush hair and get into their nightgowns.

'Mammy? Did you hear that? Does it mean they're going to start dropping bombs again? I thought they'd give up on us, honest to God I did. I hate the noise, Mammy, it frightens me ever so. Oh, I wish we were back on the farm, so I do!'

Daisy had been curled up in a chair, reading her comic paper, but now she stood up and came over to the table to put a reassuring hand on her small sister's shoulder. 'Let's peep out of the window and see if the sky's clear of aeroplanes,' she suggested.

Rose was about to remind her eldest that they must never go near windows during an air raid, and the safest place for them right now was inside the Morrison shelter, when they all heard it: the steady, menacing thrum, thrum of enemy aircraft approaching, and then the scream of descending bombs and the explosions as they hit their target.

Immediately, mince pies were forgotten. Rose seized the children and hustled them into the Morrison shelter. Petal was crying, but Daisy, though white-faced, seemed calm enough. Rose had already placed blankets and pillows beside the shelter, as well as their night clothes and Petal's almost bald teddy bear, and now she handed these to Daisy, who promptly began to make a nest. 'Don't be long, Mam,' she urged, trying to keep her voice steady, Rose thought. 'When you come into the shelter as well, you can tell us a story – or read to us if you like. I've put *Simple Susan* on the sofa and one of the *Amelia Anne* books. It'll – it'll stop us listening for the next crash.'

Rose was about to say that she would come into the shelter at once when the smell of cooking reached her. With a squeak of dismay, she rushed across the kitchen and grabbed the mince pies from the oven. They were done to a turn, and for a moment she looked regretfully at the uncooked pies before resolutely turning off the gas. If, by some awful mischance, the house was hit, then a fire in the kitchen, fuelled by the gas oven, would not be a good idea.

The thrumming was directly overhead now; she could imagine the dark and evil shapes blotting out the stars, death falling from them on to the innocent citizens below. An enormous crash almost stopped her heart, and she was still holding the tray of mince pies ten seconds later as she joined her children under the table. Daisy, looking white and frightened, had an arm round Petal and was telling her a story, but when the children saw the mince pies their faces brightened and Rose, without a word, handed them round.

'Should we go to the shelter, Mam?' Daisy asked presently, as the sound of explosions and the noise of enemy aircraft got louder. 'The house keeps shaking. I'm scared it'll come down on our heads.'

'It won't,' Rose said with a confidence she was far from feeling. 'But it will be really dangerous out in the streets, queen. Those planes are right overhead . . . we'll stay where we are this evening. But I'm afraid tomorrow night we'll just have to get to the shelter early, whether or not there's a raid. Auntie Maisie used to do that most nights when the raids were bad; says she's got used to sleeping on a concrete bunk with strangers all round her.'

'Oh. Right,' Daisy said. 'Can you read to us, Mam? Only my voice isn't loud enough, and . . . oh, look at that!'

Rose, wrapping a blanket around herself and pulling her pillow into position beneath her head, followed the direction of Daisy's pointing finger, then smiled, torn between astonishment and sheer, undiluted relief. Petal was curled up under her blanket, her thumb in her mouth and her golden eyelashes fanned out on her cheeks. She was fast asleep.

A couple of days later, Rose and Rachel met in the canteen for a chat. The raid which had caught Rose making mince pies had been followed, the very next night, by an even worse one. Bombs had rained down upon Liverpool and no one had got much sleep, though Rose and the children had gone to the shelter as she had promised. The atmosphere down there was a good deal happier than it was when you were shut up in your own house, for the older women organised sing-songs and there was a good deal of laughing, story-telling and question and answer games. Rose managed to get a bunk for herself and the children and had the satisfaction of seeing them drop asleep as the night wore on, but she herself could not so much as close her eyes. So now she was asking Rachel, in all seriousness, whether she was right to keep the children in the city when the danger was so real, so terrible.

'I expect you ought to send them into the country,' Rachel conceded as they ate their braised liver and onions. 'But where would they go, queen? It isn't as if you could trek – go into the countryside each evening and return in the morning, I mean – as lots of mothers with kids do, because you want to keep your job, don't you? Oh, I'm sure someone would have them, but finding that someone will take time. It's not as though there were a general evacuation, as there was directly war broke out.'

'No-o, but I feel so bloody guilty, letting them stay here when the danger is so great,' Rose said, spearing a potato and chopping it into the gravy. Canteen food was pretty good, all things considered, and it meant that she could feed the children better since she did not need to share their evening meal. 'My aunt and uncle, the ones who used to live in Penny Lane, have moved out to Formby, but they've scarcely any room to spare and though they've said they'd pack the kids in somehow, they're – well, they're awful old, Rachel. They used to spoil the kids, and I doubt very much if they could discipline them now, see that they went to school and so on. And when I suggested it, Daisy went all bolshie on me, and said she wouldn't leave me in danger because if she did I'd be bound to get hurt. Oh, she would go to the Williamses like a shot, but not to Aunt Selina and Uncle Frank. Kids are weird, but Petal backed her up so I said I'd think about it and left the subject alone.'

'I can understand in a way,' Rachel said, pushing her empty plate aside and pulling forward her pudding, a dish of suet roll and custard. 'When they went off to Ruthin they were with all their classmates; it was an adventure, with lots and lots of their friends and teachers around them. They made heaps of new friends on the farm and at the school, and got used to them, were truly fond of them. But going off to an ancient aunt and uncle – no, I know they aren't ancient really, but they must seem that to your little girls – without a soul they know, joining a new school, being away from you . . . well, it's a lot to ask.'

'Yes, I suppose you're right, especially at Christmas time,' Rose admitted. 'Goodness, only another couple of days and it will actually be Christmas! Oh, Rachel, surely the Luftwaffe will want to be in their own homes at Christmas, and not bombing us? I do hope so!'

'You aren't the only one,' Rachel admitted. 'Mam and Dad simply won't hear of going to the shelter and so I feel I can't walk out and leave them. But when the bombs are close, and you can hear the planes' engines overhead . . . well, I wouldn't mind a nice hefty shelter over my head, and people all around me in the same boat.'

'After what happened when bombs managed to get below that shelter before they exploded, and sent almost fifty people to kingdom come, I'm not all that sure that going to the shelter is the safest thing to do,' Rose observed, beginning to eat her own pudding. 'The trouble is, whatever I do may be absolutely wrong . . . still, it's the same for all of us. And for the moment, we'll stay put and take our chance along with everyone else. In the New Year, if things get worse, I'll have to think again.'

Steve met Alby as the watch was changed and saw at once from his friend's face that he had had good news. He loped over to the smaller man and raised his eyebrows. 'Well? It can't be a letter because we ain't in port.'

Alby grinned exuberantly. 'Signal,' he said. 'I've passed my final exams and will be a signaller, starting when we next go to sea, and I can stay with the old *Jericho*, for the time being at any rate.'

It was a nasty, grey day with snow gusting across the open deck from time to time and a bitter wind blowing, but Alby's face was alight and Steve saw that he must be glad for his pal, though inwardly he was dismayed. Ever since Alby had passed the preliminary examinations he had been fearing that the two of them would be parted, and though it was good news that Alby had been made up without, as was usual in peace-time, having to change his ship, he knew that this was now bound to happen sooner or later.

'Congratulations, old feller,' Steve said. 'And I've

heard a bit of good news, too; we'll be back in the Liverpool docks in four or five days, and we'll get a chance to see our folks this time, since unloading the merchant fleet takes a day or two. So it won't just be letters; we'll sleep in our own beds for a couple of nights.'

Alby's smile grew even broader, then faded a trifle. 'If the wolf pack don't find us and scupper half the merchantmen,' he said. 'They say the U-boats hang about just outside the Mersey estuary. And then there's the Luftwaffe . . .'

'Oh, don't be so bleedin' miserable,' Steve said reprovingly. 'We've had a good run this time. We've not seen so much as an enemy—'

'Shut your great big blathering mouth,' Alby said, suddenly furious. 'Do you want to bring every perishin' U-boat on our track? I tell you, if anything stops us getting a couple of days at home, I'll personally break both your bloody legs.'

Considerably startled, for Alby rarely swore and never lost his temper, Steve mumbled an apology and gestured to the younger man to go ahead of him, down the companionway. 'I dunno what made me say it,' Steve said humbly, as they entered the seamen's mess and went to line up at the hatch which separated the men from the galley. 'But won't it be grand to be back in Liverpool again? I told you the kids had come back from the farm, didn't I? It'll be good to see them after so long.'

To his relief, Alby grinned at him. 'And you'll see that pretty wife of yours,' he said reprovingly. 'I can't wait to see Rachel, meself, though we still haven't got a place of our own. Her parents are grand; they never interfere, understand how precious a couple of days can be when you've not seen each other for months.'

'Oh aye, it'll be grand to see Rose, of course,' Steve said, realising with some surprise that it wasn't altogether untrue. She was a good cook, was Rosie, and when she wasn't working the house was real homelike. He imagined the firelit kitchen, the soft easy chairs, the delicious smell of bread baking, or a meat pie simmering away in the oven. For the first time for absolutely ages, he thought about his mother and her ill-kept, disorganised house. He remembered dirty kids underfoot, his brothers' perpetual quarrelling, his father's violence and the fits of ill-temper, so bad that he and his brothers had dreaded his father's return at the end of each day. His father had been dead for five years, killed in a dockers' brawl, and Steve rarely visited his mother because her whining got on his nerves, though whenever he had a few bob to spare he would go round to the house in Regent Street and slam the cash on the table, grudging every penny, but knowing that the old girl would make better use of it than his hard-drinking father would have done.

Ahead of him, Alby turned away from the hatch, his tin plate full of stew and dumplings. Steve swallowed; the food both looked and smelled good, but the gravy was thin and the dumplings were not as satisfying as potatoes, which could be mashed into the gravy and would have filled him up nicely. Although they always took on supplies in New York, potatoes quite often ran out before they docked again, mainly because a convoy had to steer a zig-zag course so that they did not make a perfect target for the wolf pack, shadowing them beneath the waves.

Steve took his plate of food and went and sat next to Alby on the bench. Ever since his brief flirtation with the idea of working in submarines, he could never think of the U-boats without shuddering. At Alby's suggestion, he had painstakingly read everything he could lay his hands on concerning submarines. He knew about the cramped conditions, the bad air, the way they lay quiet in the very depths of the ocean, the men warned not to make a sound, not to move, whilst above them the enemy sat with their hydrophones clamped to their ears, listening for a man to cough or sneeze, giving away their position. And there was the sonar, whose blip, blip, blip, could detect objects lying on the floor of the ocean, and of course the depth charges, which could destroy a submarine so completely that sometimes only fragments came to the surface to prove to the attacking ship that she had made a killing.

But he also remembered that U-boats fired torpedoes, which could finish a ship off within moments of their first strike. In fact, from having been happily devoid of imagination, he thought resentfully, thanks to Alby he now seemed to have more than his fair share. He could quite see why Alby had been annoyed with him, too; the dangers were always there, either above or below you, and only a fool would tempt fate by announcing, in mid-ocean, that they had had an uneventful voyage. He turned to Alby to voice this thought, just as the ship reverberated to a shuddering crash and all the lights went out.

Chapter Seven
January 1941

There was no panic. Steve felt for Alby's arm and gripped it tightly, whilst all around them men produced torches and began to make for the nearest exit. Steve and Alby followed, clattered up the companionway and emerged on to the deck. Since they had last been up here dusk had fallen, though there was still sufficient light to see each other and to recognise the officer who was marshalling them into a line – not easy, since the deck was already at an angle of 45 degrees.

'What happened?' a burly seaman ahead of them in the line asked. 'I were in me bunk and when the crash came I were thrown out, on to the floor. I slipped and slid towards the companionway and looked down the corridor and, begod, there were water roaring towards me. It were up to me waist by the time I'd climbed the first half dozen steps . . . I doubt if another soul gorraway besides meself. If I'd realised what were happenin' . . . me bezzie, Lofty, were snorin' like a motorbike . . . mebbe I should ha' gone back . . .'

'No point,' someone said succinctly. 'It were a torpedo. No enemy shipping about, so it must ha' been fired by a U-boat.'

'Not just one torpedo, two, fired in quick succession,' someone else said. 'It's near blown us apart, which is why they're launching the boats. Our only chance, see. We're too far ahead of the rest of the convoy to swim back to 'em.'

'I hope they've scarpered, now they know we know

they're here,' a small red-headed rating said apprehensively. 'Last time I ended up in the oggin, the buggers fired at us, damn near blew me 'at off.'

Alby laughed. 'Oh well, that's all right,' he remarked. 'I'm not wearin' me hat, so I'll be okay then.'

As they talked, the line had been moving steadily forward, and now Steve reached the rail and was able to watch what was happening. Despite the difficult circumstances, the lifeboats were being launched efficiently and coolly, since this was the side of the ship nearest the water. Steve noticed, with a sick churning in his stomach, that the sea was getting closer every moment, indicating that it would not be long before the poor old *Jericho* slid quietly beneath the waves.

It was also clear that the boats could not possibly hold the entire crew, but Steve realised that a great many of the men must have suffered the same fate as that which the burly seaman had described: in their bunks, or at their stations below decks, they would have been helpless to escape the terrible inrush of water.

Ahead of him, Alby had reached the front of the queue and was clambering aboard the lifeboat. Steve glanced back. He had not realised that he and Alby were quite near the end of the line, for there were only a dozen or so blokes still to come as he took his place in the lifeboat beside his friend. In fact, within moments, the deck was empty, and the young officer, having checked that no one else was waiting, launched the lifeboat, and then jumped aboard himself, saying breathlessly as he did so: 'Grab an oar, you men, and let's get out of here! When she goes under, she'll take us with her if we don't put a good distance between us.'

Everyone did their best, and afterwards no one was

quite sure whether it was the suction of the sinking of the *Jericho* or whether the unseen enemy had fired another torpedo. But suddenly there was a huge wave, as high as a house, bearing down on them. They were at the wrong angle to ride it, even if such a thing were possible, and could do nothing when ton after ton of water, green and salt and cold as ice, crashed down upon their cockleshell craft.

Steve came ashore with nothing worse than a cut over one eye, a great many bruises and a strong desire never to return to sea again, even though he knew he was one of the lucky ones. He and the young red-haired rating had been picked up – eventually – by the SS *Coromandel Queen*, carrying grain, and he knew that Alby had been picked up, too, since there had been much frantic signalling amongst the fleet when day had dawned.

So now Steve stood on the quayside and waited, because he did not intend to make his way back to Bernard Terrace until he had seen his friend face to face.

He did not have long to wait. Alby came ashore only thirty minutes after Steve himself had landed, but his first remark proved him more alert than his friend. 'Did you see the damage as we came up the Mersey?' he said. 'The docks and Bootle seem to have taken a fair pasting. I hope to God the girls are all right.'

It was the first time that Steve had even considered that they might not be. To his mind, war was a man's business; women moaned about shortages, said there was nothing to buy in the shops, sent their children into the wilds of Wales. He acknowledged, of course, that the Luftwaffe would bomb the docks, the grain warehouses, and other such places, but it had honestly not occurred to him that his neighbours, his wife, his children even, might have been killed or injured whilst he was fighting his own battles at sea.

In fact, as he and Alby walked through the shabby streets, he realised that he still could not believe anything had happened to Rose or the girls. Bernard Terrace must be at least half a mile from the docks; there was nothing in the surrounding area to attract the attention of the bombers, so he could not bring himself to waste time worrying about them. They would be all right; he knew it in his water.

And so it proved. He and Alby said cheerio on Shaw Street and went their separate ways, and presently Steve crossed Bernard Terrace and went into No. 7. The back door was closed, but he opened it and a wonderful smell of cooking came out. He had not realised it was a Saturday, but now he knew it must be, since his daughters were seated on stools drawn up to the kitchen table, busily painting in two colouring books. Rose was cooking at the stove and, to do her credit, when his head appeared round the door there was only the slightest of hesitations before she cried: 'Steve! I'm so glad you're safe.' And, leaving the pan she was stirring, she crossed the kitchen, gave him a quick peck on the cheek and then said: 'But what have you done to yourself? Don't say you've been fighting!'

She ushered him into the room whilst he explained, briefly, what had happened and the children stared at him, round-eyed. It had been five months since they had seen him last, he thought ruefully, and that must be why they were both looking at him doubtfully. He crossed the room and bent over Petal, who had always been his favourite. 'Don't you remember me, queen?' he asked, and suddenly his voice was rough with unshed tears. This kid had been fond of him, had never shown fear in his presence, had always hugged and kissed him, but of course she was older now; would she turn against him as Daisy had done?

But it seemed as though surprise alone had stopped her running to him, for she pushed her picture away and jumped up, casting herself into his arms. 'But Daddy, Daddy, your poor face . . . but the doctor will make it better,' she gabbled, as he lifted her off her feet, settling her on his hip. 'Was your ship sunk? Was you nearly drownded?'

'The old *Jericho*'s sunk to the bottom of the sea, but me and me pal bobbed up like a couple o' corks an' gorra lift home with one of the merchant ships,' he said gaily. 'But if I'd had to, queen, I'd have swum all the way home, just to see my little girl again.'

Daisy had left her seat as Petal did, and now she reached up and patted his arm. It was a timid gesture but the nearest she had ever come to showing any sort of affection for him, so Steve rubbed her cheek, feeling foolish in a way he never did when caressing Petal. He told himself she was older, more reserved, and did not examine his own feelings for his elder daughter in any depth. He loved Petal and tolerated Daisy; what was wrong with that? He knew many men who did not care for any of their children and felt no guilt over his secret dismissal of Daisy. She's her mother's daughter, he told himself; Petal's Daddy's girl.

Whilst he talked to the children, Rose had dished up. It seemed that the meal was to be some rather odd-looking rissoles, a handful of carrots and three large boiled potatoes, and all of it was being put on one plate. He was still pondering the significance of this when Rose carried it over to the table and set it down in front of him. 'I'll just make some French toast and fry up a bit of bacon for the rest of us,' she said. 'It won't take a moment; then we can all eat.'

Oh, so that was why there were three rissoles and three potatoes, Steve thought, picking up his knife and fork and reaching for the HP Sauce. It would have been their meal had he not turned up. He began to eat; the rissoles looked rather strange and home-made but they were delicious, full of flavour and cooked crispy on the outside and soft and meaty within. Just as he liked them, in fact. The children sat down again and began plying him with questions, whilst behind them Rose dipped thick slices of home-made bread into the egg and milk mixture she had concocted, then fried the soggy slices in the pan alongside a few thin rashers of bacon. Steve, eating steadily and helping himself to a couple of thick wedges of bread and margarine, rather enjoyed being the centre of so much attention. He went over his recent experience, from the crash and thunder of the striking torpedoes to the moment when he, the red-haired rating, and Alby had been fished out of an increasingly rough sea and hauled aboard two of the merchant vessels.

'Oh, Dad, it must have been awful, really terrifying,' Daisy breathed, and Steve was gratified to see that there was hero-worship in her small face instead of the usual mixture of fear and defiance. 'Weren't you and Alby and the other man lucky, though? What happened to the rest of the men in your lifeboat? Were they rescued too?'

Steve shook his head. 'No, the rest of 'em was all drowned,' he said. 'But me an' Alby, I reckon we've got charmed lives, same as Andy – he's the rating what came home on the same ship as meself – because of the whole ship's crew, only eighteen came ashore today.'

'Why do you say Andy has a charmed life?' Rose asked, putting three more plates down on the table. She pushed Petal's chair in, then handed both girls knives and forks and sat down before her own plate. Steve saw she had no bacon but only the French toast – or eggy bread as Petal called it – but thought nothing of it, though he had not realised before that she did not like bacon. He wanted to say: *You can't afford to be fussy in wartime, you should see some of the meals I've been forced to eat aboard ship*, but decided against it. Rose might see it as criticism and the atmosphere at present would not be helped by Rose's getting snooty with him.

'Steve? Why does Andy have a charmed life?'

Steve polished his plate with the last slice of bread and looked hopefully round. Where was the pudding? But then he saw the children were still eating and held his tongue. Doubtless a pudding would appear in the fullness of time. 'Andy? Oh, didn't I tell you? This was the third time his ship had been torpedoed under him. Some fellers is like that, they seem to have bad luck in that they are aboard ships which get holed or shot up or something of that nature, but they always gerroff scot-free themselves. Well, I had me cut eye and bruises but that were only done when I were being hauled aboard the merchantman. Oh aye, I reckon me an' Alby are lucky, awright.'

'I see. Well, I'm most awfully glad Alby was saved as well, because . . . well, me and Rachel are very good friends, and – and I don't suppose it will matter if I tell you now, because it's the first thing Rachel will tell Alby. They're expecting a baby, Steve; isn't that nice? Rachel is thrilled to bits and she's certain Alby will feel the same. Apparently they've always wanted a family, and though they won't move out from her mam's place until things are . . . more settled, like, they'll do so as soon as the war's over and Alby's home again for good.'

'Grand, grand,' Steve said absently. He wondered if afters would be jam roly; easily his favourite. He decided not to ask about the pudding; instead, he contented himself with remarking that he'd enjoyed the rissoles. He tried to smile at Rose, but the way she had just spoken stuck in his craw: *Well, I'm most awfully glad*, she had said, in that annoying, smug way she had. And then she couldn't say: *Rachel's gorra grin on 'er gob what stretches from one lug to t'other*, like any decent scouser would. She had to say: *Rachel is thrilled to bits* – stuck up cow! Still, there you were. He had married her knowing her mam and dad thought she were a perishin' princess and had done his best to knock the nonsense out of her, though clearly without very much success. Oh, well; he remembered Alby saying once that you can't change people, only time and experience can do that. Then, he hadn't really understood, but now he thought he did. Once a snob always a snob; and anyway she were a good mother to his kids and a cracking cook. He watched as she cleared away the plates and felt considerable relief when she went over to the cooker and opened the oven door once more. Baked apples! She had a special way with baked apples. She cored 'em, filled the middles with sultanas, brown sugar, bits of peel and the like, then wrapped them in pastry, her specially rich pudding pastry as he always thought of it. The result was . . . oh, just grand! He hoped there would be custard; he was fond of a spot of Bird's finest.

He watched hungrily as three baked apples were removed from the oven and was a little disappointed to see that they were being put on to three plates. Not all for him, then. But he doubted he could have eaten three, though two would have gone down very nicely. There wasn't much custard, either, but it would have to do. He watched jealously as Rose poured the sauce and was pleased to see that he was getting the largest apple and a good-sized pool of custard. Well, it was fair enough; he was a hero, wasn't he, and anyway girls had smaller stomachs; well-known fact.

He had almost finished his pudding when he saw that Rose was beginning to wash up. His brows rose. Really, it seemed she had gone off baked apples and custard now; what was the world coming to? Didn't everyone keep telling everyone else that there was a war on? But the kettle had boiled and she had made the tea; it was sitting to one side of the stove, brewing, and presently she came over and poured conny-onny into a cup and then added the tea. It was dark brown and sweet, the way he liked it. He grinned at her as she handed him a large mug. She wasn't so bad . . . he knew many a man who, coming home unexpectedly, would have been told to get himself down to the fried fish shop, but snooty Rose, for all her faults, had dished up a prime meal, prime!

He began to sip the scalding tea.

It would not have been true to say that Rose regarded Steve's homecoming with nothing but pleasure, because she was still extremely wary of him, and sometimes she caught him looking at her in a very odd way, almost as one would look at a tiger which was caged behind bars of astounding frailty. At other times, she could read downright dislike in his glance and knew, sadly, that this dislike was mirrored in her own answering gaze. Yet he is trying, she told herself as she and Rachel, on the same shift for once, hurried back along Shaw Street. Ever since he stopped drinking so much – ever since he met Alby, in fact – he's been a good deal easier to live with. But now she began to listen to Rachel, who was chattering away, telling her that Alby would be starting aboard his new ship in two days' time and would be acting Signaller.

Rose had only been listening with half an ear, but now it occurred to her that if Alby knew about his new berth then Steve would probably have heard also. She wondered whether they would be aboard a corvette, a destroyer, or perhaps even a battleship, and decided that as soon as he knew for sure, she and the girls would accompany him down to the dock to take a look at what would be, in effect, his new home. It would be sensible to take an interest, she decided, and nice for the girls to be able to picture the size and strength of the ship their father sailed on. A true daughter of Liverpool, she knew that a corvette was a very small fighting ship and that a battleship was huge. But that was about the extent of her knowledge. She guessed that Steve, however, would enjoy telling the girls all the details and found herself quite looking forward to arriving home.

When she did so, Steve was lounging in a chair by the fire, with a copy of the *Echo* spread out on his knees, though she did not think he was reading it. She glanced, at once, towards the sink, hoping that he might have seen fit to peel the bowl of vegetables which stood on the draining board, but was not surprised to find them still just as she had left them, untouched. The evening before, she had mentioned that she would leave them on the draining board and had asked him, humbly, to peel and prepare them if he had time, but probably he had not given the matter a thought. Better to say nothing, she decided, hanging her heavy coat on the back of the door and making for the sink. Anyway, what did it matter? In a couple of days he'd be off again and she wouldn't have to peel a great mound of spuds, carrots and swedes in order to make up for the small amount of meat she had managed to obtain.

'Hello, Steve,' she said cheerfully, as her husband stirred, yawned and stretched. 'Have you had a good day? Alby came up to the factory and told Rachel he's got a berth, so I suppose you know which ship you're sailing on by now.'

Steve grunted, then knuckled his eyes. 'Put the bleedin' kettle on, gal,' he said thickly. 'No, I've not been to the office yet. Mebbe I'd best go down to the docks before the kids come home. Then, if they want, I can show them which craft Alby an' meself will be 'onourin' with our presence.'

He said the last four words in a strange, falsetto voice, which Rose took to be an imitation of her own since he had carped over her accent ever since he had arrived home. Sighing, she wondered why men almost seemed to want to drag you down to their level rather than applaud your efforts to speak good English and bring your children up properly, then chided herself for such a narrow view. Many men, such as Alby, her own father and Mr Edelmann, were a very different kettle of fish.

While she was thinking, Rose had filled the kettle, put it on the stove and lit the gas, and Steve had hauled himself out of his chair, grumbling that he was gasping for a cuppa and could do with a bite of something as well. Rose immediately went to the pantry and got out the loaf and a jar of mixed fruit jam, but by the time she was beginning to spread the jam on the bread, Steve had unhooked his overcoat and cap from the back of the door, and was clearly about to leave.

'You could wait for the kettle to boil . . .' Rose was beginning, but once more, Steve simply grunted and left the room, slamming the back door behind him. Rose shrugged and glanced up at the clock above the mantel. The bread and jam would do for the children, who would be in soon and always arrived starving hungry, and she could do with a cup of tea herself, so would make a pot anyway. It really was a pity that Steve couldn't be a bit more civil, couldn't at least acknowledge that she was making an effort to sustain good relations.

At the sink, Rose peeled, chopped and sliced, and then carried the pans over to the fire. Then she got down the big old frying pan in which she would gently part cook the precious onion which the greengrocer had saved for her, and the cubes of stewing beef rolled in flour, which she had prepared that morning before leaving for work.

When the back door burst open, her stomach contracted and she scolded herself for being a fool; then she realised that it was only the children. They bounced into the room full of talk about their day's doings, and pounced on the bread and jam as though they had not eaten for a week, though Rose knew for a fact that they had had a cooked dinner at school that day. 'Where's Daddy, Mam?' Petal asked, as soon as her appetite had been at least partially satisfied. 'He said he'd be home when we came out of school. He said he'd try to buy us some sweeties, if he could find a shop selling any.'

'Daddy's gone down to the docks to find out which ship he'll be sailing on in a couple of days,' Rose told them, pouring out two mugs of weak tea as she spoke.

'Alby went down earlier and was given all the details but I didn't ask Rachel the name of the ship; in fact, I didn't even ask her what class of vessel he'd be on, but we'll know when Daddy gets home.'

'Oh goody,' Petal said joyfully. 'I love going down to the docks and Daddy telled us he'd take us to look at his new ship as soon as he knew which one it was. Will we go tonight, Mammy, do you think?'

Rose shook her head. 'I doubt it, queen,' she said gently. 'I know we've not had a raid for three weeks or so, but that's no guarantee that the planes won't come over again, and no one wants to get caught out during a raid, do they?'

'Especially not down by the docks 'cos everyone knows it's the docks the horrid Germans are after,' Daisy said wisely. 'Never mind, Petal, I expect Dad will take us down there tomorrow and we wouldn't see much in the dark, anyway, what with the blackout and everything.' A sudden thought seemed to strike her. 'Do you know that a lighted cigarette can be seen from a plane hundreds and thousands of feet above the city? Dicky O'Neil told me so when we was walking home from school, and Dicky knows everything, just about, because his dad's a scuffer. Mam, why aren't you a firewatcher or in the ARP, or the WVS? Some of the other mothers are and Miss Hebden does something with the Red Cross, I don't know what.'

Rose laughed. 'It's because I've got two horrid little children to look after and a full time job,' she explained. 'I wish I could help more but the fact is, queen, it's all I can do to keep going sometimes, because I'm so tired. Now, do either of you have any homework?'

It transpired that Petal had to learn a poem and Daisy to write an essay on what her mam did to help the war effort. By the time these tasks were satisfactorily concluded, the meal was ready. Rose wondered whether she should dish up at once or wait for Steve to reappear, but decided, in the end, that she really had no choice. It would be a crime to spoil good food in wartime and that was just what would happen if she kept the stew simmering for too long. I'll warm Steve's up as soon as he gets in, she told herself, turning off the gas and beginning to ladle the stew on to her own and her daughters' plates. He won't be long, unless he falls in with a group of friends and stays to have a crack with them. Thank heaven it's not chops, or rissoles, or a nice piece of cod!

She and the children ate their portions and had bread and jam instead of a pudding, and still Steve had not arrived. He was still absent at bedtime, and Petal whined to be allowed to stay up until her daddy got home, but, at a glance from Rose, Daisy grabbed her sister and hauled her up the stairs. Giggling, Petal let herself be pulled into her bedroom, though she turned in the doorway and shouted back to Rose that at least her mammy should send Steve up to read them a story, or possibly come herself if her father arrived home very late indeed.

Rose finished clearing up the meal and looked doubtfully at the stew congealing in the pan. What on earth was Steve playing at? She supposed that he might have met a pal and bought fish and chips, but why, for goodness' sake? She knew he enjoyed the atmosphere in a pub but did not think he would spend a whole evening there, because he had admitted once, when in a mellow mood, that there was no enjoyment in watching other fellows drink.

The hours ticked by. When eleven o'clock came, Rose, who would have to be up at five next day, decided that she would simply have to go to bed. Steve would not want to eat at this hour, so she transferred the stew to a large bowl, covered it with a plate and popped it into the pantry. Then she made her way up to her room, undressed hurriedly and was soon asleep.

In her own room, Petal was still lying awake when she heard her mother mount the stairs. Usually, she slept as soon as her head touched the pillow, but tonight, for some reason, sleep eluded her. She had a most uneasy feeling that all was not well with her daddy. She knew, of course, that he was not to be relied upon, could say one thing and do another, but he had promised to take Daisy and herself to see his new ship and she guessed, from her mother's attitude, that Steve had not intended to stay out for the entire evening. This was worrying. Daisy sometimes mentioned that Daddy used to drink too much and had been known to thump both Mammy and Daisy herself when full of drink and in a bad mood. But she had also said that Daddy did not drink like that any more, intimating that this was a good thing. So why, why, why was he not home?

Uneasily, Petal lay and listened to the sounds of her mother changing into her nightdress. She heard the springs creak as Rose got into bed, heard her turn restlessly a couple of times before settling down. Then, some time later, she heard the clock strike twelve. Midnight! She had never been awake at midnight in all her years and did not think her daddy had ever come home so late before. She wondered if she should go through and wake Mammy, and when the clock struck the half-hour, slid out of bed, her warm toes curling indignantly away from the icy lino, and her warm body making it plain that it did not wish to wander the house and would much prefer to return to bed.

By now, however, Petal's blood was up. It would not be fair to wake her mother, whose alarm clock would go off at five in the morning and who would leave the house soon afterwards in order to reach the factory by six. But Daisy started school at the same time as Petal did, so she was the proper person to wake. Petal shook Daisy's shoulder vigorously, then leaned over and sang softly in her sister's ear: *'Wake up, wake up, wake up, you lazy devil, I feel so sorry for you!'* which was the reveille her father had taught her in one of his more expansive moments.

Daisy awoke groggily, knuckling her eyes and remarking, in far too loud a voice, that Petal was a little beast and it surely couldn't be getting up time yet.

'No, it ain't,' Petal said inelegantly. 'But our daddy hasn't come home, Daisy, an' I'm afraid something horrid has happened to him. He's got a cut face and lots of bruises, remember; if he fell, he might not be able to gerrup again.'

'Ye-es, but what could we do if we found him lyin' on the ground?' Daisy asked reasonably. 'We're not strong enough to pick him up; he's ever so heavy, our dad.' Despite her objection, however, she had got out of bed and was slowly following Petal's example, for Petal had begun to dress herself, pulling her clothes on over her nightie. 'Anyway, if he was at the Edelmanns' house and it got late, they might have asked him to stay the night, don't you think?'

Though Petal did her best not to show it, this suggestion was so sensible that she nearly gave up the whole idea, but having got Daisy out of bed and into her clothing, she decided to go ahead with her plan. It would not hurt, after all, to walk down as far as the docks and if Steve was nowhere to be found, then at least they had tried, and could come back to bed with a clear conscience.

So, presently, two small figures emerged from Bernard Terrace and began to make their way down Everton Brow.

An hour later, the same two small figures approached the house in Bernard Terrace, trying to be as quiet as possible. They had not been successful, despite searching diligently in all the likeliest places, and were now returning home feeling that they had done their best and that no more could be expected of them.

Daisy's hand was actually on the front door knob when both children heard someone turn into the terrace and head towards them. Petal squeaked: 'It's Daddy!' and Daisy, turning a moment later, saw that she was right. She swung open the heavy front door and opened her mouth to speak, but before she could say a word she found herself roughly grabbed and hustled inside the house, along the hall, and into the kitchen.

Petal, following, said plaintively: 'Where have you *been*, Dad? We waited and waited and you didn't come, and then poor Mammy had to go to bed because her alarm clock goes off at five, so Daisy and me decided . . .'

Daisy tried to wriggle out of her father's grasp, tried to explain that they had been searching for him, but one glance at his bleary, bloodshot eyes and one whiff of his spirit-laden breath told her that she was unlikely to get him to listen. 'Where have *you* been, you deceitful little bitch?' he shouted. 'Oh, you think you're so grand, Rose McAllister, so much better'n me, but you're just a little slut, really. Off after some other feller the moment me back's turned. Oh, I'm goin' to teach you a lesson you won't forget in a hurry!'

As he said the last words, he transferred his grip from Daisy's shoulders to her hair and actually heaved her off her feet by it, tearing a shrill scream from her lips. Daisy struggled and kicked and knew, vaguely, that Petal was joining in. She saw, through tear-blurred eyes, that Petal was attached to her father's leg like a small bulldog, but her own pain was so great that she was scarcely conscious of anything else. Steve was raving at her, calling her Rose, repeatedly hitting her across the face whilst still gripping her hair so tightly that she could feel the roots giving way. She was almost fainting, waves of black coming and going, a sick dizziness possessing her, when she heard a sound like someone striking a great gong, *doiiing, doiiing, doiiiiing!* Then she was falling to the floor, sobbing for breath, weak with terror and pain. She felt the quarry tiles come up to meet her, slapping her hard on the knees and the palms of her hands, then something large and heavy fell on top of her and, for a few blissful moments, she plunged into darkness.

Rose had entered the kitchen at the height of the fracas. She had not understood what was happening, or why, but she did not waste time in conjecture. She simply seized the frying pan and brought it down on Steve's head with enough force to make him let go of Daisy and fall, senseless, on top of her.

Rose grabbed at his seaman's jacket and hauled him, bodily, off her daughter, inadvertently treading on his hand as she did so and not giving a damn. She had never been so angry in her entire life and hoped, fervently, that she had done Steve some mortal damage, though she doubted it. His head was hard as a rock, and because he was clearly drunk as a skunk she doubted that she had done him nearly as much harm as he deserved. The devil takes care of his own, she thought bitterly, lifting Daisy up in her arms and carrying her over to the easy chair nearest the dying fire. Petal had been sobbing wildly but now she came over to her mother and they both looked anxiously into Daisy's small, white face, already beginning to turn scarlet and blue in stripes where Steve's hand had caught her.

'Oh, Mammy, it's all my fault. Will she die?' Petal said fearfully. 'It were my idea to go and search for Daddy, so I woke Daisy and made her come with me. We searched and searched and couldn't find him, only when we got home he – he sort of appeared. He were angry wi' Daisy, only he kept calling her Rose, and then he dragged her indoors and started hitting her. I bit him in the leg and I did my best to make him leave our Daisy alone, but . . . but . . .'

Daisy's eyes flickered open and Petal gave a huge sigh of relief, echoed by her mother. 'She's alive! Oh, Mammy, I'm so glad she's alive!' She glanced behind her as she spoke, to where her father sprawled face down on the floor. 'I wonder if he's alive, too?' she said, her tone so academic as to bring a quivering smile to Rose's lips. 'I hope he stays asleep, though, because he's mad, isn't he, Mammy? He *must* be mad because he thought poor Daisy was you, and you wouldn't have let him drag you by the hair, would you, Mammy? You'd have hit him, bang, wallop, with the frying pan.'

'He's not dead,' Rose said grimly. 'But he'll wish he was, when he wakes up! Daisy, darling, if I help you, can you get upstairs, do you think? You poor little thing, and you were only trying to help the great, bullying . . . I mean you were only trying to help Dad. But he's drunk, you see, and men . . . well, they don't always know what they're doing when they've a good deal of drink inside them. Oh, your poor little face, you're covered in bruises. I've a good mind to fetch the scuffers, then your father could enjoy a bit of peace and quiet in a police cell, *and* answer to the local magistrate for the way he's behaved.'

Daisy sat up, wincing as she did so, and looked fearfully around her, but when she saw Steve, still prone on the floor, her anxiety seemed to ease a little. 'Don't get the scuffers, Mammy,' she said in a small, cracked little voice. 'Only . . . only do we have to go on living in this house, where he can come whenever his ship docks? Can't we go away, all of us, and live somewhere – somewhere safer? I know we can't go back to Ty Siriol, and I know you need your job, but . . . oh, *do* let us go away from this house!'

'We'll do something,' Rose promised. 'Once he's at sea and out of the way we'll find somewhere better to live, somewhere nearer the factory, perhaps. But right now, pet, we'd best all get to bed, or no one will be going anywhere in the morning.'

She carried Daisy up the stairs, with Petal bobbing at her heels, but when she had tucked the girls up and would have gone downstairs to check on Steve, both children begged her to stay with them, not to sleep in her own bed. 'Dad's drunk, you said so. He – he might hit you and kill you by – by mistake,' Daisy said wildly. 'Please, Mam, sleep with us tonight! We'll squeeze up small as small to give you room, won't we, Petal?'

And in the end it seemed the most sensible thing to do. Rose went downstairs and saw Steve was conscious again and sitting on the sofa, though in no very amenable state of mind. He had vomited on the kitchen floor and shouted at her when she advised him to clear it up before morning, but the shouting was half-hearted and she could see that he was having difficulty in remembering anything that had happened in the previous two or three hours. 'Why were I on the bloody floor, instead of in me bloody bed?' he asked, the belligerence fainter, for once, than the puzzlement. 'I don' unnershtand . . . I met me pals for a quick bevvy, never have more than the one now I'm on the wagon . . . nex' thing I know me head's ringin' an' I come to meself on the bloody *floor*, for God's sweet sake!'

'Yes, you were on the floor because you attacked your little girl and I hit you with the frying pan,' Rose said grimly. 'You stink of drink, strong drink, not just a beer or two, and I'm locking my bedroom door against you, so don't expect to sleep anywhere but the sofa tonight. I've had enough, Steve. If it wasn't for the fact that it's two in the morning and I'm dead tired I'd have handed you over to the scuffers without a second thought. So just you kip down on the sofa and we'll talk in the morning.'

'But you'll be at work,' Steve said craftily. 'Shan' be – be able to talk to me, nag me. When a feller's drunk he don't know what he's doin', you can't blame me for what I didn't know . . . aw, to hell with it, you'll find a way to blame me somehow.'

Rose snorted but said nothing more and presently left him. He heaved himself on to the sofa, demanded a blanket in a voice which told her that he had small hope of receiving one, and was snoring fit to wake the dead before she was halfway up the stairs.

Three in a bed, when one of the three – Petal – kicked in her sleep, was no picnic, but Rose heard her alarm clock go off at five through the thin partition wall which separated her room from that of the children and got reluctantly out of bed. She would not dare go in to work today, leaving Steve in the same house as the children, for even if he behaved himself, Daisy was in no fit state to get herself up and to school, let alone that she would be terrified to so much as catch her father's eye for a long time to come. She padded out of the house, therefore, and round to the Fosters. Fortunately, both women were on earlies, so Helen was up, and proved quite willing to take a message in to work explaining that Rose's daughter was ill but that Rose would be in as soon as she had sorted something out.

'And though I don't believe a word of it, I shan't go splittin' on you,' she said, yawning behind her hand. 'Your old feller was a-screechin' and a-yellin' last night, bawlin' out that you were a tuppenny tart . . . oh, don't worry, queen, no one won't listen to his bad-mouthin', because I reckon they all knew he was half seas over, as the sayin' goes.' She looked inquisitively at Rose. 'He didn't knock you about? You're bloody lucky, queen. Most of 'em get nasty when they've a skinful.'

'No, he didn't hit me, he hit Daisy,' Rose said grimly. 'So you see, I've a lot to sort out, but thanks ever so, Helen, you're a pal. And now I'd best get back to the house just in case someone beside meself wakes up.'

Back home once more, Rose went quietly into the kitchen where she found Steve at the gas cooker, making a cup of tea. He looked up as she entered, then looked quickly down again and she saw, for the first time in her life, that he was blushing. Steve McAllister, actually blushing, showing embarrassment! She said nothing, however, going over to the dresser and taking down two mugs. Without a word, she poured conny-onny into each, then stood them next to the teapot which Steve had just filled. When the tea was brewed and poured, she took her own cup, still in silence, and sat down at the table. Steve followed suit and as he leaned forward and put both hands round his mug – it was bitterly cold in the kitchen for the fire had gone out and had not yet been relit – Rose met his eyes for the first time, her gaze steady yet penetrating. She saw that his own eyes wavered, his glance shooting from his mug of tea to her face, and then wandering, uneasily, round the kitchen. Had he not behaved so badly, she might have felt sorry for him, for never had she seen him look so hang-dog. Guilt was written all over his face and his first words proved it.

'How's the kid?' he said gruffly. 'I don't remember touchin' a hair of her head, though I know I hit you a couple o' times, but – but you said it were her . . . I dunno, I were that confused . . . what were I doin' down at the docks, anyroad? And why did I go to the pub after?'

'You went to the docks because Alby had gone down earlier in the day and been told which ship he was to join . . .' Rose began, but got no further. She saw a look of horrified comprehension dawn on Steve's face and then, to her astonishment, he buried his head in both hands and began to sob.

Once again, she felt a faint stirring of pity; Steve never showed any emotion other than anger and here he was, crying like a baby. Tentatively, she leaned across the table and touched his hand and felt an immediate revulsion, so strong that she snatched her hand back as though his had been red hot. Remember, you're in this fix because you were once fool enough to fall in love with this pathetic creature, she scolded herself, and don't let him get away with anything because he's got to know what he did, and you've got to know it will never happen again; you owe it to yourself and the children.

'Steve? Whatever is the matter?'

He looked across at her, shamefacedly rubbing the tears from his cheeks with his enormous, grimy hands. 'Alby's norron the *Harrier*, an' I am,' he said. 'He's gorr'is promotion, but he's on one of the flower class corvettes.'

'So?' Rose said coldly. She knew the two men were friends but this was ridiculous. He was behaving as though he and Alby were lovers, not pals, using the fact that they would no longer be shipmates as an excuse to drink himself silly and to punch up his daughter. She began to say as much, but was interrupted.

'But you don't understand. Alby kept me off the drink, stopped me thinking I had to have a skinful every time I reached port,' he said thickly. 'Before I met him, I always had bottles of the hard stuff stashed away somewhere aboard. I've used me pay to buy other fellers' rum rations . . . I'd do anything for a drink. Then I met Alby—'

Rose interrupted him without compunction. 'Steve, you sound like Pinocchio, as though you're incapable of existing without Jiminy Cricket to tell you how to go on. For God's sake, you're a grown man, not a child, and must learn to take decisions for yourself. You've cut down on the drink once and we'd actually begun to get along quite well, but one little setback and you almost kill your own daughter. What on earth were you thinking of?'

'I thought she were you,' Steve said sulkily, after a short pause. 'I dunno why, 'cos she's not very like you, but me brain was addled by all the drink I'd taken. They say when you come off the wagon, you can get drunk on two or three bevvies, and I'd had just about as much as I could hold.'

Rose heaved a deep sigh. 'It's not good enough, Steve, because once you're back on the drink, the same thing could easily happen again, and with worse results. Come to that, you'll probably attack me, and who will look after the kids if I'm in a hospital bed, or six foot under? I think it would be best if you stayed in the Sailors' Home next time you're in port, and kept well away from us. I've not told the scuffers this time, but there isn't going to be a next time, understand?'

Steve stared at her as though he could not believe his ears. 'But Rosie, this is me *home*. I pays the rent and you get my allotment from the Navy, same as the other wives. You can't simply kick me out of me own home.'

'I don't need your money; I'm a supervisor now, so I can cope with household expenses, the rent . . . the lot, in fact,' Rose said. 'Besides, if I don't have to feed you when you're home, I'll be a great deal better off.'

'But – but wharrabout me kids? I dare say Daisy's not feelin' too fond . . . you must tell 'er it were an accident – say I didn't mean it – but Petal's me little princess, she loves her daddy, she'll be that upset—'

His words were cut off by the opening of the kitchen door. Petal came into the room. She was rosy with sleep, her fair curls tangled, but her eyes bright. She looked across at her mother, her eyes seeming to look straight through Steve. 'Mammy? Are you awright? I heared you talking an' I thought – I thought . . .'

'Well, if it ain't me favourite little girl. Come an' sit on your ol' dad's knee an' tell your mam it 'ud break your heart if she didn't let me come home no more,' Steve said coaxingly. 'I weren't meself last night, I were ill, but I never meant to hurt nobody, only your mammy don't understand. She thinks . . .'

He put out a hand as though to pull Petal on to his knee but she eluded him easily, and went round the table to stand beside her mother. Rose, glancing down at her, saw hostility in every line of the child's face and body. Petal looked up at her. 'Oh yes, Mammy, it would be lovely if *that man* never came into our house again,' she said, pointing at Steve. 'I don't like him at all. In fact, I hate him. Poor Daisy is still asleep, but earlier, when she turned over, she cried. Her face is all red and purple down one side and some of her hair's come out. Can you make him go away before Daisy gets up?'

Rose glanced across at her husband and saw that he was crying again and felt nothing but contempt. How dared he expect Petal to love him when she had seen him beat up her older sister only hours before? But Steve was lurching to his feet, and for a moment Rose feared that he might actually attack her daughter. She pulled Petal to her, but the little girl pushed her off and ran round the table. 'Go on, gerrout of our house!' she shouted. 'We doesn't want you here after what you've done to our Daisy. Go on, beat it!'

'I'm goin',' Steve said unsteadily. He turned to Rose. 'As for not wantin' my money . . . well, mebbe a rating's pay ain't worth much for all I'm fightin' for me country. But I know a way to earn more and you and the kids shall have every penny, 'cos I don't mean to start seein' them crabs crawlin' up the walls an' droppin' off on to me bunk to try an' eat me alive. I'll stop drinkin', I swear it, an' then you'll be sorry you turned me out.'

Neither Petal nor Rose said a word as Steve lurched towards the back door, grabbed his jacket and crashed the door shut behind him. Then Petal turned to her mother. 'What did he mean about crabs eating him alive?' she asked fearfully. 'It – it sounded horrid, Mammy. Do crabs get inside ships?'

'No, queen, but if a fellow drinks too much, he has awful nightmares,' Rose said tactfully. 'We shan't have to worry about your father for a bit, though, because I've told him to stay at the Sailors' Home next time he's in port, and I shall have the front door lock changed so that he can't get in whilst we're out. Now let's go up and see whether Daisy fancies a nice bowl of porridge for her breakfast.'

By the time she and the girls had washed, dressed and eaten breakfast, Rose had made a decision. No matter how careful she was, she could not keep her job and protect the children against another attack from their father. She remembered how often, when they were first married, Steve had sworn to lay off the drink, and how such episodes had never lasted more than a few weeks. If only Mrs Williams had been able to take them back, she would have had no hesitation in sending them off to Ty Siriol, but as it was she would speak to the head teacher of the local school, and find out whether there was any sort of scheme at the moment to take city children into the safety of the countryside.

By teatime that evening, she knew that she could send the children to safety in the next week or so; she had decided that it would be best if she kept Daisy by her until the bruises had faded and the memory of Steve's attack had grown less vivid. But then, provided she accompanied her daughters and saw them safely settled, they should be happy enough knowing that they were safe from their father, as well as from more nights of horrendous bombing, and she would assure them that she would visit them as often as possible.

'You're going to Wrexham, my loves, the town which we visited when Mrs Williams was in hospital there,' Rose told them. 'It's a nice big house, I believe, just outside the town, owned by a gentleman who is working in London, so it is being run in the meantime by his wife. The billeting officer said she took four boys when war was declared, but could not cope with them, and this time has asked for nicely behaved little girls, so it sounds to me just the place for the two of you.'

'I'd rather stay with you, Mam,' Daisy said fearfully. 'Maybe Dad won't try to come home any more. Or you said we might all move – you as well – which would be grand if we could find somewhere Dad didn't know about.'

'Yes, but we will need my job more than ever if we aren't going to get your father's pay,' Rose explained. 'And that means I can't live out in the country because I wouldn't be able to get to the factory each day.'

Daisy looked undecided. 'But suppose Dad finds out where we're staying and comes there? The lady wouldn't know what he's like; she might let him take us out for a w-walk or a p-picnic. And – and you wouldn't be there to bonk him over the head with a frying pan.'

Rose hesitated. 'I had to explain to the billeting officer that your dad was a violent man and must not, in any circumstances, be given your address,' she said carefully. She turned to Petal. 'That means no letters, queen, neither from you to him, nor from him to you. Can you understand?'

'Yes, and I don't want to write letters to someone

so horrible,' Petal said vehemently. 'Nor I don't want letters from him; he's our worst enemy, ain't he, Daisy? We hate him like we hate the bleedin' Germans, and the Luft—Luftwhotsit.'

'Luftwaffe,' Rose said, as Daisy nodded agreement with her sister's sentiments. 'Right then; I'll take you to Mrs Wyn Roberts in a week or ten days, and stay there with you for a day or two, just to make sure everything's all right. I'm awfully sorry that it means yet another change of school, but I'm afraid things like that happen in wartime. And now I'm going to make you a nice big high tea and then we'll all have an early night, because we didn't get much sleep last night, did we?'

'Daisy an' me slept all right, once we got to sleep,' Petal said. She picked up her sister's hand and cuddled it against her cheek. 'I love Daisy next best to you, Mammy, in the whole world, so it won't be *too* bad going away from Bernard Terrace. But – but can you sleep in our bed again? I know there's no lock on the door but we can swing the bed round and jam the brass rail thing under the door handle, then we'll be safe as houses, won't we?'

Rose sighed inwardly; so it was not only Daisy who was going to remember Steve's attack with dread for the rest of her life. It had clearly affected the normally ebullient Petal as well. She did hope that neither would start bed-wetting once they got to Wrexham because constantly laundering sheets and mopping up puddles was enough to put the most perfect foster mother off her charges. However, there was no point in meeting trouble halfway. The billeting officer had told her that Mrs Wyn Roberts kept a spare room for the use of parents and, in view of the violence which had precipitated this move, had written a letter to the factory, explaining that Rose would need to be away for at least a week, though she gave no actual reason.

'I don't need to do so; your employer will take my word for it that the time off is needed,' she said, when Rose looked doubtful. 'You say your husband's ship sails in a couple of days, and once he has left the children will be safe. Then a week should be ample. Good day, Mrs McAllister.'

Rose carried out Petal's plan of action, and by eight o'clock the three of them were tucked up in bed, though Rose had chosen to wedge a chair from the kitchen under the door handle, rather than try to move the heavy old brass bedstead. Secure in the knowledge that their mother would protect them, the girls fell asleep almost at once, but Rose, not used to such early hours, merely snoozed. When the knocking came, she was instantly awake. With considerable care, she eased herself out of bed, gently moved the chair, opened the door and padded down the stairs. It could not possibly be Steve, because he had his own key and she had not yet had time to have the locks changed. It would be a neighbour, someone wanting to borrow half a cup of sugar, or a tin of conny-onny. After all, in normal circumstances, she was rarely in bed before ten o'clock.

Nevertheless, she opened the door carefully, clinging grimly to the edge of it, in case someone tried to force an entry, for her nerves still jangled from the happenings of the night before. In the thick darkness, she could only see the outline of a man, but when he whispered hoarsely: 'Can I come in, Rose, just for a few minutes,' she knew at once that it was Steve.

She was tempted to slam the door but knew that this would be unwise since he had a key, though he had not chosen to use it. Instead, she said in a low voice: 'I thought I told you to stay away from this house, but if you meant to disregard what I said, why didn't you use your key? We were in bed, the kids and me.'

'I didn't use me key because you telled me not to; you said to clear off,' Steve said, his voice almost a whine. 'Let me come in for a moment, Rose, I'm freezing cold and I can't stop anyway.'

Rose hesitated, then pulled the door wide and gestured him inside. She knew he was speaking the truth, though she didn't know how she knew. She ushered him into the kitchen, saying as she shut the door softly behind him: 'I'll give you five minutes, Steve, and then you've simply got to go. We can't take much more, me and the kids, and we need to get some sleep.' He slumped into a chair and, after a moment's hesitation, Rose followed suit. 'Well? What do you want to tell me that's so important you've come knocking in the middle of the night?'

'I came to tell you . . . oh, dammit, Rose, I – I'm real sorry for what happened, honest to God I am. No, don't start, I know being sorry isn't enough, that's why . . . that's why . . .'

Rose waited, brows lifted. She did not intend to make things easy for him; let him tell her straight whatever it was that was so important, or get out. After more hesitation and some mumbling, Steve seemed to pull himself together. 'You know Alby and me were bezzies, looked out for one another, kept each other on the straight and narrer. Well, when I heared he were being sent to another ship . . . that's what drove me back to the bleedin' drink. You see, Alby's been my – my luck, in a way. While we was together it seemed to me nothing real bad was likely to happen to either of us. And then they've separated us, and I went kind o' mad, I reckon. So – so I went to the shipping office just now, and wrote on a lot of papers and talked to folk, and now I've done it; I've signed on as submarine crew and I leave for Gosport – that's the training centre, and it'll be me home port – first thing in the morning. The money's a good deal better and – and it'll go to you and the kids, and I won't be able to get back to the 'Pool, mebbe not for years. The feller warned me that a good few o' the subs are sent to places like Malta, or Greece, and will stay there until the war's over or until they're sent home for repairs or refits or whatever. So you see, I doubt I'll be coming back to Bernard Terrace for – for a goodish while.'

He stared at Rose with what seemed like a mixture of misery and defiance but Rose's answering stare was, she knew, mainly one of puzzlement. 'So?' she said at last, when the silence between them had stretched and stretched. 'I don't see why a submarine can't have Liverpool as its home port . . . or why you've signed on for it, come to that. I'm sorry, Steve, but I just don't get the significance of what you're telling me.'

Steve jumped out of his chair and took two strides towards her but Rose was out of her own seat almost simultaneously and reaching for the frying pan. She would never take a chance again, not with Steve. He was as dangerous, and unpredictable, as – as a tiger; she did not mean to be caught napping. But, apparently, he had only risen in order to stride about the room, his face tormented, so she sat down again, though on the very edge of her chair this time, and with the poker at her feet where she could grab it in a moment.

'It's a whole different ball game, being in a bloody submarine, woman! They have to sail from Gosport or Portsmouth because . . . oh, I don't know, they just do . . . and that means I'm not liable to turn up here unannounced. If I'm given proper leave I can telegraph, write, let you know somehow. Not that I'm particularly keen to come back here, if me home's barred to me. As for the submarines, God, the money's good, and I dare say I'll get used to being crammed into one of 'em, though the thought of all those tons of water above and below . . . but I've done it – done it for you and the kids, done it to show you I'm sorry, that I ain't all bad, whatever you may think. I – I want Daisy and Petal to know I won't ever hit either of 'em again . . . dammit, Rose, I were mad wi' drink. I thought it were you I were draggin' into the bleedin' house!'

And I suppose if you had killed or half killed me, that would have been all right, Rose thought to herself, but did not put it into words, because it would not exactly help matters. And now that she came to think about it, she could not imagine tall, hefty Steve cramming himself inside a submarine. He would undoubtedly go for training – he probably had little choice since he said he had signed papers – but they would soon realise their mistake; this was the man who had once refused point-blank to get into the lift at Lewis's with her and the pushchair, but had run up all those stairs instead. However, it would not do to say so. Instead, she spoke soothingly. 'I see; I understand, Steve, but to be frank, it isn't money that's needed here at present, it's the promise that you won't come near us, won't pursue us if we leave Bernard Terrace. Can't you understand that? It's going to be a long while before Daisy stops being scared of her own shadow, after what you did.'

'Yes, I know, but there's nothing I can do about

that if you won't let me see her,' Steve pointed out, with a certain amount of truthfulness, Rose was forced to admit. 'But can't you *see*, Rose? If my home port is the other end of England then I can't just turn up unexpected – that's wharr I'm tryin' to tell you. And – and I'm punishing meself by signing on aboard a sub. I'll be going through a worse hell than any I've put the kid through. Oh, for Christ's sake, try to understand!'

Slowly, Rose nodded. 'I really am trying, and I – do appreciate what you're saying,' she said at last. 'But honestly, Steve, you must go now! Suppose one of the girls woke and heard me talking and came downstairs? I've promised you'll stay away, and . . .'

'All right, all right, I'm going,' Steve growled. He stopped in the doorway and glared at Rose before making his way out of the house, and in that moment she knew, with real sorrow, that his problem was insoluble. He might make an effort to reform, to become a decent person, but such a reform would – could – only last for a few weeks. In a way it wasn't even his fault, it was how he had been brought up. He had seen his father knock his mother about, been knocked about in his turn, and when he married he already deeply despised women. When Rose had stood up to him he had simply loathed her, as he had, in the end, loathed his mother for letting his father beat him. But there was no sense in saying any of this, because tigers did not change their stripes any more than leopards changed their spots. The kids had the right idea. They would all move away from here when the war was over, go abroad if necessary, and shake the dust of Bernard Terrace, and Steve, off their feet for good.

Chapter Eight

Rose waited a full week before she packed the children's belongings into a suitcase, told them to bring their favourite doll or teddy bear, and set off for the house the billeting officer had found for them. She was glad it was situated in Wrexham because she felt at least the town would not be strange to any of them; had they not visited Mrs Williams in the War Memorial Hospital, had a meal in Steven's Café and gone round the shops? It was a market town, small but friendly, Rose thought. The district was riddled with coal mines, and though she knew there were both army barracks and an airfield, these were separated from the town by some distance. There were certainly no docks, as it was at least thirty miles from the sea, so there was little to attract the Luftwaffe. In fact, she supposed it was a bit of a backwater. But a backwater was just what one wanted for one's children in time of war.

No taxis were waiting when they arrived at Wrexham station, so Rose and the children made their way to Grove Road on foot; Rose, at least, with a pleasant feeling of anticipation. She looked at Daisy and saw that the child was examining her surroundings with every sign of interest and without any of the caution which she had shown whenever they left Bernard Terrace on a shopping expedition. She had explained over and over that Steve had gone to a place called Gosport at the other end of England and that he would not be returning to Liverpool until the war was over, but though Daisy appeared to be reassured, she could not quite rid herself of the suspicion that he might be lurking behind a telephone box, or in the dark entry which ran between the shops and the jigger at the back.

Rose halted in front of a tall stone wall, with a pair of double wrought-iron gates set into it. The gates were painted black, and above them there was a stone arch upon which were depicted the words *The Larches*. For a moment, the splendour of the gates took her aback, made her heart begin to bump uneasily. Surely she must have made a mistake? This was the home of rich people, people of influence. She assumed that the rich pleased themselves in wartime as they did in peace, and if so, the owner of the Larches would have found some excuse not to have to accept evacuees. Then she remembered what the billeting officer had said. Mr and Mrs Wyn Roberts had had four boys billeted on them, but had been unable to cope. She supposed that ordinary people would have been told, pretty brusquely, to make the best of it, but these wealthy folk had used their influence to get the boys sent elsewhere, though they had said, graciously, that they would take a couple of young, nicely behaved girls. Oh, well. She supposed she should be grateful that the boys had not been satisfactory, because – she peered through the gates – this was certainly a far grander and more beautiful house than she had ever dreamed of staying in. Not that she could see much from here, as there was a shrubbery of evergreens to the right and a great many tall and beautiful trees obscured her view, though she could see that the house was very large indeed. Rose had stood down her suitcase before looking through the gates, but now she picked it up again, lifted the latch and pushed the gate wide, aware that the children had crowded close to her, awed by the gravel drive which crunched beneath their feet, and by the extent of the shrubbery and the garden ahead of them.

Halfway along the drive, Daisy jerked at her mother's sleeve. 'Look, Mam, under the trees: millions and millions of snowdrops. I've seen them on the market stalls, and there were a few under the big beech at the farm – we wasn't allowed to pick them – but I've never ever seen a carpet of them. Why, they're so thick you couldn't walk without treading on them.' She turned to her sister. 'Have you *seen* them, Petal?'

Petal glanced sideways and nodded, but she was clearly more interested in bricks and mortar than in horticulture. 'Yes, I see 'em,' she said impatiently. 'But oh, Mam, look at the house. It's – it's like a castle, or a palace, or something. It's huge.'

They had rounded a bend in the drive and now the house stood before them. It was built of stone with mullioned windows which came to a point, rather like church windows, and there were two turrets which, Rose supposed, had reminded Petal of pictures she had seen of castles and palaces. There seemed to be a great many windows, all staring out at the newcomers, and Rose was glad she had put on her best clothes and dressed the children as neatly as possible.

Three stone steps, well scrubbed but not whitened, led up to the front door, which was huge and decorated with large brass studs. There was a round, white porcelain bell push on the right and a large knocker in the shape of a lion's head in the centre of the door. Rose was hesitating, wondering which to use, when Petal forestalled her by pressing on the bell with all her strength, and continuing to do so even when approaching footsteps could be heard above the bell's shrill notes. Daisy snatched her sister's hand away just in time; the door creaked open.

'Yes?' An elderly woman stood there, looking at them as though she suspected them of planning to steal the doorsteps, Rose thought. She wore a large white apron over a black dress, stout lace-up shoes and wrinkled black woollen stockings, as well as a most unpleasant expression. Rose had begun to stammer that she was Mrs McAllister, and that she had told Mrs Wyn Roberts that they would be arriving by train this morning, when suddenly her embarrassment changed to annoyance. The old woman had eyes in her head; she could see the suitcase and the paper carrier bags the children held. She must know very well who they were and why they were standing on her doorstep; she was just being difficult for some reason which Rose, as yet, did not understand. So she cut off her stammered explanation, looked the elderly woman straight in the eye, and said firmly: 'We are the McAllisters and we have an appointment to see your Mrs Wyn Roberts; kindly inform her that we have arrived, please.'

She had meant to step forward into the hall, presuming that the woman would expect the family to follow her. Fortunately, she hesitated, meaning to take Petal's hand, and it was a good thing she did since the woman, without a word of acknowledgement, turned away, slamming the door behind her as she did so and missing Rose's nose by inches.

Rose put down her suitcase and Daisy gave her hand a squeeze. 'She's a nasty old woman, Mam,' she whispered. 'But she's only someone who works here, not the lady who owns it, isn't she? I expect she's cross because she thinks she'll have to make our dinners and show us the way to school and that.'

'I don't care what you say, Daisy, I think she's a rude old woman; a nasty, rude old woman,' Petal said. She did not lower her voice. 'If she's rude again, Mammy, I shall knock her horrible old legs with my little suitcase; that'll make her sorry.'

Rose was about to remind her that one should always be kind to elderly ladies when the door opened again. It was the same woman, but this time she held the door wide, gesturing them inside. Rose pushed the children ahead of her, then turned to the maid. 'I'm sorry, but there are four doors to choose from; where should I go?'

For answer, the maid slammed the front door shut, stalked ahead of them to fling open another, and then headed for the very last door, which was situated at the end of the hall and was covered in green baize. She was not quite through it when Petal's voice rose plaintively. 'Is she dumb, Mammy? You know, it's like blind, only it's your voice. If she's dumb, we should be sorry for her, 'cos Mrs Williams says we must be sorry for the afflicted.'

Rose smothered a giggle but thought it a pity that Petal hadn't kept her voice down for she could tell, by the look of hatred which the maid shot at Petal, that whatever the woman's afflictions deafness was not one of them; she had heard – and resented – every word.

And as Rose was soon to learn, she was not the only one to overhear Petal's words. The three of them went through the doorway and found themselves in a pleasant, high-ceilinged room, painted white with sprigged wallpaper, floral curtains and a round, plush carpet decorated with a scattering of roses. There was a beautiful fireplace with a tiled surround, in which a number of logs burned brightly, a wide well-cushioned window seat, and several comfortable-looking easy chairs upholstered in white and gold. Two of these chairs were occupied by middle-aged women, both smiling, and as Rose advanced towards them they got to their feet. 'Good morning, Mrs McAllister,' the taller of the two said, holding out her hand. 'I'm Mrs Wyn Roberts and this is my sister Mrs Franklin.' She was plump and pretty, with a round babyish face upon which was perched a pair of tiny spectacles. She had frizzy fair hair, hazel eyes and small but rather uneven teeth, which showed when she gave Rose a wide and friendly smile. Rose, shaking hands, liked her at once. She could tell from Mrs Wyn Roberts's smile that she had heard Petal's comment and was amused rather than annoyed by it.

Her companion was very different, short, skinny and dark-haired, with a pair of snapping black eyes, a long thin nose and a gravity of expression which vanished when she, too, smiled. Like Mrs Wyn Roberts, she was obviously well disposed towards the newcomers, and the sharp black eyes twinkled as she greeted Rose, then held out her hand, first to Daisy, then to Petal. 'How do you do, young ladies?' she said seriously. 'You will be Daisy McAllister and you will be Petal McAllister. I am Mrs Wyn Roberts's sister, Mrs Franklin, and as you can see, no two people could be less alike. So I am not at all surprised to see that you, Daisy, have straight dark hair and you, Petal, have blonde curls, but as I often used to say to my sister, when we were small, I could have curls if I wished, by the simple expedient of having a permanent wave, or wrapping each lock round a pipe cleaner every night, whereas my sister is doomed to curls, and cannot straighten them no matter how she tries.'

'But you don't curl your hair, Mrs Franklin . . .'

Daisy was beginning, when Mrs Wyn Roberts floated across to the fireplace and pressed the bell. 'Tea, tea, tea,' she sang out. 'Take your coats off, my dears, and sit down. You must be tired and thirsty after your long journey, so we thought a meal halfway between lunch and supper would be appropriate. Edith – that's our maid – will bring the tea trolley through directly.'

And sure enough, only moments later, there was a great clattering outside and Daisy jumped up from the tapestry stool on which she had been sitting and politely held the door open. Edith shoved her trolley through it without acknowledging Daisy's presence by so much as a glance. Indeed, she ignored everyone but her mistress, to whom she said in a grumbling tone: 'I made breakfast tea, like you said, Mrs Wyn Roberts, and I hopes as the sangwidges is sufficient. You said "little gals".'

There was a world of reproach in her voice but Mrs Wyn Roberts only laughed. 'They *are* little girls,' she said, beaming at them both. 'Thank you, Edith, that will be all.'

Edith gave the sort of fruity sniff which, had Petal done it, would have had Rose demanding that she use her handkerchief, but no one said anything until the maid had slammed the door resoundingly behind her.

Mrs Franklin tutted. 'I know Edith's been in the family's employ for forty years, but she really should learn that you are her employer; she who pays the piper calls the tune, you know. And what's more . . .' she glanced disapprovingly at the tiny sandwiches set out on the trolley, 'there's not enough food there to feed a sparrow, let alone the five of us. But never mind. You start pouring, Clara, and I'll go and have a word with Edith.'

Whilst she was gone, Rose and Mrs Wyn Roberts

chatted amicably and Mrs Wyn Roberts dispensed cups of tea and handed round pretty china plates and then the tiny sandwiches, advising her young guests to take four or five. The children obeyed but the postage-sized sandwiches disappeared in no time and Rose was relieved when Mrs Franklin returned to the room, bearing a large plate upon which were set out what appeared to be chunky and uneven cheese and tomato butties. She stood the plate down and turned to take another dish from the disapproving Edith, who was following her closely. The second dish held a fair-sized madeira cake, and presently they were all munching. Rose noticed, with approval, that when Edith left the room for the second time, she closed the door quietly behind her.

When tea was finished, Mrs Wyn Roberts glanced hopefully at her sister. 'Anna, my dear, would you save my poor legs and show Mrs McAllister and the children over the house? Mrs McAllister is to stay in the blue room tonight, but the children will be in our old nursery, of course. And then, if they would like to explore the garden, I dare say they can do so without any help from us.'

Rose followed Mrs Franklin willingly, eager to see if the rest of the house was as beautifully furnished as the drawing room. She soon found that it was, though Mrs Franklin told her that the dining room, breakfast parlour, living room and conservatory were rarely used now. 'My sister has breakfast in bed and takes most of her meals on a tray in the drawing room because it means she only has to heat the one room, but the children will eat with Edith in the kitchen,' she explained. 'I'm afraid you will have to talk to Edith regarding what time the children eat and what sort of food they prefer, because my sister has always left such matters in the hands of others. Before the war, when Mr Wyn Roberts lived here all the time, and did not have to spend weekdays in London at the Ministry, they employed a cook, a gardener, a boot boy, a scullery maid and Edith, who was the parlour maid. The gardener does his best to keep the place tidy, and in summer grows wonderful fruit and vegetables for the house. But the others have all gone. Mrs Jones, the cook, joined the ATS, but the scullery maid and the boot boy took more remunerative posts, at the Royal Ordnance factory in Marchwiel. I believe they make munitions there but it's awfully hush hush, you know. However, Edith is too old and too set in her ways for anything but domestic work, so she has stayed on.'

'I see,' Rose murmured. 'But – will Edith be able to manage, Mrs Franklin? As you say, she is no longer young and seems very set in her ways. I realise that you must do a great deal to help her, but . . . but . . .'

'Oh no, I do nothing, because I don't live here,' Mrs Franklin said quickly. 'I thought you realised; I'm simply on a visit. I live in Chester and I work at the Ministry of Supply, so I have little opportunity to come back to Wrexham, let alone to help my sister out. But as for managing, Edith must do quite well or my sister would not continue to retain her services.'

They had been climbing the wide staircase and now Mrs Franklin threw open a white-painted door. 'Your room,' she said briefly. 'The children are on the next floor up. I think my sister felt that the old nursery, containing, as it does, a great many of the toys and books which she and I enjoyed as children, would be more suitable than a bedroom on the lower floor.'

Rose said nothing until they were once more descending the stairs. The children had stayed in the nursery, fascinated and intrigued by the rocking horse, the doll's house, and the large bookcase, packed with shabby but beautifully illustrated books. Now, greatly daring, Rose put her hand on her companion's arm and drew her to a halt. 'Mrs Franklin, my girls are good girls, but even so, they will make extra work for everyone. They can make their own beds, bath themselves, get ready for school and so on, but they can't cook their own meals or wake themselves up in time to get to school. And they have normal appetites. If you'll forgive my frankness, the tea Edith had prepared for the five of us would have left Daisy and Petal feeling very hungry, even if they'd eaten it all themselves. I'm sure Mrs Wyn Roberts will do her best to see the children are cared for, but if too much is left to Edith . . .'

'Naturally, Mrs McAllister, you are worried that your children might not find Edith very . . . sympathetic,' Mrs Franklin said tactfully, 'but I'm sure such worries are needless. The fact is, the authorities told my sister, when the other evacuees left, that they meant to requisition the Larches for the use of senior management at the Ordnance factory. The alternative was to house at least six evacuated children here, so you see, my sister will make every effort to keep your girls happy and content. Indeed, she has already applied for more evacuees, only stipulating that they should be girls, since this is an all-female household.

'I see,' Rose said slowly. 'And – and will Mrs Wyn Roberts employ more help when the other children arrive?'

'She may well do so; but surely two women can manage six small girls?' Mrs Franklin said, beginning to descend the stairs once more. 'Don't worry, Mrs McAllister. Your children will be both safe and happy here. It's a wonderful house for children and, when spring comes, a wonderful garden. There is a Wendy house, an orchard with a swing hanging from a branch of an old pear tree, a tree house built in the big copper beech . . . a sandpit . . . I assure you, it's a paradise for children, and I should know because I lived here myself from my birth until I married.'

Rose had to be content with this, though before she left the following day, she did manage to have a word with Edith. Finding the maid alone in the kitchen, she approached her, trying to smile pleasantly, though the older woman's features did not soften and her gaze was distinctly aggressive. Rose thought that Edith looked like an angry toad with her long thin mouth tightly folded and her pale eyes bulging.

'Yes?' she said baldly, as Rose approached. 'I'm very busy, Mrs – er – Mrs McAndrews, so if you've anything to say, you'd best say it at once, and no beating about the bush.'

To say that Rose was taken aback was an understatement, but she held the woman's gaze. 'I just wanted to tell you, Edith, that I am very sorry for the extra work my children will cause, but I think you will find them co-operative and helpful. However, I have written my name and address on this envelope, together with the telephone number of the factory in which I work. If there is anything I can do, or if you need to get in touch with me, you can contact me there.' She handed Edith the envelope which contained, beside the details mentioned, a ten shilling note. 'And by the way, as you will see, our name is McAllister, not McAndrews.' Rose was tempted to add 'Ethel', but did not do so. She felt sure that the older woman would take it out on Daisy and Petal if she did any such thing.

The children walked with her to the station, chattering happily as they did so. Daisy had fallen deeply in love with the Wendy house and said that she and Petal meant to carry one of the doll's tea services down from the nursery in order to have tea parties there. Petal, for her part, could not wait to climb up to the tree house, and both children anticipated the arrival of four more small girls with pleasure. 'I expect we'll all go to this Alexandra School,' Daisy said cheerfully, as Rose climbed aboard the train and turned to give her daughters a last kiss. 'Mrs Wyn Roberts's house isn't like the farm because there are no animals, not even a dog or a cat, but perhaps they'll get one if we suggest it.'

Rose opened her mouth to warn Daisy to do no such thing, but at that moment the guard came along the train, slamming doors and shouting to those not travelling to stand well clear, and almost immediately the train began to chug out of the station. Rose waved and waved at the two tiny figures until they were out of sight, then sat back in her seat, blew her nose, and told herself that Daisy and Petal were a couple of lucky kids. That beautiful house! And all the wonderful toys which children in their position would never normally see, let alone play with. And then there was the garden, the Wendy house, the tree house . . . yes, they were lucky children indeed.

Nevertheless, the eyes that she turned on to the magazine she had bought for the journey were full of tears.

On the way back to Bernard Terrace, Rose decided that she must fill her life with activities; preferably those which would help with the war effort. Loneliness was a bad thing because it gave one too much time to think; she would be better fully employed spending her spare time, such as it was, helping others.

So, as soon as she got home, she went and visited Maisie and asked her where she should go to volunteer for part-time war work which would fit in with her factory shifts. Maisie said, frankly, that she had no idea but, as usual, knew someone who would be able to help. 'Remember Muriel Jones, who were a couple of years above us in school? She works full time at the Civil Defence Control Centre; it's a real important job, so if you go round to her place one evening – she lives in Upper Beau Street – she'll soon put you right.'

Deciding that there was no time like the present, Rose went round to Muriel's house that same evening, and by the time she was eating her solitary supper she was all fixed up. She had decided she would become a firewatcher or, if the need was elsewhere, a shelter warden. Muriel was a tall, thin woman, square-shouldered and energetic, and had understood about both Rose's factory shift work and the loneliness which she felt now that the girls had been evacuated for a second time.

'I'm glad you came to me, because I do believe that you'll be a good deal happier fitting in with other people and getting to make new friends,' she said, her rather horsy face suddenly transformed by a broad smile. 'Alone, one cannot help but imagine dreadful things during the raids – I did myself – but in company with others, everything is easier to bear. I share this house with three other war workers, all women of course, and usually we are too busy to feel afraid. How is your husband, by the way? I seem to recall someone telling me he was a seaman, so I don't suppose you see much of him.'

Rose smiled. She knew enough about the local grapevine to realise that Muriel must know she had married Steve McAllister; a man who drank too much and probably ill treated his wife. Simply answering the question, she replied: 'Yes, Steve's in the Royal Navy, so naturally I don't see very much of him . . . and now, apparently, I shall see even less. He recently volunteered for submarines, so his home port will be down south. At the moment he's on a training course in Gosport.'

Muriel looked her squarely in the eye. 'Is that bad? Will you miss him?'

Before she had thought, Rose had answered with complete honesty. 'No, it isn't bad and I shan't miss him at all. He – he is not an easy man to live with. I've put up with it for years, learned to defend myself, and to keep out of the way when he was really drunk, but after Christmas he attacked one of the children and as far as I was concerned, that was the end. I've managed to evacuate them and won't give him their country address, but by the time the war is over I hope I'll have found a permanent home for us, somewhere far away. Perhaps even abroad.'

'I see. I'd heard rumours – you know what this place is like – but whenever I've seen you in the street you've always looked smart and happy, and the children content and well cared for. Some women in your position would let themselves go, take the easy way out.'

'I did that at first,' Rose said honestly. 'I was too frightened of him to think of making a stand. Then one day I was cooking at the stove . . .'

She told Muriel the whole story, half ashamed, half proud, and was delighted when the older girl smiled broadly and held out her hand. 'Shake, Rose! My father was violent, and after my mother died he thought he could start on me. He was a scuffer; I hit him so hard with his own truncheon that he had to have five stitches in a scalp wound. That was years ago but he's still alive, and though we've not shared a house since '36, he seems to respect me now and wouldn't dream of saying a word out of place, let alone raising his hand against me.'

The two women talked a little more and then Rose left, having made out a schedule of her shifts for the next four weeks or so. Muriel had agreed to put together a programme of firewatching for Rose to follow, taking her shifts into account, and promised to push it through the door of No. 7 in the next couple of days.

So when Rose met Rachel in the canteen on her first day back in work, she was full of news. Over macaroni cheese and boiled potatoes, she told Rachel all about the Larches and Mrs Wyn Roberts, and about Edith, who had seemed so grumpy but would doubtless improve upon further acquaintance. Then she talked about the voluntary war work which she would be starting as soon as her schedule arrived. It was almost as an afterthought that she mentioned Steve's transfer to submarines.

Rachel stared at her, round-eyed. 'Oh, Rose! Alby told me Steve had thought about it once before only he was put off by the *Thetis* sinking,' she said. 'Alby said Steve was all wrong for submarines; he said he's not too keen on enclosed spaces and – and he's so *tall*. Alby said he'd have been ducking his head all the time. Whatever made him do it? Volunteer, I mean?'

Rose took a deep breath. 'It's a long story; it goes right back to when we first married, which was when Steve began to hit me when he was drunk, or in a bad mood,' she said quietly. 'I've never said a word before, Rachel, because Steve and Alby were such friends that it didn't seem fair to tell you about Steve's other side, the side only his wife and kids knew.' She looked thoughtfully across at Rachel's appalled face. 'If you'd rather not know, just say, but it's why he ended up volunteering for submarines.'

After a long and very tense moment, Rachel nodded. 'I'd rather you told me,' she said. 'Once, Alby hinted at something of the sort but I suppose I didn't want to understand, because Alby is such a grand fellow that it seems strange he should choose to befriend someone – someone who wasn't just as grand.'

So Rose told her story and at the end of it Rachel nodded sadly. 'I see. Things are a lot clearer: the lump on your forehead, and your black eye . . . the way Steve sometimes talked . . . oh, Rose, I am so sorry. If I'd known, perhaps I could have done something to help. But one thing I don't understand. Why should Steve volunteer for submarines?'

'He said that it was partly the money, which is very much better, and partly he's punishing himself for what he did to Daisy,' Rose explained. 'Also, his home port will be down south, so he won't be able to simply walk into number seven whenever he's in port. And oddly enough, I think it's partly because he and Alby were to be separated and he feels fate has kicked him in the teeth by taking his pal away. So perhaps he's kicking back by volunteering to do something which Alby had warned him against.'

There was a long silence, then Rachel got to her feet and Rose followed suit. 'I'll never understand men if I live to be a hundred,' Rachel said ruefully, as they left the canteen. 'But I'm so glad you told me everything, Rosie, and I hope you and I will always be bezzies. I wouldn't mind helping with the firewatching meself. Could you put in a word for me?'

Rose laughed and shook her head chidingly. 'They'd have to buy a bigger van just to squeeze you inside,' she observed. 'No, don't hit me, I was only teasing. I'll have a word with Muriel the next time I see her. 'Bye for now, Rachel.'

Several weeks later, Rose came home from work to find two letters on the doormat. She carried them through into the kitchen but did not bother to light the fire since the March weather was quite clement at the moment. She sat down at the kitchen table, wondering which missive to open first, and decided on the children's. She loved their letters, which were always chock full of their news, each one writing a few lines. Now it seemed that they were going to have what Petal called tests, and what Daisy called examinations, before the Easter holidays, so both girls announced that they were studying hard and that Mrs Wyn Roberts had volunteered to 'hear' such things as tables and the rules of grammar. Because of her new responsibilities, Rose had only visited the Larches once since that first time and had been delighted with the children's enthusiasm for their new school and their obvious contentment with Mrs Wyn Roberts. Daisy informed their mother that they did lots of work round the house, making beds, dusting and using the carpet sweeper as well as occasionally going into town for messages. Rose smiled indulgently, thinking that a carpet swept or a room dusted by Petal would have to be done again by someone a little more meticulous, but congratulated them on their hard work.

Rather to her surprise, Edith had not been at home when she visited and when she had asked the children where the maid was, they had exchanged quick glances and said they did not know but thought she would be home around six.

'Ah, then I suppose Mrs Wyn Roberts will be making your supper,' Rose had observed. Daisy had nodded vaguely but Petal had piped up that supper was always cold when Edith was away, and then the subject had been changed and Rose thought about Edith no more. She guessed that the woman's attitude would lead to the children's avoiding her as much as possible, but since she had asked them, tentatively, whether they were happy or had complaints, and had received an emphatic yes to the first and no to the second, she decided that Edith's attitude must have softened.

She did wonder why no more evacuees had arrived at the Larches, but Daisy told her that Mrs Wyn Roberts thought the authorities had forgotten about them. 'Only I 'spect they'll remember soon,' Daisy had said hopefully. 'Not that it matters, 'cos we've both got friends in school, haven't we, Petal? Mine's called Gwennie and Petal's is called Sian. The four of us play together at weekends, and now the evenings are getting lighter we'll probably play after school as well.'

So Rose received letters from the children with pleasure, and now she eyed the second letter with considerable curiosity. It was from Steve – she knew his writing well – and it was postmarked Portsmouth which, she knew, was near Gosport. But it was also fat, and in the past Steve's communications had never run to more than a single page of his untidy – and rather illiterate – scrawl. So she slit the envelope and pulled out the contents with more interest than usual. Immediately, she saw the reason for the thick envelope; there was a letter to herself, but he had also enclosed letters to the children. Each one had the name printed on it, though no address, and both were stamped. Rose smiled a little; clearly, Steve's intention was still to win back his children's trust, and when she felt the envelopes she was pretty sure that something more than a letter was contained therein. It might be money, or a little brooch or badge. He had obviously enclosed a small present with each letter.

But right now, the most important thing was to read her own epistle and find out whether he had become a submariner or if he had already changed his mind, so she bent her head and concentrated.

Dear Rose,

Well, here we are, nearly at the end of our training and though it's been tough, it was certainly no worse than I expected. We've done all sorts, learned how to operate the controls, stared through the periscope until we could make sense of what we could see and used the escape hatch . . . a nasty business. But we're settling down, learning to trust one another – and trust is real important aboard a sub. I can't tell you too much about the sub we'll be joining except that she's called Centurion *and has a crew of thirty-three. I say 'we' because I've got a mate, a grand feller. His name is Ted and he's from Southampton – married, like myself, with two little girls; what a coincidence, eh? There's a rumour that the* Centurion *has come into dry dock for repairs and will go back to the Med, with us aboard, when she's fit again. Not bad, eh? All of them lovely beaches and gorgeous Maltese girls . . . but you don't have to worry about them, not looking the way you do. I think about you all the time, and the girls of course. Write often, my love, and tell the girls to write as well. I know they aren't with you but I know, also, that you'll be in close touch.*

All my love, Steve.

Rose stared at the letter, her chin dropped on her fists. There was something . . . something not quite right here. Submarine training was all very well but surely it would not have altered the style in which Steve wrote? It was his writing all right, but there was something strange . . .

Carefully, she conned the letter again, examining each word, then gave a whoop as realisation dawned; when she looked closely, she could see that, originally, the writer had begun to write one name and had replaced it with *Ted*. Suspicion growing, she realised that *Southampton*, too, had originally been something else. She sat back in her chair, scarcely knowing whether to laugh or cry. Steve had copied another man's letter, word for word. She had no doubt that, in the original, the friend's name had been Steve, and the town in which he lived Liverpool. She could imagine, all too clearly, how Steve would sprawl across the table in the mess, tongue curling out of the corner of his mouth, concentrating so hard on his copying that he had almost forgotten to transpose Ted for his own name and Southampton for Liverpool. Once, she might have been really annoyed, but now she could understand why he had done it. He had no ability with a pen, insufficient imagination to pass on to someone else what he had seen and done. Yet he had clearly wanted her to know that he was not unhappy, that he was looking forward to joining the *Centurion*, and that he had found a good friend. If he had to cheat a little bit to get the news across to her, so what? People did many worse things – Steve had done worse things himself; she should be grateful that he had taken the time to write, even if he had copied his friend Ted's letter. As she went to put the letter down on the table again the last page folded itself and she saw there was something written on the back of it. She turned it over, then grinned. *PS Rose – I miss Alby, course I do, but this feller Ted's real grand. He's goin to help me keep off of the drink.*

He had only signed the postscript with his initial, which was far more typical than the *All my love, Steve* with which the main letter had ended.

Rose carried the letter over to the dresser and put it in the drawer on the right, where she kept such things. Then she returned to the table and looked long and hard at the letters Steve had sent to their daughters. It seemed awfully sneaky to open them, but the kettle was steaming on the hob and no one need ever know. Presently, she tipped the contents of both out on to the table, keeping them separate so that they would both go back into their original envelopes. Then she read the letters which, she thought, were pretty much as her own letter had been . . . probably copies of what Ted had written to his own daughters. There was no mention of the fracas which had sent Steve off to volunteer for submarines, but she was extremely annoyed, when she opened the little cotton-wool-wrapped parcels, to find that Petal's contained a shiny new shilling and Daisy's a sixpence and a threepenny joe. She did not believe that this was meanness – it must have been the only cash he had had on him at the time – but the fact that he had sent more money to the child he had not attacked, but who happened to be his favourite, hurt her so much, for Daisy's sake, that she jumped to her feet, fetched her own purse, and found a silver shilling, thinking Steve's ninepence a fair enough exchange for peace of mind. Then she carefully resealed and addressed the envelopes; she would post them in the morning, as she went to work.

She was on her way up to bed when a thought which had never entered her head before stopped her in her tracks. When he was sober, men liked Steve. Alby had considered him good company, a grand person to be with, and Ted clearly felt the same. When they had first married, Steve had been popular with the crowd who went to the football matches on a Saturday afternoon, with his workmates, with the boy cousins he had played with as a youth. When he was drunk, they avoided him, which was both natural and sensible, but when he was sober, they actually liked him.

Slowly, Rose began to mount the stairs once more. She had heard girls in the factory speak of someone as being 'a man's man', and now she thought that this description fitted Steve perfectly. He could admire and respect a man, but never a woman, so it stood to reason that he should never have married.

And his marrying, she could admit it now, had been partly, at least, her own fault. She had found his good looks, the sheer size of him, as well as his swaggering attitude, irresistible. And then there had been the heady pleasure of defying her parents, insisting that Steve McAllister was the only man she would ever love, dogging his footsteps. He had been flattered, she was pretty sure of that. The best-looking girl in the neighbourhood, a well-brought-up, intelligent girl, albeit only sixteen, crazy about him – who would not have been flattered? She had virtually thrown herself into his arms – could one entirely blame him for catching her, marrying her . . . and then reverting to type?

But now it seemed that, having come to his senses at last, if only temporarily, he was trying to behave as other, better, men did. He had tried to imitate Alby, when the drink had been getting the better of him; and then their ship had gone down and they had been assigned to different vessels and fear, superstition, call it what you will, had sent Steve staggering off to the nearest pub to drown his sorrows. And then, of course, he had become violent, had attacked Daisy . . .

And now, in a sense, he had come full circle, she thought as she undressed and slipped into bed. Though he was still trying to reform, it was too late. When he emerged from the Navy he would be a single man once more because his wife and children would be far away, and safe from him for ever.

And on this thought, Rose slept at last.

Daisy and Petal had discussed what they should write in their letters, how much to tell their mother, and had come to the conclusion that they had best tell her only the good things about their new foster home. Indeed, most of what they wrote, and what they had told her when she visited, was no more than the truth. Mrs Wyn Roberts was kind, in her way, and was always asking them if they were happy, making friends, getting enough to eat. To be sure, they did do a great deal of housework, but they were also allowed to play with their friends in the garden or in the big attic nursery at the top of the house.

What they did not mention to either Rose or anyone else was that Edith hated them, not because they were children, or a nuisance, but because they were from Liverpool, and this meant that she hated their mother, too, and everyone living in Bernard Terrace, everyone attending St Ambrose School.

From the moment that they had returned to the house after Rose's departure, the maid had made it plain how she felt. 'Two dirty little scousers,' she had said malevolently. 'Not fit to clean my shoes, you ain't, with your thievin' ways, your filthy language. Makes me sick, you does, sick just to hear that 'orrible accent, them 'orrible expressions! I tell you, if them bloody Huns did one good thing it were to drop bombs on Liverpool. I wish they'd flatten the whole stinkin' city, that I do.'

Against such outright loathing, what could they do? Tell Mam that Edith hated them, wanted them dead? Well, they could, Daisy thought, but all it would do would be worry Mam, make her strain every nerve to get them billeted with other people, and other people might be worse. Edith fed them on the leavings from Mrs Wyn Roberts's table; once she had given them each a bowl of thick vegetable soup (she called it *cawl*) and when they had eaten it, had told them she had pissed in the pan before pulling it over the fire.

Daisy had gone green and rushed for the sink, where she had vomited the soup up, but Petal had looked coldly at Edith and said: 'I don't believe you. You say scousers are liars, but you are worse. You look like a toad and you behave like one too. You're slimy and nice to Mrs Wyn Roberts because she's important, and you're horrible to us because we aren't. Don't you know the poem: *Taffy was a Welshman, Taffy was a thief, Taffy came to our house and stole a leg of beef*? Well, I thought that were just a cruel lie, but it's true about you. You steal the food that our ration books buy, and you tell lies. I can't imagine you squatting over that little pan and piddling into it – your knees would give out, so they would!'

It had made Daisy feel better, but she realised that they had to make a stand. Edith gave them bread, potatoes and leftover scraps, but never made them a proper meal, and though they had a hot dinner at school they often went to bed hungry. She wondered about telling Mrs Wyn Roberts, tried timidly to point out that their breakfast and tea were makeshift meals, but Mrs Wyn Roberts arched her fair brows and stared at Daisy, disbelief written all over her face. 'But last night we had a beautiful mutton stew. The night before it was vegetable pie with a tiny piece of liver each, and the night before that—'

'We didn't have any of that,' Daisy had said boldly. 'We had potato and a bit of cabbage one night, and bread and jam the other. And – and not very much bread and jam, either,' she added, her voice sinking almost to a whisper.

'But Edith has assured me that she's too busy to cook nursery meals so we all have the same,' Mrs Wyn Roberts said, with an air of finality. 'Of course, I know that rich food would be bad for children – it would give you nightmares – but Edith is very careful never to overload your little stomachs. And besides, so much food is rationed that eating truly well is next to impossible. Though I do believe the food Edith has provided these past few weeks has been better than it was earlier in the year. I suppose it's because, as the weather grows finer, things become easier, though I'm sure I don't know why.'

Daisy murmured that the fact that Edith now possessed her own and Petal's ration books might have something to do with it, but Mrs Wyn Roberts was not listening. 'I've put Edith's wages up because she's trying so hard to make us good, nourishing meals,' she informed Daisy. 'After all, now that there are no other servants, she has to do all the marketing, and she goes from butcher to butcher trying to find someone who has got something available which isn't rationed.'

Daisy was so indignant at that remark that she spoke up. 'Edith gets the ration stuff but we do the rest of the messages,' she informed Mrs Wyn Roberts. 'It takes us hours after school and on a Saturday, going round the shops. We even walk out to the farm on Cefn Road for some of the messages.'

Mrs Wyn Roberts looked surprised. 'Messages!' She laughed gaily, then patted Daisy's cheek. 'Now I wonder what sort of messages my dear old Edith sees fit to send around the shops with two little girls as couriers? I expect she wants to know when various foodstuffs will become available, eh?'

Daisy stared at her, completely baffled. But before she could even try to explain, the front doorbell rang and Mrs Wyn Roberts got slowly and gracefully to her feet, shooing Daisy out of the room before her. 'Off with you to the kitchen, and tell Edith not to bother to come to the door, since I am on my way there myself,' she said briskly. 'I expect it will be Mrs Prothero with a knitting pattern which she is lending me.'

Daisy was still wondering what she should do about Edith and their meals, when Mr Wyn Roberts came home for what his wife described as 'a short break from routine, an end-of-year refresher'. The children, with the memory of their own father and his recent behaviour very fresh in their minds, regarded the announcement of their unwitting host's imminent arrival with considerable concern and Edith, seeing this, did her best to portray Mr Wyn Roberts as some sort of monster before his actual arrival. Petal said stoutly that she didn't care; if Edith didn't like him he was sure to be as nice as anything, and anyway, Mrs Wyn Roberts would not have married someone as horrible as the person she depicted. Nevertheless, both children nursed a secret dread of this 'short break from routine'.

Mr Wyn Roberts was arriving on the six o'clock train from London on Friday evening, and though the children suggested that his wife might like to meet the train she said, with a heavy sigh, that because of the war train times were no longer reliable, so she had instructed her husband to catch a taxi from the station.

'Only there isn't always a taxi,' Daisy said, remembering their own arrival. 'Suppose he has to walk, carrying his luggage? You can drive, can't you, Mrs Wyn Roberts? And there is a car in the garage, isn't there?'

'Yes, I can drive, but the car hasn't been used for months and months . . . there's probably no petrol, and anyway, as I said, the times of the London trains have been so disrupted by the bombing that I might be waiting for *hours*!'

Daisy heard the petulant note creep into Mrs Wyn Roberts's voice and realised that she should not ask any more questions; there was no point. Their hostess did not want to fetch her husband from the station and Daisy was realist enough to remember that it was, in any case, a pretty short walk, even carrying a heavy suitcase, and also that the porter had told them that the taxis were always there to meet the London train, but did not bother much for more local ones.

'We'll have dinner whenever Mr Wyn Roberts arrives . . . that is, he and I will dine then,' Daisy overheard Mrs Wyn Roberts telling Edith. 'And what should we have? I think . . . something special, but something which can be kept hot in the Aga, because heaven knows what time the train will actually reach the station. And a nice pudding, I think . . . there are still some apples in the loft over the garage, but they're past their best . . . do we have marmalade? I don't know whether you remember, Edith, because before the war you were never called upon to cook, but marmalade roll with custard was quite one of Mr Wyn Roberts's favourite puddings. Could you manage that, do you think? And perhaps cheese and biscuits with a nice cup of coffee to round the meal off?'

Edith said obsequiously that she would do her best, though she went on at some length about the difficulty of getting most of the ingredients her mistress had asked for, but since this was not at all unusual Mrs Wyn Roberts merely waited until Edith stopped telling her how hard life was and then said: 'That seems satisfactory; goodnight, Edith,' and sailed gracefully out of the kitchen and back to the white drawing room, where she spent most of her time.

On the Friday, Mr Wyn Roberts duly arrived. He was about the same height as his wife, which surprised Daisy for, without really thinking seriously about it, she had concluded that men were always taller than their wives – look at her parents! Rose was at least six inches shorter than Steve, and a great deal slimmer and more – well, more fragile, Daisy supposed. But Mr Wyn Roberts, though of a height with his wife, was downright skinny. 'You wouldn't think he were a feller whose favourite grub was marmalade pudding and custard,' Daisy whispered to her sister from their spy-hole halfway down the gracious staircase. 'He must be awful old . . . he's got hardly any hair and there are lines all over his face.'

In the days that followed, however, they found Mr Wyn Roberts, though strict, to be a good deal less fierce than Edith had led them to believe. He expected certain things of them – punctuality, particularly at mealtimes, and at getting up and bed times – politeness to all grown-ups and instant obedience when asked to perform some small task. But so far as Daisy and Petal were concerned, the happiest result of his week-long stay was a change in their routine which benefited them greatly. On the second day, Mr Wyn Roberts came into the kitchen, his wife trailing behind him, and glanced frowningly round. Edith and the children were preparing vegetables, and stopped their work as the master of the house addressed them. 'I've decided we shall all benefit if, in future, everyone, including myself and my wife, eats all their meals in the kitchen. It will save Edith carrying heavy trays up the stairs, but most of all it will save fuel. I expect you know that a great many miners – the younger, fitter men – are now in the armed forces; their place has been taken by conscientious objectors – conchies, folk call them – but they don't have the experience or the strength of the men they have replaced. So, as the war goes on, coal will become a rarer and rarer commodity. To have a fire in three rooms is ridiculous, a wicked waste, so in future, Edith, the only fire you kindle must be that in the kitchen.'

Mrs Wyn Roberts gave a bleat of protest. 'Oh, but, Henry, I can't possibly get myself up early enough to share breakfast with the children. They have to eat before eight in order to get to school on time. And how can I possibly perform all my many tasks in a room without a fire? I shall simply freeze to death!'

'No you won't,' Mr Wyn Roberts said robustly. 'You will bring whatever work you may have down to the kitchen. I've arranged with the GPO to come in and re-route the telephone so that it can be placed on the kitchen dresser. That will save either yourself or Edith having to run all the way to the white drawing room whenever it rings. As for breakfast in bed, my dear, that is a luxury no one can afford in wartime. Surely you've heard that song the soldiers all sing . . . now what are the words?'

Petal's hand shot up. 'I know it!' she squeaked. '*This is the army, Mr Jones, No private rooms or telephones, You've had your breakfast in bed before, But you won't get it here any more.*'

Mr Wyn Roberts actually smiled, though his wife stared stonily before her. 'Well, well, it seems we have quite a little songstress among us,' Mr Wyn Roberts said. 'Now I hope I'll hear no more objections to what is, in truth, sheer common sense.'

His wife stared at him with scarcely veiled hostility and Daisy realised that these arrangements had come as as much of a shock to Mrs Wyn Roberts as they had to Edith and themselves. She gazed at Mr Wyn Roberts with dawning respect. He might be old and skinny, with weak eyesight which needed the help of heavy horn-rimmed glasses, but he was not afraid to take unpopular decisions.

When no one spoke, Mr Wyn Roberts continued. 'I shall write out a timetable and suggest some menus which will be a good deal easier for everyone,' he said, in his deep, unaccented voice. Daisy had noticed that Mr Wyn Roberts, though a Welshman to the core, did not speak with a local accent. He had told the children he had never learned Welsh as he had gone to a local prep school in Chester until he was eight and from there been sent to an English boarding school.

Mr Wyn Roberts turned back towards the kitchen door, but before he could leave the room his wife spoke again, her voice unnaturally high. 'And I suppose you are going to have the front door lifted off its hinges and brought round to the back so that we shan't have to go along all those passages whenever someone rings or knocks?'

Daisy expected an outburst of anger from Mr Wyn Roberts, but instead he beamed at his wife with what appeared to be genuine pleasure. 'Clara, my dear, you think of everything. I am a lucky man to be married to someone with such a keen brain. Oh, I know you were only joking, but you've got the right idea; we will affix a large, permanent notice to the front door, instructing all callers to take the side path round to the back of the house and knock loudly upon the kitchen door.'

Daisy thought there was a rather tense moment whilst Mrs Wyn Roberts made up her mind how to take this remark. But either discretion was the better part of valour, or their hostess had decided to accept the praise as her due. She inclined her head graciously, then addressed the maid. 'Well, Edith, it seems that we are to learn to share this beautiful kitchen in future. I shall be able to help you with meal preparation far more easily than I have done in the past.' She turned to her husband. 'Come along, my dear; you promised to accompany me to Chester to visit my sister this morning; she won't like it if we're late.'

For several moments after the Wyn Robertses left the kitchen, Daisy and Petal sat uneasily at the table, continuing to shred cabbage. Daisy half expected an outburst from Edith, for when the older woman realised the full import of Mr Wyn Roberts's changes she was sure to be cross. With all of them sharing a meal, Daisy was sure it would not be possible for Edith to give them nothing but cabbage whilst she and her mistress feasted on stew, or chops, or sausages. Edith had stomped over to the sink and started peeling potatoes, so Daisy could not see her face, but soon the old woman dropped the last peeled potato into the pot and carried the latter across to the Aga, though she stood it to one side since their main meal was always taken in the evening.

She said not a word, but presently Daisy heard a very odd sound issuing from the old woman's direction. She looked across and saw that Edith's shoulders were shaking; surely she was not crying? Mr Wyn Roberts's changes would make her life very much easier, though of course she might not relish sharing her kitchen with her mistress.

But as Edith turned away from the stove, Daisy saw that she was laughing, laughing so helplessly that tears ran down her cheeks, uttering great whoops as though the laughter had been locked inside her for so long that it could not come out in a quiet and orderly fashion, but must emerge in whoops and gasps.

When, at last, the laughs hiccuped to a halt, Daisy gave Petal a nudge in the ribs. 'You ask her,' she muttered. 'You gerraway with more'n I can, 'cos you're only a kid still.'

Petal nodded. 'Edith, why's you laughing?' she asked baldly. 'We've never heard you laugh before, me an' Daisy.'

'I never had cause before,' Edith said. 'But the thought of that idle, fat cow havin' to get up for breakfast, which she hasn't never done since I've known her, and havin' to live in the kitchen along a' me . . . well, it was enough to make a cat laugh.' She glared ferociously at Petal. 'And don't you go tellin' no tales, sayin' that I called the mistress names, because that I never would. I – I'm . . . *hee-hee-hee* . . . I'm her devoted slave, everyone knows that.'

Later that day, on their way to the shops to purchase some bones for stock, Daisy and Petal discussed the enigma that was Edith, but came to no very definite conclusion; the only thing they did realise was that, thanks to Mr Wyn Roberts, life would be a good deal easier for them from now on. They knew Mrs Wyn Roberts was lazy but she was not unkind. Once they were all eating together, she would see that they got a fair share of the food.

'But suppose Mrs Wyn Roberts goes back to breakfast in bed and so on and doesn't live in the kitchen any more when Mr Wyn Roberts leaves?' Petal asked rather apprehensively as they came out of the butcher's market and headed for Chester Street. 'She might, you know.'

But Daisy had already thought this out and shook her head. 'Mrs Wyn Roberts is really very fond of Mr Wyn Roberts and she wouldn't do anything to upset him,' she observed. 'Besides, she has lots of visitors, you know, and most of them are friends or relatives of his who might easily let slip that they'd been given tea in the white drawing room, or something like that. And then there's Edith. You bet she can tell tales with the best.'

Petal admitted that this was so and the children returned home feeling that life had definitely taken a turn for the better.

Chapter Nine
April 1941

Steve's training was finished and he and the rest of the crew of HMS/M *Centurion* had been sent to Malta by the submarine service – or 'the Trade' as it was known to the submariners – whence they scoured the Mediterranean, attacking enemy shipping, and sometimes coming back to port after a ten-day patrol with the skull and crossbones flying and two or three more definite kills to their name.

Oddly enough, the thing that he had most dreaded had not come to pass. Steve had always disliked – feared – enclosed spaces yet he had no such feelings aboard the *Centurion*, even when she was sailing at her maximum depth. He felt safe from the terrors he had known aboard HMS *Jericho*, almost began to think of the sea as a friend. Now, *they* were the lurking peril searching for prey. *They* were the wolf pack, the terror which struck from below on a calm, blue day; it was their torpedoes which streaked through the water whilst men were relaxing, asleep in their bunks, eating a meal.

He said as much to Ted as the two of them were sprawled in the mess. 'I never thought I'd say it, but I prefer subs to surface ships,' he remarked. 'We're like – like invisible to them up above. They don't even know we're there until they feel the deck moving under them and hear the explosion. Oh aye, I'd rather be a wolf than a sheep, if you see what I mean.'

Ted was writing to his wife; Steve to Alby. The

correspondence between the two men was, naturally, of a sporadic and infrequent nature but, whenever he got into port, Steve looked as anxiously for a letter from Alby as Rachel would have done. He had been parted from his friend by fate and the exigencies of war, but he did not intend to lose touch with the other man. They were both Liverpudlians and would both return to their native city when hostilities ceased. If they kept in regular touch, then they would simply pick up their friendship where it had left off. So Steve was determined to keep up the correspondence, hard labour for him though it might be.

Ted looked up from his own letter with a grin. 'So you like being the hunter, rather than the hunted, eh? Just you wait, me old china, until we're lyin' on the bottom, pretendin' to be a rock with ten battleships circling above and depth charges goin' off all round us. I know they fired at us yesterday, but that was nothing compared to what some subs go through.'

Despite the fact that he and Ted were, so to speak, in the same boat, their attitudes were totally different. Steve paid very little attention to words or warnings. It was actual personal experience which had taught him the lessons he had learned in life. His mother had told him to be gentle with women, but his father had shown him how the force of a blow could give him power over others; showing, not telling, was what counted for Steve.

Now, Steve agreed with what Ted had said, but was only paying lip service since, so far, the *Centurion*, ably captained by their young skipper, had nipped into dangerous situations, struck with deadly accuracy at fat merchantmen, or at the warships surrounding them, and had nipped out again, untouched.

Their most recent attack had been almost unsporting

since they had sneaked into a smallish Greek harbour, sunk three caiques, and left before their presence had been so much as suspected. Steve had heard some of the men muttering but the skipper knew best and he said the caiques were being used as gun boats and were probably manned by German sailors, which made them fair game.

Steve signed off with a flourish and slipped his letter into an envelope, but did not seal it down. The censor would have to see it before it could be sent, and since he had no idea in which theatre of war Alby's new ship operated, he had no idea, either, how long the letter would be on its journey. Ted, finishing his own letter at the same time, stood up and stretched. 'Do you want me to check that for you?' he said, indicating Steve's missive. 'I will if you like . . .' but at that moment the skipper sent the crew to action stations and Steve went to his position by the forward plane controls. Taking up his position, he thought, regretfully, that this would probably delay their meal by some while. On a small submarine, there was no regular cook, the men taking it in turns to prepare the meals. Today it was his turn and he had planned to make Cheese Oosh: a delectable mixture of milk, cheese, powdered egg, tomato and mustard which was much prized by the crew of the *Centurion*. But Cheese Oosh would have to wait; Steve sat down, resting his hands lightly on the wheel before him, and prepared for action.

This time, even Steve realised that they were in a sticky situation and would need phenomenal luck to get out of it. The *Centurion* had gone in low and deep, believing the ships above them to be in a half-circle, intending to do the maximum amount of damage in the shortest possible time, whilst relying on surprise to get them out of the half-circle before any ship could retaliate.

It had not been a half circle but a full one, and since it was daylight they had been spotted through the crystal clear waters of the Mediterranean, probably by their shadow on the sandy bottom, for the Mediterranean was a tricky sea. There were hills and valleys, plateaux and rifts on the sea bed, and they had not stuck to the valleys and rifts because the skipper had been too intent on the prey and had not realised that he could be seen. Everyone had been at battle stations but they had not had a chance to fire as much as one torpedo before the depth charges began.

At times, these were too close for comfort, so the skipper had decided to make a run for it; to go deeper. Fortunately, they had almost immediately found just what he was looking for: a sea valley so deep that when they reached the bottom, it was at their maximum depth of two hundred and fifty feet and they knew they could no longer be seen, although the ships above probably had a shrewd suspicion that they were still somewhere around.

'They'll go presently,' Ted murmured in Steve's ear. 'They've got a destination to reach; they can't hang around on the off chance that we're still here. In a couple of hours, Skip will bring us up to have a look around.'

The hours passed; every now and then, a depth charge exploded, giving the lie to the hope that the enemy would move on. Once it grew dark, they would have a better chance of getting away, but turning propellers was the sort of thing the hydrophones would pick up on immediately, and then the depth charges would start in earnest. Steve guessed that most of the convoy would have moved on, intent on reaching their destination, but probably leaving a destroyer behind to deal with them when they tried to surface.

The air was growing fouler; Steve's chest ached with every indrawn breath. He had been on the forward plane waiting for the signal to move his controls. But, like every man aboard, or all the ones he could see at any rate, he was now lying prone, conserving energy, conserving air, praying to God that they would be able to surface before the air ran out completely.

Beside him, someone moved. Jacky was throwing up, almost silently, into the bucket of diesel. A sour stench filled the air – what air there was – but the diesel dealt with that, and presently the skipper came quietly amongst them. He wanted a volunteer to go and change the batteries, which would give them perhaps half an hour more of breathable air. The trouble was, the space through which one had to wriggle to reach the batteries was extremely shallow – a bare twelve or fourteen inches. The skipper was sturdy, even though the men always reckoned to lose at least a stone of weight in the course of a ten-day patrol.

The skipper had written on a sheet of paper, *I want a volunteer to change the batteries*, and Steve immediately raised a hand. He had always prided himself on his slim figure and knew he was perfectly capable of wriggling through the narrow space and changing the batteries; he had done it often enough before, heaven knew.

Skip gave him the thumbs up sign and Steve stood up with great care. As the atmosphere had thinned, it had grown hotter and hotter, and he was already stripped down to singlet and shorts, his feet bare. He squeezed into the narrow space and was disconnecting the batteries when he heard, behind him, a muffled thud and an unwary exclamation. Startled, he tried to turn, then scolded himself for stupidity. He had gone in forwards but must retreat backwards; he would find out who had made that God-awful din when he was back with the others. He was actually trying to wriggle out of the narrow space when there was a tremendous explosion and the sea came roaring in. For a moment, he fought to escape. He tried to hold his breath but the sea was too strong. It roared in, unstoppable, stronger even than the *Centurion*, the old, remorseless enemy. Oddly, as he realised that this was the end, a picture of Rose as she had been on their wedding day came into his mind. The wide, innocent eyes, the adoring look in them as they fell on her new husband. What had gone wrong, he thought confusedly. She had changed; hardened. It had all been her fault, the failure of their marriage, the fact that his daughters no longer loved him.

Then the water forced itself into his lungs, stomach, ears, eyes and nostrils. Darkness was merciful as the sea took him.

Rose came out of the house in Bernard Terrace, tin hat in position, gas mask on one shoulder and two cheese sandwiches in the left-hand pocket of her coat. It was a fine, clear night, the stars bright in the dark heavens above. Because she had been on early shift that day, Rose had had a good rest in the afternoon, so when the siren sounded she had not been to bed and was able to leave the house at once, fully dressed and ready, she told herself, for anything.

She headed for the tall building where she would be firewatching as long as the raids lasted. The streets were full of scurrying figures, some making for the air raid shelters, others for their posts, and Rose was greeted by several people as they hurried along. Reaching her destination, she climbed the long flight of metal stairs to the roof. The moonlight was too bright, she thought apprehensively, settling herself in the shadow of a large chimney stack. By now, everyone knew all about the bomber's moon and indeed, as she looked up at the great silver disc, Rose saw the first enemy aircraft silhouetted against the stars, heard the steady thrum of its engine. Then she saw others and her heart gave an uncomfortable jump. Great black, lumbering shapes; they came on relentlessly, and soon she heard the first bombs fall, though they seemed to be some way off. Birkenhead docks? She could not say for sure, but of course they would be aiming for the docks, for the unprotected shipping lying there, for the warehouses, full of desperately needed supplies, which lined the quayside.

Usually, there were two of them firewatching from this particular position since the roofs covered an enormous area, but there was no time to check round for Violet Pierce, her opposite number. Rose saw a fire blossom, calculated its position, and made for the stairs at a run, almost colliding with a figure coming up them. It was Violet, looking shaken.

'Sorry I'm late,' she gasped. 'But I'd just got into bed when the sirens started so I had to dress and that. Anything happened?'

Rose swung past her, calling back over her shoulder as she did so. 'Big fire over towards the docks; a warehouse, I should think. I'll report it to the warden's post and come straight back because, by the sound of those engines, we're going to have a busy night of it!'

* * *

It was a bad night, but worse was to follow. Rose was kept constantly on the go, both on the Thursday night and the Friday night, and greeted Saturday with real relief. It was her day off and she would be able to rest instead of having to work, for though many shops, factories and other buildings had been hit her own place of work was pretty much untouched, and uniforms, the boss had told them severely, were always needed; production must not be allowed to fall just because the Luftwaffe had decided to give the docks a pasting.

Only it wasn't just the docks, as the people of Liverpool soon realised. Bombs were falling everywhere. Homelessness was commonplace – you would go out to the shelter at night and come home to a smoking ruin.

Rose came off firewatching duty in the early hours of Saturday morning and went home to Bernard Terrace – and straight to bed. Once, she would have found it impossible to sleep during daylight, especially on a lovely May morning, with the sun shining from a cloudless sky, but now she was far too tired to appreciate the fine weather. She crawled into bed and slept the clock round, then got up, made herself a quick meal of beans on toast, and sat down at the kitchen table to write a reassuring letter to the children. She realised that the BBC might well mention the raids on Liverpool, though she did not think the children listened to the wireless much. A set was kept in the white drawing room so that Mrs Wyn Roberts could keep abreast of the war, but the children, busy about their own concerns, were not likely to be told worrying news by their kindly hostess.

Rose wrote steadily. She told them that she had visited Aunt Selina and Uncle Frank, who were enjoying country life. They had purchased a piglet and four hens and had intended to fatten the piglet for the table, but had grown so fond of it that she doubted they would ever bring themselves to do the necessary. There was a woman called Mrs Higgins – did the girls remember her? – who lived three doors further along Penny Lane; she had offered to run the shop for a fifty per cent share of the profits. Uncle Frank thought he could trust Mrs Higgins and had taken up her offer and now only visited the shop once a week.

Rose finished off with the usual line of kisses. Last time she wrote, she had enclosed Steve's latest letter for, to her secret astonishment, he had begun to write regularly and cheerfully, and had made it clear that he was happier as a submariner than he had ever been aboard ordinary ships.

Rose had wondered whether to send the letter to the children but, in the end, had decided to do so, in fairness to Steve. Submariners were highly regarded by the rest of the Navy, and Steve had signed on to try to show his children, and his wife, that he wasn't all bad, as he had put it. So Rose thought her daughters should know that life aboard the *Centurion* was not everyone's cup of tea and that their father, in his own way, was a brave man.

In fact, having thought long and hard, Rose had concluded that Steve loved the life, partly because of its total masculinity, and also because the thirty-three men aboard the *Centurion* were like an extremely close-knit family; something Steve had never known, or appeared to want, before. If he had had sons instead of daughters, things might have been easier at home, but as it was it had taken the Navy – and most of all HMS/M *Centurion* – to show him what he wanted from life. Having been the target of German U-boats, he was obviously prepared to put up with a good deal in order to be the wolf rather than the sheep.

When the knock came on the door, she glanced at the clock on the mantel and wondered whether Violet had come to visit. The sky was still clear and the moon would be bright later, but that did not mean there would be yet another raid. She hurried to the front door and pulled it open, and there was Rachel, smiling a little apologetically. 'Rachel! It's lovely to see you; I miss you dreadfully at work. But what on earth are you doing here . . . oh, for goodness' sake, where are my manners? Do come in. I've got the kettle on, and I dare say you'd like a cup of tea.'

She ushered Rachel into the kitchen, sat her down in an easy chair and then began to pour the tea, talking as she did so. 'Have you seen the doctor lately? You're due any time now, aren't you? I know how they keep changing one's dates – at least they did with me. When I was expecting Daisy, I told my mam I thought there was a conspiracy and that my pregnancy was going to last for at least ten years.'

Rachel laughed. 'It does seem a bit like that,' she said ruefully, running a hand over her enormous stomach. 'But I'm actually due tomorrow, and that's why I've come.'

'Tomorrow!' Rose said, staring at her friend. She could not help thinking that this was not a good time to be giving birth, with the Luftwaffe trying so hard to flatten the city. But of course no one could choose when their baby was born; it was pot luck. 'Rachel, if you don't mind, I'll work while we talk, because if there's a raid I shall be going to the shelter and I usually make myself a few sandwiches and a bottle of cold tea to take with me.'

'Oh!' Rachel said. 'Well, let's hope there isn't. The

thing is, Mam and Dad have moved out to the country – they didn't want to, not with the baby due so soon, but I told them I'd be more worried about them if they stayed than they would be about me if they went, so they agreed to go. It was a relief, I can tell you, because my mam kept telling me I was eating for two and trying to pile my plate until I told her that if I ate any more I'd burst; but you know what mams are. She's so keen to have the perfect grandchild that she doesn't care how uncomfortable I am so long as the baby's fine. And that's why she made me promise not to stay at home alone at nights once the baby was due; she made me swear on the Bible – the Old Testament, of course – that I wouldn't, and I did – swear, I mean . . . well, promise, anyway,' she finished.

'But what if there is another raid tonight?' Rose said, feeling harassed. 'I think you ought to go along to the hospital, honestly I do, Rachel. I believe they've got cellars where patients can shelter during raids, and then if anything did happen – if you started to have the baby, I mean – you'd have doctors and nurses all around you; don't you think that might be best?'

'Oh, but, Rose, the hospital might not like it,' Rachel said, looking distraught. 'I – I don't want to put their backs up, if you know what I mean. After all, I'm not a patient until my pains start.'

'Ye-es, I see what you mean,' Rose said, though a trifle doubtfully. Although she'd had two children herself, she had never seen another woman in labour, let alone helped to deliver a child, and found herself hoping, devoutly, that she never would. She honestly thought that Rachel would be very foolish to risk having the baby under any but ideal conditions. However, it was clearly useless to say so now. If there was a raid – and a glance at the kitchen window confirmed that it was another fine evening – then that was the time to decide just where her friend should spend the hours of darkness.

It was around quarter past ten when the sirens went off, interrupting Rose and Rachel, who were having a lively discussion over babies' names. Rose jumped to her feet and began to struggle into her coat, for though the day had been warm and the night was mild, she knew that the wind would be cold. Rachel stood up at the same time and began to pull on her own coat.

'I'll come with you to the shelter. I'm not going to have the baby for at least twenty-four hours,' Rachel said authoritatively. 'They told me at the hospital that babies stop moving twenty-four hours before they decide to get born and my little chap has been kicking and pounding all day, so let's get going.'

'All right, if you're sure,' Rose said, rather doubtfully. She did not recall that either Daisy or Petal had stopped bounding around inside her twenty-four hours before their arrival. And indeed, halfway to the shelter, Rachel suddenly stopped and clutched her arm. 'Rose! Oh, Rose, I feel . . . I feel . . .'

They had been about to cross Everton Brow and they could hear the planes, the thrum, thrum of their engines sounding all too familiar. Rose tried to hurry Rachel on, but her friend resisted. 'I'll have to stand still for a minute . . . there was a horrid, tearing pain . . . oh, my goodness!'

'What is it, what is it?' Rose said anxiously. Then her eyes followed Rachel's gaze downwards. In the moonlight, there was a dark stain spreading across the pavements beneath her friend's feet. 'Oh, Rachel, don't say you're bleeding! You *must* get to hospital. Really you must.'

She looked wildly around her, but already the street was almost deserted, save for a tall figure – probably an air raid warden – coming towards them. But Rachel was answering, shaking her head. 'No, I'm not bleeding, or I don't think so, at any rate. I think my w-waters have broken. You were right, Rosie, I really ought to be at the hospital.'

Rose gazed at her friend in an agony of indecision. They were a long way from the hospital but quite near the air raid shelter. The trams and buses would have stopped running when the sirens sounded and she did not think she could get Rachel to the hospital by herself. Her friend would very soon be unable to walk, but if she could reach the shelter, at least there would be others there who could help her if the baby really was about to be born. She was starting to say so, to urge Rachel towards the shelter, when a voice broke across her words.

'Excuse me, ma'am, but can you direct me to the nearest warden's post? I've offered my services but I got caught out and what with the blackout and the searchlights and the noise, I'm well and truly lost.'

Rose heard the soft American drawl with real relief. If he had been willing to help at the warden's post then surely, if she explained their desperate situation, he would be equally happy to help her to get Rachel off the street. In the moonlight, she could only see that he was tall and dark and wore a uniform of some sort.

She turned towards him, speaking briskly. 'Thank you so much, but my friend and I need your help far more urgently than the wardens could possibly do. Rachel's expecting a baby and I think it's started. She's booked into a hospital, but it's a fair way off and I'm simply not strong enough to help her to cover such a distance. If I could get her to the nearest shelter, though . . .'

The young man grinned; she could see the flash of his white teeth in the moonlight. He began to speak, but the foremost planes were overhead now and the roar of their engines and the whistle and crash of descending bombs made conversation impossible. The American looked round wildly, then put an arm round Rachel, motioning Rose to do the same. Then he shouted, 'Lead the way, ma'am. This is no place for any of us to be lingering. Point me to the shelter.'

They didn't make it. A few yards further along, someone opened a door, then hastily slammed it shut as light streamed out, for a second, on to the pavement. A man stood there, a tin hat on his head, struggling into his jacket. This time it was a real air raid warden and he addressed them angrily, wanting to know what they were doing in the street during an air raid. Rose began to explain, but the American said brusquely: 'This woman's giving birth, officer, and she needs a roof over her head. Open that durned door!'

The man complied, grumbling beneath his breath, and less than a minute later they had been ushered into the warden's sizeable kitchen. The warden did not like leaving them there – he was a small, ferrety man with mean, suspicious little eyes and a whiffling pink nose – but he had little choice, he told them. The nearest public shelter was already full to overflowing. His wife and children had taken their places on the bunk beds there some three hours previously, and they had not been the first by a long chalk. 'Don't you go touchin' nothin', nor stealin' nothin' neither,' he said nastily, turning to leave. 'I've got me duty to do, but when I checks the shelters I'll see if there's a nurse or a doctor what might pop along, give you a hand, like.'

'Thank you so much,' Rose said sarcastically. 'I take it you won't object if we boil some water. After all, water doesn't cost much and you've still got a decent fire in the stove.'

'Ah, I dare say you think she'll be wantin' a cup o' tea,' the warden said knowledgeably. 'Well, if you use any of my missus's tea, you'll have to pay us back. And don't go messin' up me kitchen or the wife'll say I were a fool to let you in and clack me head off.'

Nobody answered him. Rachel sat on a small easy chair by the hearth, moaning gently. Rose filled the kettle at the sink and carried it across to the fire, and after the warden had left and she had leisure to look around, she saw that the American was wearing Royal Air Force uniform. She also saw that he had a pleasant, craggy face, short, light-brown hair, and eyes of almost exactly the same shade. As she watched, he was removing his greatcoat, which he spread over Rachel, telling her that she was not to worry; he was going to fetch help.

He straightened up and Rose clutched his arm. 'Don't leave me,' she said in an urgent undertone. 'I've never seen a baby being born. I won't know what to do . . . and where will you find help with a raid going on?' Even as she spoke, an enormous explosion drowned her next words, so that she had to repeat them. 'The warden said he'd send a nurse.'

The American smiled and patted her shoulder. 'I'll get help of some sort,' he assured her. 'I wouldn't trust that mean little feller to remember any of us once he was out of here. Now you just keep your friend company; I'll be back before you've missed me.'

Despite Rose's fears, the American was as good as

his word. The kettle had scarcely boiled before the front door opened once more and a practical, grey-haired woman came briskly across the room towards them, a small black bag in her hand. The American hovered behind her. 'This is Sister Dawson, the local midwife,' he announced. 'She was in the shelter and volunteered to come at once.'

'Oh, thank God,' Rachel muttered. She tried to sit herself up in the chair, then collapsed back once more, but she smiled with determined brightness at Sister Dawson. 'They – they told me at the hospital to time the pains, sister, and not to start bearing down until they were coming every two or three minutes. So far, it's only every five or six, but I feel – I feel . . .'

Sister Dawson smiled reassuringly at her patient but looked disapprovingly round the kitchen, then addressed Rose. 'You'll be the friend who was taking her to hospital,' she said. 'Run upstairs and fetch bedding – and don't tell me Mr Parsons won't like it because I'll deal with him – and this young man here can bring the sofa through from the front room. I seem to remember a sofa in the front room the last time I visited here.'

Rose rushed to obey her, and when she came back to the kitchen with her arms full of blankets, the sofa was pulled up near the fire and Rachel was lying on it, her head supported on cushions. There was no sign of the American, which was fortunate since Sister Dawson had helped Rachel out of most of her clothing. As soon as she saw Rose, she took the bedding, wrapped Rachel in a sheet, and then folded it back in order to examine her patient thoroughly. Then she pressed a stethoscope against the mound of Rachel's stomach. Rose started to speak, to ask where the American had gone, but Sister Dawson shushed her impatiently and after a few moments removed the stethoscope and hung it round her neck, then patted Rachel's shoulder reassuringly. 'Well, the head is engaged, but he won't be born for an hour or two yet,' she said. 'Now, I'd best take a few details before the actual birth begins.' She took a notebook out of her capacious black bag and began to ask questions: Rachel's full name, age and address, the name of her doctor and details such as the hospital she should have entered, the names and addresses of her next of kin, her blood group, and so on.

In the middle of all this there was a small tap on the door. Rose hurried across and opened it. The American stood there, looking awkward. 'She turned me out because she said she had to get her patient prepped, whatever that might mean,' he whispered. 'She seems pretty competent so I'd have left and made my way to the warden's post, only she wouldn't let me take my greatcoat, not until you'd brought the blankets down, and I guess the air force would likely court martial me if I lost my uniform before I'd even reached my airfield.'

Rose smothered a giggle and glanced cautiously behind her, then gestured to him to enter the room. Rachel had the blankets up round her chin and was perfectly respectable, and Sister Dawson was putting away her notebook and getting to her feet, saying that they'd all be the better for a nice cup of tea, telling Rose to see if she could find a tin of biscuits in the pantry, and commanding the American to bring another chair through from the parlour, since they might as well make themselves comfortable.

She had already enquired Rose's name, but now she asked the American just who he was, and such was the authority of a pencil poised above a small notebook that he gave the information immediately.

'I'm Luke Nadolski; I'm a flyer, come over from the States to join your RAF,' he said. 'I was making my way to the nearest warden's post to see if I could help any, when I came across these young ladies. So if you've done with me, I'd best be getting along . . .'

All the time they had been speaking, the whistle and roar of descending bombs had been sounding outside, and now Sister Dawson shook her head at him. 'You're not going anywhere, Mr Nadolski,' she said reprovingly. 'For a start, there's no point in sending you out to the warden's post, because you'd never find it, not with bombs dropping everywhere and the streets full of flying glass.' She lowered her voice. 'And if anything goes wrong here, which is always possible, then I may need you.'

'Oh. Right,' Luke Nadolski said at once. 'Only I've never seen a baby born, ma'am, and I don't reckon I'll be much use.'

'You'll likely not see this one born either,' Sister Dawson said. 'But whatever happens, Mrs Cohen will have to go to hospital, even if it's after the birth, and someone will have to fetch an ambulance. Personally, I think it may be many hours before Mrs Cohen is delivered, but with first babies you can never tell. So pull up a chair and sit down.' She smiled suddenly at the American's obvious unease and winked at Rose. 'Don't worry, I'll send you out when the action starts. And now let's have that cup of tea!'

The baby, a boy, had been born as the sirens wailed the All Clear, by which time Rose felt as if she had known Luke all her life. She and he had accompanied Rachel and her baby to the hospital in the ambulance but had decided to walk back, since public transport would undoubtedly be in a state of chaos as the raid had been an extremely heavy one.

Luke had told her that he was not due at his airfield for a couple of days, so she had invited him back to Bernard Terrace for breakfast and a wash and brush-up. He had insisted upon leaving a message – and a ten shilling note – for the warden whose house they had commandeered so ruthlessly, and now they strolled along in the sunrise of a fine May morning, talking companionably, though the destruction around them was incredible; it seemed a miracle that the warden's house, and those of his neighbours, had escaped even from blast. As she and Luke walked along the littered road, glass crunching beneath their feet, she clutched his arm and pointed. 'My God! See that building over there? The one you can see right through because there's nothing left except the façade and the window frames? That . . . that was my firewatching post. If I'd been on duty last night . . .' She did not bother to finish the sentence; the hollow shell of the warehouse spoke for itself.

'My God,' Luke said softly. 'But I guess war is like that. I mean, if you'd directed me to the warden's post, I could have been killed on my way there. See what I mean?'

Rose nodded dumbly. What he said was true, but somehow the narrowness of her own escape had been like a kick in the stomach. She knew she would grow accustomed to what had happened, but felt that she needed time – and some sleep – before she would be able to come to terms with it. Meanwhile, she and Luke made their way steadily across the city, appalled by the extent of the destruction and by the fires which still raged.

They were deeply, dreadfully tired, for neither had got a wink of sleep all night. Rose had worked with Sister Dawson once the birth was imminent, pulling against Rachel's hands as she strove to give birth to her child, and when he arrived, scarlet-faced and furious, she had bathed the baby in the sink whilst Sister Dawson did all the important things and saw to the new mother.

Naturally, the American had been consigned to the front room whilst all this was going on, but as soon as Rachel was respectable once more, and the child tucked into the curve of her arm, Sister Dawson had dispatched him, with Rose as his guide, to the warden's post to get an ambulance. They had got Rachel and the baby to hospital, seen her comfortably settled, and then the two of them had set out to walk to Bernard Terrace.

When they reached Salisbury Street, Rose felt a tightening of her stomach muscles as apprehension gripped her; it would be too terrible if a bomb had landed on her little house. But there was no dust, no broken glass, no obvious destruction; Salisbury Street and its environs snoozed in the May sunshine, and as she turned into the terrace Rose felt a surge of relief. The short rows of houses faced each other, calm and undamaged, as though there had been no raid, no bombs, no raging fires.

Because Luke was a visitor, Rose did not head for the jigger but went straight to the front door, unlocking it and waving Luke hospitably inside. 'There won't be a fire, I'm afraid, but I've a nice modern gas stove, so I can heat you up some water on that,' she said cheerfully. 'Oh, but I am so tired and so thirsty! I could drink the Mersey dry and sleep the clock round . . . only we'll have breakfast first. You'll want to get back to where you're staying and sleep there before you go off to . . . Lincolnshire, was it? I'd offer you a bed but you'll want your stuff – you left your kit bag in your lodgings, I take it?' She had lit the gas under the kettle as she spoke and now turned and looked up at her companion, seeing for the first time the dark circles round his eyes and the exhaustion which carved lines on his face. She was suddenly aware that she felt light-headed with tiredness herself and realised that if she sat down and relaxed, she would almost certainly fall asleep. And it must be worse for him, she told herself, bustling across to the pantry to fetch bread and margarine, porridge oats, tea and condensed milk. He had returned the previous day from America where the air force had sent him to train as a bomber pilot. He had tried to make light of his journey back to Britain but she guessed that the strain must have been considerable; no wonder he looked so weary.

Rose worked quickly and presently they sat down to porridge, tea and toast. They talked little as they ate and drank, but by the time the meal was over and Luke had pushed back his chair and stood up, Rose had made up her mind. He began, haltingly, to thank her for the food and to ask for directions, but she interrupted him. 'Luke, there are perfectly good beds upstairs and you are far too tired to go roaming the streets and so am I. We'll both go upstairs and sleep until, say, four o'clock. I'll set my alarm so you needn't worry on that score. Then we'll go to your lodgings and make sure they haven't been bombed. Don't you think that's more sensible than forcing ourselves to go on being wakeful and alert when we need sleep so desperately? I'm on the night shift tonight, and tomorrow I'll be visiting Rachel in hospital and then doing my firewatching stint. What do you say?'

She had risen when he did. Rose was tall, but even

so, she had to look up to catch Luke's eye. He was staring at her, looking undecided, but then a wide smile lightened his face for a moment, and he nodded. 'Sure, Rose, if you don't mind my borrowing a bed, I'd be downright glad to crash out for a few hours. I am pretty well jiggered, to tell you the truth.'

'Good,' Rose said, leading the way up the stairs. They had each had a brief wash at the sink, but right now all she cared about was getting some sleep. She opened her bedroom door, then paused on the threshold. She had meant to let Luke use Daisy and Petal's bed, but now she realised that this would be unfair. Like Steve, he was long-legged and would be horribly cramped in the children's small bed, so she guided him into the room, picked up her alarm clock as unobtrusively as possible and then backed out of the room again as he stood there looking almost owlishly around him. 'I'll bang on the door at four o'clock and we'll have a cup of tea and a sandwich, and then go along to your lodgings,' she said. 'Sleep well, Luke.'

Closing the door softly, she crossed the narrow landing and went into the children's room. By now, she was so tired that undressing seemed out of the question, but she pulled off her thin jersey and wriggled out of her grey skirt, noticing how dusty both garments had become and wrinkling her nose at the smell of burning which still clung to them, for several times during the walk from the hospital they had had to make their way through smoke from burning buildings. Sitting on the edge of the bed, she set the alarm for four o'clock, doing so with such exaggerated care that she might have been a drunk, striving to appear sober. Then, smiling at the thought, she tumbled into bed and pulled the blankets up round her ears. For a moment, she lay there, enjoying the crisp cleanness of the sheets and the softness of the pillows beneath her head, thinking that she was probably too tired to sleep. She thought about Daisy and Petal, safe and secure in the Larches, and wondered what Luke was thinking about. Then, abruptly, with his face still before her inward eye, she fell deeply and dreamlessly asleep.

Luke took off his outer clothing, folding tunic and trousers carefully, rolling his socks into a ball and stuffing them into the toe of his boot. Then he sat down on the bed and contemplated the room. He had guessed immediately that it must be Rose's, and not that of the small daughters. He also guessed why she had let him use it, and as he climbed between the sheets and stretched out his long legs he was grateful to her. Beds in England – or the ones that he had slept in, at any rate – were made kind of short, so that he always felt he was stubbing his toes, but this bed was grand, with plenty of space for a guy to stretch out. Carefully, he snuggled his head into the pillow and was immediately aware of a faint, sweet perfume. Even as he breathed it in, he remembered Rose's face. It was a nice face with widely set brown eyes, a small straight nose and a mouth which, when she smiled, tilted upwards and formed a deep dimple in one cheek. Her chin was small but determined, her figure neat, with curves in all the right places. She had told him she was the mother of two girls, but he thought there was no sign of it in either face or figure; she might have been no more than twenty. He wondered what the children were like; whether they favoured her or her husband. She had told him that her submariner had blond curly hair and had shown him small photographs of her husband and the two children, though he had not looked closely at either. Rose had told him that the younger child had Steve's blond curls but had not commented on the older one, and the photograph had been too small and fuzzy to tell him much. Rose's own hair was a shining, chestnut brown, not curly or even wavy, but cut in the pageboy style which some film star had made popular. When the sun fell on it, its russet hue gleamed with touches of gold, fawn and copper; yes, it was the sort of hair which could be described as a crowning glory.

Luke yawned and put one hand beneath the pillow, feeling something soft enmesh his fingers. He grinned to himself; it was her nightie, of course, pushed under the pillow to be out of the way. Doubtless there would be pyjamas – Steve's – under the other pillow. He slid his hand further along to check, but found nothing and supposed that the submariner had either taken his pyjamas away with him or stowed them in the chest of drawers beneath the window. Thinking of the chest of drawers made him remember that he had forgotten to draw the drapes before getting into bed. He opened one eye a slit; yes, sunshine was streaming in, making it quite impossible to get to sleep. He must certainly remedy this – in a moment, he would climb out of bed and pull the drapes across. In a moment . . . but right now it was so comfy . . . he felt so relaxed, so at home . . .

He slept.

Chapter Ten

It had been Edith's weekend off, so the children had enjoyed a rest from her constant nagging and nastiness. But all good things come to an end and on Sunday evening, when they came back from playing with some schoolfriends near the allotments on Chester Road, there was Edith, cooking a meal in the kitchen. She turned as they entered the room and said snappishly: 'The mistress has gone a-visitin', so you'll have an early tea and then go straight to bed. I can't be doin' wi' the pair of you under me feet all evenin'.'

'All right, Edith,' Daisy said peaceably. She had no desire to start a row with the older woman, especially when there was no Mrs Wyn Roberts to put Edith smartly in her place if she became openly aggressive towards the children. 'But is there anything we can do to help you? We could lay the table, or . . .'

Edith turned and stared at them for a moment and Daisy saw, with some surprise, that the woman's face held a strange expression she had not seen on it before. It was not a nice expression. She had a sort of half-grin on her face, and Daisy thought it was a gloating sort of grin. But perhaps, she told herself, as Edith said she needed no help, not from the likes of *them*, it was better than the look of truly evil bad temper which Edith frequently wore when her weekend off approached. Come to that, she usually came back to the Larches in a foul mood, which often lasted a couple of days, so perhaps the peculiarly pleased look was some sort of improvement.

'Well, if we can't help then we'll play in the garden for a bit,' Daisy said, turning away from the stove and heading for the back door. 'Come on, Petal.'

Petal, however, lingered. 'What's for tea, Edith?' she enquired hopefully. 'We went over to Laura's house after Sunday school and her mam was out so we didn't get anything to eat. I'm starving, so I am.'

Edith turned and gave them a particularly nasty look. 'Snot sangwidges and sick soup,' she grated. 'That's all you bleedin' well deserve, you grubbin', grabbin' little pair. Now gerrout o' me kitchen and don't come back till I calls you.'

Daisy turned to leave the room without a word but Petal stood her ground for a moment. 'You're a rude old woman,' she said calmly. 'And if Mrs Wyn Roberts were at home you wouldn't dare say such things. If you say 'em again I'll tell on you . . . to Mr Wyn Roberts, I think. He wouldn't care if you left, you know . . . he'd probably like it, so just you watch out, Edith!'

Edith turned and began to speak, but Daisy grabbed her small sister and dragged her from the room. They both dashed into the garden and right down to the bottom of it, where a sooty brick wall, at least twelve feet high, separated the Larches' garden from that of the house at the back. Daisy was pink and furious, but Petal, giggling, told her not to get in a fuss over old Edith. 'She hates us, I don't know why, but she really is scared of Mr Wyn Roberts, because she knows he doesn't like her much, and he isn't nearly as lazy as his wife and wouldn't mind if the old horror left,' she said cheerfully. 'I know that's true, because last time he was home he said he didn't know why his wife put up with her. He said that when the war's over the first thing he'll do is send old Edith back where she came from. So you see, she won't want us telling Mr Wyn Roberts about the things she says and does when there's only us kids to hear.'

Daisy smiled, but agreed that Petal was probably right. 'And she shouldn't talk to us the way she does,' she admitted. 'Only she's got us in her power in a way . . . she can make things jolly uncomfortable for us – and for Mrs Wyn Roberts – if she puts her mind to it. After all, she cooks and cleans and so on, and I can't see Mrs Wyn Roberts doing it for herself, can you?'

'No. But I say, Daisy, I *do* wonder where Edith goes on her weekends off, don't you? She doesn't seem to enjoy herself much, does she? And she nearly always comes back here in a nasty temper.'

'I used to think she lived somewhere lovely, like the farm, or perhaps even by the Welsh seaside,' Daisy said thoughtfully. 'But if so, you'd think she'd at least set off with a smile, wouldn't you? Yet she even puts off leaving on a Friday evening, quite often, and doesn't set out for the station until Saturday morning. Still, never mind her. Let's climb up into the old tree house; tea won't be ready for a bit.'

The tree house was Petal's delight, so the two of them spent a happy half-hour high in the branches of the big copper beech, but by the time Edith called them they were quite glad to descend, for their midday meal had been a sketchy one; Mrs Wyn Roberts had already left for her friend's house but had made some honey sandwiches and some paste ones, and had put them with a jug of milk on the kitchen table. She had left a note telling the children that Edith would make them a hot meal that evening, so by the time they were seated once more at the kitchen table they were eager for the food which Edith was dishing up.

It's a pity she's so horrid, Daisy told herself as she dug her fork into the slice of meat pie on her plate, because she really is a good cook. And she gets round the people in the shops, too, because I'm sure we have more meat than some folk do.

Edith took her place beside them and, catching Daisy's eye, gave her a creaky smile. Daisy thought her resemblance to a toad even more marked when she smiled but did not mean to do anything to annoy the old woman. After all, neither she nor Petal wanted to be enemies with Edith; life would be so much nicer if only the maid could bring herself to regard them with less malice. But Edith was smiling now, though with glittering eyes, so Daisy decided to see what reaction a friendly overture would receive. 'Did you have a nice weekend off, Edith?' she enquired. 'The weather has been lovely, hasn't it? Mrs Wyn Roberts got out our cotton dresses and said we might wear them for school tomorrow instead of our serge skirts and woollen cardigans.'

She half expected a snub, but instead Edith positively beamed at her. 'Oh aye, I had the best weekend of me life,' she said. 'I went to bed last night but I were woke up at ten o'clock by the sound o' bombs droppin'. So what did I do? I gorra coat on and went down to the Mersey – I go back to Birken'ead, you know, on me weekend off – an' what d'you think I saw?' She cackled triumphantly, blotchy colour rising in her unhealthy-looking face. 'I saw bloody Liverpool on fire, that's wharr I saw. I saw them great black bombers a-hammerin' of that stinkin' city until it were flattened. I saw the docks on fire and the big warehouses, and the little houses of them filthy scousers.'

She cackled again. 'I stayed up all night, cheerin' the bombers on, tellin' 'em to do a good job of it, to kill every bleedin' scouser what ever opened his mouth. Oh aye, the Jerries have taught 'em a lesson they won't forget in a hurry – 'cept I doubt there's anyone left alive to benefit by it.'

'I don't believe you,' Daisy said stoutly, after an incredulous moment. 'I think it's what you'd *like* to happen, though I'm sure I don't know why.' She squeezed Petal's hand reassuringly. 'It's just Edith's lies, Petal, like the snot sandwiches; she's trying to frighten us, that's all.'

Petal's face was white but she glared with hatred at Edith and raised her own small voice. 'You're a wicked liar, Edith. Why, if Liverpool was burned down, it would be on the news.' She glanced quickly up at the kitchen clock. 'It's nearly six now . . . turn it on, Daisy.'

'It'll be on the news awright,' Edith said gloatingly. 'But they won't say the whole place were flattened because they know the Jerries listen in an' they don't want the good news to get back to old Hitler.' She laughed, a sound the children had seldom heard before. 'I'm tellin' you, I could ha' read the *Echo* by the light of the fires blazin' and reflectin' in the water. Oh, it were a grand sight, a grand sight!'

'We still don't believe you,' Daisy said bravely, but there was a quiver in her voice. Somehow, the remark about reading a newspaper by the light of the fires rang horribly true and presently, when she turned on the wireless, the announcer's voice gave credence to what Edith had been saying. Liverpool had been heavily bombed on the previous night. Daisy did not resume her seat at the table but held out a hand to Petal, who had stopped eating as soon as Edith had dropped her bombshell. Then she looked steadily across at the old woman. 'Our mam is in Liverpool,' she said in a trembling voice. 'And all our friends . . . they're all there. And what have any of them done to you, Edith?'

Edith got to her feet and ambled across to the kitchen door, preventing the children from leaving by that route. 'You just get back to that table and eat the good food I've prepared,' she hissed. 'What have they done to me, you ask? Oh, nothin', of course! They just dismiss anyone who don't live in their stinkin' city as bein' third class citizens. Why, they even call Birken'ead the one-eyed city! They hates us . . . but not nearly as much as I hates them. I tell you I danced wi' delight as them bombs rained down. I prayed the Air Force wouldn't stick their long noses in, and nor they did. I cursed the bloody balloons and the fellers on the searchlights, an' I cheered on them Jerry pilots, wharrever they call theirselves. As for your mam, I dare say she might have gorrout somehow; you never know. Rats desert a sinkin' ship, they say, and—'

But Daisy had had enough. She ran full tilt at Edith, her head striking the old woman in the stomach and sending the air out of her lungs with a whoosh. Then, as Edith wheezed and gasped and began to curse, Daisy pushed her bodily away from the door, grabbed Petal's hand, and towed her out of the kitchen. The two of them raced up to their room and slammed the door. For a moment they just stared at each other, chests heaving, and then Petal hurled herself into Daisy's arms and the two little girls wept as if their hearts would break.

After ten minutes or so, Daisy pulled herself together and began to mop Petal's tears and tidy her small sister up. 'We know Liverpool was bombed 'cos the wireless said so,' she said. 'But it was bombed at

Christmas . . . it's been bombed quite a lot . . . and the old Germans didn't flatten it then, so I don't suppose they have now. It was just Edith being horrible and spiteful and trying to upset us.'

'Ye-es, only suppose she *were* telling the truth,' Petal said dismally. 'Suppose our mammy is hurt and wanting her little girls? Suppose she's in hospital? Oh, Daisy, suppose she's dead an' we're orfings!'

'Orphans,' Daisy said automatically. 'But I'm sure she's wrong. I'm sure our mam's all right, and all our friends as well. Only . . . only we've got to make sure. I'm going to go back right now. I'll leave a note for Mrs Wyn Roberts, telling her what's happened. I'm afraid I'll have to steal some money but you know what Mrs Wyn Roberts is like. She might not be home for hours and hours. And I want to go *now*!'

'I'm coming with you,' Petal said stoutly, rubbing the tears off her face with her dirty hands. 'Besides, if we wait for Mrs Wyn Roberts, you know what she'll say: she'll say we can't possibly go back to the city. She'll say she's sure our mammy's fine. She'll say we're in her charge and she'll promise to send a message and it'll be days before we find out what's really been happening.'

Daisy stared at Petal; for a kid of seven she was remarkably cool-headed. And presently she proved even more cool-headed, producing from her pocket two pieces of rather squashed pie, and handing one to Daisy. 'I took it off our plates while Edith were ranting,' she said cheerfully. 'I knew we'd be hungry later and wouldn't want to go back to the kitchen. Only why do we want money, Daisy?'

'Train tickets,' Daisy said briefly. 'Get me a bit of paper – tear a sheet out of your homework book – and I'll write the note. Then we'll go.'

Without a word, her small sister complied, and Daisy wrote a note in her neatest handwriting to Mrs Wyn Roberts, telling their foster mother what Edith had said and explaining that they had to go home to Bernard Terrace, but would return when they knew their mother was safe.

'In books they always pin notes to the pillow, but I don't know where the pins are kept and we can't waste time looking,' Daisy said, placing Petal's old teddy bear on top of the note. 'He'll hold it down, though, so it doesn't blow away.'

Petal gave an indignant squawk, snatched the teddy bear off the pillow and replaced it with a copy of *Five Children and It* which Daisy had been reading to her, a chapter at a time. 'Teddy's coming too,' she said firmly. 'Why, if I left him behind, Edith might cut his dear ears off, or throw him on the kitchen fire.'

Daisy realised that Petal might well be right and picked up her rag doll, pushing it into the satchel which she had just emptied out on to the floor. 'Put Teddy in your satchel, along with a cardigan and anything else we might need,' she said authoritatively. 'I expect Edith will be shovelling meat pie into her gob and thinking up more horrible lies for later, so we'll get going before she begins to wonder what we're up to.'

As quietly as they could, the children stole down the attic stairs and went into Mrs Wyn Roberts's bedroom. They knew she kept a small supply of cash in her bedside cabinet, though both children felt guilty as they opened the drawer. However, they need not have done so, for it was empty. 'Oh well, at least it's saved us from being thieves,' Daisy whispered, as they crept down the main staircase, carefully avoiding the creaky step three from the bottom. 'We'll nip out of the side door because our coats – the winter ones – hang there. If we have to sleep out of doors, then we can cover ourselves with those.'

Outside, it was still broad daylight, and the children felt almost happy as they hurried along towards Chester Road. 'If we were on the train, we'd go through Chester, or, at any rate, in that direction,' Daisy said as they walked. 'Are you hungry, Petal? If so, we'll nip into the allotments and get ourselves some peas and some new carrots. People wouldn't mind if they knew what's happened to us today.'

However, they were not destined to become vegetable thieves either, since several of the allotments were being worked by their owners, and anyway, as Petal said, the chunks of meat pie which they had messily devoured in their bedroom had filled them up quite nicely.

'I expect we'll get a lift soon,' Daisy said cheerfully, as they left the town behind. 'We'll tell people we came to visit our auntie for the weekend, but lost our return train tickets. Someone's bound to take us most of the way to Liverpool, even if not all the way. Best foot forward, Petal!'

They reached Liverpool in the early hours of Monday morning. They had been given several lifts, including one by an ATS officer and her driver on their way to Blackpool, and ended up being driven in a baker's van through the outskirts of the city. It was then that they discovered that Edith had not exaggerated, for fires still burned, lighting up the darkness, and the roads were covered in debris. Their driver, an elderly man with a thin humorous face, enormous porcelain teeth, and no more hair than a day-old baby, knew the city, he told them, like the palm of his hand and actually delivered them to Salisbury Street. The girls got out of the van, thanking him profusely, and waving until he was out of sight. Only then did they begin to look apprehensively around them. But though the sky was clear, they could see very little damage in the bright moonlight, and made their way to Bernard Terrace considerably relieved. They were approaching their own dear, familiar front door when a figure stepped out from between two houses, checked, then came towards them, wagging a disapproving head. It was a neighbour, Mr Bright, who lived further down the terrace, though at first the girls did not recognise him for his tin hat was pulled well down over his eyes, and his ARP uniform was covered in dust. He greeted the girls cheerfully, however, saying: 'What have we got here, young ladies? Oh, it's Daisy and Petal McAllister, isn't it? Why aren't you down a shelter somewhere? Don't you know there's a raid on? The All Clear hasn't gone yet.'

'Yes, it's us, Mr Bright,' Daisy admitted. 'We heard about the raids from someone who had been visiting over the weekend and we've come home because we had to know if our mam was all right.'

Mr Bright tutted indulgently. 'Oh well, I can understand that,' he said. 'Your mam's norrin, but I saw her yesterday evening and she were all right then; I reckon she were on her way to work. She stopped for a word – very cheerful she was – and I'm perishin' certain she had no idea you were headin' home. If you ask me, the worst of the raid's over, so mebbe you'd best go home an' have a few hours' sleep afore your mam gets back. I dare say she'll be awful mad wi' you, but no doubt you did it for the best. Come along, I'll see you inside. D'you have a Morrison shelter?'

'Yes,' Daisy said. 'I'll just fish the key up through the letter box . . .' By this time, they had reached the front door and Daisy realised, with some dismay, that there was no key dangling on a piece of string, to be fished up and used by any member of the McAllister family who needed to get inside. She turned wide, dismayed eyes up into Mr Bright's face. 'It's not there,' she quavered unhappily. 'How's we to get in, Mr Bright?'

It seemed like a knotty problem, but Mr Bright accompanied them down the jigger and across the small backyard where, to the children's great relief, he found that their mother had left the pantry window slightly ajar. It was the work of a moment for Mr Bright to hoist Petal through the window, and seconds later both children stood in the familiar kitchen, whilst Mr Bright, shouting a cheery goodnight, left them at last to their own devices.

'We'll have some bread and jam and a drink of milk, and then get to bed,' Daisy said, ushering her sister towards the kitchen table. 'And we'll have to go back to Wrexham in the morning because . . . well, because we'll have to.' She did not add that one of the many buildings missing from the familiar skyline had been the school she and Petal had attended. Petal had been very brave but there was no point in letting her see how near disaster had come. The school was only a few streets away; Bernard Terrace had been lucky.

Daisy cut thick slices of bread and spread them thinly with jam, filled a couple of mugs with a mixture of milk and water, and watched her sister drink and eat hungrily, following suit herself. The Morrison shelter had the same blankets in it which had been there at Christmas and Daisy smelt the familiar odour of brick dust, soot and damp – reminding her sharply of the Christmas bombing, when she and Petal had spent so many nights in the shelter, their mother beside them.

However, both children, utterly exhausted, slept for a couple of hours before waking abruptly to find that morning had arrived. Daisy sat up. The atmosphere of the house, which had once been so pleasant and friendly, seemed to have changed, to have become full of brooding menace. She sighed and crawled out of the shelter, not surprised that Petal followed her so swiftly that she could feel the little girl's nose bumping against the back of her legs. 'It's time we found out what's happened to Mam,' she said, straightening up. 'We can't stay here not knowing, so why don't we try to make our way to the factory on Long Lane? We can meet Mam out of work and explain what's been happening as we walk home.' She looked hopefully at the younger girl. 'Of course, if you'd rather stay in the house—'

'I wouldn't,' Petal said quickly. 'It 'ud be different if Mam were home, but – but it doesn't seem like our house, does it, Daisy? And were that the All Clear? If so, folk'll be comin' out of the shelter and someone might know if Mam's all right.'

'Right, I'm going to take the stuff out of my satchel and fill it with food for our breakfast,' Daisy said, suiting action to words, and presently the two children emerged on to Bernard Terrace once more. Daisy took a deep breath of the early morning air which, despite smells of burning, brick rubble and dust, seemed downright pleasant. No one was about yet but she still felt as though they had both escaped from some peril and smiled joyfully as they entered Salisbury Street. 'It's a lovely day; why don't we go to the gardens and eat our breakfast there? Why, we might meet

Nicky on his way to school . . . oh no, perhaps . . . or he might be coming up from the shelter any minute. I've really missed Nicky.'

Happy to be out of the house, which had suddenly seemed such a dangerous place to be, the children set off in the direction of Long Lane.

Rose woke early and looked around the small room in which she lay, totally confused for a moment. She had not gone to work after accompanying Luke to his lodging house, which was mercifully intact, because there was no work to go to. The factory had been bombed in the early hours of Sunday morning and damaged far too extensively for there to be any question of the workers returning there. Instead, she had visited Rachel in hospital to explain that some other premises would have to be found before the staff could make uniforms once more, and Rachel had begged her to spend the night in the little house which she had abandoned the night before.

'Mam and Dad won't be coming home for weeks; not until it's a lot safer than it is now,' Rachel had said. 'I'm so afraid that I may have left windows open or doors unlocked, and you know how dreadful people can be. If someone gets in and steals all our nice stuff, or wrecks the place, I'd never forgive myself, so would you be a dear and check up for me? It'll only be for a day or two; once they release me from here, I'll go straight to the house myself, though with the factory gone, it's tempting to take little Luke out into the country to stay with Mam and Dad.'

Rose had not been able to conceal her surprise, though she was pleased, too. 'You're going to call him Luke? What will Alby have to say to that?'

'Well, after big Luke was such a trump last night,

it seems the least I can do; if the baby had been a girl I'd have asked if I could call her after you. And I know Alby won't mind at all; he'll be just as grateful to big Luke as I am when he hears what happened, I'm sure. But, Rose, you will go and check on the house for me, won't you? I'll be really anxious until I hear that everything's all right.'

Rose had agreed, and when she left the hospital she had gone straight to the Edelmanns' house. She had checked all the windows and doors and then had gone round to the neighbours for a chat, explaining that she would be staying in the house to keep an eye on things for her friends until Rachel and the new baby returned from hospital. The neighbours had been really nice, friendly and helpful, but since they were in the habit of 'trekking' out of the city each night, they were not able to promise to look after anyone else's property. 'In fact, to be honest, my dear, we've been relying on Mrs Cohen to stop anyone breaking into our house,' Mrs Carruthers had said. 'She was adamant that she could not leave the area until after her baby was born, so she was quite willing to keep an eye on our place.' She was a small, wrinkled walnut of a woman, trying to do her best for her daughter and her four grandchildren, who had been bombed out of their own home and had come to live with her. She looked hopefully at Rose.

'Whilst I'm staying here, I'll do my best to keep your house safe as well as the Edelmanns',' Rose had said gently. 'But after the very heavy raid last night, I imagine the authorities may simply take over houses which are not occupied. Folk have got to live somewhere, after all.'

Mrs Carruthers had nodded sadly, her bright little brown eyes filling with tears. 'Me and my family have got to live somewhere too,' she had pointed out. 'Oh, Mrs McAllister, this is a wicked, wicked war.'

Rose had agreed and gone back into the Edelmanns' neat home, reflecting that her own house in Bernard Terrace would also be unprotected whilst she remained at the Edelmanns'. But I'll go back for a time each day, and the neighbours will make sure that no one takes it over, she had told herself. Yes, now that there's no factory, I'll be able to look after two homes until Rachel is on her feet again.

But right now, waking in Rachel's nightdress to see the May sunshine pouring between the Edelmanns' curtains, life did not seem too terrible. She felt all the better for a good night's sleep, able to cope once more with whatever lay ahead. Stretching luxuriously, she rolled out of bed and made her way downstairs to get some breakfast.

The sun was climbing as the children crossed Shaw Street and headed for Netherfield Road, and it was at this point that Daisy remembered that they could not catch a bus, even if one was running, because they had no money. Furious with her own stupidity, for the teapot on the mantelpiece always had cash in it, Daisy pulled Petal to a halt. 'We'd best go back to the house and find some pennies so's we can catch a tram or a bus when our legs is tired,' she said. 'Oh, *do* come along, Petal, don't drag!'

But Petal was tired and not at all keen on retracing her steps. However, a bus ride certainly had advantages when you were tired, so she followed her sister obediently. After all, being without any money whatsoever was not a good idea. Sighing, she tagged along behind Daisy.

* * *

Overhead, a lone Dornier bomber crippled by ack-ack fire sustained while attacking the shipbuilding yards at Barrow-in-Furness passed over the city of Liverpool, the crew no doubt rejoicing as they looked down on the fires still burning brightly below. Now, returning home, the pilot knew that the condition of the plane was so desperate that he must jettison the one remaining bomb he carried to lighten it. He pressed the bomb release and watched it plummet to earth, saw the enormous explosion in a part of the city which, from this height, looked relatively undamaged. Then he turned back to resume his interrupted conversation with the navigator.

Rose had her breakfast, checked the house once more, and then set off for her own home. There were a great many people about, some on their way to work, others hopefully carrying shopping bags, children going to school and air raid wardens and council workers roping off unsafe buildings and trying to answer a thousand questions as to the state of their homes from those returning to the city.

Rose greeted a good many people she knew, but continued on her way. She wanted to get back to the terrace as soon as she could, make sure that all was well there.

She crossed Netherfield Road, which was littered with debris, picking her way carefully around great shards of shattered glass. Men with brushes and shovels were clearing it as fast as they could, but there was nothing they could do about the tram lines which reared out of the road like angry snakes; there would be no trams running on this route today. When she reached Salisbury Street she could see no new damage and entered Bernard Terrace with a light step. She told herself that she would have to begin to look about her for another job, for though Steve's money arrived pretty regularly, she needed her own contribution and besides, she wanted to do her share towards ending this dreadful war so that life could return to normal again. She had always fancied the women's services, but because of the children – and her job in the uniform factory – she had never seriously thought of joining up. The children seemed happily settled with Mrs Wyn Roberts, however, and she certainly would not bring them back to this war-torn city.

In fact, as soon as Rachel gets out of hospital, she would . . . Rose's thoughts stopped dead, and she stopped too, unable to believe her eyes. The terrace was crowded with people, many of them friends and neighbours, but there were officials there, too, roping off . . .

No. 7, Bernard Terrace, was no longer there. Instead, there was a deep pit out of which reared a shaky-looking brick wall with the tattered remains of a double bed hanging from a beam which thrust out into empty air at what once must have been first floor height.

Rose took two tottering steps forward, then stopped again, her hand flying to her throat. It was incredible, impossible! Other houses in the Terrace showed gaping windows and someone's front door . . . it was her own . . . lay forlornly in the roadway, but otherwise, it was as though No. 7 had been scooped up by a giant hand – a hand which had taken care not to brush against Numbers 5 or 9, and had left them relatively unharmed – and crushed into dust. 'Mrs McAllister! Oh, my dear, what a relief! We thought . . . well, you can guess what we thought. Oh, thank God you're safe, but wharra terrible shock for you, to come home to this.'

It was Mrs Gray, looking white and strained. Rose

smiled tremulously. 'I couldn't believe my eyes when I came round the corner,' she said shakily. 'But why the crowd? And – and why does the rope stretch along your frontage and that of number nine? Your homes are all right, aren't they?'

Mrs Gray uttered a sound between a snort and a moan. 'You want to see the back, chuck,' she said. 'It were a lucky thing we were down the shelter 'cos the kitchen's only got three walls and no ceiling, and the back bedroom's gone. The warden just telled me your place received a direct hit, but number nine and our place got the blast. They say it ain't safe to go back in and that we've gorra find somewhere else to live for a while.'

Suddenly, her face was lit up by a wicked grin and she nudged Rose in the ribs. 'Mind you, we come up from the shelter afore the wardens an' them realised yours had been hit and me sons went into ours an' took out as much as they could. A' course we couldn't budge the beds but we got most of the small stuff out – food, pots an' pans, bedding, clothes and that – afore they roped it off.'

'I'm glad for you,' Rose said rather feebly. She wondered what the Grays would do now, how they would manage, but was aware, suddenly, that she already felt detached from Bernard Terrace. This catastrophe had made up her mind for her. Homeless now – and jobless too – she would be a liability not an asset if she remained in Liverpool. But if she joined up, then she could be truly useful, truly valuable.

One of the men who had been gingerly roping off the one tottering wall of No. 7 came over to Rose. 'Mrs McAllister? A neighbour pointed you out. I'm real sorry, queen, but I reckon you're a very lucky woman. Oh, I know the house is gone, along with all your goods and chattels, an' I know you've got nothin' left in the world but the clothes you stand up in, but Mrs Gray told me your children were evacuated to Wales a few months ago and your husband is in the Navy, so at least you've got your lives . . .'

Rose felt someone tugging her arm and looked round. Old Mr Bright stood there, his face grey with fatigue, his tin hat and uniform grey with cement dust. He said urgently: 'Missus, I'm that sorry and it were all my fault . . . honest to God, missus, I thought I were doin' it for the best. Oh, I'll never forgive myself if . . . if . . .'

For the first time since she had returned to the terrace, Rose smiled. 'I don't see how you can blame yourself for what the Jerries did, Mr Bright,' she said gently. 'It's a dreadful thing to have your home destroyed, but at least there wasn't any loss of life, so far as we know.'

'But – but there were; that's wharr I'm tryin' to tell you,' Mr Bright said, and to Rose's horror she saw tears brim up in the old man's eyes and trickle down his dust-covered cheeks. 'Them little girls o' yourn, missus, they come back last night. They wanted to make sure you hadn't been hurt, so I told them I'd seen you, and the planes had all gone, so . . . so . . .'

Rose stared at him, trying to take in what he was saying. 'The – the girls?' she quavered. 'But they're miles away, miles and miles. It couldn't have been Daisy and Petal. They're in Wrexham, in Wales. And – and they couldn't have got in. I always lock up pretty carefully before I leave the house and I did so last night. Honest to God, Mr Bright, you're mistaken, you have to be.'

Mr Bright shook his head dolefully. 'They were in there. You'd left a window open round the back and

I lifted the littl'un up so's she could squeeze through. She unbolted the back door and I told the pair of 'em to get inside the Morrison, just in case. Oh, missus, you'd best tell the fellers to start diggin'.'

Rose felt waves of faintness threaten to overcome her, but pushed them resolutely back. The Morrison shelter! People in Morrison shelters had been known to survive after their whole house had fallen on them . . . but a direct hit? She pushed her way through the thinning crowd until she could look down into the pit that had once been her home. If she could just see a corner of the Morrison shelter . . . but surely Mr Bright must be mistaken? He was old and did not know the children well. Some other child must have persuaded him that it was her home . . .

Rose looked down. There was something . . . something covered in dust, filthy and torn, but with bright brown glass eyes staring up at her. Her mind gave an unbearable jerk as she recognised Petal's teddy, and then waves of merciful darkness overcame her as she slid to the ground.

Rose came round and looked up, dizzily, at the circle of faces about her. She started to struggle, to try to get up, and found herself being lifted from the ground in a pair of strong arms. She had no idea what had happened or why she had fainted, but even as the man who held her began to speak, everything came rushing back and she burst into a storm of weeping.

'Rose! Now, Rosie, don't take on so. I know it was your home and you loved it, but . . .'

She recognised the soft American drawl at once, remembered the young airman who had been so kind, had helped her with Rachel. She wondered why he had come back, but it hardly seemed to matter. Nothing mattered but the terrible fear that her children were dead, buried beneath the ruins of their home.

She began to struggle and he set her down gently, putting both arms round her, trying to comfort her without knowing the reason for her distress. She tried to fight free of him, breaking into panicky speech. 'The children! My children! Oh, Luke, they were here. I thought Mr Bright was confused, but Petal's teddy . . . it stared up at me. Oh, Luke, they might be down there this minute, choking to death under all that rubble! I must get in there, I must!'

She would have ignored the rope barrier, scrambled down into the pit, but Luke held her firmly, but when she would have screamed and attacked him, another voice broke in, and a small and extremely grimy hand grabbed at her arm. Rose looked down and saw Nicky Bostock. He was filthy, as always, but his eyes were shining and he was shaking his head vehemently. 'They ain't dead, missus. Daisy and Petal ain't dead,' he said with emphasis. 'They gorrout of the house 'cos they were scared of bein' there without you, Daisy said. I met 'em earlier on. They'd been on their way to Long Lane when one of 'em thought to come back to the terrace to fetch a few pennies so's they could catch a bus. It's the divil of a long way out to Long Lane on foot, so they turned back, which was when I fell in with 'em. We were walkin' back to the terrace when we saw a plane kinda low; we actually saw something fall from it. We stopped where we was, starin' up – we were on Salisbury Street – and there was this huge explosion. It blew us off our feet – I cracked me elbow on the kerb an' young Petal grazed both knees and the palms of her hands. But that were all, honest to God it were.'

Rose stared at him, wanting desperately to believe

what he was saying, yet unable to forget the teddy bear, Petal's most dearly loved possession. 'But – but the teddy bear's lying there, amongst the rubble,' she said uncertainly. 'Are – are you sure they didn't go back to the house after the explosion, Nicky?'

'Course I'm sure,' Nicky said scornfully. 'Not that it would have mattered if we had gone back, because that explosion was the bomb that landed on the terrace, it must have been. But the bomb made Daisy decide not to bother about a few pennies, so we all turned back again and headed for Long Lane. I went with the kids as far as the recreation ground off Rice Lane. We had a great breakfast there, 'cos Daisy had stuffed her satchel, and Petal's, with grub. But then I remembered there might be trouble if Ma Ryan found out I'd not gone to the shelter, so I come back.'

'Oh, Nicky,' Rose breathed, almost fainting, but from relief this time. 'You don't know . . . I can't explain . . . oh, Nicky, thank you, thank you!'

She would have hugged him but Nicky, seeing the intention in her eye, stepped back smartly, holding up a grimy paw like a policeman halting traffic. 'No you don't,' he said reprovingly. 'I give you the good news but I don't expect to have you a-huggin' of me. What do you want me to do, missus? I reckon them kids will have found out you ain't at work by now.'

Rose began to answer him, to say that no doubt the children would soon return, when another thought occurred to her. She clapped a hand to her mouth, then lowered it again. 'Oh my God,' she said brokenly. 'The factory was bombed on Saturday night; they're going to think – they're going to think . . .'

Luke had released her but he still had a comforting arm round her shoulders and now he gave her a squeeze. 'I know what you were going to say, but I'm sure you're wrong; they won't conclude that you're dead or badly hurt,' he said bracingly. 'I don't know this Long Lane, nor your factory, but they've only got to ask anyone in that neighbourhood when the factory was bombed and they'll be told that it was Saturday night. And remember, they know you were alive and kicking on Sunday because they met Mr Bright and he told them so.' He turned to the old man who was still sniffing dolefully and mopping his eyes with a large checked handkerchief. 'Isn't that so, Mr Bright?'

The old man nodded. 'Aye, I telled 'em you were all right when I met you on Sunday evening, when we'd had a word,' he admitted. 'And I thank God that I didn't send them to their death, oh, I thank God.'

Edith was still in a good mood when she came downstairs on Monday morning to make breakfast. She got out the porridge oats and began to measure them into a large saucepan, adding water, a little milk and then a good dollop of black market butter; she had obtained it herself, though Mrs Wyn Roberts had paid for it, so she knew it was black market. Then she added a hefty spoonful of brown sugar and carried the pan over to the stove. Mrs Wyn Roberts loved Edith's porridge, frequently remarking that no one else, not the best hotel in the country, could make better porridge than her Edith. Folk had asked Edith for the recipe but she would never give it since she was well aware that the soft life she led could only be maintained so long as Mrs Wyn Roberts could not find a better cook anywhere in the area. She lit the gas under the pan, fetched a wooden spoon and began to stir. She reflected that, in peacetime, the porridge would have been just the beginning of an excellent breakfast which would have gone on to eggs, bacon and kidneys, perhaps a nice pair of kippers or a flavoursome piece of smoked haddock, and would have finished up with freshly baked bread, lashings of butter, and as much Seville marmalade as you could pile on each round of toast. Now, of course, breakfast began and ended with porridge, so she made a great deal.

Presently, Edith began to wonder what the children were up to. Usually, at this hour of the morning, there was a considerable racket from upstairs as the girls got out their school clothes and put their weekend things into the laundry basket. Edith reflected, grimly, that she did not mind how much washing the girls made since it was done by Mrs Llew. Mrs Llew took the washing home on a Monday and brought it back cleaned and ironed on a Tuesday. Then she stayed for the whole of the rest of the day, doing what Edith called 'the rough work', scrubbing floors, brushing acres of carpet, polishing furniture and washing down paintwork, tiles, and anything else which needed cleaning.

The porridge began to simmer gently and Edith put the lid on the pan and began to pour a cup of tea, just as she heard Mrs Wyn Roberts's step on the stair. Her mistress came into the kitchen, smiling brightly. 'Good morning, Edith,' she said. 'Aren't I kind to you today? It's so beautifully bright and sunny that I woke early and thought I'd save you having to climb the stairs by taking my morning cuppa in the white drawing room. Has the post been yet? Oh, and I thought the children would already be up, but since they obviously aren't I fear you'll have to climb the stairs anyway, to rouse them. We can't have them late for school, can we?'

'No, m'm; I'll go up at once, m'm,' Edith said agreeably, but with murder in her heart. Bloody kids!

As if she didn't have enough to do without waitin' hand and foot on a pair of slummies. Still, Mrs Wyn Roberts seemed quite attached to the dirty little tykes, so she'd best go up and wake them. She would quite enjoy giving them a good shake and a slap round the face, and then saying her hand had slipped.

Edith carried Mrs Wyn Roberts's cup of tea through to the white drawing room, thinking resentfully that it would not have hurt her mistress to carry her own cup. But of course she did not voice her thoughts aloud. She never intended to let the younger woman know the depth of her dislike and resentment. She was as near happy as she could be at the Larches, and did not mean to jeopardise her position by an unguarded word.

Presently, she stomped up two flights of stairs and threw open the door to the girls' room. She was astonished to find the bed neatly made and no sign of either child, and though she had not investigated she was pretty sure they had not been in the bathroom on the first floor of the house. She supposed, angrily, that they must have gone off to meet friends before school, but then she remembered that neither child had had breakfast and thought it unlikely that they would have left the house, because it would have given her an excuse to deprive them of the meal.

She was just about to stomp off downstairs again, brimming over with righteous wrath at such ingratitude, when she saw the note. Even without reading it, she felt sweat start on her forehead, felt her hands grow clammy. She crossed the room and grabbed the note, then read it.

Dear Auntie Clara,

Edith went back to Birkenhed for her weekend

off and told us about the bombing. She told us all of Liverpool had been flattened and she thinks heaps and heaps of people have been killed. She is glad of this as she does not like scowsers but we are afraid for our mam and our friends who are scowsers too. We could not wait for you to come home as Edith said you were always late when you went to call on that silly old woman, so we have gone now (six o'clock). We will come back when we know our mam is safe. Please do not worry, we shall be all right.
With love from Daisy and Petal xx

Edith read the letter a second time, rage mounting in her so fast that her breathing grew short and her cheeks hot. Then she scrumpled the letter up and pushed it, viciously, into her skirt pocket. Mrs Wyn Roberts was certainly not going to read that! If she had done so, Edith might have been blamed for the children's disappearance, and what was more, Mrs Wyn Roberts would have discovered that Edith thought her mistress's sister a silly old woman. She might even have guessed that Edith had deliberately frightened the children, though she had never dreamed that they would run away, silly little fools. She would just have to brazen it out, remember that she had heard something on the wireless about the bombing of Liverpool, pretend it had been that which had sent the children off on what was sure to be a wild goose chase.

She was halfway down the stairs when a cheering thought occurred to her. If the children had reached Liverpool and there had been another raid the previous night, then they might easily have been killed or badly injured, which would mean that she would be shot of them at last.

Edith descended the rest of the stairs with a spring

in her step, arranging her expression to read alarm and puzzlement. She entered the white drawing room, dramatically flinging the door wide and saying in a hollow voice: 'Oh, Mrs Wyn Roberts, their bed ain't been slept in. They've gorn orff, God knows where.'

Mrs Wyn Roberts was deeply distressed by the sudden disappearance of her young guests but did not know what to do for the best. Fortunately, she went first to the school and spoke to Daisy's teacher, who immediately gave it as her opinion that the girls must have heard about the bombing of Liverpool and wanted to see for themselves whether friends and relatives were safe.

'But how could they do such a thing?' Mrs Wyn Roberts wailed. 'They said nothing to Edith and didn't leave me a note, which is most unlike Daisy, who is a very thoughtful child. They had no money, they took nothing with them – well, apart from Petal's teddy and Daisy's rag doll – and it's an awfully long way to Liverpool. And then there's the Mersey. How could two little girls cope with that?'

The teacher, Miss Rhoda Jones, admitted that it seemed almost impossible that two penniless children could cross such a wide tract of country. 'But both girls are bright and resourceful, and in these difficult times folk are not slow to give lifts,' she reminded the other woman. 'I know the bombing was bad because a friend of mine visited her parents in Wallasey over the weekend, and said the fires from bombed buildings and shipping could be seen for miles. If someone told the children, I'm sure their one desire would have been to get back to their mother. Do you happen to know where Mrs McAllister works?'

'No, not really; I believe she makes uniforms for

the forces,' Mrs Wyn Roberts said vaguely. 'And it isn't as if they're on the telephone, otherwise I could ring.'

'Send a telegram, Mrs Wyn Roberts,' the teacher advised. 'I take it you know Mrs McAllister's Liverpool address? And you can send a prepaid reply, you know, which would mean you'll know what has been happening by the end of the day.'

'Oh, but suppose they haven't gone home? Mrs McAllister will think me careless and unfeeling to lose her children,' Mrs Wyn Roberts pointed out. 'I'm really very fond of them both – they are dear little girls, polite and helpful – but I can't be everywhere at once. I spent yesterday with my sister, but the children weren't alone. Edith – my housekeeper – was with them. She assures me she put them to bed and saw that they had everything they wanted before going to bed herself.'

'I'm sure no blame will attach to anyone,' the teacher said reassuringly. 'If the children have not yet reached home, though, the police must be alerted to keep a lookout and find the girls before harm comes to them. In fact, I think you should inform the local police in any event.'

'I'll do so at once,' Mrs Wyn Roberts said. 'Thank you so much for your help and advice, Miss Jones. I shall, of course, let you know what is happening as soon as I know myself.'

The teacher smiled. 'I shall be most grateful,' she said. 'Daisy is one of my favourite pupils – though teachers are not allowed to have favourites – and Petal is both lively and affectionate. You are lucky in your evacuees, Mrs Wyn Roberts, and I'm sure they are lucky, too.'

Chapter Eleven

There was a glorious reunion, of course. Luke had insisted on hailing a taxi to take himself and Rose out to Long Lane, and it was a good thing he had done so, since they arrived at their destination to find two terrified, ashen-faced children staring at the shell of the factory with tears running down their cheeks. Clearly, they had not had time to make enquiries about the raid which had done such damage and assumed it must have taken place the previous night. The taxi drew up with a squeal of brakes and Rose hurtled out of it, screaming: 'Daisy, Petal! Oh, my darlings, you're safe! Thank God you didn't stay in Bernard Terrace this morning.' She hugged the children convulsively, kneeling down on the pavement amidst all the rubble and glass, to get to the children's level. 'But whatever made you come back to Liverpool? Did someone tell you about the bombing? My loves, the bombing was the reason you were sent away in the first place; I wanted to keep you safe.'

'Mammy, oh, Mammy,' Petal sobbed, burying her face against her mother's shoulder. 'We did hear about the bombing – horrible Edith told us – and we had to make sure you were all right.'

'Oh, Mammy, if you'd been in the factory, you might have been killed,' Daisy sobbed. 'Can't we stay with you? Can't we all go away from the bombing? There must be somewhere safe and you can't say you've got to be near your factory, 'cos it's all in bits.'

Rose was suddenly aware that she was kneeling on something horribly sharp and got hastily to her feet, as an agonising pain shot through her knee. Glancing down she saw, to her horror, that a jagged sliver of glass was sticking out of it and that blood was pouring forth. Petal and Daisy squeaked with fright, but Luke was more practical. He crouched on the pavement and gently removed the glass, then squeezed at the wound, causing it to bleed even more freely. 'The blood will wash out any fragments of glass left in,' Luke said. 'I've got a clean handkerchief, but it's a long cut and quite a deep one; I think we should make for the nearest first aid post. I told the taxi to wait, so he can take us.'

As he spoke, he was knotting a large white handkerchief round the injury, tying it so tightly that Rose doubted if she would be able to walk, but in seconds the handkerchief was scarlet with blood and though she said, faintly, that she was sure she would be all right, did not need hospital treatment, she made no objection when Luke half carried her to the taxi and thrust her and the girls inside, then climbed in after them. 'The lady's knelt on some glass; take us to the nearest first aid post, please,' he said.

Luke did not say so to Rose, but the depth and position of her wound, and the fact that the jagged piece of glass which he had removed from it might have left splinters behind, worried him. The pavement and the glass were both filthy, and from the amount of blood pumping forth he feared that Rose might be in real trouble if she was not dealt with quickly. However, it would not do to let the children see he was worried. So he smiled reassuringly at them and introduced himself. 'I'm a friend of your mom's. My name's Luke

Nadolski. We'll get your mom some treatment, where they can put a couple of stitches in her knee, and then we'll decide what to do next.'

'When the doctors have made Mammy all right, we could go home and have some dinner,' Petal said longingly. 'We did have breakfast, didn't we, Daisy? But it were an awful long time ago.'

Luke glanced at Rose. He felt it should be she who told the children that their home no longer existed, but the poor girl was leaning back against the cracked leather upholstery, eyes closed and face ashen. He did not think she was listening to the conversation; she was probably half fainting. Sighing inwardly, he squared his shoulders and spoke as gently as he could. 'Your home was bombed this morning, honey. But we'll get you a meal somehow, as soon as your mom is better. Then, of course, we'll have to find you all beds for the night, though you'll be going back to Wales tomorrow, I expect.'

Daisy's small face set in lines of sheer obstinacy. 'We're never going back to that place again,' she said. 'Mrs Wyn Roberts – Auntie Clara, I mean – is quite a nice woman, but Edith is really, really horrible. I think Mrs Wyn Roberts is afraid of her; at any rate, she never stops her being beastly to us. Why, the reason we came home was because Edith told us that Liverpool had been flattened and that almost everyone was dead. She said the docks were on fire and she said she danced with joy as the bombs fell. We told her she was a wicked woman, but she didn't mind at all. She hates us, just because we're scousers, and we'd far rather risk being bombed than go near her ever again.'

'I see,' Luke said slowly. 'But what in God's name are scousers? Is it another word for little girls, honey?'

'It's what folk call Liverpudlians,' Rose said, in a thin, faint voice, and Luke saw that she was actually smiling. 'Has Edith been nasty to you before, pets? You've never said.'

'She's always been absolutely *awful*,' Daisy assured her mother. 'But we didn't want to upset you so we never said anything. Only this time, when she said she danced with joy to see the flames . . . oh, Mam, we just couldn't bear it.'

'The evil old witch,' Luke said feelingly. 'Doesn't that Mrs what's her name, Auntie Clara, have any control over her?'

Daisy sighed patiently. 'Mrs Wyn Roberts is kind but very lazy; Edith does all the cooking and most of the housework, so I suppose Auntie Clara closes her ears to Edith's nastiness for the sake of her treacle tart,' she said ingenuously. 'Edith is friendly with all the black market spivs – I heard someone say that – so she gets all sorts of extras. Auntie Clara has to pay for them, but she doesn't have to . . . to . . .'

'Doesn't have to dirty her hands or admit to herself that she's cheating,' Luke supplied. 'I think the sooner you're away from that place, the better; don't you agree, Rose?'

But, to his alarm, he saw that Rose was in no state to answer. Her head had fallen sideways and even as they drew up, she fell heavily against his shoulder.

Luke felt cold with fear for a moment, but then common sense came to his aid. She was breathing gently but quite normally, so far as he could judge, and one way and another she had been through quite an ordeal. So he scooped her up in his arms and ducked out of the cab, then spoke to the taxi driver. 'Wait for me,' he said briefly. 'And you kids stay in the cab until I come back. I shan't be long.'

He glanced at the girls' frightened faces and hesitated, then turned back towards them, giving them his most reassuring grin. 'It's all right, babes, your mom's fainted, that's all, and no wonder! She thought the pair of you were in the house when it was bombed, and then there's her poor leg, which must have hurt like— like nobody's business. So just you stay there and I'll be back in two minutes, see if I'm not, and your mom with me, right as rain once more.'

Because Rose insisted, they went to Bernard Terrace. She hustled the children past the remains of No.7, telling them not to look, but of course she guessed that they had done so when she saw them staring at each other wide-eyed, perhaps realising for the first time what a narrow escape they had had.

Rose meant to call on Miss Ada Finch, who was living on her own at No. 14. Rose was hopeful that Miss Finch might be able to let them have a room for a few nights, just whilst they made alternative arrangements, but this proved impossible. 'My dear, if I could help, I would, you know that,' she said warmly, clasping Rose's hand. 'But my sister Freda, her two daughters and the baby were bombed out on Sat'day night, and my brother Tom's house was hit on Sunday, so I don't have an inch of space to spare. But there must be someone else who could take you in . . .' Turning away from No.14, Rose felt her shoulders droop. It seemed she had no alternative; the children would have to return to Wrexham and she would have to find herself some sort of place to go, even if it were only an air raid shelter.

She said as much to Luke and he offered to go with her to take the children back to Mrs Wyn Roberts, though they were declaring, stoutly, that they would not leave their mother. 'If you make us go back, we'll run away again,' Daisy said tearfully. 'That Edith is the wickedest woman in the world; she spits in the soup and tells us there's snot sarnies for tea. Last week, she told Petal the sausage rolls had dog turds in and I couldn't eat my tea even though I knew it was lies. Petal told Auntie Clara that Edith had said there were turtles in the sausage rolls – she got the word wrong – but Auntie Clara just said that Edith was teasing.'

'Then Auntie Clara gobbled up the sausage rolls herself, so they weren't wasted,' Petal said dolefully. 'Mrs Wyn Roberts is greedy, Mammy, that's why she buys black market stuff and won't ever tell Edith off, or get rid of her. Oh, I won't, I won't go back!'

Rose looked, speakingly, across at Luke, as they walked back towards the ruin of No. 7. 'I don't see how I can possibly keep the children with me, since I simply have to work and we've got nowhere to live,' she murmured, drawing closer to Luke and keeping her voice low. 'I had hoped to join up – after all, I could still visit them regularly whenever I got leave – but if they won't go back to Mrs Wyn Roberts, I just don't know what I should do.'

'I guess the kids have a point, though,' Luke said. 'You wouldn't want to send them back knowing what that Edith is like, would you?'

Rose looked up into his troubled face and realised that he was absolutely right. Her children had always been truthful and it was pretty plain that no matter how kind Mrs Wyn Roberts might be, it was really Edith who had the most to do with Daisy and Petal. I must be going mad, she thought remorsefully, to consider for one moment letting them return to the Larches. But dear God, what can I do?

'No, I wouldn't – want to send them back, I mean – now that I know the situation, and I'm ashamed that it took you, a virtual stranger, to make me see sense,' she said humbly. 'My children mean more to me than anything else and I am so keen to ensure their safety that I can't have been thinking straight. Thank you, Luke, for making me see clearly.' She turned to the children as they approached No.7, looking down at Petal and smiling encouragingly. 'If there's a warden or a worker handy, sweetheart, I'm going to ask if they can fetch out your teddy bear and Daisy's rag doll, because they were both visible when I came over earlier. Otherwise, the chances are they – and everything else – will be looted as soon as the authorities leave the terrace.'

'Oh, good,' Petal said, beaming. 'I love my teddy next to you, Mammy – no, next to you and Daisy. I wonder if we might go back to Auntie Blod's? D'you think we could, Mammy?'

'That would be an ideal solution, of course . . .' Rose was beginning, when Luke pointed. There were men working on the tumbled ruin of the house, and already a number of artefacts were neatly lined up on the pavement: several saucepans, a pile of dust-covered blankets, some extremely chipped and dirty ornaments, a handful of cutlery, several Bakelite mugs and plates, and next to them – oh joy! – Petal's patched and faded teddy bear and Daisy's beloved rag doll.

The children pounced on their possessions with cries of joy and Rose was just about to approach the workers to thank them for their efforts when a telegram boy skidded into the terrace and came to a halt outside No. 7. He stared hard at the ruined house, then looked across at Rose. 'You Mrs McAllister? Telegram for you.'

Rose gave a little gasp. All her life, she had been afraid of telegrams, but she took the small yellow envelope, saying brightly: 'I am silly. Of course, it will be from Mrs Wyn Roberts. I know you left a note, darling, but you could only tell her you were coming back to Liverpool; she must have been half out of her mind with worry, imagining you lost, or in bad company.' As she spoke, she slit open the envelope and pulled out the sheet within and began to read.

The Admiralty regrets to announce that HMS/M Centurion *is ten days overdue and must be presumed lost with all hands stop.*

Rose stared blindly down at the ground whilst pictures formed in her mind. Steve, on their wedding day, proud and sure of himself, giving her a hug as they emerged from the church. Steve holding Daisy in his arms when she was about a week old, looking down at her tiny face with affection; he had wanted a boy but had seemed fond of Daisy at first. Steve playing football with a crowd of kids and young men, kicking the ball so hard that it had sailed right over the rooftops and disappeared into Mary Terrace. Steve bursting into the house after his first long voyage, with a fluffy toy for the baby and a necklace of polished stones for herself. But there were other pictures, of course, pictures which she would have to try hard not to remember. Steve, red-faced and angry, punching her in the mouth, kicking her as she lay on the floor, dragging her up by the hair and screaming at her because she had annoyed him in some trivial fashion. Steve swearing at the neighbours if they knocked on the wall because of the drunken din he was making. Worst of all, Steve holding Daisy up by her hair with one hand while he hit her across the face with the other, and Petal tried in vain to drag him away. She saw them all, the incidents, petty and horrendous which had ruined their marriage, turning Steve into a monster and herself into a victim.

She realised she was folding the telegram into a tiny square, unfolding it, pleating it into an accordion, then folding it up again. Anything rather than having to take in the implications of the words on the buff-coloured paper between her hands. Oddly, Steve had been happier aboard the submarine than he had ever been in his life before, or so she had grown to believe. The cramped and dangerous life lived by the thirty-three men aboard HMS/M *Centurion* seemed to suit him completely. Shared danger, shared excitement, the new skills he was learning, combined to make him truly proud. It was sad and terrible that Steve, the submariner, was dead and maybe, in the fullness of time, she would be able to weep for him, but Steve McAllister, husband and father . . . her mind shied away from the truth, then faced it steadily. She, and her daughters, would be infinitely better off without him.

'Mammy?' It was Daisy, eyes anxious in her small, pale face. 'Mammy, is it from Mrs Wyn Roberts?'

Rose shook her head dumbly and felt Luke take the small piece of paper from her fingers and spread it out. 'No, it's not from Mrs Wyn Roberts,' he said gently. 'It's – it's bad news, kids. HMS/M *Centurion* is ten days overdue and that almost certainly means . . .'

'Our dad's on that boat,' Petal said at once. 'Does that mean he's overdue, too?'

'It does,' Luke said diffidently. Rose saw him glance hopefully at her, but shock seemed to have deprived her of speech and she listened as he went on: 'It – it may mean that your dad won't be coming home any more.'

'Well, he isn't coming home any more,' Daisy said at once. 'After he hit me and dragged me indoors by my hair, Mam promised he wouldn't come home ever again. So why is someone sending us a telegram, telling us what we know already? And why is Mammy upset?'

Rose pulled herself together with a big effort. It was not fair to leave Luke, who was almost a stranger, to try to explain to Steve's daughters that their father was dead. So she said: 'The Admiralty have sent a telegram to tell us that your dad was almost certainly lost at sea . . .' and was amazed at the firmness of her own voice. 'Can you understand that?'

Daisy nodded solemnly but said nothing, though she put out a hand and took Petal's small paw in her own. Petal's face crumpled and she turned her head away but Rose saw the tears on the child's cheeks and thought how sad it was that only Petal could cry for her father's death. She bent and lifted the child up, trying to give what comfort she could, but after a moment Petal gave an enormous sniff, knuckled her eyes and wriggled out of her mother's arms. 'I wish Daddy had just gone away like you said he would, but perhaps he'll be happier in heaven than he would have been in Portsmouth,' she said philosophically. 'Mammy, couldn't we just get on a train and go and see Auntie Blod? We did so love it there, me an' Daisy, and – and we hated the noise and the fires and that, last night.'

Rose had recently acquired a wristwatch and now she glanced down at it. It was still early and what was to keep them here, after all? It was quite possible that someone else in the Ruthin area might be able to take the children, even if the Williams family could not. A personal visit would be quicker and much simpler than trying to get in touch by letter. 'I think you're right, Petal,' she said slowly. 'Even if Auntie Blod can't have you, someone else might have a spare bedroom. There are pubs which do rooms so we could stay there for a couple of nights at least, whilst I sort myself out.'

The children beamed with satisfaction and ran ahead, beginning to chatter excitedly, and Rose turned to Luke, pulling a wry face. 'I'm so sorry to have involved you in our troubles,' she said formally, holding out her hand. 'Thank you so much for all your help; we'll never forget you, the girls and I. Goodbye; perhaps we'll meet again some day.'

Luke laughed. 'You aren't getting rid of me that easily, ma'am,' he told her. 'Any chance of me getting to this Ruthin and back in a day? If so, I'll come with you; why not? After all, I've got nothing else to do until I catch the 10.35 to Lincoln tomorrow morning. If the trains are still running by then, that is,' he ended.

Rose was guiltily aware that her heart gave a decided leap. Adult company, in her present state, would be very welcome and she both liked and trusted this young American serviceman who had come to her aid at one of the worst moments in her life so far. So she smiled up at him, assuring him that the train journey was unlikely to take more than a couple of hours, and thanked him again for his kindness.

Luke, however, would have none of it. 'I'm not being kind, I happen to enjoy your company and, as I said, I've nothing much else to do,' he told her. 'Besides, I really don't think you're in any state to cope with whatever else life might throw at you. You've lost your home, your husband and your job and whether you know it or not, you must still be in a state of shock. It'll hit you later, believe me, and when it does,

I'd be happier if you were with friends, or at least with people who are well disposed towards you and the children.'

Rose could only thank him again. At his prompting, she sent a telegram to Mrs Wyn Roberts, explaining what had happened and asking her to send the children's possessions to Ty Siriol. She knew kindly Mrs Williams would pass their stuff on as soon as they had a permanent address.

Lime Street station was closed because of unexploded bombs so they caught the boat over to Rock Ferry where they got on a train to Chester. There, the four of them got aboard the train which would take them to Ruthin. Luke had bought sandwiches from the buffet at Chester station and a rather stale-looking pork pie, and the children regarded this unexciting fare as a picnic and began clamouring to eat it almost as soon as the train drew out of the station. He had also provided himself with a notebook and some stubs of pencil, and soon the four of them were playing word games, and I Spy, and gazing out at the sunny countryside speeding past. The journey seemed to pass in a flash and they reached Ty Siriol before noon, to be greeted with rapture by Auntie Blod, who wept with happiness as she hugged the children and Rose. Before anyone could explain, she also hugged Luke, exclaiming that it was grand to meet Mr McAllister at last and telling him that he had the best wife and the nicest children in the world.

Petal laughed wildly, but said sunnily that this was Mammy's kind friend and that Daddy had gone to Jesus that very day.

Poor Auntie Blodwen looked very confused, as well she might, Rose thought. But when the children raced into the yard to find Dilys, she was able to explain the whole situation to the older woman. Luke, ever tactful, had left the kitchen in the children's wake, so Rose and Auntie Blod settled themselves at the kitchen table with cups of tea and home-made scones, and Rose told her everything that had happened, including the unsuitability of the evacuation home which had been found for the children in Wrexham. 'It was a lovely house and the Wyn Robertses are lovely people, but they employ a housekeeper called Edith . . .'

Blodwen Williams was shocked by the story but assured Rose that she had done right to bring the children back to Ty Siriol. 'We had three Land Girls, but now I'm back on my feet and able to cope we've only got the one, so the children's room is empty again,' she said cheerfully. 'I'm afraid I can't offer to put you and your gentleman friend up – that's to say, you could share the children's room, as you used to, but—'

'It's all right, Luke is going back to the city tonight, since he is due on his airfield in Lincolnshire sometime tomorrow,' Rose said. 'But Blodwen, I wouldn't expect you to accommodate a man I hardly know myself! I did tell you we only met on Saturday night . . .'

'Of course, of course, cariad,' Blodwen said, looking embarrassed. 'I'm an old fool, but when the four of you came into the kitchen . . . well, you looked such a happy little family . . .'

'Yes, I know what you mean,' Rose said, nodding. 'Now there's something else we must discuss, because you must realise that the children have nothing, no clothes, no ration books, not so much as a penny piece between them. I didn't think when we simply headed for the train, but I suppose we should have gone to a centre somewhere, to get emergency ration cards and some sort of clothing. I have telegraphed Mrs Wyn Roberts asking her to forward the children's stuff to this address, but I don't know how long it will be before it arrives. I had planned to ask you if I could stay for a night or two, but will the authorities in Ruthin be prepared to do anything for us, or shall I have to return to Liverpool?'

'You leave it to me, my dear,' Blodwen said, getting to her feet. 'There's a centre in Ruthin, manned by the WVS . . . you stay here and give an eye to the children and get some dinner on the table. I'll take the pony trap into Ruthin and sort things out . . .'

Next day, Rose stood on the platform at Edge Hill station, seeing Luke off. The children had been so happy to be back at Ty Siriol once more that she had decided to return to the city when the American did. She knew she should have contacted the authorities and was actually able to do so before the offices closed for the day, and then she and Luke had visited Rachel, and Rose had brought her friend up to date with everything that had happened. Rachel had been deeply sympathetic, both about Steve's death and the bombing of the house in Bernard Terrace, and offered the use of her parents' house for as long as Rose needed a roof over her head. Rose had thanked her, saying that it would be lovely if she could stay there one more night, but that after that she was taking over Luke's room in his lodging house until she could make more permanent arrangements.

Luke had seen her settled into his lodging house, assuring her that she could pay him back as soon as she had sorted out her affairs. 'I'll give you my address, the telephone number of the base and the name of the nearest train station; then you can write with your own address, as soon as you've got one, and that will mean we don't lose touch,' he had told her, scribbling on a piece of white card and handing it to her. 'Put that away safely and don't you dare lose it. I've enjoyed being with you and the kids more than I can say – yesterday was just like a holiday, if a rather eventful one – so I refuse to let you chuck me out of your life, or disappear into the wide blue yonder.'

Now, they were standing on the platform, being jostled by people, mainly service men and women, hurrying to get aboard the waiting train. Luke took hold of her upper arms and swayed her gently from side to side, smiling down into her face as he did so. 'You're a grand person, Rose McAllister, and you've taken the sort of punishment which would have had a lesser woman on her knees, but you're still in there, fighting. I know there was maybe friction between you and your husband, that there wasn't much love lost, but even so, I guess there were good times and you'll want a bit of space before you let anyone else get close to you. But when you do feel you need a – friend, I want it to be me. Is that asking too much?'

Rose stared at him, then gave him a push towards the train. 'Get in, Luke, or you won't find a seat, and it's no fun standing in a crowded corridor for miles and miles,' she said urgently. 'I – I know what you're trying to say, or I think I do, and you're right. My marriage turned sour years ago and it's made me . . . well, not scared of men exactly, but – but wary of them. But if friendship is all— Oh my God, they're shutting the doors! Get in, or you'll be left behind.'

Luke grinned, grabbed her and planted a resounding kiss on her astonished mouth, then leaped into the train just as it began to move. The guard shouted at him, but he slammed the door and leaned out of the window, at what seemed to Rose a perilous angle. 'Write as soon as you're settled,' he shouted. 'And join the WAAF, if that's what you really want. Remember, Rosie, your new life starts here . . .'

But whatever words might have followed, Rose heard none of them above the clatter of the departing train and the long blast of the guard's whistle. She waved until the train was out of sight and then made her way, thoughtfully, out of the station. All she had in the world were the clothes she stood up in, her gas mask in its case, and a few shillings which Luke had insisted upon lending her. If she joined one of the services, they would provide her with everything she needed, including accommodation, and, of course, a uniform. They would pay her a wage, feed her, give her leave when it was due so that she might see her children, and transport her, free, from one place to another. What felt more important than anything else at present, however, was that, when she put on a uniform, the responsibility for her future would be hers no longer. The army, the air force or even the Navy would take that responsibility from shoulders which, she felt right now, were no longer capable of bearing the weight. Resolute at last, she began to walk towards the recruiting office.

Within three days of bidding Luke farewell, Rose also said goodbye – for the time at least – to Liverpool, and her civilian life there. She had joined the WAAF and set out for the nearest training centre with a light heart, feeling Luke had been right: her new life was beginning.

Chapter Twelve

By the time America entered the war on 8 December, 1941, Rose was a fully fledged WAAF, about to take a week's leave before going to her first permanent posting, which was to an airfield in Norfolk. She went first to Liverpool to visit Rachel, who was once more established in the little house in Langsdale Street. It had suffered some blast damage while Rachel was still in hospital, and although the roof had been roughly patched up and some of the glass in the blown-out windows replaced, it was no longer the cosy, well-furnished home it had once been, for there had been not only destruction, but also looting, and the Edelmanns – who had moved back in – and Rachel had had to refurnish the place with anything they could find. Utility furniture was available, but it was poor stuff so in the main, the family bought second hand and managed well enough.

Rose only meant to stay one night in the city and then go on to Ty Siriol, but in fact, Rachel begged her to stay a little longer so that she might see Alby, whose ship was due in any day. Rose was pleased enough to do so for the baby, now seven months old, was a delightful little chap, and since she had been made his godmother, though by proxy, she felt she ought to spare him some time. Also, Rachel wanted to know all about life in the WAAF. She told Rose that had it not been for little Luke, she, too, would have joined up. But circumstances had made it impossible and anyway, the uniform factory was flourishing once more, though it was no longer in its original building but in a huge hangar which had been converted so that the girls might continue their work. Rachel complained that it had been rather stuffy in summer and was draughty in winter, but she was good at her work and the money came in useful.

Rose was willing enough to tell Rachel all about the WAAF because she felt she had found her niche at last. The WAAF had taught her to drive a car, a bus or a large lorry, had sent her on courses to learn how engines worked and had trained her in the art of telling others what to do without appearing either bossy or self-opinionated. She had only been at the training centre for three months, then had spent three months as a sort of roving driver, being sent around to any airfield which needed her. But this posting was to be a proper one; she might remain there for the rest of her service, or of course she might be moved on. Everything depended on the needs of the air force.

'So far, I've been billeted in all sorts of places,' she told Rachel. 'Mostly, we're in what they call huts, which are pretty basic affairs. They usually hold around twenty WAAFs, and each one of us has a small iron bedstead, a very small locker for personal possessions, and a bit of wall where we can pin up photographs or posters . . . stuff like that. Most huts have ablutions either attached or a short way away, but one of our billets provided us with a tin basin each, and two of the girls would be told off each morning to go and fill great big enamel jugs with water and each girl got about a pint to wash in. Then, once a week, they marched us to the public baths, where we could have a good soak and get properly clean.'

'Lord, I wouldn't like that,' Rachel said disapprovingly. 'Don't they give you curtains or anything so you can have a good wash in privacy?'

Rose laughed. The two girls were sitting in the Edelmanns' kitchen, with baby Luke asleep in his wickerwork cradle and a vegetable stew simmering on the stove. Mr and Mrs Edelmann had gone to the cinema, knowing that their daughter and her friend would have a lot to talk about, so Rose had no hesitation in assuring Rachel that modesty was simply impossible when twenty or thirty girls were crammed into a hut like sardines into a tin. 'But believe me, queen, it's a good deal better than civvy street, when you've been bombed out,' she added. 'I'll never forget the three days I spent in Liverpool after Bernard Terrace was bombed; I knew what it was then to be a Displaced Person. The authorities sent me to a church hall where I was allocated an emergency ration card, free passes for the British Restaurant and the Public Baths, and a pillow and a couple of rather thin blankets. The WVS were marvellous, and the folk in the British Restaurants, but you couldn't help feeling you were accepting charity. If I hadn't known I would be leaving it behind me, I think my self-esteem would have disappeared without trace.'

Rachel smiled affectionately at her friend. 'I think the war has changed everyone, though not always for the better,' she said. 'But it's changed you most of all. You always seemed a little bit unsure of yourself, a bit apologetic. You always dressed nicely but you didn't have the pride in your appearance which you've obviously got now.' She hesitated. 'I – I know your marriage wasn't always a very happy one, but I think it isn't just being widowed that has changed you. I really do think it must be the WAAF.'

'It is the WAAF,' Rose acknowledged at once.

'Steve had almost convinced me that I was useless, just another silly female, good for nothing but scrubbing floors and making meals. Then the war came along and I got a proper job, and earned proper money, and I began to think that there was more to me than Steve thought. His death didn't really change anything, but joining the WAAF . . . oh, Rachel, it's been the making of me. I never thought I'd learn to drive, be taught how engines work, be a truly useful member of a big community, but I've done all those things and I don't believe I've come to the end of what I can do yet.'

'And what about Luke what's his name?' Rachel asked curiously. 'I know you exchange letters, but have you met up? He seemed to like you a lot, I thought.'

'No, we've not met since May, but he's just a friend,' Rose said at once. She stood up and went over to the cradle where the baby was beginning to stir and pucker his lips in a suggestive sort of way. 'I think the young master is hungry; can I pick him up and have a play with him whilst you get his bottle?'

In March 1942, Rose was posted to Coltishall, in Norfolk.

Now, she took the big camouflaged lorries up to HQ when supplies were needed and spent quite a lot of time in denims. She had told Rachel that she and Luke had only exchanged letters, but as she entered the mess one dank October afternoon someone called out to her that she was wanted on the telephone. Rose hurried across to the instrument and recognised Luke's transatlantic drawl immediately. 'Well hello, honey! I've been posted, along with my whole crew. We've moved from Lincolnshire to East Wretham in Norfolk, so I reckon we could meet up, if you're willing? D'you realise, it's almost eighteen months since we first met, so I thought it was high time I made contact. I'd like to take you out for a meal if you can get away this evening. Your liberty trucks will take you to Castle Meadow in Norwich I guess, same as ours?'

'That's right,' Rose said, half reluctantly. She was not sure that meeting Luke again was a good idea at all.

'I thought so. Then how about it?'

Rose hesitated. Writing to Luke was fine, but actually seeing him might be going a bit too far. Since joining the WAAF, she had discovered the joys of independence and found she had no wish to change them. She had been asked out by a great number of men and had turned them all down without compunction. She had seen other girls get involved, seen how their normal cheery dispositions changed as anxiety for the safety of the young men who flew off almost nightly on their dangerous missions began to affect them. Because she had had no strong feelings for Steve, she had not allowed herself to worry overmuch when he went into danger, but she knew, instinctively, that it would be very different if she allowed herself to love someone. Loving anyone brings anxiety in its train; she had seen how fear for Alby had made even the placid Rachel jumpy and nervous, watching the dock gates as though staring in that direction would bring Alby safely through them. But she could scarcely say this to Luke, who had been such a support to her during the May Blitz. So, since she was not on duty that evening, she arranged to meet him on Castle Meadow at around seven o'clock.

As she made her way to her hut to get ready, she told herself that sharing a meal was not like going to the cinema or to a dance hall. They would sit on opposite sides of a small table, eat good food and tell each other about their lives. She supposed that he might give her a friendly kiss on parting, but perhaps, if she were quick enough, they might shake hands instead. At any rate, he had said he wanted her friendship and that was something which she might rather enjoy. She had a good many friends amongst the girls in her flight, but young men did not seem content with friendship and wanted something more. If Luke was really different . . .

Rose went to the rendezvous and did not immediately recognise Luke among all the other RAF personnel, but as soon as Luke grinned at her she knew him and was surprised at the warmth of her own pleasure upon seeing his tall figure approaching. She thought he looked somehow older since their last meeting, but she knew from her own experience that bomber pilots, with the responsibility for getting their crews, as well as themselves, to and from their targets in safety, were apt to develop worry lines ahead of their time. Luke flew Wellington bombers, she knew, though because of the censor his letters had usually dealt more with his life on the ground than with his time in the air.

But he was coming to meet her, a broad grin on his craggy, attractive face, both hands held out. 'Rosie!' he said warmly. 'I hardly recognised you. You look tremendously smart. How have you been keeping? How are the kids? Gee, we've got so much catching up to do . . . I've booked a table at the Castle Hotel for seven fifteen, so if we hurry we'll be able to get ourselves a drink before we eat. How well d'you know Norwich?'

He took her hand as he spoke; it would have seemed churlish to snatch it away, so Rose left her fingers in his as they crossed the width of Castle Meadow, avoiding a couple of buses and a swarm of cyclists as they did so. As soon as she reached the further pavement, however, she gently disengaged herself, pretending to fuss with her gas mask case. 'I know the city quite well, but I've never risen to the heights of the Castle Hotel, not even been inside its doors,' she admitted. 'I've been round the cathedral and visited several churches – there's supposed to be one for every day of the year, did you know that? – and of course, I've been to most of the cinemas and pubs. How about you?'

'I scarcely know it at all; this is only my second visit,' Luke explained. 'But there's heaps to do here, not counting cinemas, dance halls and pubs.' He hesitated. 'Things a couple of pals could do together. In the summer, there are the Broads – we could hire a boat and take ourselves off for a whole day – and the fellers tell me there are still places on the coast where the beach isn't mined, so one can swim. It's a great place for birds – waders, sea birds and the like – so we could take my binoculars and spend a day down on the salt marshes, watching for summer visitors. Still, for now, it's just a meal and a chat; is that right?'

Rose smiled at him. His words seemed to imply that he really did want friendship – only friendship. He really was most awfully nice and was not put off because she was not looking for a boyfriend, and that was good enough for her.

'There are a great many stately homes as well,' she said eagerly as they entered the Castle Hotel. 'Did you know Anne Boleyn was born and brought up just down the road from here, in Blickling Hall? I don't suppose it's possible to go inside the house in wartime, but there's nothing to stop us looking at the outside, only I don't know about buses and how often they run, and I expect it's too far to walk.'

'That's no problem,' Luke said at once, leading her to a softly lit bar, already full of men and women in service uniform. 'I've a seventh share in an old car – what the fellers in my crew call a jalopy – so we can get about in that, provided you can give me a day or so's notice of your off-duty time. The whole crew chipped in and we take it in turns to use it, but Toby – he's my tail gunner – and myself have it most often; the rest of the fellers seem to want the city more than the country, so they use the liberty truck mostly. Now, what would you like to drink?'

It had been a grand evening, Rose thought, as she climbed into the liberty truck and took her place on the little tin ledge which served for a seat. The meal had been good – as wartime meals went – and the company, she thought, had been even better. Luke had talked a great deal, filling her in on all the details of his life before the war, when he had been 'Stateside' as he called it. He had explained that he came from what he dubbed Middle America, a small introspective town where his father ran a gas station and garage, and his mother had managed the grocery store attached. Just before the war in Europe started, his father had taken his elder brother Max into the business, bought the empty lot next door, and started selling new cars. Max was good at it, using all his considerable charm to persuade folk to buy from them rather than going forty miles further on to the only other dealer in the area.

'Did you work for your father?' Rose had asked, but Luke had shaken his head so vigorously that his dark brown hair had flopped across his brow. 'No way, sister! I've always wanted to fly, ever since my Uncle Bob took me for a flip in an old string bag which was part of an air circus. I would have joined the American Army Air Force as soon as I left school, but I was too young; they wouldn't take me. So I went into what you might call civil aviation, only they wouldn't let me fly – too young again – so I learned all about aero engines. By the time the war broke out over here, I was a pretty useful aero engine mechanic. I'd done some flying on the side, mind you, pretending I had to test the engines which I'd just repaired, but then your war came along, and I volunteered for the RAF.'

'And walked straight into the Blitz,' Rose had said, smiling at him. 'Poor old Luke, what a ghastly beginning!'

Luke had smiled too, showing the amazingly white teeth which seemed typical of all American servicemen. 'No, you've got that wrong,' he had assured her. 'I came over by sea and joined up in '40 and what d'you think they did? They looked at the forms I'd filled in and listened to how I'd been involved with aviation ever since leaving school, and sent me straight back to Texas to get myself trained as a flyer. I don't believe I said, but my mom came over from the old country – England, I mean – when she was only four, and she's still passionate about the place.'

In return, Rose had told Luke something about her own childhood and adolescence, though she had steered clear of her marriage, save to talk about the children. She had told him that she had received a somewhat stiff letter from Mrs Wyn Roberts but had not let it worry her since she felt that both she and her daughters had done the right thing. Mrs Wyn Roberts had claimed that the girls had left her no note, had not even told Edith of their plans, but though Rose was certain that Daisy and Petal had told her the truth, that they had left a note, she did not think it worthwhile telling Mrs Wyn Roberts so. Neither had she pointed out that Edith had lied when she had claimed to have checked on the children last thing at night since, had it been true, Daisy and Petal would not have had time to reach Bernard Terrace in the early hours of the morning, before their house had been bombed.

'And I'm sure the Wyn Robertses and that horrible Edith soon forgot all about my girls and would probably have been happier having no evacuees at all,' she had commented. 'And the children are happy at Ty Siriol, so happy that their letters are far shorter than they were when they were living at the Larches. In fact, I believe Auntie Blod has to sit them down at the kitchen table once a week and make them write a page each, so that I know what they're up to.' She had smiled across the table at Luke. 'Not being a parent, you can't imagine how it eases my mind to know that the girls are both safe and happy.'

Luke had clicked his tongue at her. 'Just because I'm not a parent, it doesn't mean I've no imagination,' he had said gently. 'I thought Mrs Williams a very great lady, but of course I wouldn't know Mrs Wyn Roberts if we met face to face on the sidewalk.' He had cocked an intelligent eyebrow at Rose. 'I wonder what sort of evacuees she got next,' he had said musingly. 'Whoever they are, I bet she isn't finding them as easy as Daisy and Petal.'

'No, I bet she isn't,' Rose had said with a chuckle. 'I never replied to her letter because I felt she was criticising the children when she said they had not left her a note, but she was pretty nice to us, really. She always put me up when I went visiting and I believe she was fond of the girls. I wonder if it's too late to drop her a postcard, just telling her that I'm in the WAAF now and that the children have gone back to their first foster home.'

'Good idea,' Luke had said, approvingly, just as the waiter approached the table and handed them both the dessert menu. 'Gee, they've got ice cream . . . and apple pie; I wonder if I could have both?'

When the postcard arrived, it took Mrs Wyn Roberts several moments to realise who Rosemary McAllister was, for it was nearly eighteen months since Daisy and Petal had left. When she remembered, she could not help thinking that the great changes which had happened in her life would never have occurred but for those two little girls. Then she scolded herself for the thought, which she knew to be unfair. It had not been their fault that Edith had been caught out in a lie – several lies – and even though Mrs Wyn Roberts had been forced to tell the authorities that the girls had left it was not exactly their fault, either, that she now had two boisterous and unmanageable teenage boys and a mother and young baby, both of whom whined and wept more often than they smiled, living under her roof. So Mrs Wyn Roberts sat down at the table and read Rose's card and let her mind go back to what had really started it all.

She had been sitting at the kitchen table, placidly shelling peas whilst Edith peeled potatoes at the sink. It was only a couple of weeks after the girls had left and Mr Wyn Roberts was coming home, so they were preparing a special dinner for that night. She remembered she had been singing a little song under her breath, whilst Edith had been chuntering on about the rudeness of the butcher when she had suggested he might produce some kidneys for the master's breakfast. A brief knock on the back door had interrupted her thoughts and Mrs Llew had entered the room carrying two linen pillow cases full of clean washing.

'Mornin', Mrs Wyn Roberts. There you are, all nicely ironed, with the master's collars starched as good as any laundry,' she had said breathlessly. 'I put the clothes in one pillow case and the bed linen, along o' towels an' that, in the other.'

'Thank you, Mrs Llew; you're a treasure. How much do I owe you?' Mrs Wyn Roberts had asked, although the sum was invariably the same.

'Three and sixpence, if you please, ma'am,' Mrs Llew had said. 'Unless you want to wait and pay it all together at the end of the week.'

Mrs Wyn Roberts smiled but shook her head. Mrs Llew always made the same offer, but she was dependent on the money she earned and would have been dismayed had her employer not paid up at once. 'Right you are, three and six it is,' she had said, reaching across the table and abstracting her purse from her handbag. She produced two half-crowns. 'Have you any change, or would you put the extra one and six towards what I pay you at the end of the week?'

It was polite to ask the question, but again she had known what the response would be. 'I've got change,' Mrs Llew had said at once, dipping into the pocket of her wraparound overall. She fished out a handful of loose cash, then gave an exclamation. 'Bless me, I meant to give you this as soon as I walked through the door. I found it among the washing when I were sortin' it into whites and coloureds. A bit crumpled it were, so you may ha' read it and throwed it away, but even so . . .'

She had handed over a creased piece of paper, clearly torn from an exercise book. Mrs Wyn Roberts had glanced at it incuriously, then flattened it out on to the table and read every word. Only when she had done so did she turn to Mrs Llew, saying in a cold, emotionless voice: 'Where did you find this, Mrs Llew?' As she spoke, she had glanced across to the sink where Edith was still peeling potatoes, but the older woman had not so much as turned her head.

'Oh, it were in the pocket of that old grey skirt, the one with soup stains all down the front,' Mrs Llew had said blithely. 'And a rare job it was, getting those stains out, but I done it, as you see.' And on the words, she had produced a droopy grey skirt from the nearest pillow case and spread it out so that Mrs Wyn Roberts could see that it was clean.

The movement must have attracted Edith's attention for she had swung round, stared at the skirt and then at the piece of paper spread flat on the table, and even as Mrs Wyn Roberts watched, her neck and face had become blotched with scarlet and her hands had begun to writhe together.

Mrs Wyn Roberts had been so angry that she felt the heat rise in her own cheeks. 'There *was* a letter from Daisy and Petal,' she had said, her voice shaking. 'And you denied it, Edith. You went up to the children's room, read the note they had left for me, realised that it implicated you and hid it away in your pocket. Well, you weren't as clever as you meant to be because you never destroyed it and now I know what sort of person you really are.'

'I – I kept it from you because – because it weren't none o' your business . . . I mean, none of what they said about me were true. All that rubbish about spittin' in your soup puttin' dog turds in the sausage rolls . . . it were just kids' lies to get me into trouble. So why should I hand it to you, eh?'

Considerably bewildered, Mrs Wyn Roberts had stared from Edith to the note and back again. 'You were glad that Liverpool was bombed and told the children so, even though you knew their mother lived and worked in the city,' she had said slowly, choosing her words with care. She realised that, in her panic, Edith had actually forgotten what had been written in the note. 'So it is none of my business if you spit in the soup, Edith? None of my business if you put dog do in the sausage rolls? What a very odd idea you must have of me! But the reason that I'm telling you to leave my house at once, and never to darken my door again, is because you deliberately tried to terrify two little children by telling them their home had been flattened and their mother was probably dead, and you were glad of it, to say nothing of the lies you've told me. Go on, pack your things.'

Edith had stared at her as though she could not believe her ears, her eyes bulging and her tongue flicking in and out to moisten her big, flat lips. For several moments, she had not spoken, then words came out of her in a torrent. Horrible words. All the spite which she must have been harbouring for years against her mistress came out in a flood of foul language and fouler sentiments, until suddenly Mrs Llew had surged forward, caught Edith by the shoulders, shoved her physically out of the kitchen and slammed the door on her. Then she turned to her employer. 'What a wicked woman; how dared she use such filthy language in front of you, ma'am,' she had said, patting her employer's shoulder with one huge, work-roughened hand. 'I hope as you won't blame me for giving you the piece of paper, but it were addressed to you and

I thought it only right. Truth to tell, I never even read it, so I'm not too sure what the children said.'

Silently, Mrs Wyn Roberts had handed her the paper and Mrs Llew had read it to herself, her lips forming each word as she did so, for Welsh was her first language and clearly reading English was a chore. When she had finished it, she turned her puzzled red face towards Mrs Wyn Roberts. 'But – but there's nothing about spittin' in the soup,' she had said wonderingly. 'Nor nothin' about dog do in the sausage rolls; why ever did Edith say . . .?'

'She'd forgotten what was in the note, but she remembered some of the nasty things she'd said to the children,' Mrs Wyn Roberts had explained. 'Well, my husband never liked the woman, so at least someone will be pleased.'

'You'll be wantin' another housekeeper, though,' Mrs Llew had said brightly. 'I know a nice, respectable woman who'd be willing to come in daily, though I doubt she'd want to live in. Want me to have a word?'

Mrs Wyn Roberts had employed Mrs Llew's friend within a couple of days of Edith's outraged departure, for the woman had not left quietly. She had threatened to take revenge on the Larches, to burn it down, to tell the police that there were illegal goings-on, to do her mistress some mischief in the fullness of time. Then she had stormed out and it was only much later that Mrs Wyn Roberts had discovered that her housekeeper's suitcase had contained, besides Edith's own possessions, the Meissen figurines from the white drawing room, the silver cutlery used for best, all the loose change from Mrs Wyn Roberts's bedside drawer and the garnet necklace and earrings which Mr Wyn Roberts had given his wife on their wedding day.

Now, sitting at the kitchen table with Rose's card

before her, and the din of the evacuees preparing for school and thundering up and down the stairs making her wince, Mrs Wyn Roberts decided that in fairness she must write to Rose McAllister and tell her about the discovery of the note and Edith's subsequent departure. Smiling to herself, she got up and went to the white drawing room to fetch pen, ink and paper, just as Joshua and Simon came charging down the stairs, skidded across the hall leaving boot marks on the black and white tiles, and disappeared into the kitchen. For a moment, she wondered whether she should go back and dole out the porridge which was simmering on the stove, for the new housekeeper arrived at nine o'clock, after the boys had gone to school. But as she was turning back, Evelyn Brown, with her squawking baby under one arm, came down the stairs and also headed for the kitchen. Let her do it for once, Mrs Wyn Roberts thought rebelliously, closing the door of the white drawing room behind her. She's idle and discontented and it's about time she learned to pull her weight. Oh, how I long for Mrs McAllister, Daisy and Petal. Those were the days! But no matter how difficult life was for her now, she never longed for Edith.

Chapter Thirteen
January 1943

'Come along, Petal, stop mooning or we'll be late. Miss Hastings is ever so nice but she does hate it when someone comes in in the middle of prayers.'

'Oh, but the hedgerows look so beautiful with frost on everything and the sun making each twig glitter,' Petal said reverently. 'Now that Mam is away from the city and out on that airfield, do you suppose she sees beautiful frosts like these?'

Daisy was a cold little creature; no matter how warmly she was wrapped, her nose, toes and finger-tips always went numb when it was frosty, and when she got to school, and into the comparative warmth, they would throb and ache with the returning blood, and if she were unlucky she might get a crop of chilblains. Even so, she could not help admiring the beauty of the delicate frost tracery on every branch and twig and decided, on the spur of the moment, that if it was still cold at the weekend, they would go into the hills. There was a stream up there which sometimes froze in severe weather and a cavern where icicles formed, some of them as long as a foot.

She put the thought into words, adding that they would ask Nicky to accompany them. She still remem-bered her delight when Nicky had turned up once more in Ruthin.

It had been three days after their own return, and at first Daisy had scarcely believed her eyes. She had only caught a glimpse of him as he crossed the playground after classes had started, and since she had only seen his back view she told herself, sternly, that it could have been anyone. But when playtime had arrived, and the whole school had erupted into the yard, she saw at once that she had not been mistaken. Nicky was surrounded by a group of friends, all of whom clearly remembered him from his first brief stay amongst them, but as soon as he saw Daisy he had come across to her, his face splitting into a wide grin.

'Bet you never expected to see me, queen,' he had greeted her. 'In fact no one expected to see me, norrin this neck o' the woods, but we was bombed out on Monday night – poor old Bernard Terrace is beginnin' to look like a gob full of teeth with half of 'em missin'. I'm thirteen now, old enough to be useful, which is why the Ryans took me back to Bernard Terrace in the first place. They'd ha' kept me there, too, if the house hadn't bought it, so they had to go an' live wi' Mr Bob Ryan and his wife, and there weren't room for me, an' when I saw the WVS ladies about a billet, I said I'd come back to Mrs Foley, if she could have me. They telephoned to the Town Hall and someone went round to the butcher's shop in Clwyd Street and Mrs Foley said if I'd give a hand in the shop an' help with her vegetable garden, she'd fit me in. So a' course I agreed, an' they give me a spare pair of kecks, a jacket an' shirt and an emergency ration card, and one of 'em put me on the train, and here I am.'

He had grinned down at Daisy and she realised, suddenly, how much he had grown since the two of them had last played Relievio in the school yard. She had said as much, but Nicky had only laughed. 'You see'd me when your house were hit and we had our picnic in the rec, and that were only a few days ago,' he had reminded her. 'I don't reckon I've growed much since then.'

Daisy had laughed. 'I know what you mean but I'm not talking about *then*, I'm talking about the last time we were in this playground. I've got taller as well, so has Petal, but you've really shot up, Nicky.'

But that had been over eighteen months ago and as she and Petal had settled happily into the farm, Nicky had done the same with the Foleys. He slept in a little attic at the top of the tall, tottery house, and worked pretty hard for his foster parents. However, they were very fair with him, allowing him time off so that he could go around with his friends, and treating him more like a son than the Ryans ever had. 'It's because their sons is both growed up,' Nicky had explained to Daisy. 'The Ryans have got a heap o' kids which are *really* their own, so they didn't need me at all, except to look after the younger ones and now Bert can do that – he's next to me in age. I were just another mouth to feed, a nuisance really. But the Foleys have only got me, so they can take time to get to know me. And they notice that I work hard and want to get on; I reckon I'm in clover!'

So now, Daisy and Petal hurried into school, and when playtime arrived Daisy suggested that Nicky might like to go up into the hills with them at the weekend. He agreed enthusiastically, as she had known he would, and reminded her that the tops of the hills, at any rate, were covered by a blanket of snow. 'We can nab a couple o' trays from somewhere and go down the hills on 'em, like on a sledge,' he said eagerly. 'It'll be grand, better'n Havelock Street, 'cos once when I went down there on me tray, I couldn't stop an' I shot straight into Netherfield Road and nearly got flattened by a coal lorry.'

Daisy nodded wisely, though she and Petal had never been allowed to sledge anywhere in the city, let alone down Havelock Street, which was known to be both steep and dangerous. 'We'll get the trays . . . we might even get a proper sledge,' Daisy said, with a vague memory of Dilys telling her how she and her brother had taken their sledge up into the hills every winter. 'Have you ever made a snow house, Nicky? They're called igloos. When Dilys was a little girl, she and her brother used to make them when the snow was deep enough. I'd like to do that.'

'Me too,' Petal chimed in at once. 'We could take a sort of winter picnic; Auntie Blod always has a cake, or some sausage rolls or something, tucked away in her larder.'

'That 'ud be grand,' Nicky said. 'Tell you what, I'll get Uncle Bill to look out some bits and pieces of meat and that, to give to Mrs Williams.' He grinned at them, tapping the side of his nose and winking as he did so. 'There's always some farmer, somewhere, what's hid away a pig or a sheep for slaughter, which won't go through the Ministry books. Oh aye, Uncle Bill will gi' me a parcel o' bits when I explain Mrs Williams will be feedin' me.'

The bell rang at this point and the children had to return to their classes, but before she left to go to her own room, Petal gave Daisy's hand a squeeze. 'Couldn't we ask Maldwyn if he could come to the hills with us as well?' she whispered. 'It'll be much more fun if there are four of us.'

Daisy and Petal had made all the arrangements for a day in the hills by Thursday evening. They would not be able to set out until around noon, because Nicky was needed in the shop on a Saturday morning, but since Maldwyn also worked on the farm at weekends, and the two girls did their share of any tasks of which

Auntie Blod thought them capable, this was no bad thing. Petal pointed out that if they had waited until Sunday they could have started earlier, immediately after church, but having made their plans they decided to stick to them.

On Friday, coming back from school in the pony trap, Dilys, who was driving, remarked that Petal looked flushed. 'I've got a perishin' cold,' Petal said, energetically blowing her nose into a rather inadequate handkerchief. 'But a day in the open air will do me lots of good because it's that stuffy classroom which has made me sneeze; the chalk dust and that, you know.'

Dilys laughed, but said that she would make Petal a hot cup of tea with a spoonful of whisky in it, as soon as they reached home. 'And if I were you, I'd go straight to bed after supper,' she advised the child. 'Then you'll be fighting fit for your expedition tomorrow. It don't do to ignore a cold, cariad.'

For once, Petal did as she was told and went snuffling off to bed, clasping her rubber hot water bag, as soon as supper was over. But next morning, when Daisy hopped out of bed and swished back the curtains and pulled up the blackout blind, she turned a disappointed face towards her small sister, still cuddled down in bed. 'Oh, Petal, can you see? It must have been snowing for hours; the yard's inches deep and there's still quite a few flakes falling. I bet Auntie Blod won't let us out of the house on a day like this.'

Petal shot up in bed, indignation written all over her small face. 'But we *must* go,' she wailed. 'I went to bed early and drank that beastly drink so's we could go to the hills today. And Nicky and Maldwyn will be coming over as soon as they've done their jobs. Oh, Daisy, we must, we must go!'

'Well, we might as well get up and dress,' Daisy said tactfully. There was no point in letting Petal get in a state for no real reason, for though the snow in the yard looked deep, it was probably only three or four inches and might be no impediment to their plans. The girls got up, washed and dressed with an anxious eye on the weather, and by the time they had made their beds and descended into the kitchen, things looked a good deal more hopeful. The snow had stopped, the dark grey clouds had blown away, and the sun was shining out of a clear blue sky, although it was still extremely cold.

As soon as breakfast was finished, Daisy and Petal did their chores. Petal dusted and swept the carpet in the living room with the Ewbank whilst Daisy, muffled in her thick winter coat, went and helped Dilys to clean down the dairy and sterilise the big milk pans and the butter-making equipment. Then she went into the cowshed and collected the stainless steel milk pails, taking them back into the kitchen where Auntie Blod cleaned them out with boiling water and a good deal of elbow grease. After that, the two girls helped Auntie Blod in the kitchen until noon, making themselves and the boys a mound of sandwiches and cutting up a whole fruit cake into large wedges, as well as popping a couple of bottles of lemonade into the haversack which Daisy sincerely hoped that Nicky, as the eldest, would carry. A rap on the door heralded his arrival, complete with an old and battered tin tray under one arm and a brown paper parcel under the other. He marched into the kitchen, handed the parcel to Auntie Blod, telling her that it came from Mr Foley, and accepted her thanks graciously before turning to beam at the girls. 'Ready for the off, then?' he said cheerfully. 'It's a grand day – the air is being warmed by the sun till you could think it were summertime if it weren't for the snow. And the snow's gettin' a grand crust on it, so it'll be as slippery as hell – I mean slippery as anything – when we get into the hills.'

Auntie Blod looked surprised. 'Oh, but I thought you'd be staying here for your dinners,' she said. 'I know Daisy and Petal have made a picnic, but you can eat that for your tea. Why not eat your dinners here? I've got a casserole in the Aga.'

The smell of the casserole was enticing and for a moment Daisy wavered, but Nicky was firm. 'No, it gets dark too early in January to purroff leavin' right now,' he explained. 'Ah, here's Maldwyn; he'll tell you the same, Mrs Williams.'

Auntie Blod sighed, but when Maldwyn assured her earnestly that it would take them almost an hour to reach the best slopes, she gave in. 'I'll save some of that there casserole and you can have it when you get back,' she promised them. 'And don't you forget, you're to be home here afore dark, or you'll be in trouble. And if the weather turns bad on you, or looks like doing so, come straight home. Is that understood, fynwy fechan i?'

Daisy smiled to herself as she agreed that they would come home at once if the weather changed, because she had suddenly remembered that when Auntie Blod had first used that Welsh expression she had thought it sounded like swearing, or some sort of insult. Now, of course, she knew that it merely meant 'my little ones', because she and Petal – and Nicky, too – understood the Welsh language well and could speak some Welsh without having to think about it.

Having promised to be sensible, the children presently found themselves trudging up the lane in the sunshine, Maldwyn towing a small, home-made sledge, whilst Daisy and Nick carried battered tin trays and Petal, wellington-booted and rosy, kept trying to take the sledge's strings from Maldwyn, or darted ahead to pelt them with soft snowballs from the shelter of snow-laden gorse bushes.

By the time they reached the cavern where Daisy had thought they would eat their picnic, they were all pretty hot and only too willing to accede to her suggestion that they eat their food here, though Maldwyn pointed out that they still had a good twenty-minute walk before reaching the best sledging place. Snow had driven into the cavern, and icicles as long as Daisy's arm hung round the entrance like jagged teeth. But they pushed their way inside, Nicky loudly lamenting that they had not thought to bring a supply of kindling up with them. 'We could have made a fire and toasted the sandwiches on sticks,' he said wistfully. 'We could have hotted up the lemonade an' all, and warmed our hands and feet.'

'Well, we didn't,' Daisy said, rather crossly. It would have been fun to light a fire all right, but she thought it was almost as nice to squat inside the cavern, eating sandwiches and drinking lemonade, and watching the sun strike a million diamonds of brilliant colour from every icicle. Besides, simply being out of the snow whilst still in the sunshine was warming her up. 'Anyway, a fire would have melted the icicles and that would probably have put it out, which wouldn't have been much fun.'

Maldwyn laughed. 'And the breeze is blowing towards us, so the fire would have smoked us out like rats out of a barn,' he pointed out, in his soft Welsh voice. 'Tell you what, though, Petal was telling me about the snow houses that Dilys and Gareth used to build when they were kids. I know how to build a snow house with a sort of chimney, so next time we come up here I'll bring some dry wood and we can light a fire in that, once it's made.'

Nicky gave a crow of derisive laughter. 'Oh aye?' he said mockingly. 'If a fire will melt icicles, then I should think your old snow house would be a puddle ten minutes after you lit the first match. I'd ha' thought a farmer's lad would know better than to fill a gal's head full o' nonsense.'

'It's not nonsense . . .' Maldwyn was beginning quietly when Petal sprang to his defence.

'You don't know nothin', Nicky Bostock, you're just a stupid city scouser,' she said angrily. 'Maldwyn knows everything about the countryside. He can tell a blackbird's nest from a thrush's by the way it's built; he knows every bird's egg, every single one. He can put his hand in a stream and bring out a trout. I've seen him – it's called ticklin'. So, if he says you can build a fire in a snow house, then you bleedin' well can.'

'Yes, I reckon Maldwyn knows all sorts,' Daisy said pacifically, 'though it does sound unlikely, Petal, you must admit. I mean everyone knows heat melts snow, so why shouldn't a fire melt a snow house? But there won't be time for building such things today, not if we're to get some sledging done, so don't let's argue.' She glanced around her, then began packing the remains of the food and drink back into the haversack. 'Everyone ready to move on?'

They agreed to do so, though Daisy intercepted the baleful look which Nicky shot at Maldwyn, and was sorry for it. Maldwyn was a nice boy and never tried to show off, particularly to Nicky, a good three or four years older than he, but Daisy appreciated that Nicky was doing his best to learn country ways and probably could not help resenting the younger boy's knowledge.

However, nothing more was said as they toiled up

the steep incline, and presently they reached the field which both she and Maldwyn had had in mind. Nicky glanced approvingly at the long gentle slope, though he could not resist pointing out that the field ended in some low, scrubby bushes with a stream beyond them. 'If we go crashin' through those bushes, we'll likely end up in the stream,' he said. 'Ain't there a place where we can slide wi'out catchin' our death of cold at the finish?'

Maldwyn, however, assured him that the bushes were thicker than they looked and in fact were growing out of a deepish hollow. 'You'll never hit the stream unless your tray takes off and soars over the bushes like a pheasant on the wing,' he said, with a chuckle. 'Before my brother Eifion joined the air force, he and meself came up here every winter, and neither of us ever got so much as an inch past them bushes.'

Nicky accepted this wisdom, though grudgingly, and soon the four of them, Maldwyn and Petal on the sledge, and the other two on their trays, were swooping and shrieking their way down the field, and tumbling off into the bushes. Despite the sunshine, the snow in the shadowed hollow was dry and powdery, so all that was necessary to rid oneself of it was a good shake, before climbing the hill again and repeating the experience. After a while Maldwyn offered the sledge to Nicky and Daisy, and he and Petal took a turn on the trays, though after watching Petal, who was small and light, descending the hill at a frightening pace, he told Daisy that her sister was far safer on the sledge since he could use his feet to brake and his hands to steer, thus making certain that Petal did not descend the hill like a rocket. 'I thought she was going to do what I told Nicky me and Eifion never did; that is go so fast that the tray took off, flew over the bushes like a bird, and crashed into the stream,' he said, chuckling again. 'But she's safe enough with me, and you and Nicky manage grand on the trays.'

'Don't we though?' Daisy said, trudging up the hill with her tray in her arms. 'This is the best thing I've ever done, Maldwyn, easily the best. Well, the best of the winter things,' she amended, remembering picking primroses and violets from banks sweet with the scent of spring; long, warm days in the hayfield, learning when to turn over the piles of drying grass with her small pitchfork; and riding the rough little pony round and round a grassy meadow whilst Dilys told her to grip with her knees, to keep her hands down, and to rise to the trot. 'You are so lucky, Maldwyn, to live here all the time; I wish we did.' She glanced around her. Nicky and Petal, talking earnestly, were following them but out of earshot. Daisy lowered her voice. 'Nicky wishes he did as well, you know. That's why he's – he's sometimes a bit sharp with you; it's because you're a lot younger than he is, but you already know all the things he's trying to learn before he gets sent back to Liverpool,' she ended.

Maldwyn's thin brown face broke into a smile. 'Oh aye, and I don't blame him, but if you ask me, he won't go back, him, not ever. Why should he, after all? Petal told me he's got no family of his own – them Ryans aren't even related to him – and so far as I can make out, he's rare good at all the jobs the Foleys need doing. Oh, I'm not saying he'll work in the shop or deliver meat for the rest of his life, 'cos he'll want to better himself, I dare say, but I think he'll stay in Ruthin. Can't see no reason why not, meself.'

Daisy gazed at him, round-eyed. 'I reckon you're right,' she said slowly. 'Why, I'll be able to get a job in a couple of years and I'd like to live here, just like

Nicky. Mind, if the war ends soon, Mam will take us back to Liverpool in a trice.'

'Why?' Maldwyn said baldly. 'Your home's been bombed, your dad's been killed – Petal told me that – so why shouldn't your mam settle here as well? You like it here, you said you did, and young Petal likes it too, she often says so. She says she's going to be a farmer and keep pigs and hens, and have her own pony and trap,' he added, grinning at Daisy.

Daisy opened her mouth to reply, but at that point they reached the top of the slope and Petal came panting up beside her. 'If you and Nicky get on the big tray, and me and Maldwyn use the sledge, we could have a race,' she said breathlessly. 'Bet we could beat you, even though we're younger.'

The first swoop down the hill was won easily by Maldwyn and Petal because, of course, they were lighter and their sledge was more manoeuvrable than Nicky's tin tray, so the second race was a handicap one, with the tin tray getting a six-yard start. This time it was a dead heat, and it was only as they reached the top of the slope once more that Daisy noticed that it was getting difficult to make out the shapes of the bushes in the hollow below them. Even as she opened her mouth to say that they must get home before dark, a snowflake landed on her nose. She began to point out to the others that the daylight was fading, but before she could say more than a few words, snowflakes began descending thick and fast, and she saw that the wind was getting up. The boys realised it at the same moment and stopped discussing the handicap which should be applied on the next race, suggesting instead that they should make all speed towards the farmhouse. They set off at once, but very soon Daisy noticed that Petal was lagging behind, even though Maldwyn was doing his best to help her along. 'I'm tired and most awfully hot,' she whimpered, when Daisy dropped back to ask her how she felt. 'I'm aching all over and I feel sick. It's all your fault, Daisy McAllister. You shouldn't have brought me out when you knew I had a nasty cold.'

Daisy felt outraged at the unfairness of this remark, but saw that Petal was not quite herself and gave her sister's shoulders an encouraging squeeze. 'That's right, queen, it's all my fault,' she said. 'Let me put my arm round your waist and Maldwyn and I will help you along.'

She had to shout the words above the worsening gale and presently, when Petal pushed her away, saying that she was dragging on her and not helping at all, Daisy went ahead once more to where she could just make out the shape of Nicky, with the hump of the haversack on his back. She caught his arm, saying urgently as she did so: 'Nicky, Petal's worn out and not at all well. D'you think we should make for the cavern and shelter there until the storm passes? She's only a kid, after all, and probably she's right; I shouldn't have brought her out when I knew perfectly well she had a nasty head cold. Oh, do let's make for the cavern; it's ever so much nearer than Ty Siriol.'

Nicky was against the plan at first because he said what they all wanted was a decent fire to dry out their clothing and a hot meal in their bellies, but presently he agreed that perhaps the cavern might be a better option and the two of them turned back to tell Maldwyn and Petal the change of plan.

There was no one behind them; only the whirling flakes and the rapidly falling dark. Nicky turned back to Daisy. 'That's bleedin' well torn it,' he said, and there was panic in his voice. 'I can barely see me hand in front o' me face and I've not gorra clue in which direction that cavern lies. Have you, queen?'

Dumbly, Daisy shook her head. With the snow underfoot, she could not tell whether they were on the stony little track which would lead, eventually, to the Ty Siriol lane, or whether they had strayed far from it. She raised her voice in a loud shout. 'Petaaaaaaal! Maldwyyyyyyyyn!' But even as she called, she heard her voice being whipped away by the wind and muffled by the falling snow, and knew there was little chance of being heard. Desperately, she turned back to Nicky. 'We'd best go back, Nick,' she said urgently. 'We've simply got to find them. I wonder if they've made for the cavern? If so, and we come across it, at least we can huddle together for warmth and wait there until the storm passes.'

This time Nicky did not even hesitate. He shook his head firmly and grabbed Daisy's arm, pulling her after him. 'Don't talk daft,' he adjured her. 'Our only hope of finding any sort of shelter is to keep on going downhill. We'll never find the cavern, norrin this snow and not without Maldwyn to guide us. If they make it, they'll be okay until the storm passes, and if we make it – to Mrs Williams's place I mean – then we can send out a search party to fetch the others in.' Daisy still hung back and Nicky gave her a shove. 'Don't be a fool, Daisy; once we turn back, we'll use up all our energy searching whilst the kids will be getting colder and colder. Can't you see we've got to have help? I reckon the Williamses will know that cavern and be able to go straight to it, even through the snow, and if the kids aren't in it, there'll be torches and more folk to shout their names, and a better chance of finding them before . . . well, before something awful happens. So best foot forward, as Mr Foley would say, and no more hankerin' after turning back, understand?'

When she heard it put so succinctly, Daisy realised

at once that Nicky was right and fell into step beside him once more. After a few moments, he took her arm, saying gruffly that they must not get separated. Once or twice he encouraged their onward progress by remarking that he was pretty sure they were still going downhill and, hopefully, were still on the track. It was impossible to say for certain whether he was right, but Daisy hoped that he was. She thought they might easily have left the track but knew, as they neared level ground, that there would be trees and bushes on either side of them and presently, despite the swirling snow and the fact that it had frozen on to her eyelashes and had to be impatiently dislodged every few minutes, she thought she saw a shape looming up before her and realised that it was a great old oak tree, the one which grew closest to the track. She must have spotted it at the same time as Nicky did for he gave a hoarse shout, then looped an arm about her waist and began to hurry her along. 'Only another fifty or sixty yards to go and we'll be in the farmyard,' he said exultantly. 'We've near on made it, queen. I say, suppose Maldwyn and Petal are already in the kitchen, toasting their toes by the fire? Wouldn't that be grand, eh?'

'They couldn't possibly have passed us without us noticing,' Daisy said, a trifle peevishly. She felt as though her legs were made of lead and wanted nothing more than to rest for a bit before tackling the remainder of the journey. 'Can't we rest just for a little while, Nicky?' she asked plaintively. 'I'm so tired, I'm sure I could curl up and sleep under that oak tree, if only for a few minutes.'

'No you could not,' Nicky said, his voice outraged. 'That's how people die in the Arctic, you stupid girl. Just you keep a-moving, or you'll feel my boot behind you.'

Daisy gave a stifled sob but in her heart she knew Nicky was right. She had heard the stories of gallant Captain Oates leaving the Scott expedition and saying that he 'might be some time', knew that he had frozen to death in the snowy wastes of Antarctica, and had no desire to follow his example. Presently, she was rewarded by the sound of voices and the sight of torches, and next moment she was in Dilys's arms, sobbing out that Petal and Maldwyn were missing, that she had lost them in the snow and would never forgive herself if harm came to her little sister. Dilys picked her up and hugged her tightly and Daisy saw that there were tears on the older girl's cheeks. 'It's all right, cariad,' Dilys said comfortingly. 'Mam's in the kitchen warming blankets before the fire and soup on the stove. She'll have you and Nicky here warm as toast and well fed in five minutes, and don't you worry yourself about Petal and Maldwyn. Shanna's got a wonderful nose on her so I brought out your pixie hoods so she can have a sniff of them and know she's looking for a person and not a lost sheep. Can you cross the yard yourself, love, or do I have to carry you all the way? Only the sooner we fetches the other two back to the farm, the better it'll be for us all.'

'I can walk,' Daisy said, struggling out of Dilys's arms with some reluctance, for the older girl felt as warm and comfortable as a feather bed. 'Come on, Nick.'

Nicky, however, hesitated. 'I oughter go back wi' the others, show 'em the way to the cavern,' he mumbled. 'I just wanted to see you safe indoors, queen . . .'

But Dilys was having none of it. 'You'd be more hindrance than help, boy,' she said brusquely. 'We've got three strong men and meself, as well as Shanna, and we're none of us soaking wet, nor yet wore out, so just you get into that kitchen and no more argufying and we'll be back with Petal and Maldwyn afore you know it.'

Daisy waited for Nicky to object, to say that he was good for many hours yet, but to her relief he just heaved a sigh, nodded and grinned at Dilys, and followed Daisy kitchenwards. Daisy had scarcely raised her hand to the doorknob before the door was flung open and she found herself clutched to Auntie Blod's warm bosom and carried across the kitchen to be set down before the fire, blinking in the strong light of the oil lamp.

'Oh, my dearest Daisy, what a fright you've give us, but you're home an' safe, and that's the main thing.' Auntie Blod was stripping Daisy of her soaking clothing as she spoke, and as soon as she had done so she turned and began to do the same for Nicky, for it was clear to Daisy that what with the cold and the wet, neither of them could move their numbed hands to any practical purpose. 'Where's Petal and Maldwyn?' Auntie Blod went on, seizing blankets, hot from the fire, and wrapping one round Daisy and another round Nicky. 'I'll warrant they ain't far behind you – I dare say Dilys is giving them a bit of extra coddling, them being nobbut babies – so the pair of you can sit on the sofa while I pour you a nice mug of hot soup.'

'P-P-Petal's lost; sh-sh-she wouldn't let me help her; she s-s-said I was dragging on her,' Daisy explained, through chattering teeth. Oh, Auntie B-B-Blod, if anything's happened to P-P-Petal . . . I should've made her l-l-let me help her . . .'

Auntie Blod patted Daisy reassuringly but the look of worry deepened on her rosy face. 'That young 'un! Obstinate as a whole herd of mules, she is; if she were in one of her independent moods, you'd not have had a chance, cariad, so don't go blaming yourself. Besides, with all the men out looking, as well as our Shanna, she'll be sharing the fire with you in no time, as well as this lovely thick soup.'

She was pouring soup into two mugs as she spoke and would have handed one to each of them, save that Nicky spoke before she had time to do so. 'Don't, Mrs Williams,' he said urgently. 'I can't even keep hold o' the blanket; our hands is so cold, they couldn't go round the mug handle, lerralone take the weight of it to our lips. But if we could sit up to the table and have a bit o' bread to dip, like . . .'

'It's an old fool I am,' Auntie Blod said remorsefully, standing the steaming mugs on the scrubbed wooden table. 'What's more, it's a deal too hot to drink, so while it cools I'll nip upstairs and fetch you down some dry clothing. Daisy can have her own, of course, but I reckon an old pair of Gareth's winter trousers and one of the thick old jerseys I knitted for him to wear on the farm will do you a treat, Nick. Shan't be more'n a moment.'

She disappeared and could be heard ponderously ascending the stairs, and Nicky turned and grinned at Daisy. 'I'll be rare glad o' them kecks,' he whispered. 'I'm bare as a babe beneath this blanket; she even took off me underpants, an' socks, an' everything. I hope you weren't watching, young Daisy.' He was grinning and Daisy grinned back.

'I'm bare, too; I were too busy shiverin' and aching when the fire started to warm me up to bother about what were happening to you,' she pointed out righteously. 'Besides, I seen you with no clothes on more'n once, swimming in the Scaldy.'

'Oh aye, but I've – I've growed a bit since then,' Nicky said, a trifle awkwardly. 'Mrs Foley were shocked when I told her we swam naked at home. She said I were too old for such things and gave me a pair of her Ernest's old bathing drawers.' He chuckled. 'She knitted them for him and they've stretched a bit, I reckon, over the years, but the other fellers usually wear something similar, so I don't complain.'

'I've never learned to swim,' Daisy said regretfully. She got up, still blanket-wrapped, and approached the table, gazing longingly at the mugs of soup. 'I can't wait to get some of this down me . . . what's that?'

Even as she spoke, Auntie Blod re-entered the kitchen, dumped some clothes on Nicky's lap and handed a thick jumper, a brown woollen skirt and a pair of stockings to Daisy. 'It's back they are; I heard Shanna barking and that's a sure sign she found what she were looking for,' Auntie Blod said briskly. 'Get into them clothes before the kitchen's full of folk needin' a warm. I'll just cut some bread, then you can be sitting down and eating your soup by the others come in.'

Nicky and Daisy scrambled into their clothes and Daisy rushed to the back door and pulled it open. Looking across the yard she saw that Auntie Blod had been right; Dilys was carrying Petal, the child's face pressed against her neck, and Uncle Gwil had an arm round Maldwyn, whilst Shanna danced around the small group, grinning and barking as if she knew she was the cleverest dog in the world. Behind them, the farmhands shouted farewells in Welsh and turned to go back to their own cottages, clearly anxious to be home before the weather worsened again, for the storm had eased and only a few large curled-feather snowflakes continued to float down. But the cold was still very much with them; it nipped at Daisy's face and at her stockinged feet and she was glad to close the door on the night as the last person entered. She looked on as Auntie Blod took Petal's small form in her arms and began to strip off the child's soaking clothing, whilst Dilys performed the same service for Maldwyn. Daisy went over to Auntie Blod, looking anxiously into her sister's small face. Petal was very flushed, her eyelids heavy and her mouth drooping, and Daisy heard her hoarse breathing. She realised, all in a moment, that Petal's eyes were not focusing on her, did not seem to see her.

'Auntie Blod? Is – is she all right? She looks so strange and she's making a sort of wheezing sound. Is she asleep?'

She could easily have been asleep for she made no move, either to help or hinder, as Auntie Blod stripped her to the skin and wrapped her in a blanket, but at Daisy's anxious words Auntie Blod tried to smile reassuringly before turning back to the task of chafing Petal's cold body. 'She's like ice,' she said quietly. 'But at least she's alive . . . *this my son was dead, and is alive again; he was lost, and is found.*'

Daisy stared at her, bewildered. 'But Petal isn't your son, nor even your daughter,' she said in a puzzled voice. 'Though of course, she was lost and now we've found her. Dear, dearest little Petal, I'll never be cross with her again.'

Auntie Blod smiled and smoothed back the tumbled hair from Petal's forehead. 'That were a quotation from the Bible; remember the Prodigal Son?' she asked. 'But the child's head is like a furnace, though the rest of her is still cold as ice.' She turned to her daughter. 'Dilys, cariad, I'm afraid someone will have to go for the doctor; the child's got a fever, and a high one if I am any judge.'

Dilys came over and looked down at Petal, a worried frown on her face. 'But will I get into Ruthin with all this snow on the road, and will Dr Clitheroe come back with me?' she asked doubtfully. 'It's awful dark, Mam, and I don't reckon he'd get his car out of the garage because it's at the bottom of a slope. By tomorrow, there'll be mebbe more chance of him visiting.'

Auntie Blod looked undecided but Uncle Gwil cut in in his usual quiet way. 'I'll go. I'll take Sweep, 'cos he's the larger of the two shires, and he's amenable to being rid bareback. Dr Clitheroe's a good man; when I tell him he's needed urgently, he'll come, even if he has to ride Sweep pillion behind me.'

Auntie Blod's face cleared. 'You're a good man yourself, Gwil,' she said quietly. 'Tell him she's hot as fire and unconscious; tell him I'm truly worried. And I'll pack you a flask of tea with whisky in so's you can have a nip whenever you feel inclined. Get that wet coat off and them wet boots; I'll fetch dry.'

She bustled out and Daisy's heart gave a startled leap as she saw that all the colour had drained from Maldwyn's face. Whilst Auntie Blod loaded Uncle Gwil with dry clothing, the promised flask and a huge muffler, as well as a great deal of advice, Maldwyn sidled over to Daisy. 'All my fault, it was,' he muttered wretchedly. 'We lost sight of you in the blizzard and Petal said she couldn't go no further, so I lifted her up and took her to the cavern, knowing it were nearby. I couldn't have reached the farmyard carrying her,' he added sadly. 'The snow was too thick, and by then I was too weak myself to take her weight.'

'Oh, Maldwyn, you did wonderfully well to get her into shelter,' Daisy said, clasping his cold hand between her two warm ones. 'Nicky and I meant to make for the cavern ourselves but we were lost and dared not turn aside from the track. I'm sure you saved Petal's life by reaching it. If you'd collapsed in the snow trying to carry her to the farm, you'd both have been dead by now.'

Maldwyn returned the clasp of her hand just as Uncle Gwil pulled open the back door. Daisy caught a glimpse of madly swirling flakes, heard the howl of the wind and realised that the blizzard had started once more. She hoped Uncle Gwil and the doctor would soon return and knew she would feel much happier about Petal when they did so, for she thought the doctor both kind and clever – had he not cured her sore throat and mended Elias's broken ankle? But now, inside the kitchen, all was bustle. It was clearly impossible for either Maldwyn or Nicky to return to their own homes, so Auntie Blod and Dilys were creating makeshift beds from the sofa and two of the armchairs. At present, Petal was lying on the sofa, but Auntie Blod meant to kindle a fire in her own room and have Petal share her big feather bed. 'Then I can keep an eye on her, my love,' she explained to Daisy. 'I wouldn't be easy, knowing she were liable to cry out and me not hear her. Uncle Gwil can sleep in the Land Girl's room, since young Heather's away for the weekend and won't be back till late tomorrow or early Monday.' She glanced at the window, almost obscured now by snowfall. 'If she gets back at all,' she added ruefully. 'We've been snowed up here for weeks at a time in the past; I reckon it's going to happen again.'

By the time Dilys had carried Petal upstairs to the now warmed bedroom, the kitchen had been converted for the boys' use and a meal – casseroled beef and Auntie Blod's delicious floury dumplings – had been set out on the table. Daisy joined the others at the meal, though she felt almost guilty doing so, since Dilys and Auntie Blod took it in turns to sit upstairs with Petal. Dilys assured Daisy that though horribly hot and feverish still, her sister was awake and as cheerful as one could be in the circumstances. 'But there's no denying Mam and meself will be a lot happier once the doctor's seen her,' she admitted. 'All finished? Who's for a nice piece of apple pie with custard, eh?'

The boys responded eagerly but Daisy felt she could not eat another morsel and begged Dilys to let her go up and sit with Petal whilst Auntie Blod came down and enjoyed a share of the apple pie. Dilys hesitated, but clearly seeing Daisy's anxiety told her that she might run upstairs and have a few words with Petal. 'Only you can't look after her the way meself and Mam can,' she said bluntly. 'She can't shift herself in bed – she aches all over – and we're bathing her forehead with the lavender water you gave Mam when she were in hospital and wiping her hands with a wet cloth. You tell her as you and Nicky are safe, and Maldwyn's fine, 'cos that does seem to worry her that she can't remember seeing you in the kitchen.'

Daisy nodded and made for the stairs, glancing hopefully towards the window as she went; you never knew, Uncle Gwil and the doctor might be crossing the yard at this very moment. But she could see nothing through the blackout blind, though she could still hear the howl of the wind.

She entered Auntie Blod's room softly, then walked quietly towards the bed. Almost as though she were aware of her sister's presence, Petal's eyes flew open, but they went straight to Auntie Blod's face. She moaned softly, turning her head restlessly on the pillow as though searching for a cool spot, and Auntie Blod gently reached out and stroked a large wet handkerchief, redolent of lavender water, around the sufferer's strangely flushed face. Daisy went and stood close to Auntie Blod. She was frightened because she had never seen Petal looking like this before. Her sister's eyes were bright with fever, the blonde curls damp with sweat; and whenever she moved, she groaned. Petal had closed her eyes while Auntie Blod applied the lavender water, but now she opened them again. Her wide blue gaze fixed, vacantly, on Daisy's face, but even as Daisy clutched at Auntie Blod's arm, beginning to say 'She doesn't know me', Petal's gaze sharpened and focused and her lips curved into a tiny smile.

'It's you, Daisy,' Petal murmured, in a thread of a voice. 'Oh, I'm so glad you aren't dead. Is Maldwyn . . .?'

Daisy saw that Petal's lips were cracked and dry and that speaking was difficult for her. Auntie Blod picked up a spoon, dipped it into a mug of something which stood on the bedside table, and would have trickled it between her patient's lips except that Petal moved her head in a gesture of negation and then cried out shrilly, as the movement hurt her.

Daisy spoke quickly. 'Maldwyn's fine; and Nicky's fine, too, and so am I,' she said reassuringly. 'You mustn't worry about any of us, darling Petal. Nicky and I got back to the farmhouse quite quickly, and you and Maldwyn were so sensible! Maldwyn says you went straight to the cavern, which was what Nicky and I meant to do only we didn't know the way, so Nicky said just to keep going downhill . . .'

She stopped; a frown was creasing Petal's brow and her eyes had closed, almost involuntarily it seemed. 'Cavern? We didn't go to no cavern,' she said in a puzzled voice. 'Oh, Auntie Blod, I hurts all over, so I does. Even my perishin' toes hurt. I think someone's pulling my head off my shoulders so's my neck will be as long as a g'raffe. Can't you give me something to make me better?'

'I dussent do much until the doctor arrives, but he won't be long,' Auntie Blod said reassuringly. 'Now how about a little sip of the nice beef tea in this here cup? Or there's lemon and glycerine; it's grand for sore throats.'

Petal did not answer; she seemed to have sunk into an uneasy dose, muttering senselessly, and to her dismay Daisy saw tears squeeze out from between her sister's closed eyelids and soak into the feather pillow.

Auntie Blod turned to her, her voice sinking to a whisper. 'Go you off downstairs, cariad,' she said. 'No sense in staying up here when sleep is what she needs. I've melted an aspirin in the lemon and glycerine and another in the beef tea, 'cos an aspirin will do nothing but good. It'll ease the pain and mebbe even send her to sleep. But the quieter she's kept, the better. Run along now, me love.'

Daisy was only too glad to obey; the sight of Petal, so obviously ill, frightened her and she could not help remembering how they had all promised to return to the farm immediately if the weather worsened or before darkness fell. The trouble was, she told herself, rejoining the others in the kitchen, that everything had happened so quickly. None of them had had a watch, but if they had only remembered to glance at the sky, they would have seen that the sun had gone and the snow clouds were rolling over. Unfortunately, the excitement of racing the tin tray against the sledge had completely absorbed them, making them indifferent both to weather conditions and to the lateness of the hour. As a result, Petal, who had had a nasty cold anyway, was now extremely ill and causing a great deal of worry to everyone, for Daisy knew Auntie Blod would not willingly have sent her husband out in such dreadful conditions, had she not feared for Petal.

As she entered the kitchen, every eye turned to her, but she took her place at the table, still trying to command her voice and blink back tears. After a moment, she told them that Petal was 'sort of awake' and had known her, though she had seemed to be sleeping once more when Daisy left the room.

'Sleep's the best thing for her,' Dilys said bracingly. 'Besides, it won't be long before . . . what's up, Shanna?'

Daisy looked down at the dog, who had risen quietly from her place before the fire and was standing in front of the back door, the plume of her black, white-tipped tail beginning to wag gently from side to side. 'They're back,' Nick said joyfully, jumping to his feet. He swished the blackout curtain back and opened the door a crack, making sure that the curtain fell in place behind him. 'Dammit, I can't see a bleedin' thing.' He turned to Dilys. 'Can I nip out and tek Sweep from him, Miss Williams? Then he and the doctor can gerrin and start thawin' out whilst I rub the old feller down and dry off his saddle and bridle.'

Dilys looked a bit doubtful, but Nicky was already pulling the door open wider and letting in a quantity of the snow which had piled up against it. 'Hang on, Nick; you aren't dressed for the weather and you've got no more dry clothes,' Dilys said firmly. 'I'll show the doctor up to Mam's room and then I'll go and give Dad a hand. I've got dry clothes a-plenty, but I'll wear my rain cape and wellies, so's I won't get soaked.

Nicky went to shut the door once more, but it was abruptly pushed wide, almost knocking him over, and Uncle Gwil appeared in the doorway, slamming the door behind him. He was so coated with snow as to be almost unrecognisable, but he spoke with his usual calm authority. 'I couldn't get through; the wind's piled the snow in the lane into drifts higher than my head, and up on the main road it's the same. We tried to take to the fields, me and Sweep, but no chance. The drifts there are worse if anything, and treacherous. Like the North Pole, it is, with not a landmark to warn of hedge or hollow, till you blunder into it. I can't risk Sweep breaking a leg, so we turned back. I've put him in his stall but he needs rubbing down. I just came in to let you know we're back.' He shook snow off himself. 'How's the littl'un?'

'Not so brave, but she'll do,' Dilys said briefly. 'I'll bring old Sweep a bucket of hot mash; reckon he deserves it.'

'Aye, that he does; he's a heart like a lion, has Sweep,' Uncle Gwil said. He turned back to grin at his daughter. 'I wouldn't mind a bucket of hot mash meself,' he said, ducking his head and pulling the heavy oak door shut behind him.

In moments, the kitchen was all in a bustle. Maldwyn made the hot mash and Dilys tipped soup into a pan and pulled it over the fire, then checked that the casserole which she had saved for her father had not dried out. 'Have that when he gets indoors, he can,' she remarked, taking her shiny cape off the back door and pushing her feet into her wellingtons. 'Can you pour some of that soup into a mug, Daisy, without burning yourself? Only I know my dad. He should come indoors, of course, and get some food inside him, put on dry clothes, but he won't leave me to fettle Sweep. No, he'll stay out there till the horse is as warm and dry as he should be, and as well fed. Then he'll come indoors and see to himself; we don't want two invalids about the place.'

Daisy, carefully pouring soup from the pan into Uncle Gwil's large tin mug, had been stricken with dismay upon realising that the doctor had not been fetched, but she told herself, resolutely, that Auntie Blod had nursed her own children through any number of ailments and would doubtless be able to cope with Petal. It was only because Petal was not her own little girl that Auntie Blod had felt obliged to send for the doctor. Having poured out the soup, she handed the mug to

Dilys and then hurried up the stairs, knowing that Auntie Blod would have heard her husband's voice and would be eagerly awaiting Dr Clitheroe's appearance.

She entered the room to find Auntie Blod sitting Petal up against her pillows and trying to administer a spoonful of the lemon and glycerine, though Petal was saying, fretfully, that she would not swallow the horrid stuff and that she wanted her mam, so she did. Auntie Blod looked round eagerly as the door opened. 'I heard Gwil's voice; is Dr Clitheroe coming up?' she asked. And then, as though she had guessed what the answer was to be, her face fell. 'Oh no! He didn't get through, did he? Well, now the fat's in the fire, and no mistake. Still, if you'll send Dilys up to me, love, the pair of us should be able to get the young madam here to swallow some of this concoction, then she'll feel more the thing.'

Dreadfully worried, Daisy scampered down the stairs, pulled Auntie Blod's rain cape off the back door and wrapped herself in it. The boys were at the sink, Nicky washing the dishes and Maldwyn wiping them, and took no notice until she began to drag the door open, when they both turned to stare at her in astonishment. 'Wharron earth are y' doing, kiddo?' Nicky asked incredulously. 'Mr Williams and Dilys – I mean Miss Williams – will be managing fine without any help from you. You don't want to go out in all that—'

The slamming of the door cut the sentence off short and Daisy was out in the yard, feeling the force of the blizzard for herself, terrified by the strength of it, by the depth of the snow and by the shriek of the wind, yet still determined to slog her way across the snowy waste of the yard and take Dilys's place in the stable. She ducked her head as far into the huge cape as it would go and was pleasantly surprised to find herself entering the stable, having been neither blown off course nor defeated by the blizzard. Both Dilys and her father swung round as the stable door creaked open and Dilys began to berate her, but stopped when Daisy gasped out her errand.

'I telled Auntie Blod that the doctor wouldn't be coming – well, I didn't have to tell her; she guessed – and she asked for you to go up and give her a hand with Petal, Dilys. She's trying to give Petal medicine, but it needs two.'

Dilys had been rubbing the big horse down with a wisp of hay and Uncle Gwil, the soup finished and the mug empty, had been teasing the tangles out of Sweep's thick, black mane, but now he took the hay from his daughter and began energetically plying it over the patient animal's damp coat, saying briskly as he did so: 'Aye, I reckon it 'ud take two to get that young madam to do anything she didn't want! You go off, Dilys, my love; the young 'un and meself will be finished here in ten minutes.' He turned to Daisy. 'Brush out his fetlocks, there's a good gal, and give his legs a good rub, 'cos you ain't tall enough to reach his mane.'

'Right you are, Uncle Gwil,' Daisy said cheerfully. Dilys had shed her rain cape in order to attend to the big horse but now she donned it again, then cast an amused look at Daisy. 'You *were* in a hurry,' she remarked, heading for the stable door. 'You've got your boots on the wrong feet, so you have!' And with a chuckle, she left the stable, shutting the door firmly behind her before more snow could swirl in.

By the time Gwil and Daisy returned to the house, both boys were in their makeshift beds, though not actually asleep, and there was no sign of Dilys. Uncle Gwil dished himself up a huge plate of casseroled meat and dumplings and then told Daisy to make her way to bed. 'I'll fill you a hot water bag and you can pop your nose into your Auntie Blod's room and make sure your sister's all right, else you'll never sleep,' he said kindly, pouring hot water into Daisy's blue rubber hottie. 'I know we wanted the doctor to come, no doubt we'll fetch him tomorrow, but in the meantime your sister couldn't be in better hands. My Blod's nursed kids through whooping cough, quinsy, septic throats and croup,' he added bracingly. 'She only asked the doctor to come out because Petal's not her own kin, but she'll see her right, so don't go worrying yourself.'

His smile was so kind, so understanding, that Daisy felt tears prick behind her eyelids, but she did not mean to cry before Nicky and Maldwyn, and contented herself with replying that she was sure Petal would be fine, before hurrying up the stairs. She hovered outside Auntie Blod's room for a moment, not quite liking to enter without knocking, yet fearing that a knock might rouse Petal if she slept. She had turned the handle and pushed the door perhaps an inch ajar when she heard words which made her blood run cold. 'Neither you nor Gareth ever had rheumatic fever, but I remember Maldwyn's brother Billy bein' mortal ill with it,' Auntie Blod was saying in a low voice. 'The thing is, to keep 'em cool and quiet, and to give plenty of fluid, so we'll do that for tonight. But tomorrow someone will have to get through to Ruthin, 'cos there's modern medicines we'll need.'

'Oh, Mam, not rheumatic fever!' Dilys said, her voice breaking on the words. 'Why, it killed young Emily Pritchard from Llanbedr.'

'Aye, but that were years back . . .'

The door creaked as Daisy entered the room and both women swung round, giving Daisy what they no doubt meant to be reassuring smiles. 'Quietly, my love; your sister's asleep. She took the medicine, and by tomorrow morning . . .'

'Rheumatic fever. You – you said it were rheumatic fever,' Daisy faltered. 'Oh, Auntie Blod, a girl in my year had that and now she can't run, or play games, and her lips is blue and – and folks say she ain't long for this world. And Petal's so – so lively, she'd never quiet down and go slow, not if you were to tell her a hundred times.'

'No, no, you've got the wrong end of the stick, cariad,' Auntie Blod said, but her eyes slid away from Daisy's entreating gaze. 'Feverish she is, from the head cold and the snow, but nothing worse. Dilys and meself were just talking about other cases where – where a fever's been neglected. We'll take good care of your sister; she'll be right as a trivet in no time, just you wait and see.'

Daisy took one hasty glance at Petal's flushed face, mumbled that she was sure she hoped Auntie Blod was right, and hurried to her own room where she found temporary respite in a hearty bout of tears. She told herself over and over that she was doing no good by worrying, but it was a long while before she slept.

By the time day dawned next morning, Auntie Blod and Dilys were longing for the light to strengthen so that someone might go for the doctor. Petal had slept, but fitfully, and every time she awoke she had complained of aches and pains and had demanded her mother's presence, had not seemed to understand when Blodwen or Dilys had reminded her that she was at Ty Siriol, many miles from Liverpool.

Dilys was bathing the child's face with lavender water when her mother drew back the curtains, letting in the wintry reflective whiteness of a countryside several feet deep in snow. As the curtains swished back, Petal gave a sharp cry and pushed Dilys's hand, and the lavender-soaked handkerchief, away. 'Don't!' she said crossly. 'I hate that stuff when it goes on my neck; it stings like anything.' She turned her head, apparently without pain, to glare at Auntie Blod. 'And I don't want the curtains back, I want them closed tight as tight. The light hurts my eyes turble bad.'

Auntie Blod gave a squawk and crossed the room so fast that Dilys found herself being pushed away before she could move for herself. She saw her mother bend over the bed and snatch back the neck of Petal's winceyette nightdress. For a moment Auntie Blod peered at Petal's skin, then she sat heavily down on the bed and turned to beam at her daughter. 'It's the measles!' she said joyfully. 'Why didn't I think of that?' She gave Petal a triumphant hug. 'Oh, my little love, it's only the measles, so today you can have a nice bowl of porridge to your breakfast – and a boiled egg, if you fancy that – and tomorrow you can have a proper dinner and in a few days you'll be up and playing downstairs with your sister, though you'll not leave the house until the snow clears, 'cos even the measles mustn't be neglected.'

'Well I'm blessed,' Dilys said, examining the rash which pretty well covered Petal's body and was beginning to show on her cheeks and forehead. 'Fancy us not thinking of that, Mam, for I'm sure Merion who drives the milk lorry told me both his girls had got 'em a week ago, and they're all at the same school. Oh lor', I wonder how soon Daisy will get them?'

'I don't know and I'm blessed if I care,' Auntie Blod said joyfully. 'Measles I can cope with; I wouldn't call the doctor out for measles. I'd best go and tell Daisy, because the poor child will have been worritin' herself to flinders. She'll be mightily relieved to learn it isn't rheumatic fever, even if it does mean that she herself will be the next patient.'

But Daisy, when Auntie Blodwen hurried into her room with the good news, was able to assure her that she had had the measles a year before Petal was born. 'I'm so glad it's only that, Auntie Blod,' she said, sitting up and clutching her bedding round her, for it was a bitterly cold morning. 'I don't think I've slept for more than a few minutes all night because – because Mam expects me to look after Petal and I didn't do very well at it yesterday, did I?'

'Yes you did, you looked after her as well as anyone could,' Auntie Blod said firmly. 'If anyone is to blame, it's meself. No one knows better how suddenly the weather can change up here in the hills. Yet I let the four of you go off as if you knew the conditions as well as I did. And anyway, you weren't to know that Petal was about to come out in a rash of measles, were you?'

'No, and nor were you,' Daisy reminded her. She gave an enormous yawn then snuggled under the covers again. 'Is it all right if I go back to sleep for a bit, Auntie Blod? It's Sunday, so there's no school and the church service doesn't start until ten.'

'You can sleep all day, if you've a mind, cariad, since we're snowed in good and proper,' Auntie Blod informed her. 'Maldwyn might get home if Gwil can get the tractor started, or he might saddle up the shire and take him back, but Nicky's here till the snow clears and that could be days . . . weeks, even.'

'Gosh, weeks!' Daisy said sleepily. 'That means no school for weeks, either. I wonder if Nicky's had measles? I wonder . . . I wonder . . .'

She slept.

Chapter Fourteen
March 1943

Because Mrs Williams had been unable to contact Rose for a couple of weeks after Petal's measles had started, Rose had not asked for leave to visit her daughters at the time. It had seemed downright foolish to trek across the country just to see the girls for a few hours, particularly in bad weather, so she had decided to put off visiting them until the spring, when she would be able to ask for a week's leave. Instead, Rose had written a cheery letter, explaining that she would visit when the weather was better. She had enclosed a postal order for three and sixpence, instructing Daisy to buy Petal a colouring book and pencils, or something else which would help her to pass the time spent in bed.

Daisy, bless her, had replied promptly. She said that Petal was up and about again, and would be back in school in another week, and that at Petal's request she had spent some of the money on a pack of Happy Families cards; a game that everyone could play whilst sitting round the table in the evening. The rest of the money had gone on knitting wool since Auntie Blod had beguiled the long hours when Petal had been listless and weary, not well enough to play games, by teaching her to knit. Daisy told Rose that all the older girls were knitting for the forces and Petal had decided to do the same. She had managed to knit squares without dropping too many stitches and proudly handed them in at school, for the teachers to crochet into blankets. The teachers had told the children that folk who had been bombed out were very grateful for the lovely warm woollen blankets, which had made Petal look a little pensive. Daisy said that Petal thought that since their house in Bernard Terrace had been bombed, they ought to be allowed to keep at least one of the blankets themselves, but her sister had reminded her that they now lived with Auntie Blod and did not need such things.

Daisy, herself, was growing up amazingly, Rose considered. She was knitting socks – great big thick ones for air crew who needed all the warmth they could get – doing well at her lessons and learning a certain amount of cooking, so that she might help Auntie Blod and Dilys. Rose loved getting her letters, now so full of her doings, but sometimes she could not help having a little weep because she was missing so much of the girls' growing up.

However, Rose realised that the WAAF was changing her as much as the passing months were changing her daughters. She had recently successfully completed examinations which had earned her the rank of corporal and this had meant a small increase in pay, a slightly larger increase in responsibility and a really big increase in her self-esteem.

Now, Rose sat in the cookhouse with Kate, Jen and Mo, her particular friends, discussing their forthcoming leave. The four girls had arrived at Coltishall more or less simultaneously over a year ago and spent most of their off-duty time together. Mo was married to a tail gunner at present flying from an airfield in North Africa, Jen was the wife of a naval rating and Kate, like Rose herself, was a widow and still unattached, though as she somewhat reproachfully told Rose, at least she had a decent social life and every intention of marrying again. 'When the right feller asks me, of course,' she always added, grinning wickedly at her friends. 'The wrong 'uns are always far too keen and the nice fellers are usually married, but one day the perfect feller will go down on his knees and you won't see me for dust.'

But right now, the vexed question of what to do with a whole week's leave was the subject of conversation. Rose had announced her intention of going to see the girls, though she admitted it was a shame that she could not wait till Easter, when they would be on holiday and, of course, the weather would be better.

'Only it's such ages since I've seen them and when Petal was ill with the measles, the farm was cut off so I couldn't go down and do my share of the nursing,' she explained. 'What's more, the Wing Officer doesn't much like it if you hang on to your leave until it's convenient for you; she would rather we took it when it suits her and I don't want her putting a black mark against my name.' She smiled round at her friends, her eyes twinkling. 'And I'm simply longing to see my kids again and to make sure that Petal's eyesight hasn't been affected by the infection, because it does sometimes happen, you know,' she finished.

Kate smiled at her. 'You go; you'll have a lovely time, even if they are in school. But why don't you get on the blower; you might be able to persuade your Luke to see if he could get the same week off. You were moaning about the long train journey, saying you'd be wasting at least two days travelling back and forth, changing trains and hanging about on draughty platforms,' she observed. 'But your feller's got a car, hasn't he? If he could wangle the petrol, I bet he could get you to Wales in half a day or less, and you could spend time with him as well as with your daughters. What about it?'

'He's not my feller and I don't want to ask him for favours,' Rose said slowly. 'If he's got a week's leave due – and I'm pretty sure he has, I remember him mentioning it – then I dare say he's got plans of his own.'

Mo, who was a small, sturdy girl with dark hair and narrow, snapping black eyes, wagged a reproachful finger. 'Talk sense, woman,' she admonished. 'That Luke of yours is a stranger in a strange land. He won't be going home to his mum and dad, or visiting his sister and her family, or going to stay with old friends, and well you know it. I reckon he'd jump at the chance of visiting your Welsh farmhouse and spending some time with you and the kids.'

Jen, who had been rapidly eating baked beans on toast, nodded approval before scraping the last piece of toast round the plate and popping it into her mouth. She was a skinny, fair-haired girl with a narrow, rather serious face. She was packed with energy and never still for long and when she spoke, it was with decision. 'Mo's right, Rosie, and as for Luke not being your feller . . .' She snorted derisively. 'Pull the other one, it's got bells on! If he's not your feller, then why is he always on the phone, asking you to see a flick or go to a dance, or take a drive somewhere?'

'He may ask, but that doesn't mean I go, not every time,' Rose said defensively. 'He's a nice chap, not pushy or grabby, if you know what I mean, but taking him on leave . . . well, that would be giving him the wrong idea.' She glanced across at Kate, smiling apologetically. 'You see, Kate and meself are very different. Kate was only married to Bobby for three months, but they were a happy three months, weren't they, Katie, old dear? I were married to Steve for – oh, years – and I can't say we made a go of it. In fact, I married in haste to repent at leisure, as the saying goes, which is why I don't want to repeat the dose, get involved again with any man.'

'Not even a nice chap like Luke?' Kate said curiously.

She was easily the prettiest of them, Rose thought, with her smooth, ash blonde hair and pink and white complexion. Most of the men on the airfield – the unattached ones – wanted to date her, but Kate was extremely choosy. She kept a photograph of her husband pinned to the inside of her small locker and though he had been killed almost two years ago and Kate seldom mentioned him, Rose thought that the love between them had been a very strong emotion and one which Kate could neither forget nor push to the back of her mind. She measures every man she meets against her Bobby and they all fail to come up to scratch, Rose thought sadly. I never thought I was lucky to have married a man I couldn't love until I got to know Kate.

'I've only met your Luke a couple of times but he seemed . . . oh, reliable, and sensible, and it's easy to see he's really fond of you, Rosie,' Kate continued.

'That's because I'm almost the only person he really knows in England,' Rose said wryly, but this remark was greeted with jeers.

'The only girl he knows in England? He's air crew, he's got a car and there must be fifty or sixty WAAFs on his station, all panting for a look from him,' Jen said. 'You may be kidding yourself, Rosie, but you can't kid us. He likes you and you jolly well like him. Why are you afraid to admit it?'

Rose pondered the question seriously. Her friends were at least partly right; she did like Luke and knew he liked her, but she also suspected that he was growing weary of being kept at arm's length. If he was to decide to stop seeing her, she also knew that she would miss him, but then if Kate or Mo or Jen were moved to another station, she would miss them too. And there was no doubt about it, a week spent on the farm with her daughters at this time of year would be restful but scarcely exciting. If Luke came along as well, she knew they would all have a much better time. It wasn't just the car, though that would be extremely handy, it was Luke himself. He was good fun, humorous and always full of ideas. The girls did not know him very well but would soon do so and Rose knew that the Williamses would welcome him to their home and find a corner for him, even if he could only sleep on a makeshift bed in their front room.

The trouble was, inviting him to spend a week's leave at the farm with her was tantamount to admitting that there was more between them than simple friendship and Rose was still very reluctant to make such a move. It was ridiculous and she knew it, but the moment she saw Luke's face soften, saw him reach out a hand to touch her, she would move away, blow her nose, do anything to prevent any sort of intimacy. But you can't go through life being afraid of a handshake, she scolded herself now, sitting with her friends in the crowded cookhouse. You've got to remember that the children will come back to you when the war's over, and what are they going to think if there's no man – not even a man friend – in your life? They'll grow up influenced against men by my feelings, and that isn't fair on either of them. What's more, a family should be a partnership because the girls need a father, even if I think I don't need a husband. It isn't as if they ever see their uncles, or male cousins. No, I simply must stop believing men are my enemies. And then there's the practical side of it. I don't know what sort of work will be available for women after the war. I might have to consider marriage from sheer necessity, you never know.

Abruptly, Rose made up her mind and got to her feet. 'Right; you've talked me into it,' she said briskly. 'Luke's a good bloke and I know he's got nowhere to spend his leave and I'm pretty sure he's due for some. He was probably flying last night, but I'll give him a ring around four o'clock.'

Luke had returned from his night raid and landed just as dawn was greying the eastern sky. He got stiffly out of his seat, then glanced across at the woods on the perimeter of the airfield, seeing the first and most beautiful signs of spring: catkins and pussy willows in the hedge which surrounded the wood and the new grass beginning to cover bank and pasture. He checked that his crew were preparing to leave the aircraft. They were good guys and had been together now for longer than most. They had been lucky and had not lost a crew member; a fact of which few skippers could boast.

'Ready, fellers?' Luke said, heading for the outside world. He looked up at the sky. It was clear and cloudless; a pale milky blue which would deepen when the sun came up. It was going to be a lovely day.

Phil, the wireless operator, stretched and yawned hugely as the men made their way towards the gharry which would take them to the admin office for debriefing. 'After a spot of breakfast, I'm going to sleep the clock round,' he said, in his soft Lancashire voice. 'We're due for some leave now, you know that, don't you, Luke? We've reached twenty-five sorties, so we're entitled.'

'Yeah, I guess so, but I don't fancy going off alone

somewhere,' Luke said softly. 'Oh, I know everyone says *you can come home with me*, but being a guest . . . I reckon it 'ud be more of a strain. I suppose I could go up to London, see the sights . . . anyway, it's something I'll have to think about.'

Brendan, the navigator, blew a raspberry. 'Why not give the go-ahead to that flighty little WAAF who's been making eyes at you for the past six weeks?' he suggested. 'Go on, make her the happiest woman on earth.'

'Shut up, you,' Phil said. 'I've got my eye on her! I've always fancied blondes, even if it does come out of a bottle. She'd be wasted on Luke.'

Luke grinned but no more was said until the debriefing was over and the crew had gone into the cookhouse for a hasty breakfast before seeking their beds. Then Phil asked Luke why he didn't take his week's leave with the young woman he occasionally took to the flicks.

'Because she hasn't suggested it,' Luke said lightly. 'I told you before, Phil, she's got a couple of kids. They were evacuated to a farm in Wales so I guess when she gets leave, that's where she'll go.'

'You could go as well,' Phil said, though he didn't sound particularly convinced. 'Aw hell, Luke, we all need a break now and then, even an iron man like yourself.'

They all laughed, but when Luke climbed into his bed, having first drawn the blackout curtains and closed the window tight against the clatter of a working airfield, he thought seriously about the situation between himself and Rose. He thought her a beautiful and desirable woman but was uneasily aware that their relationship was not progressing as he would have liked. She may have thought he did not notice, but he dreaded the way she drew back from him if he tried to make even the simplest gesture of affection, and winced if he made a sudden movement. Once, aboard a country bus, he had raised his hand to lift their gas masks down from the overhead rack and Rose had positively cringed, as though expecting a blow. He knew she had not had a happy marriage and guessed that Steve might have hit out at his wife when he'd had a few drinks, but told himself that she could not put him in the same category as her dead husband. He had never raised his voice to her, let alone his hand, and found himself resenting the implication that he might do so. Dammit, Rose would not even let him hold her hand in the flicks and though she had danced with him, it had been like dancing with a wax model, so stiff and unbending had she seemed. And yet . . . and yet there was a warmth and a gaiety in Rose and a sweetness of character which he longed to share. He reminded himself that he had only really got to know her since she had joined the WAAF; in a civilian situation, things might be different. If he suggested that they went on leave together, she might unbend a little.

That's not a bad idea, Luke told himself drowsily, shrugging the covers up round his ears. I'll give her a ring this evening and arrange to meet; then I'll tell her about my leave, explain that I have no family or friends to go to, though she knows that well enough, and ask if we could spend the time together. After all, she can only say no.

Almost before the thought was formulated, Luke slept.

Luke saw her waiting on Castle Meadow as his gharry drew to a halt behind hers and waved cheerfully. They had not said an awful lot when they had spoken on the phone earlier that day, but he had told her he wanted to take his leave now that spring had arrived, and without prompting she had suggested he should go with her to the farm.

It had been tempting to reply that he would be delighted to go with her but he had held back. Instead, he had said he thought they ought to talk and had been honestly astonished when she had agreed.

Now, however, jumping down from the back of the truck and seeing her welcoming smile, the colour rising in her cheeks, he thought that perhaps everything would be all right. She was so pretty and had recently become so much more self-confident that surely she would begin to be less cautious in her dealings with him. At any rate, he intended to put his feelings into words and see how she responded. He had tried the friendly approach and it really hadn't worked; now he would see what plain speaking would do. So, for a start, he took her hand as they crossed Castle Meadow and went down Davey Place, telling her as he did so that he meant to take her to Lyons where they could have a good meal and a good talk. 'And don't try wrenching your hand away,' he added, feeling her instinctive withdrawal but not letting go, as he had on previous occasions, 'because I don't like being treated like a leper, darling Rose.'

He was watching her face as he spoke and saw her bright colour rise up, but he also saw the little smile which touched her lips and felt her fingers relax in his.

'Sorry,' she said, and sounded as though she meant it. 'I don't mean to be rude, or to hurt your feelings. It's just . . .' She sighed. 'Oh, it's so difficult to explain without being . . . well, disloyal, I suppose you could say.'

He squeezed her fingers lightly as they turned on to Gentlemen's Walk, almost immediately entering Lyons Restaurant. It was still early evening and the place was not crowded, so they found a quiet table for two and talked inconsequentially until the nippy, in her neat black and white uniform, had delivered their food. Only then did Luke raise the subject which he was beginning to believe was uppermost in both their minds.

'I know you mentioned you were going to spend a week at Ty Siriol and you suggested that I might like to join you. It was very generous of you, honey, but the reason I didn't jump at it was because I wasn't sure why you had asked me,' he said carefully. 'You see, you've never given me much encouragement to believe that I'm anything more than a chance-met acquaintance.'

Rose began to murmur a protest, flushing even more deeply, but Luke cut her short. 'I know it's not easy to talk about such things, Rose, but I'm – I'm real fond of you. You're a beautiful, desirable young woman, yet I'm not allowed to take your hand without feeling . . . well, that I'm being fresh. If I spent a whole week with you, I'd like to think it was because you were growing fond of me and wanted to further our relationship. But quite frankly, I'd be half afraid to try to give you a kiss in case you repulsed me.'

'I thought you understood,' Rose muttered. She took a mouthful of food, chewed and swallowed it before speaking again. 'I've been happy in the WAAF and I was pretty happy in Bernard Terrace whilst Steve was away. I – I thought you knew Steve was violent when he'd had a few drinks. I thought you understood.'

'I do know,' Luke said gently. 'But I'm not Steve,

as you very well know. Have I ever raised my voice to you? Why, I've never even told you how it hurts me when you cringe at any sudden movement I make. You can't believe I'm the sort of guy who would hit *any* woman, let alone the one I love.'

Rose looked up quickly, and for a moment Luke thought he saw in her eyes a reflection of the love which he knew must be in his own, but then she glanced down at the food on her plate. 'I know you aren't like Steve – but it isn't just that,' she muttered. 'If Steve had always been violent, I wouldn't have married him, would I? He was grand when we were courting; it was only after we got married and Daisy was born that he began hitting me. At first, I couldn't believe it; I kept telling myself that it was my fault, that I was doing something wrong. It was ages before I realised that Steve had always been a bully but had kept it hidden from me for as long as he could.' She had kept her eyes down while she spoke, but now she raised them to his. 'I don't *want* to spend the rest of my life alone, because of what Steve did to me,' she said, her eyes bright with unshed tears. 'I want to be able to love someone properly, the way my friend Kate loved her Bobby – but I'm so afraid of making another mistake.'

Luke looked at her with real compassion. What an awful fix she was in, and through no fault of her own. He said quietly: 'But don't you see, honey? You've got to learn to trust again, because there's no other way. You can't have a trial marriage with half a dozen different guys to see which of them isn't likely to turn into a wife beater. And anyway, since you seem to regard an arm slipped round your waist as being dangerous, I don't think you'd take kindly to a trial marriage!'

He spoke lightly, trying to make a joke of it, and Rose gave him a tremulous smile. 'I know you're right, and I really will try,' she said. 'For one thing, I want the girls to have normal, happy lives, and that means boyfriends in a few years and husbands after that. So if you will come to the farm with us, I'll truly do my best to behave normally, the way you would expect a girl to behave.' To his astonishment, she reached across the table and took his hand, holding it firmly in her own. 'And I'm sorry for the way I've treated you, Luke, because I like you better than any man I've ever met.'

'That's wonderful,' Luke said. 'And will you do something for me, honey? Will you just tell me exactly how Steve was when he was courting you? I never met him, of course, but from what you've told me, he wasn't a lot like me. Now think; did he make you laugh? If you were carrying a bag, did he take it from you? Was he as nice to your mam and dad when they weren't there as he was to their faces? And last, but not least, did he think he was one hell of a guy who could have any woman he wanted, so you were real lucky to get him?'

Rose looked at him for a long moment and then she began to laugh. When she could command herself once more, she mopped her streaming eyes with a handkerchief and gave him her answer, ticking her replies off on a finger as she did so. 'You ask if he made me laugh and the answer to that is pretty straightforward. He was the sort of man who took himself seriously and was always slightly suspicious of laughter. To be fair to him, I think he thought you were laughing at him and not with him . . . a kink in his self-confidence, I suppose. As for carrying heavy bags, an awful lot of Liverpool fellers would say that was women's work . . . Steve was certainly one of them. What was the next question?'

'Was he as nice to your mom and pop—?' Luke began, but Rose cut him off short.

'Oh, yes, I remember: was he as nice to my parents when they weren't there as he was when they were present.' She giggled again, clearly finding the question amusing. 'That's a difficult one, Luke, because thinking back, he was pretty horrible to them every time he came to our house. He sneered at Mam's cooking, argued with Dad over any subject that came up, and was generally difficult. I'm ashamed to admit I let him get away with it because, little fool that I was, I took him at his own valuation. He swaggered into our house as though he owned it and I was so afraid of losing him that I never told him off or criticised him in any way. Even then, I knew how deeply he would have resented it,' she ended.

'And the last question? Did he think he was one hell of a guy who could—'

Once more, Rose interrupted, her eyes sparkling. 'Oh yes, he thought he was God's gift to the universe, but not particularly to women. It sounds awfully odd, Luke, but I don't think Steve really liked women, not any of them. I remember my father once saying that Steve was a man's man and that fellers like that didn't make good husbands and by golly, wasn't he right? If I'd been as meek as Steve thought me – never giving an opinion, never arguing, never saying no when he wanted yes, it's just possible that the marriage might have worked, though I doubt it.'

'Ah, but you had the girls to protect and guys like that end up beating their kids as well as their wives,' Luke said shrewdly. 'From what you've told me, I think your marriage was doomed from the start. But now, honey, why not ask yourself the same questions, only put the name Luke instead of Steve. Go on, don't think you'll embarrass me if I fall short.'

But Rose was smiling at him with sparkling eyes and shaking her head so that her long dark hair swung violently from side to side. 'No, no, I don't need to; you're always making me laugh and it's the same with all the rest. You're as different from Steve as chalk from cheese, and it's about time I realised it and valued you for what I know you are. Dear Luke, come to the farm with us and I promise you the length of my arm will be so short, you'll scarcely notice it's there.'

Luke gave a whoop and, forgetting his surroundings, leaned across the table and took Rose in his arms, kissing her resoundingly. 'That's my girl,' he said exultantly. 'Oh, Rosie, we're going to have the best week's leave in the whole world! And now let's get out of here and go somewhere where I can kiss you properly without an audience.'

Going back to Coltishall that night Rose was astonished at how warm and happy she felt. I've been an absolute fool turning Luke's love away because I was too scared to take a risk, she told herself as the truck began to bounce along the narrow country roads. They had discussed their forthcoming leave at some length and had both agreed that it was a wonderful opportunity to put right the things that had been wrong – or rather lacking – in their relationship.

'When we get to know one another better, we may decide it's all a mistake and prefer to remain simply friendly acquaintances,' Luke had said but not, Rose thought, as though he had meant it. 'That means we'll enjoy ourselves but be prepared to go our separate ways at the end of the week with no hard feelings.'

Rose thought it generous of him but, as she now

acknowledged, Luke was a generous person. He had given her friendship and affection without any sort of return; in future, Rose told herself, things would be very different.

The journey to the farm in Luke's old car was a revelation. Crossing the whole countryside, it was as though spring was always one step ahead of them as they neared the west of the country. In Norfolk and the Midlands, buds were still tightly furled and the glorious hedgerows which lined the roads barely showed a touch of green, but as they entered Wales and headed for the hills, there was a riot of blossom as well as the brilliant green of hawthorn, and Rose knew that soon the steep banks would be starred with primroses and sweet, purple violets.

She was as excited as any child. She told Luke how Daisy and Petal had gone out with their friends in February, dipping for frog and toad spawn. Uncle Gwil had given them an old battery case which they had speedily converted into an aquarium, and now it contained a number of fat tadpoles, most of which were turning into tiny, jewel-bright frogs. 'I never had any country fun like that when I was a kid,' Rose said wistfully, as the car turned into Ty Siriol lane. 'When I was Petal's age, I didn't know a hazel catkin from a pussy willow, nor a frog from a toad, because of course I was an only child and Mam and Dad kept me pretty close. Why, I thought Princes Park was real country. I used to tell other kids that Uncle Frank and Aunt Selina lived in a country cottage, though of course it was really a terraced house in Penny Lane.' She turned to look curiously into Luke's face. 'What about you, Luke? I know you come from a small town in the middle of America, and you've got a brother, and your dad runs a garage and your mum a grocery store, but is that country? I suppose it can't be because you wouldn't sell much petrol or mend many motor cars out in the country, would you?'

Luke gave her an indulgent glance. 'It is country, though it's on the outskirts of a small town,' he told her. 'When we were kids, my brother and I, and a whole gang of us from the local school, used to ride off on our bikes and get into all sorts of mischief. In the fall, we stole apples and pears from the orchards and feasted like kings. We made ourselves catapults and either drew a target on a tree, or hid behind a hedge and tickled up grazing cattle with an acorn or a little smooth pebble. There were prairie dogs on the plains and, of course, fields and fields of maize, which grew a good deal higher than a boy's head. We had some fun in that maize, playing hide and seek, catch, anything you'd like to name. I don't suppose you've ever sat down, on a hot afternoon, and bitten into a corn cob and felt sweet white liquid running down your chin, but it's something us kids took for granted then, yet now it seems like the taste of Paradise.'

Whilst he spoke, he swung the car off the lane and into the farmyard, and as he drew up the back door flew open and two small figures emerged to hurl themselves joyfully upon Rose.

'Mammy, Mammy, Mammy!' Petal shrieked, whilst Daisy clung on to her mother's arm and nestled her head into the hollow of Rose's shoulder. 'Oh, Mammy, Felix the cat has got kittens. I'm going to have the black and white one, and Daisy wants the ginger. We're going to call them Nib and Nob.'

'I always thought Felix was a boy's name,' Luke said mildly, getting out of the car and receiving a hug from Petal, though Daisy hung back a bit, looking awkward. 'But I suppose names are different over here.'

Daisy laughed. 'No, it's more because it's difficult to tell a boy cat from a girl cat when they're kittens,' she explained. 'When Auntie Blod saw Felix getting a round tummy, she said we'd made a mistake and wanted to call her Phyllis, only the name Felix sort of stuck.' She glanced, shyly, up at Luke. 'Do you want to see them? The kittens, I mean, and Felix of course. They're in the end stall of the stable, up one corner of the manger.'

Luke said that he would be delighted to see the kittens but felt he ought to greet his hostess first, and presently the small party repaired to the kitchen where Auntie Blod poured out cups of tea, cut wedges from a fruit loaf, which she told Luke was called bara brith, and settled down for a good gossip.

'You've chosen a lovely time of year for your visit,' she told them. 'We've had a bit of a turn round upstairs so's I can put everyone up. I've put Daisy and Petal into the apple store because there isn't much fruit in it at this time of year and there's plenty of space for a couple of makeshift beds.' She turned to Rose. 'You are sharing Dilys's room, if that's all right; I haven't moved Heather, because she's in our Gareth's room anyway, and that leaves the children's room for Mr Nadolski – or should I call you Flying Officer Nadolski?'

'No indeed; please call me Luke, Mrs Williams,' Luke said quickly, which made the older woman laugh.

'If I'm going to call you Luke then you must follow Rose's example and call me Auntie Blod,' she said easily. 'Now, what plans have you got for this coming week?'

* * *

They had five glorious days on the farm. Auntie Blod spoiled them dreadfully, Rose told Luke, as each meal seemed better than the last, though the children assured them that they seldom had a meal which did not include meat, or eggs, or fish.

'I think things are easier out here,' Daisy said wisely. 'Nicky Bostock works for the local butcher in town and seems to be able to get hold of all sorts of things which you wouldn't even see in Liverpool. He says it used to be called bartering, only we call it swapping these days. If someone in the town who sells – oh, hardware, or knitting wool or something – needs eggs for a cake, then they'll go to one of the farmers in the hills with knitting wool, or a pound of nails, and exchange it for the number of eggs they want. See?'

Rose did see, and when she explained to Luke, adding that the Ministry did their best to stop such transactions but were mostly outwitted by the canny farmers, he said he thought it was fair enough. 'Townsfolk don't realise how hard a farmer works to rear his lambs and pigs and calves, to till his fields, lift his potatoes and cut his wheat,' he said. 'Why shouldn't he get some of the benefit as well?'

So, for five days, they lived on the fat of the land, and since their visit included a weekend Rose was able to enjoy the girls' company and to assure herself that Petal's eyesight was unaffected by the measles. 'And all the spots have gone as though they had never been,' Daisy assured her mother. 'It were a good job you couldn't see her when she were first took bad though, Mam. She looked terrible. Her eyes were all swolled up and she had so many spots, you could scarce fit a pin head between them. She was pretty good about not reading and not pulling back the curtains to look out, because the snow was so dazzling. It were a good thing I couldn't go to school, though – no one could get through, not even the milk lorry – because I sat by the bed for hours at a time, reading her all her favourite stories. And for the first few days, you know, Nicky was snowed up here with us. He were ever so good, helping out on the farm, carrying trays up so we could have our dinners with Petal, and playing games when she were well enough. I really do like Nicky; if we go back to Liverpool when the war's over, I'm going to miss him like anything.'

'But surely, Nicky will go back too?' Rose asked. 'Surely he'll want to return to the Ryans when the war's over?'

Daisy gave a derisive snort. 'Oh, Mam, why on earth should he? He's got a good job with the Foleys and they really like him, treat him like a son, he says. The Ryans never wanted him; he weren't no kin of theirs, they just kept him out of charity . . . well, if you can call it charity to treat someone the way they treated poor Nicky. No, he'll never go back.' She shot her mother a quick glance then looked rather intently down at her hands. 'Anyone who has lived in the country would think twice about going back to the city,' she muttered. 'I do meself.'

Rose had been astonished and slightly affronted by her daughter's words, but it had made her look at Daisy more closely. When she did so, she saw how her daughter was changing and maturing. When the war started, the child's figure had been almost sticklike, with no shape to it at all; now she had a proper waist, slim but gently curving hips and the beginnings of a bust, and it's not only her figure that's changing, Rose told herself ruefully. Daisy was becoming a real help around the farm. She understood about broody hens, knew how to control the great grey and white geese, whose noisy approach still scared Rose half to death, and could knit and sew, cook and clean almost as well as a woman grown. Seeing her with new eyes, Rose was also forced to see that Daisy had a will of her own. If she decided to get a job in Ruthin when she was old enough, Rose very much doubted whether she would be able to override the child's wishes and force her to move back to the city.

Petal, of course, was a different matter. At nine years old, she had little thought for the morrow and would, Rose was sure, do as she was told, though possibly not without grumbles.

Rose began to worry over these things but Luke, when she confided in him, told her not to meet trouble halfway. 'Both Daisy and Petal are your children and they love you very much. It's all very well for Daisy to talk about staying in Ruthin when the war's over, but who can tell when that will be. And for that matter, who knows where *you* will be. Your house has been destroyed and most of your neighbourhood. Oh, I'm not saying it will never be rebuilt, but judging from what I saw of Liverpool after the May Blitz, it's going to take quite a time to put things right there. Why, you yourself might prefer to live and work in Ruthin, when you leave the WAAF, which would solve everyone's problems.'

Rose realised that this was true and stopped worrying, bending her mind instead to relishing the company of the young woman Daisy had become, as well as enjoying Petal's artless conversation and refreshing outlook on life.

When Luke suggested, however, that they should leave the farm and make their way back to Norfolk a couple of days early, she was astonished and rather hurt. 'But, Luke, we've both got seven days' leave; it won't be much fun mooching round the station when we could be here, with the Williamses and the kids,' she said reproachfully. 'I thought we'd leave at about eleven o'clock on Wednesday, so that we were back in time to settle down and hear all the gossip before going to bed. Neither of us has to be back before midnight but I wouldn't want to leave it as late as that.'

The two of them had gone for a stroll up towards the hills after the children had gone to bed. They had formed the habit of doing this because it was the only time they had to themselves and Luke usually put his arm round Rose, saying that it was safer in the dark in case one of them should trip over an unseen obstacle.

At her words, Luke gave her a quick squeeze. 'I'm not suggesting we go back to the station, honey. I thought we might stop off in a pub, or a small hotel somewhere, take a look around. You see, though it's been a wonderful few days, we're not much nearer getting to know one another properly, are we?'

Rose stopped short, pulling him to a halt as well, and turned to face him. It was a clear night for once and they had got their night eyes, so Rose could see his face looming above her, catch the glint of his teeth as his lips parted in a slow smile. 'Luke Nadolski, just what are you suggesting? If it's what I think it is, then you can jolly well forget it! I don't want to be drummed out of the WAAF because I'm in trouble.'

'But I see no reason why you should be drummed out of the WAAF just because we've taken a bit of time for ourselves,' Luke said. 'Look, if you hate the idea of a couple of days alone with me, just say so, but oh, Rosie, I guess you must know by now how I feel about you, and I was beginning to believe . . . to hope . . .'

As he spoke, he cupped her face tenderly in both hands, and very, very slowly, giving her every opportunity to pull back, he bent his head until their mouths met.

It was a gentle kiss, almost passionless, yet Rose felt her heart begin to beat faster and her stomach to perform unusual gyrations. She returned the kiss, then broke away from him, saying rather breathlessly: 'Oh, Luke, you're right. We'll leave early and – and have some time to ourselves. Oh, Luke, oh, Luke, I'm almost sure . . . it's just that . . .'

Luke laughed and put a finger against her lips. 'Hush, honey,' he said in a low voice. 'Make haste slowly. Now let's get back to the farm and tell Auntie Blod we'll be leaving Tuesday morning, early. That will give you another full day and no one will be surprised at our leaving, since I've told everyone that old Henrietta needs nursing along and that doing the whole cross-country journey in one day was hard on her elderly constitution.' Luke had christened the car Henrietta after an aunt of his who, at ninety-six, was still working her small farm without assistance, save at harvest time.

Rose laughed and put a hand up to stroke his cheek as they turned back towards the farm. 'Has anyone ever told you you're a devious devil, Luke Nadolski?' she asked him. 'I *wondered* why you kcpt on shaking your head and saying we mustn't expect too much of Henrietta, when we both know full well that she sailed across the country without so much as a hiccup.'

Luke captured her fingers and kissed them; an action which sent more thrills tingling up Rose's spine. She snatched her hand back, however, saying breathlessly:

'Just you behave yourself, Luke! You're getting me all hot and bothered when I want to be cool, calm and collected. Race you to the kitchen door!'

On Tuesday morning, Luke insisted on running the children to school in Henrietta, so that they might have a few moments more with their mother. Since Rose had assured the girls that she would be arranging for them to come across to Norfolk sometime during their summer holidays, they were reconciled to her leaving them a day sooner than they had expected, but even so, when it came to the moment of parting, they clung to Rose and then, to their mother's pleasure, they both insisted upon hugging Luke and kissing his cheek. 'We think you're the nicest man our mammy has ever had,' Petal said, squeezing Luke's hand tightly in both of hers. 'Auntie Blod says the same; I heard her telling Uncle Gwil the other night that you'd make a grand daddy.'

Daisy felt the heat rise up in her cheeks, but gave her small sister a shake. 'I don't know why you say that because, apart from our dad, Luke's the only feller Mam's ever brought home,' she said. 'You name me one other, Petal McAllister!'

'Oh! Well, if Mam had had other fellers, Luke would be the nicest and *I* think he'd make a lovely daddy,' Petal said. She turned back to Luke. 'Do you have children of your own, Luke? Are you a daddy?'

Luke was beginning to say that since he had never been married he had no children of his own either, when Daisy once more took a hand. 'For the Lord's sake, stop prattling, Petal, and gerrinto your class,' she said crossly, giving her small sister a shove. She turned to follow her, then turned back. 'I'm awful sorry, Luke; if I've telled her once, I've telled her a hundred times not to repeat what she only half hears as though it were gospel. Only – she didn't mean no harm, she just wanted you to know she likes you very much. And I do, too,' she added hastily. 'I think you're almost as nice as Uncle Gwil.'

Luke thanked her, gravely, for the compliment, assured her that his feelings were undamaged and his withers unwrung, and then watched with a smile as she scampered into the school, waving as she went.

'Two nicer kids you couldn't find if you searched the length and breadth of this island,' Luke said, as he put the car into gear and drove out of the small, grey town, cupped between the soft green hills. He turned his head to smile down at Rose. 'Now where do you fancy stopping for lunch?'

Rose blew her nose vigorously and dabbed at her eyes before replying. She loved the girls so much and had realised, this time more than ever, how she was missing them. Daisy's adult awareness had come far earlier than Rose's own had done and she thought that this was because Daisy had had to take responsibility for her little sister whilst she was still only a child herself. But what could I have done, she asked herself miserably. I had to earn money and I had to do my bit towards the war effort. Oh, but now Petal will start to change, and I shall miss that, too.

'Rose?' Luke asked gently. 'You're upset because you're leaving your children behind, but you mustn't be. No one could be kinder or more generous than the Williamses, and you said yourself that you could never have given them the sort of country childhood they're experiencing now.'

Rose sniffed dolefully. 'I know you're right and I suppose I'm really crying for myself,' she admitted. 'I've missed so much, Luke – so much of their growing up, I mean. And they never come again, those special years which turn a little girl into a young woman.' She took a deep breath, put away her handkerchief and smiled across at Luke. 'I don't mind where we stop,' she said. 'Any nice little pub where they make sandwiches will be fine.'

Luke spotted a pleasant-looking pub just outside Melton Mowbray and they stopped there for their lunch. The fat and motherly landlady provided them with cheese and pickle sandwiches and a large piece of apple tart. The day was fine and sunny, though there was a real nip in the air, but they sat in the bow window of the pub, which overlooked an attractive garden dotted with wooden tables and chairs where, had the weather been warmer, they could have eaten their food. Both pickles and apple pie were home-made and they did not hurry over the meal, finishing up with a cup of coffee each and then enjoying a chat with the landlady, whose son was also in the air force.

'We'll be lucky if we find anywhere half as good as this to spend the night,' Luke said casually, handing Rose into the front passenger seat and then taking his place beside her. 'I thought we'd break the back of the journey today, if we can, by pressing on for a bit. Then we can have our evening meal wherever we stop and go up to bed at our leisure. There'll be no rush in the morning, so we can lie in for a bit – if that's what you'd like, I mean.'

'That sounds lovely,' Rose said vaguely. Not for the first time, it occurred to her that Luke might mean them to share a room and she looked across at him speculatively. How would she feel if he suggested it and what should she say? She was no shrinking violet and knew that in one way it would be natural for Luke to want to sleep with her. After all, he did a highly dangerous job and one never knew . . .

Horrified, she pushed the thought out of her mind. She was not going to agree that she and Luke should become lovers just because he piloted a Wellington bomber and was in danger every time he flew. There were girls in her hut who must have slept with a dozen different men, using the excuse that they were giving the fellers a taste of life – and love – because it might be the feller's only chance. Rose had never subscribed to this, thinking it an excuse for behaviour of which they would otherwise be ashamed. But now, when she suspected it was about to become an option for her, she realised she felt differently. She also realised she was close to falling in love with Luke, and if one loved, then surely one wanted to give? The greatest gift, she thought confusedly, was the gift of oneself, but she had given herself to Steve and look where that had led.

'Rosie? A penny for your thoughts.' Luke's voice cut across her musings and Rose felt the hot colour flood into her cheeks. Was this the moment to ask him . . . well, what exactly? She could scarcely say bluntly, *Do you want me to share your bed tonight?* He had told her that the folk amongst whom he had grown up were good church-going people, with a great regard for moral values. He might be shocked and horrified at the mere suggestion that they should sleep together – or rather, not sleep – before marriage.

Rose glanced quickly across at him, hoping he had not noticed her flush. Anyone would think I was an eighteen-year-old virgin who knew nothing about men and didn't want to learn, she scolded herself. Luke's a good man, he's let me set the pace for our relationship; I think we'll just let things take their course.

'Oh, my thoughts aren't worth a penny,' she said aloud, meeting his eyes and seeing the quizzical gleam in them. 'Hasn't it been a lovely holiday, Luke? I don't mind admitting that I'm going to miss you almost as much as I miss the girls.'

Luke's eyebrows shot up and he slowed the car in order to reach across and pat her knee. 'That's the nicest thing you could have said,' he told her. 'I shall miss you horribly but we must meet whenever we get the opportunity. After all, I'd say we were more than just friendly acquaintances now, wouldn't you?'

Rose, agreeing, suddenly noticed that many of the sheep in the field past which they were driving had lambs beside them. 'Oh, Luke, pull into that gateway so we can have a proper look,' she said eagerly. 'Auntie Blod said that lambs in the Lowlands district came earlier than in the hills . . . oh, aren't they sweet?'

Luke complied, and Rose was able to steer the conversation back to farming. In discussing such matters, she was able to put out of her mind how they would spend the coming night.

As they drove away from the fascinating lambs, Luke could not help glancing quizzically at Rose but her face was still averted as she enjoyed the countryside, drowsing in the early April sunlight. He wondered what she had been thinking to bring such a burning blush to her cheeks when he had offered her a penny for her thoughts. He himself had been wondering whether it would completely spoil their relationship if he suggested that they might share a bed. The maddening thing was, he could not think of a way to ask her which would leave him an escape route if she refused – an escape route which would mean he could say, *No, you misunderstood me; as if I would make a suggestion like that!* He glanced across at Rose again and battled with an almost irresistible urge to stop the car, slide his hand round the back of her neck and pull her gently towards him. Then he would kiss her flushed cheek, the line of her jaw, the firm white skin of her neck. He would cuddle her, tell her how beautiful she was, explain that he had never felt like this about anyone . . . oh, oh, oh, it had been dreadfully hard at the farm, to keep his kisses gentle, to see her disappear into the room she shared with Dilys whilst he made his way to his own bed.

Not that he would have missed the days he had spent at the farm, not for anything. The more he knew of her, the more he loved her and he found her daughters delightful, even though, at times, he could not help wishing them elsewhere, because he realised that kissing and cuddling Rose was not possible when the girls were present. He had no wish to alienate them and knew that a show of the sort of affection he felt would probably both annoy and embarrass them. So, enjoyable though their stay at the farm had been, it had also been frustrating. And now that he and Rose were alone, he realised he was afraid of letting her see how he felt in case she honestly could not share his feelings. Perhaps a woman needs more time than a man to make up her mind, he told himself. If only it were possible to explain that he loved her unconditionally, but somehow he did not seem able to find the words.

He drove on. Sometimes they talked, commenting on the scene through which they passed, sometimes they were companionably silent, and presently Luke told Rose to keep an eye open for a comfortable-looking inn or public house. 'We'll need a meal and it would be nice to stay the night in a village, or perhaps by a river, so we can have a walk, stretch our legs, before bed,' he said. 'Um, Rosie . . .'

'Yes?' Rose said, as the silence lengthened. 'What were you going to say, Luke?'

'Um . . . there's a pleasant-looking pub; the one with the thatch, by that little stone bridge. See it? Shall we stop there? We'd get the best of both worlds. That bridge must cross a river, yet it's only fifty yards or so from the village itself.'

Rose looked across at him, raised her eyebrows, began to speak and then seemed to change her mind. 'It looks lovely,' she said briskly. 'I wonder if the landlady makes home-made pickles?'

Luke drove the car in under an arch leading into a small courtyard, slowed to a stop, applied the handbrake and turned off the engine. He got out but left their suitcases locked in the boot. 'Better make sure they've a room – rooms, I mean – for us before we march in with our luggage,' he said. He could have kicked himself for not being bolder, but it was no good now; he would ask for two single rooms and then, when they had eaten and were taking the walk he had promised himself, he would tell her how he felt about her.

They went into the inn through the back door, along a corridor and into a pleasant little hall. There was a bell on the counter and Luke rang it and, almost immediately, an elderly woman appeared. She was wearing a fold-over floral apron and there was a smudge of flour on her nose, and she carried with her, as she approached them, the comfortable smell of food cooking. 'Glad you rang the bell 'cos I'm cooking the evening meal and I'm by meself this evening till the village girl comes in to help serve, and me husband gets back from visiting his old mother,' she said, beaming at them. 'Now what can I do for you, my dears? Is it a room you're wanting? I thought I heard a car drive into the courtyard, a few minutes since, but Mr Symes – he's a travelling salesman and a reg'lar – is stayin' here a couple of days so it might of been him.'

Luke opened his mouth to speak but Rose forestalled him. She put her left hand on the counter, smiled at the landlady and said: 'Yes, we would like a room. We didn't bring our luggage out of the car in case you were full, but if you have a room free, my husband can fetch it in right now. Oh, I didn't ask your terms.'

'Ten bob for me best double what overlooks the river, seven and six for the others, and I'm Mrs Rogers.'

'Nice to meet you, Mrs Rogers. Luke, darling, shall we spoil ourselves and have the best room?'

Luke was so astonished that he could only open and close his mouth and Mrs Rogers, plainly interpreting this as horror over her high prices, said quickly: 'The ten bob includes your breakfasts, o' course, and I does a grand breakfast: eggs from me own hens, a pile of fried potatoes, toast and home-made marmalade, o' course, and as much tea as you can drink.'

Luke pulled himself together. 'That sounds just fine and dandy,' he said. 'And we'd like dinner tonight, please.' He turned to smile down at Rose. 'It certainly smells delicious, doesn't it, honey?'

'It's onion soup, followed by steak an' kidney pudding, mashed potatoes and peas, with an egg custard or apple snow for afters,' Mrs Rogers told them. While she spoke, she had been fishing under the counter and now produced a large, leather-bound book. 'If you wouldn't mind signin' in, sir . . . at one time, no one ever bothered, but it's different now. Just your name . . .' Her eyes travelled over their uniforms. 'And where you're stationed, o' course.' She chuckled richly. 'Your home address wouldn't be no manner o' use since I can tell from your voice you're an American, though you're wearin' our uniform and not theirs.'

'I joined your air force before America came into the war,' Luke said, well used to answering this particular question. 'I'll just fetch our luggage in. Rose, will you sign in, honey?'

He left Rose filling in the visitors' book and returned, presently, a bag in either hand. Then he and Rose followed the landlady up the creaking oak staircase, along an uncarpeted corridor and into a delightful, low-ceilinged bedroom, whose window overlooked fields and meadows as well as the willow-girt river. There was a washstand, a square of carpet and a large, brass bedstead, as well as a couple of easy chairs and, of course, a dressing table.

Luke glanced towards the bed, then quickly away, but Rose walked calmly across to it and examined the number of blankets before turning to thank the landlady. 'It's a lovely room,' she said sincerely. 'We'll settle ourselves in, have a wash and brush up, and then come downstairs. When do you serve dinner, Mrs Rogers?'

Mrs Rogers told them, adding that there was a bathroom at the end of the corridor. 'The water's always hot because it's fed by the Aga and we never let that go out,' she told them. 'See you in a moment, then.'

She went out, closing the door behind her, and Luke turned and lifted Rose into his arms in one swift, exuberant movement. 'Rose Nadolski, I love you more than I've ever loved anyone in my entire life and I want to marry you just as soon as it can be arranged,' he said huskily. 'I was standing there wondering why you'd put your left hand on the counter . . . oh, Rosie, Rosie, Rosie!'

* * *

Rose had expected to feel shy and awkward when she and Luke made their way up to their room after they had had an excellent dinner and a long, meandering walk through the soft April evening. The river smells had been sweet and in the comforting darkness, under the willow trees, they had kissed and cuddled passionately so that, in the end, going to their room seemed both easy and a natural thing to do. Once there, Luke's matter-of-fact, loving attitude made shyness seem both foolish and unnecessary.

They went to the bathroom separately, to change into their night things, clean their teeth and wash. Rose got into bed first, and when Luke came in he turned off the light and fumbled his way across the room in the darkness, cursing as he cannoned into one of the chairs, so that they were both laughing when he joined her under the blankets.

'It's all very well for you to laugh but I might have broken my toe,' Luke said ruefully, trying to rub the injured member and making Rose gasp as his knee struck hers sharply. This set them off laughing again until Luke put a stop to such nonsense by kissing her.

Looking back on it afterwards, Rose could only marvel at how sweet love could be with the right person. She and Luke, she decided, were made for each other. Next morning, as they got themselves ready for the day ahead, she told Luke, shyly, that she had never known, had never guessed, that loving could be so sweet.

Luke, carefully shaving in front of the small mirror on the washstand, turned to smile at her. 'It was the same for me,' he told her. 'Oh, Rosie, we're so lucky to have found one another! Let's make a vow never to lose our way again.'

Chapter Fifteen

Luke dropped Rose off at the gates, waved a quick farewell, and turned the car about. They had said their proper farewells parked on the side of the lane which led to the airfield and Luke was glad they had done so. It would not have been the thing for two people in uniform to start exchanging fond farewells where anyone might see them.

Luke drove back to his own station noticing, with some alarm, that he was having to fight to keep the car on the road. The wind had been getting up all day and now it was really bad; he pitied whoever was flying tonight. If this wind kept up, taking off – and landing again – could be a tricky business. However, he told himself as he went to park the car, since his leave did not end until midnight he, at least, would be safely out of it.

The thought had scarcely formed in his mind when he heard himself hailed. It was Fred, his squadron leader, walking rapidly across the hard standing towards him, a grin almost splitting his good-natured face. 'Thank God you're back, Luke,' he said as soon as Luke had alighted from the car and dragged out his grip. 'Your crew have agreed to just one more sortie tonight to help out, and since you were supposed to be on leave we'd put young Masters down to pilot Bouncing Betty, but he's not really experienced enough for this kind of weather.'

'But my leave doesn't finish till midnight,' Luke

pointed out. 'Still an' all, I guess I don't want to see Bouncing Betty slammed into the runway or shot up over the target, if I can help it. What'll y' do with young Masters, though?'

'Oh, he can go with you as second pilot; he'll learn a thing or two just watching you,' Fred said breezily, twirling the waxed ends of his moustache. It was the largest moustache on the station and Fred was always playing with it; Luke knew the other man was proud of it, despite the jokes which abounded, the men referring to it as 'Fred's spare propeller' and daring him to shave it off so that they could see whether he really had teeth.

'Okay, he's welcome to travel as supercargo; if I'm hit, he could come in useful,' Luke said jokingly, then wished he hadn't. He had never considered himself superstitious but since flying the Wellington he had noticed that none of the crews liked going on a sortie on their birthdays or special anniversaries, and no one liked being put in at the last minute, in case the vengeful god who watched over aircrews decided to pick on someone who should not have been in the air at all on that day. But you couldn't let superstition dictate your movements, so he gave Fred a big grin and reminded him that they would be a pack of sandwiches short, since he could scarcely take over young Masters's grub if he was actually going to fly with them. Fred frowned thoughtfully, then said he would consult Masters, see how he felt.

Luke made his way to his room, where he undressed and got into bed, after a glance at his watch. It was barely two o'clock; he could sleep for four hours and still be in plenty of time for the briefing.

He awoke to find that the wind still howled around the hut, if anything noisier than before, though fortunately it had not woken him. He got up, padded along to the bathroom for a wash, then went back and dressed himself in his flying gear. Another glance at his watch told him that he should go down to the anteroom for a cup of char and a bun before the briefing, especially as, if Masters was coming with them, he would have to plead with the head cook for extra rations for the flight.

However, as he emerged from his room, he met young Masters coming towards him, holding out a packet of sandwiches and a bottle of cold tea which the cookhouse had provided. He grinned cheerfully at Luke, handing him the food and drink with a flourish. 'Fred explained that you were back early and going to fly Bouncing Betty yourself, so I've got a night off since my own kite isn't scheduled to go on this raid,' he said. 'It was quite a relief; no one likes taking another feller's place.'

'Thanks,' Luke said, taking the sandwiches and bottle of tea. He did not remind Masters that any sort of last minute change was also considered unlucky. What was the point? The younger man was clearly relieved to be let off the hook; it was both cruel and unnecessary to mention that Luke himself was now in the invidious position of actually flying the kite when he should have been sleeping soundly in his own bed.

However, it was a blessing that he and Rosie had decided to break the back of the journey the previous day! At least it had given him time for four hours' solid rest, which meant that he was not starting off tired and stale. On the other hand, of course, had he been later arriving, Fred might not have spotted him, might not have suggested he should fly Bouncing Betty tonight. Still, he was truly fond of his crew and knew they would be a good deal happier with himself in charge than with the young, and relatively untried, Masters.

'By Jupiter, am I glad it's you handling the old girl and not that young feller,' Phil, the wireless operator, bawled in Luke's ear as the heavy plane left the ground. It had been a fearful take-off with the wind now gusting, now dropping, now coming at them from the wrong angle; Bouncing Betty had not been the only bird to have to make several attempts before she became airborne. Now, however, Luke eased back the stick, pulling her nose up into a steep climb to get above the clouds – say five thousand feet. They knew their target was the factories which abounded along the Rhine and that these were always well defended, not only by gunners on the ground but by every fighter the Nazis could put up. Still, if he kept as high as possible until they were right over the target, then laid their eggs quickly and turned for home, they should be all right.

The plane droned on and the men became absorbed in keeping themselves warm and alert, for it was extremely cold. They had to keep radio silence so could not chat over the intercom, but when it was time for Luke to eat his sandwiches and drink his tea, he had a few murmured words with Phil. Phil slid into the co-pilot's seat, checked the instruments, then bawled above the noise of the engines: 'How did your leave go?'

Luke smiled reminiscently. 'It couldn't have been better,' he said dreamily. 'We're going to get married, Rosie and me.' He shoved a sandwich into his mouth, noticing it was bloody Spam again, and spoke rather thickly through it. 'Damn, I told her I'd ring her tonight. I wonder if she'll guess I'm flying? I told her I wasn't, but I'll ring her tomorrow, first thing, before breakfast – hers, I mean, not ours.'

Phil nodded. 'Well, that's just great, skip,' he said. 'Tell you what, though, I'm damn glad it'll be you and not me who has to land if the wind stays at gale force. You'll be fishtailing all over the runway, trying to put her down without losing a wing or smashing the undercarriage.'

Luke nodded grimly. 'It was hard enough getting her up,' he reminded the wireless operator. 'If the Met boys knew about this hurricane, I'd have thought we'd have been grounded. But there you are, they'll be full of it tomorrow morning when it'll probably be dying down.' He took a swig of cold tea, then belched. 'I almost envy young Masters, snug in his bed.'

'Almost? I envy anyone who's asleep in their bed,' Phil said frankly. 'Not long to go now though; another hour and we'll be over the target.'

When they reached the target, there could be no doubt that it was the right one. Throughout the flight, they had been aware of the dark shadows of the rest of the squadron, and as soon as they saw the moonlit river below them, and the enormous flat-roofed factories on either bank, the quiet night became a very noisy night indeed. The flares which lit up the scene below them so that they could drop their bombs accurately were joined by the bursting shells of flak some of which came near enough to Bouncing Betty to make her name seem entirely appropriate as she rocked about the sky. Below them, they could see the fires caused by the first bombs to drop, and all too soon they saw the leading Wellington go down in a mass of screaming flame, whilst a Ju88 followed her, machine guns blazing as she sought to slaughter the crew. Not that the crew had had a chance, Luke thought grimly, fighting to keep Bouncing Betty steady as they approached their particular target. Below them, several factories were on fire, but one large one seemed undamaged and it was for this that Luke was heading. He tried to ignore the attentions of the German fighter planes, only jinking from time to time when it became a matter of survival to do so, but mostly he held the great plane steady. He knew that Neville, the bomb aimer, was waiting for exactly the right moment and swept a little lower, reducing speed and, because of the extra drag, having to fight the kite like a recalcitrant horse as her nose dipped and she seemed about to stall.

But it was all right. From behind him he heard the cry, 'Bombs away!' and hastily reached across to increase engine power and pull her nose up. Even as he did so, he heard Neville shout, 'Let's go, let's go, let's go!' and knew that their task was accomplished; knew it even more satisfyingly as the plane banked in a turn and he caught a glimpse of the huge factory, with smoke and flames pouring through three enormous holes in its roof.

All around him, chaos still reigned. It was a clear night but the smoke and the flak and the constant attacks from the German fighters turned the sky into bedlam. Luke felt profoundly grateful that their job was done; now all they had to do was get home safe and face the difficulties of trying to land, without mishap, in a hurricane.

All around them, the shapes of other bombers heading for home could be seen, but he knew the German fighters would follow them as far as they dared and hoped that the Spitfires and Hurricanes would soon appear to harass the Luftwaffe.

Behind him, the men were settling down, beginning to discuss the raid, wondering what the weather would be like in four or five hours' time when they reached Norfolk. The fires and confusion of the Rhine were far behind them now, the great planes droning quietly on beneath the stars. When a Ju88 suddenly flashed in front of Bouncing Betty, Luke was so surprised that, for a fatal instant, he did not jerk the stick into immediate avoidance, and in that moment the two planes actually collided. Luke heard himself scream at the chaps, telling them to get out, as the plane began to lose height. Then he was battling to tighten his own parachute straps, which he always loosened before climbing into his seat, and following the crew out through the hatch.

One moment it was all noise, bright lights, fear and confusion. Then there was rushing air, ice-cold against his face, and the certainty that this was the prelude to dying. Frantically, his fingers felt for the ripcord, found it, tugged gently, then a good deal harder, and he felt the shock in every part of his body as the 'chute opened and jerked his mad downward career to a painful, blessed stop.

Luke glanced around him and felt an almost crazy relief flood through him as he counted the opening 'chutes. They were all there, floating downwards as he was, some ahead of him, looking like pale mushrooms against the dark of the ground beneath, others to his left or right . . . but all there, all apparently in one piece. He had been last out and had noticed, with what small, cool part of his mind had been noticing anything but the danger, the kite's doomed glide earthwards. Luke thought that his crew were a pretty cool bunch. They had answered his urgent shout to bale out in a sensible and orderly fashion; grabbing for their parachutes and jumping as soon as they were able to do so . . . and it could be the saving of them. For one moment – a horrid one – it occurred to him that they might not all have got out after all; that one or two, or maybe more, of the parachutes he had seen might belong to the crew of the Ju88 which had crashed into them. Then he dismissed the thought with a shudder. Poor devils, they hadn't had a chance. The collision had simply annihilated their craft; what was left of it had gone down in flames, falling faster than the Wellington . . .

His thoughts were interrupted. From below them came an almightly crash, then he saw the flames and knew it was Betty's funeral pyre. That would give their position away all right, he told himself, but found that he could not worry overmuch about what lay ahead. It was so strange, so peaceful, floating gently earthwards, with the sky above them dark as the stars began to dim, and the earth beneath them totally black apart from the flames from the aircraft. Luke found himself relishing the silence; quiet was something totally absent from the experience of flying a Wimpey, particularly once they drew near their target, and as he looked down once more it occurred to him for one horrifying moment that all that blackness might be sea.

Then he chided himself for an idiot; had poor Betty plunged into the sea she would scarcely still be burning, and besides, they had had hours to go before they would have been over water. Gently descending, he realised that the moon had disappeared, perhaps behind a mountain top, and the starlight was not strong enough to show the ground beneath in much detail, but he remembered that one could steer a parachute to a certain extent, and hoped to be able to keep clear of any trees. He could see no lights and hoped they were in open country – moorland for preference – but was still too high to be able to make even an informed guess. They had been extremely lucky, he reminded himself, that the fighter which had collided with them had been by itself, not accompanied by other aircraft which might have followed them down, machine-gunning both men and 'chutes as they descended. He knew it happened sometimes, had seen it himself, and thanked God for their own escape from such a fate. What was more, because they had flown some distance from their target before the accident happened, there was a strong chance that they would be captured and imprisoned and not quietly killed as had happened to many an airman parachuting down amongst the houses and factories he had just bombed. If he'd been able to choose, it would have been better to parachute into France, but choice, unfortunately, was seldom available, and life as a prisoner of war would be infinitely preferable to death by howling mob.

So when the ground grew close enough to identify what was beneath, Luke felt he could not complain when he saw that it was forest, stretching as far as the eye could reach. He stared over to his left, where Betty had burst into flames, but could no longer see even smoke. Either she had not flamed for long or the wind was stronger than he had thought and had carried him well away from the crash, he told himself, even as he became entangled in an extremely tall beech tree and heard at least one of his crew crashing into a similar specimen, though at some distance. Fate had dealt pretty kindly with them, he thought, as he began, as speedily as he could, to unbuckle himself from his harness. In a way, it was the most hazardous act he could have contemplated, since he was pretty near the top of the tree and might easily plunge to earth without the parachute to hold him up, but he did not intend to simply swing here, like a damn fool butterfly caught in a spider's web, until some German or other came to cut him down. No siree, he would take his chance on a speedy – but not too speedy – descent to the forest floor.

One glance at the parachute itself told him that he was unlikely to be able to disentangle it. He knew he was supposed to bury the 'chute, though no one had ever explained how one dug a fairly long and deep hole in the unyielding ground beneath large trees without so much as a teaspoon to help. Still, the question was academic and did not trouble Luke at all. Looking around him – for he was still in the upper branches of the tree – he realised that he, and at least one of his crew, had landed in a very extensive forest, most of which was still leafless, though the buds would be bursting in a few days. By screwing up his eyes and staring in all directions, he thought he could make out another 'chute in the branches to his left, and presently, as the light grew stronger, he was sure of it. Gingerly, he began to descend from his lofty perch, wondering as he did so at his own calm acceptance of the situation and concluding that, after the hell of the bombing raid, almost anything else would seem positively pleasant. It was the first time he had descended by parachute – the first time he had ever been so high in a tree, come to that – and because the night was balmy and there had been no enemy fighters to shoot him up, he had rather enjoyed the experience. The peace of the forest could not but affect him and he remembered, gratefully, a childhood spent scrambling up and down trees as he began the long descent. Had he been able to see just exactly how high he was, he might have panicked, for several times he missed his footing in the dimming starlight and once he seized upon a branch too thin to bear his weight and crashed ten feet before landing, far too abruptly, upon a wide and spreading branch.

He told himself, afterwards, that he might have got down uninjured, had it not been for the voice which hailed him from below. 'Hey, skip! Is that you?' Luke gave an almighty start, lost his hold on the branch, and crashed some fifteen feet to the ground, his fall only partially broken by landing on the crew member who had shouted to him. Cursing, he got to his feet, only then discovering that his left ankle would not support him and seemed to be at a very odd angle.

The man who had called him proved to be Neville, the bomb aimer, and Luke addressed him crossly as the other man scrambled to his feet: 'You bloody fool, you scared the life out of me shouting like that. I wouldn't be surprised if I've busted my ankle.'

'Well, you knocked all the breath out of me, and I wouldn't be surprised if you've broken a couple of my ribs,' Neville grumbled, but he grinned as he did so. Luke saw the flash of his teeth in the grey dawn light. 'What'll we do now, skip? Where's the rest of 'em, d'you think?'

'Dunno,' Luke said shortly. His ankle was beginning to hurt like hell and even the thought of putting it to the ground made him wince. 'I'm gonna sit here, see if the pain goes off if I stay still for a moment. You go and see if you can find the others, only don't lose me, for God's sake, because with this ankle I'm goin' no place, not without help.'

'Right, skip, and I'll see if I can find you a couple of stout branches to use like crutches,' Neville said. He fished a penknife from the pocket of his flying suit. 'I'll blaze a trail so I get back to you. Sure you're all right to be left? You're beginning to look pretty green.'

'It's the pain, and shock I suppose,' Luke said, as laconically as he could. 'Off with you, Nev.'

For a while after Neville had left, Luke simply sat and surveyed his foot. He knew he ought to take his boot off in case the ankle swelled, but he found he was not at all keen to so much as touch it. However, it had to be faced, so he began to draw his foot up, the breath hissing between his teeth at the sheer agony of even such a small movement. When he could reach his boot, he untied his laces and began to try to get it off, but already his whole foot, and the lower half of his leg, was swollen and shiny, as well as turning an increasingly deep purple. Luke groaned aloud and retied the lace, though loosely. He imagined that if Neville could find the other crew members, they might somehow manage to get him to the edge of the forest. They would have to leave him then because they would want to try to reach France, and must know they could scarcely do so while burdened with an injured man. All right, so he was clearly destined to spend the rest of the war as a prisoner – for you, the war is over – but that did not mean his entire crew must suffer.

Presently, Neville returned. He was alone but he carried what looked like two stout cudgels, one under each arm, and announced proudly that his trusty knife had come in useful for stripping the branches from a couple of young saplings to make the skipper a pair of crutches.

'Well, I dunno,' Luke said doubtfully. 'If there were a few more of us . . . but with only us two, and me with only one foot . . .'

'P'raps I ought to take your boot off,' Neville said doubtfully. 'I wish Brendan were here. He's done a

First Aid course – he'd know what's best to do. If I tried taking your boot off, I might be doing more harm than good without knowing it.'

'I've already tried; it won't come off. My foot's already too swollen, and anyway, the boot sort of contains it – if you know what I mean. Without the boot, it would flop around too much. So you didn't see any of the others? How far did you go?'

'Not very far,' Neville said, rather evasively. 'To tell the truth, I was afraid of getting lost and not being able to find you again.' He grinned deprecatingly at his skipper. 'I know I blazed a trail but a penknife doesn't leave a huge mark and, of course, I only marked one side of each tree. If I'd walked past a marked tree on the wrong side, it would have been all up with me; real babes in the wood stuff.'

'And you didn't come across a road, or the end of the trees, or any sign of habitation?' Luke asked, rather helplessly. He remembered stories of the enormous German forests which stretched for mile after mile, without so much as a track between the trees. It was all very well talking about escaping to free France, or even trying to make their way back to England, but that would mean living on the country, and since they had no gun with which to shoot squirrels, and the forest seemed to consist mainly of beeches and oaks, they could scarcely survive on acorns and beech mast, even had such things been available in April.

Neville shook his head. 'Nothing but trees,' he said gloomily. 'Look, skipper, are you up to trying to move, because I've a nasty sort of feeling that if we just stay here, it's only our bones that the searchers will find. I've got my compass so we shan't walk round in circles, but we'd better move on while you've still got the strength.'

The light was getting stronger all the time, though

it still came dimly to them beneath the almost leafless branches. Luke looked doubtfully at his bomb aimer's rough crutches and then at his horribly swollen and painful foot. 'I'll have a go . . .' he was beginning, when a thought struck him. He had no idea where Neville had landed after leaving the plane, but doubted that he had been at the very top of any of the surrounding trees, since he seemed to have escaped without any obvious bruises or abrasions. He said as much and Neville replied, cheerfully, that he had been lucky; he had come down in a clearing, had shed his parachute, buried it, sketchily, in leaf mould, and had then walked towards the sounds of crashing which had been, he realised now, his skipper's far from effortless descent. 'But first, old feller, I think you should shin up one of these trees – go as high as you can without risking a fall – and see what you can see from up there,' Luke said. 'When I was at the top of my beech, it was still pretty dark so I couldn't see much, but you might be able to pick out some sort of landmark, or even a thinning of the trees. Why, you might even see other parachutes, because I'm sure I can't be the only one who got tangled in branches. Then we could meet up; we'd have a much better chance of finding civilisation if we were all together.'

'Right, I'll have a go,' Neville said, though his voice was doubtful. 'Whilst I'm doing it, skip, do you want to have a go on the crutches? A sort of practice, like?'

By now, Luke's foot was on fire with pain and his ankle sheer agony. He only had to make the tiniest movement for bone to grate against bone, and even the thought of trying out the crutches brought drops of sweat standing out on his forehead. 'I'll wait till you come back, if it's all the same to you, Nev,' he said hoarsely. 'I wouldn't dare try alone in case I fell.

And if I fell, I don't think I'd ever manage to get up.'

'Right you are; stay put until I get back,' Neville said breezily, but Luke could see that his bomb aimer was worried. Neville was a short, stocky man, which might make it difficult for him to assist his much taller skipper if they had to walk further than a few paces. But it was no use worrying over what might never happen, so Luke leaned back against the trunk of the beech, closed his eyes and tried to think calming thoughts whilst listening to Neville grunting with effort as he began to scramble up a big old elm tree, with branches spaced a good deal closer than those of the beech through which Luke himself had descended.

Presently, he opened his eyes and saw that Neville was out of sight, though the movement of the upper branches showed that he must be nearing the top of the tall elm. Luke felt rather guilty; it had been his idea for Neville to climb a tree and he had not thought to suggest a beech, an oak or a sycamore, but now he remembered that elms were tricky, that their branches could appear stout but break off easily, earning them the nickname of coffin wood.

However, ten minutes or so later, he felt the ground shudder slightly as Neville jumped down from the lowest branch. His face wore a beam. 'There's a 'chute in a tree and someone tugging at it no more than a hundred yards off,' he said gleefully. 'Don't worry, I noted the direction, and whoever it is, I'll have him back here before you can say knife. With two of us, one each side, we can move you to a better spot in no time. Oh, and I forgot to mention, I've seen a road and the trees on the other side of it are definitely more sparse. Skip? You all right?'

Luke had closed his eyes again as soon as he saw his friend was safe, but now he opened them, trying to fight off a feeling of total weariness. 'I'll live; I never heard of anyone dying of a broken ankle,' he said weakly. 'I'll just rest for a moment while you go and find the owner of that 'chute.'

Luke must have dozed, for he awoke to the sound of voices and saw, with real pleasure, Brendan accompanying Neville across the short distance to the foot of the great beech. 'I've bust my damned ankle,' he said wearily. 'I tried to get my boot off, but no luck. Still, if you and Neville can help me to the road . . .'

They got him there. It took them two full hours and if the journey was tedious for them, it was sheer agony for Luke. When they reached the road, and propped him against a convenient tree, he told them they must begin to make their way towards the French border if they meant to try to escape.

'We can't leave you here alone,' Neville said firmly. 'God knows when you'd be found, if at all. Besides, we're miles and miles from the border, so I think we'd best stick together. We can try to take you a bit further . . .'

'You'll leave me here,' Luke said, with all the firmness he could muster. 'Let's face it, I'm no use to anyone with a busted ankle, I'd only hold you back. Someone's bound to come along and I'll end up in hospital. We're always being told how efficient the Jerries are, so I guess they can set an ankle as well as any Yank or Limey.' He grinned at them. 'Good luck, fellers, see you back in Blighty when the war's over. Oh, and can you get the news to my girl? I don't want her thinking . . . thinking . . .'

He was looking at his crew as he spoke and suddenly realised he was seeing them as though through water. Brendan was speaking, asking him which girl, but he was no longer capable of replying. He was descending a long slope which ended in darkness, and he was glad to enter it.

Luke came round with a shout of pain and a jerk which, he thought afterwards, might very well have been the last move he ever made, for when he managed to focus his eyes he saw that he was looking down the barrel of a rifle. He realised that the throbbing pain in his forehead must mean that the owner of the rifle had jabbed him there, quite viciously, to bring him round; he could feel a trickle of blood running down the side of his face.

The man standing in front of him spoke, but since it was in German, Luke could not understand a word. He was an old man, wearing breeches, long leather boots laced up to the knee, a faded shirt and an ancient tweed jacket. He wore a pair of tiny, much mended spectacles behind which his eyes glared, the whites showing all round the irises and proving, to Luke's secret dismay, that his questioner was scared out of his mind and might easily decide that shooting someone as dangerous as himself was his best option.

The man butted him with the rifle again, this time in the chest, and Luke groaned and tried to pull himself upright, then gave a shout of pain as the movement disturbed his ankle. Hastily, the old man levelled his rifle once more, this time pointing it at Luke's head. He heard the safety catch click off, saw the old man's finger tighten on the trigger, and gave himself up for lost.

Despite the fact that she was very tired, Rose got little sleep that night. The wind increased to such an extent that all hands were called out to either hold the aircraft down or get them into hangars, if there was sufficient room. Rose, with her companions, battled across the airfield, trying to keep their eyes half closed, for a veritable dust storm had arisen to make things even harder for the would-be rescuers. Whilst out there, they saw two pines and a sturdy elm tree come crashing to earth, and one of the storage huts simply blew away, leaving the cardboard boxes of supplies to bowl merrily across grass and runways, with anyone who could be spared from the aircraft in hot pursuit.

'How on earth will the kites get down safely in this?' Kate asked Rose, as they staggered to the cookhouse, bearing a large cardboard box full of cornflakes between them. 'Our fighters didn't go up, did they – too light, I suppose – but I bet the big bombers, the Wimpeys and Lancs, took off on their raids.' They had reached the cookhouse by now and dumped their burden amongst the other assorted boxes and bundles which had been brought into the shelter of the brick building. 'You'll be wanting to ring East Wretham in the morning to make sure your Luke got down safely.'

'Luke wasn't flying tonight; he was still on leave until midnight,' Rose explained. She pushed the damp hair off her forehead and whistled: 'Phew! I doubt the poor bloke has had much sleep though, because they'll turn everyone out, even the officers, to save as much as possible from being smashed to bits by the wind. Have you ever seen anything like it, Kate?'

Kate shook her head, then chuckled. 'Did you see ACW Franklyn, though? She's only a little thing, she can't weigh more than six stone, and the wind picked her up as though she was a feather, bowled her six feet along the ground, and might have taken her further if LAC Roberts hadn't grabbed her as she passed. I've never seen a girl so furious. She was weeping with temper.'

'Who can blame her?' Rose said, as the two of them

emerged from the cookhouse. The wind seized Rose's once neat brown hair and flung it across her face so that she was forced to stop, gather it up and hold it back with one hand. 'What'll we do next? I'm dead tired and we seem to have done all we can do to help but, to tell you the truth, I'm scared our hut will blow away, taking us and our beds with it, like Dorothy in *The Wizard of Oz*!'

Kate had opened her mouth to answer when a voice came booming and crackling over the tannoy. 'All personnel to take themselves to the cookhouse, for tea and a wad,' it announced. 'The Met Office tell us that the gusts should die down by evening.'

Kate and Rose turned with one accord, and made their way back to the cookhouse, relieved to be out of the wind and in a solid building, though the roof, Rose supposed, was as liable to blow away as anything else on the airfield.

Across the room, Jen and Mo hailed them. It appeared that they had been working in the cookhouse helping to get the tea brewed and the wads on the go, so were comfortably ensconced at a table for four by the time the other two entered. They greeted the newcomers cheerfully, and for some moments the talk was all of the destruction the storm was wreaking on their airfield and what must be happening on other stations.

'We saw a barrage balloon going past at one hell of a speed; it took the chimneys clean off Grundy's farm as it went and is probably halfway to France by now,' Mo said cheerfully. 'And Bates had washed a pair of stockings and some knickers and hung them on that bit of a line behind the hut. She said even the line's gone and God alone knows if she'll ever see her knickers again.'

'Was your chap flying tonight, Rosie?' Jen asked,

taking a large bite out of her bun and speaking, rather thickly, through it. 'If so, landing will be pretty dicey, won't it?'

'No, he's not flying, he's still on leave,' Rose told her. 'But I'll ring first thing in the morning because no doubt he'll have been up most of the night, like us, and with a bit of luck he'll know when he's flying again so we might have a chance to meet.'

Jen waggled her eyebrows. 'How a week's leave can change a person,' she remarked. 'Before you went, you even objected to Luke being spoken of as "your feller" but now, you're actually talking . . . well, like the rest of us.'

'He's asked me to marry him,' Rose said proudly. 'I think I must have been mad not to realise that life with Luke would be totally different – wonderfully different – from life with Steve. Oh, I know it's wrong to speak ill of the dead, and I don't meant to do so, and besides, it's all over; Steve is a part of my pre-war past that I want to forget, and Luke, believe me, is my future.'

The three girls nodded, clearly impressed. 'Lucky old Rose,' Kate murmured. 'I hope and pray that one day I'll meet someone who can mean as much to me as Bobby did. As for you two . . .' she pointed a derisive finger at Mo and Jen, 'it's about time you settled down and made the current flame the happiest man on earth. Who are the current flames, by the way?'

Jen giggled. She was notoriously free with her affections but had been going out with the same mechanic for five months, and this time seemed to have no urge to move on. Mo, on the other hand, was true to her peacetime boyfriend, who had joined the army and been sent to Burma. They exchanged letters, but many months elapsed before such letters arrived and lately Mo had had a couple of dates with a Hurricane pilot, though she assured her friends that Joe and herself were simply marking time until her Norman and his Mandy were back in England; for Mandy was a Wren up at Scapa Flow and her leaves were never long enough to allow her to come this far south.

'When we're as old and withered as you two, we'll probably marry and have kids and that,' Jen said airily, and seeing the wistful look in Mo's eyes, Rose felt guilty. She was so lucky to have Luke close at hand; poor Mo must have heard about the terrible fighting in Burma, where the troops were using jungle warfare against the Japanese, whilst the Burmese did their best to avoid both combatants. She must know that, even as they spoke, her Norman might be dead, or in a Japanese prisoner of war camp, which would be almost as bad. It wasn't fair to tease her when her future was so uncertain.

Rose was still congratulating herself on her luck when she went to the mess immediately before breakfast next morning, hoping to be able to get to the telephone before others had the same idea. She was lucky and the voice at the other end of the line informed her, crisply, that she had reached East Wretham and asked her to whom she wished to speak.

'Flying Officer Nadolski, please.'

There was a short, awkward silence, then the voice at the other end said, cautiously: 'I'm sorry, who is that speaking?'

Rose's heart plummeted. Why had he asked who she was? Why had he not just gone and fetched Luke? Of course, it would be better if he told Luke who was calling, but the chaps usually simply sang out that so and so was wanted on the phone.

However . . . she cleared her throat. 'I'm Corporal Rose McAllister, ringing from Coltishall airfield,' she said, as crisply as she could. 'Luke and I only came back from leave yesterday, so I know he wasn't flying, but I thought I'd have a word . . .' Her voice tailed off.

The voice the other end cleared its throat in its turn. 'Sorry, corp, thought I'd better ask,' he said. 'Flying Officer Nadolski took his Wimpey over Germany last night; he went as a favour to the CO really, because the only pilot spare, so to speak, was a youngster, three months out of training school.'

'Oh, I see,' Rose said, with a most uncomfortable feeling beginning to tie her stomach into knots. 'Have they got down yet? Is . . . is he safe?'

'It's been a wild night and the wind's been gusting at well over eighty mph,' the voice said evasively. 'Several of the kites haven't come in yet, but at least one was blown far enough off course to end up in Kent, so no need to worry too much yet. Give it a go later, corp.'

Rose put the receiver down slowly and walked back across the mess, heading for the cookhouse. She told herself that it was too much to assimilate in one go, that she must sit down and think about what she had been told. Oddly, there was anger mixed with her anguish. How could he have agreed to fly when he had no need to do so, was officially on leave? How could he risk his life which, she now realised, was as precious to her as her own? But by the time she reached the cookhouse, her common sense had begun to reassert itself. His crew meant a great deal to him, perhaps more than they would have meant to someone who had been born and brought up in Britain. Luke was not a loner from choice and his crew had taken him to their hearts, realising, as Rose had only just begun to do, how solitary he was, without so much as an old school friend, let alone a relative, for thousands of miles. So naturally, when the chips were down, his crew would come first; he would never willingly leave them in the hands of a stranger.

In the cookhouse she gravitated, like a pin to a magnet, towards the table where Kate, Mo and Jen sat. She gave them what she thought was a cheerful smile, but there must have been something in her face which told its own story, for as she sat down Kate spoke at once, her eyes anxious. 'What's up? I thought you said Luke wasn't flying last night? God, girl, you're white as a sheet. Has he landed yet?'

'He flew last night and no, he hasn't landed yet,' she said wearily. 'I spoke to some chap . . . I didn't recognise the voice . . . who said that they'd put a young fellow on to fly Bouncing Betty, a young fellow who'd only had three months' experience. So when Luke turned up, all bright-eyed and bushy-tailed from his leave, his squadron leader asked him if he'd fly Betty instead of the new chap. And – and he'd not landed when I rang, or not at East Wretham at any rate. The bloke I talked to said another bomber had landed in Kent, so I suppose . . .' Her voice trailed away.

Jen leaned over and gave Rose's shoulder a comforting squeeze. 'Think of the gale. It's enough to blow anyone off course,' she said briskly. 'You stay where you are and I'll fetch you some brekker; got your irons?'

Dumbly, Rose handed her cutlery over, though she said that she knew she would be unable to eat a thing. 'Still, tea would be nice,' she admitted. And presently, with a large pile of scrambled egg and a small piece of bacon before her, she found that she was ravenously hungry and cleared the plate, as well as drinking two cups of tea.

While she ate the girls chatted, making suggestions as to how Luke might have got down perfectly safely, either on another airfield, or possibly on his own, though since her phone call, of course. Rose knew that this was an attempt to keep her spirits up, but she appreciated it none the less and went out to work still feeling worried, but determined to put a good face on it. Today she was driving the Winco up to Lincolnshire where he would be part of a large group watching an experimental aircraft giving a display of its powers. She might ring East Wretham from there, because she would not be wanted whilst the trials were being performed. Usually the Winco, a pleasant fair-haired man in his forties, with a neat little toothbrush moustache and humorous grey eyes, told her to go to the cookhouse for a meal and then to take a good book into the mess and amuse herself until he called for her, but today, Rose thought, she would simply have to keep telephoning East Wretham until someone could give her news. That it might be bad news, she did not dare contemplate.

By four o'clock that afternoon, Rose imagined that every officer on East Wretham airfield must be heartily sick of the sound of her voice. She contemplated going for a walk along the perimeter but knew, the moment she did so, that she would be called on the tannoy to take the Winco home, so stayed where she was. I'll have one last go, she told herself, as the clock hands crept slowly round to half past four. The wind had died down earlier than the Met Office had anticipated, but there were stories coming in from all over East Anglia – barns, sheds and even roofs blown away, trees uprooted and hedges battered, crops ruined and telephone wires torn down – so Rose convinced herself that there was still a chance that Luke, and Bouncing Betty, had landed safely somewhere in England. Because of the chaotic conditions, he might be unable to get in touch with his own station, might even now be crossing the country on public transport, not dreaming that she even knew he had been flying because, after all, he had still been on leave and she might have been too busy to telephone his mess until quite late that evening.

But at half past four, the phone was answered by Chubby Davies, who flew a Wellington bomber, and was a member of Luke's squadron. Rose had met him a couple of times and greeted him as cheerfully as she could, asking for news of Luke. If he had known her better, if he had realised that the relationship between herself and Luke had deepened into something more than casual friendship, he might have answered her less frankly. As it was, he said quite breezily: 'Shot down I'm afraid, old girl; saw it myself. But they all got out – I counted the parachutes – and they were over open country, so they ought to be okay.'

'Shot down?' Rose quavered, her voice rising, despite her determination to stay calm. 'Oh, Chubby, was anyone injured? Did you . . . did you . . .'

'Well, they weren't really shot down; a Ju88 came at them but what went wrong I don't know, because he crashed straight into them. We hung about to make sure no one tried to shoot them up and we saw the kite hit the ground and burst into flames some way from where the crew baled out. They were lucky really,' he added, in a ruminative tone. 'Bouncing Betty was a goner from the time the Junkers hit her, but she didn't burst into flame, or break up, until she hit the ground, so the crew were able to bale out all right. And I think her engines couldn't have packed up either, because she went down in a long glide and that means that the Germans will look for them a good few miles from where they'll actually have landed. So maybe, even now, they're making their way back to England. England, home and beauty,' he added, sounding almost envious, as though he himself would have enjoyed such a trek.

For Rose, however, it was a different matter. She tried to tell herself that since there had apparently been no exchange of fire, Luke would have landed safely, unwounded and perhaps even eager to pit his wits against the enemy and get home – or at least to a neutral country – before he was captured, but it was uphill work. Hideous pictures kept appearing before her inner eye. Stories of English bomber crews parachuting safely to earth only to be torn to pieces by an angry mob, or of men landing in icy seas or lakes and dying of exposure, filled her mind. When she was called over the tannoy, and drove her staff car across to where the Winco waited, her mind was so full of horrors that she could scarcely answer his cheerful questions as to how she had spent the day, and very soon began answering so completely at random that the Wing Commander guessed something was up.

'I'm afraid you've had bad news, corporal,' he said quietly, after they had travelled a dozen miles in almost complete silence. 'Do you want to talk about it? Is it your young man?'

'Yes,' Rose said, after a moment. 'He flies a Wimpey – a Wellington, I mean – from East Wretham airfield. He was over Germany last night and had turned for home when a Ju88 flew into him. Flight Lieutenant Davies watched them all bale out and said all the 'chutes opened, so he hung round to make sure they weren't shot up, and said they all got safely to the ground. Only – only I can't help worrying. You hear such awful stories and – and Luke was on leave, he shouldn't have been flying at all . . .'

Despite her resolve, Rose's eyes had filled with tears, blurring her vision of the road ahead. The Winco obviously realised this for he told her to pull in at the next gateway, and when the car was stationary he produced a large, pale blue handkerchief and handed it to her, telling her to have a good cry and then to mop her eyes and blow her nose, and remind herself that her young man had been most awfully lucky to get down safely and would undoubtedly return to her as soon as he was able. 'And you can't spend the rest of the war worrying about what might never happen,' he told her, 'because I remember you telling me, when you first started driving me, that you had been making uniforms for the forces but decided that that was not sufficient, so in order to help the war effort even more you joined the WAAF.' He grinned across at her, his funny little moustache tilted up at the corners. 'So you see, you must put your worries to the back of your mind, say a prayer for him night and morning, and in between, concentrate on your job. It'll be hard, I know that, but you're a brave young woman, and a darned good driver and I don't mean to lose you. All right?'

Rose gave a watery sniff, put the handkerchief away in her pocket, promising to let him have it back when she had laundered it, and started the car. 'I know you're right,' she said in a subdued tone. 'Other girls have worse problems, but they keep cheerful. And – and thank you, sir, for being so – so understanding. I'll remember what you've said.'

The watery-eyed peasant did not shoot Luke, largely because the rifle was not loaded, but also because before he could do anything, Neville had burst out from the covering trees, causing the old man to drop his gun from fright. At this very moment, a lorry had come careering along the road, driven by a hard-faced young soldier. He saw the small drama being enacted by the roadside and pulled up with much dust and a screech of brakes and jumped down, calling something to the slightly older soldier in the passenger seat.

Neither had a word of English, but said: 'Engländer? Sprechen sie Deutsch?' and upon nods to the first question and head shakings to the second, promptly loaded both men into the back of the truck. The merest movement hurt Luke so much that he was unable to stifle a yelp of pain and then a great many groans, but this was all to the good, as it turned out, since the soldiers took them straight to the nearest civilian hospital, where, to Luke's amazement, he was greeted by a doctor who spoke excellent English, though with a strong Scottish accent.

'I took my medical degree in Edinburgh in 1936,' he said briefly. 'We're going to have to set that ankle before you can go on to a prisoner of war camp, but your friend has no business here. We will dispatch him as soon as we can find transport.'

Luke, lying on a stretcher, trying not to move a muscle, had a word with Neville before his friend was taken away. 'Get a message to Corporal Rose McAllister – she's based at Coltishall – and tell her I'm alive and in hospital; say I'll write just as soon as I'm able,' he said urgently. 'Tell her not to worry; I'll be just fine.'

Neville agreed to do so and shortly after that Luke was taken to the operating theatre and anaesthetised, coming round some time later to find his left leg in plaster from toes to knee and his right arm in a similar condition.

'You cracked the radius in your right forearm when you broke your ankle,' the doctor told him. 'But you're lucky, both injuries should mend without leaving you unduly incapacitated. And as soon as you're out of plaster you'll be joining your friend in the nearest POW camp.'

After that, there were all the formalities of being

taken prisoner, the filling in of forms, and so on. And a few weeks later, he was hustled from the hospital to an ancient army lorry and taken to the prisoner of war camp, where he found Neville, Phil and rear gunner Toby already gloomily ensconced, though they told him, as soon as they got him alone, that Brendan had not been taken so far as they knew. 'Lucky beggar will be back in England in a few weeks,' Neville said enviously. 'Oh well, I suppose the worst we'll have to suffer now is boredom. Unless we can think of a plan to break out, of course. There's an escape committee, but they haven't managed to spring anyone yet.'

'Well they aren't going to start with me,' Luke said firmly. 'My ankle still won't bear my weight and I don't imagine I'd get far on two sticks. What's the food like?'

'Basic,' Neville grunted, 'but there's Red Cross parcels; they're all right. And you can write home, of course.'

'Great! I wrote to my folks, and to Rose, from hospital, but God alone knows if the letters even got posted. Not one of the nurses spoke a word of English and they just said jah, jah, jah, and bustled off whenever I asked a question. So I'll write straight away; anyone got a sheet of paper and a pencil?'

'Hello, Rose, what's up?' Jen had intercepted Rose as she shot out of the mess, her face pink with excitement. Rose skidded to a halt and flung both arms round her friend, giving her a hard squeeze.

'He's alive! I've just had a letter from him,' she squeaked. 'He broke his ankle when he parachuted down, and they put him in a civilian hospital, which is why he wasn't reported as being a POW. But now his ankle is mended, and he's at the same camp as the rest of his crew. Oh, Jen, I'm so *happy*!'

Chapter Sixteen

1945

'Petal, Daisy! If you two girls don't get a move on, we're going to miss your mam's train. Well, I declare, anyone would think you didn't like parties.' Auntie Blodwen was shouting up the stairs and was presently rewarded by the sight of Petal and Daisy, in their best summer dresses, beginning to descend the flight. Blodwen noticed, with a little stab of anxiety, that both girls' faces wore that 'contained and sulky' look which seemed to come over them whenever their return to Liverpool was mentioned. She could understand it in a way – she loved the children as much as if they'd been her own, and knew she would miss them dreadfully when they went – but, as she frequently reminded them, Liverpool was only a few hours away on the train, and even if their mother was too busy to bring them to Wales, their Auntie Blod and Uncle Gwil would be quite happy to do the journey in reverse, to find out how they were.

It was now September, and though one could scarcely say things were returning to normal, everyone was getting used to the thought of living in a country at peace. There had been celebrations when the war in Europe had ended in May, more celebrations when the Japanese had accepted defeat on 14 August. The girls might have expected to go home then, except that they had no home to go to and their mother was still in the WAAF. But now she had said, in her last letter to the Williamses, that it was time for her small family to be together once more. She had been 'demobbed', as they called it, a couple of weeks ago and had found herself a job in an office in Liverpool's Renshaw Street, though what she did there she had not fully explained. Apparently, however, she was earning sufficient money to rent a tiny, tumbledown terraced house, not too far from her work, and thought that this would do for the family for the time being, at least.

The last time she had visited the farm had been in early August, when she had been full of excitement because Luke Nadolski had been told he would be repatriated to England, where he would be officially demobbed from the Royal Air Force. Rose had explained that the two of them meant to marry, but that Luke would probably go home first to see his parents and his brother, before returning to claim his bride.

Blodwen had felt a little doubtful when Rose had outlined this plan because she had heard of several cases where American servicemen had left British girlfriends, or even wives, behind whilst they returned to the States to be demobbed there. The wives and girlfriends had never heard from them again, and the United States Army had proved to be exceedingly tight-lipped over the whereabouts of such men. However, Rose had seemed so happy and confident that she had not voiced her fears, and now it appeared they had been groundless. Luke had come back and he and Rose meant to marry by special licence in St Peter's church in Ruthin, with the girls as bridesmaids, and Uncle Gwil to give her away.

Blodwen straightened the large ribbon bows in each girl's hair and checked their appearance. Yes, they looked neat and very pretty. Petal's hair was naturally wavy, but Blodwen had rolled up Daisy's darker locks in pipe cleaners the night before, and now curls bobbed on her shoulders.

Blodwen reached her own coat down from the back of the door and ushered the children into the yard where Dilys was waiting with the pony trap. Today was Tuesday and the wedding was fixed for Saturday so, in the time-honoured manner, Luke was to stay at the Castle Hotel, in the Square, until then. This delighted him, for he was intrigued by the old half-timbered houses, the narrow streets and the ambience of the small Welsh town. Luke had only returned to Britain a couple of days earlier, but Blodwen remembered him from his previous visits as a pleasant, easy-going young man and thought the children liked him, so why were they showing such glum faces? Blodwen had moved heaven and earth to produce pretty bridesmaid's dresses and had managed to acquire some parachute silk, which she had dyed to a beautiful shade of pale blue. The village dressmaker had made it up into two delightful dresses, but even that had not brought genuine smiles of pleasure to the children's faces. Blodwen felt a little impatient with them, had lectured them on how their mother deserved some happiness, had reminded them that they liked Luke, that they had been happy in Liverpool before the war and would undoubtedly be happy there again.

'Only once Luke has got a good job, I dare say you'll move into the country, or at least into the suburbs,' she had said comfortingly. 'Last time your mam came to stay, she was asking me about rearing chickens and pigs . . . all sorts. Just you wait, you'll find yourselves having a whale of a time and hardly missing the farm at all.'

Daisy had spoken then. 'It – it isn't just the farm,

or you, Auntie Blod,' she had mumbled. 'It's all our pals. People like my friend Phoebe, and – and Nicky. People who are staying here.'

'I've told you before, Liverpool isn't a million miles away,' Auntie Blod had said. 'You'll come back regular, I'm sure of it. Why, your mam knows how much you mean to us; she isn't going to take you away for ever.'

The girls had exchanged glances which Blodwen had been unable to interpret, but then Daisy had murmured that she was probably right and changed the subject.

Now, however, Blodwen hustled the girls into the pony trap and asked Dilys to have dinner on the table in an hour. 'Unless the train's very late we'll be back by then, and though Luke is staying in Ruthin I'm sure he'll come back here and have a meal with us,' she told her daughter. 'Still, perhaps it might be better if you stood the spuds to one side of the stove and moved the casserole from the main oven to the side one, because there's no denying that trains are a bit unreliable.' She beamed at her daughter. 'Oh, I do love a wedding, and since they're having the reception at the hotel, I'll be able to sit back and enjoy myself without having to worry about the food.'

''Bye, Mam, and don't worry about the dinner, I'll see to it,' Dilys called, as the trap rattled out of the yard.

Making their way along the lane, where already the nuts on the hazel trees were beginning to turn brown and the hedges were starred with hips and haws, Blodwen chatted to the girls about the wedding. Receiving only monosyllabic responses, she felt her annoyance returning. What was the matter with them? Could they possibly resent their mother's marriage? After all, they had had to live without her for the past few years, and had seemed to understand that she was doing her bit for her country but still loved them dearly. Blodwen glanced across at them and made a sudden decision. She pulled the pony trap on to the verge, slowed and stopped, then turned to stare accusingly at her passengers. 'Just what is the matter?' she demanded baldly. 'If you show your mam and Luke those long faces, you're going to make them very unhappy and I'm going to feel ashamed. It might seem to them as though I've tried to take your mam's place, and that I would never do. So far as you're concerned, I know your mam must always come first and that's fine by me. Now come along, and tell Auntie Blod why you're not even happy about being bridesmaids.'

Once more, the two girls exchanged glances, and rather to Blodwen's amusement first Petal and then Daisy gave a little nod before Daisy began to speak. 'Auntie Blod, they aren't just going to take us to Liverpool; it's only a rented house and Mam's giving it up at the end of the month. They're going to America, to the little town where Luke was brought up, and Mam says we've got to go with them, because we're only kids. Last time she came to stay, we begged and begged to be left behind, but she got so upset – she *cried*, Auntie Blod – that we had to give in and say we'd go, only – only we don't want to, not one bit. It's – it's such a long way, and so different! Oh, I know they speak the same language, but it truly is different. So you see, you won't be able to pop on the train to come and visit us, and we shan't be able to visit you. It may not be so bad for Petal because she's younger, but I'll be in a class with girls and boys of fifteen . . . oh, can't you understand? They'll have made all their friends and they'll only be in school for another year so they're not likely to accept me, a stranger . . . *can* you understand, Auntie Blod? Mam couldn't – or wouldn't – she said I was being foolish and would soon have a heap of friends, and probably an interesting job as well. Only – only it's not what I want! I shall hate it, I know I will!'

Auntie Blodwen stared from face to face, feeling the heat creep up into her cheeks. I must have been mad not to have realised, she thought. Of course he'll want to take them back to his own place, his own country, and Rose will want it too. She had a pretty hard life before the war, what with that bully of a husband and that dreadful damp little house, and no job worth speaking of until the war came along. But it's different for the girls; they've had a wonderful country childhood, and they've made a good life for themselves. Of course they love their mother and want to be with her, but they're torn. I wonder why Rose never said that they would be going to the States? But of course, she took it for granted that I would guess the farm she talked about couldn't possibly be in Liverpool. And the girls said nothing because they knew that Gwil and I would be upset, because there's no denying, we're mortal fond of them and not getting any younger. In fact, we'll probably never see them again, as they'll be starting new lives and, whether they know it or not, we'll simply become a part of their past, as they will become a part of ours.

But she could not say this to the children, of course. For a moment, she wondered how she could make it more bearable for them, then decided the honest approach was best, though she chose her words with great care. 'I expect you must have guessed, my loves, that I had no idea your mam was going to take you so far away,' she said, trying to keep the quiver out of her voice. 'But I suppose I didn't want to face up to losing you quite so soon. It *is* hard on you, but just think for a moment; think what life has been like for your mam, not just during the war, not just while Luke was a POW, but for many years before that. When she was little more than a girl herself, she married a man who – who turned out to be thoroughly unsuitable; isn't that right now?'

Both girls nodded vehemently. 'He were a beast and a bully,' Daisy said forthrightly. 'He hit our mam – oh, often and often. We hated him, didn't we, Petal?'

Petal nodded until her curls bobbed, but both children kept their eyes fixed on Blodwen's face.

'Right. So your mam had to set out to bring her children up, not just without any help from her husband, but with actual hindrance. He drank the money she earned when he was on leave – and towards the end he attacked you, didn't he, Daisy?'

More nods, and Blodwen saw, with some distress, that Petal's eyes had filled with tears. 'Yes, he pulled Daisy's hair out by the roots and smacked her about, and I wanted to kill him,' she said, in a small, choking voice. 'I prayed to God to get him killed, and when He did – get him killed, I mean – I wished I'd just prayed to gerr'im sent away. I didn't *mean* him to be dead, but I were too little to protect Mam and Daisy, so I guess God did the right thing, after all.'

Blodwen was appalled by the weight of guilt which Petal must have carried, but realised that the child had very sensibly decided that her father's death had been God's decision, not her own. So she smiled at Petal and patted her hand before resuming. 'Well, what I'm trying to say is that your mam has walked a long and lonely road for a great many years but now she's going to have a loving partner to walk with her. Luke is a good man, gentle, generous and full of humour. He'll make her very happy and take from her shoulders the burdens which must have seemed so heavy. But, fynwy fechan i, your mam couldn't be happy in America, knowing that you had been left behind in Britain; you are her real family, the only family she's got, apart from Aunt Selina, since Uncle Frank died. So you see, for your mam's sake, you've got to make the best of America. They call it the land of opportunity and I'm sure it is; you'll have chances there that you'd never have here because we're struggling just to keep our chins above the flood, whereas over there, the war didn't touch them. They know nothing about rationing, or air raids, or being homeless.' She smiled brightly at them. 'So now, my dear ones, you have a choice. You can give something back to your mother for all that she's done for you; you can show her happy, glowing faces and be sweet to Luke and look forward, and not back. Or you can be mean and miserable and ruin her wedding day, and go to America complaining every inch of the way. Which is it to be?'

The girls once more exchanged glances, but this time, to Blodwen's relief, smiles hovered on their mouths. 'We'll be happy and make Mam happy – and Luke,' Petal said.

'Yes, we'll do that. And when we get there, we'll make the best of it,' Daisy added, with decision. 'Luke *is* nice and we don't really want to make anyone unhappy. But I'm telling you, Auntie Blod, the moment I'm old enough, I'm going to come back. Don't you think I shan't, because I shall. You haven't seen the last of me and nor has Ty Siriol.'

Auntie Blod leaned forward and gathered both girls in her arms, and there was a lot of hugging and kissing, and a little bit of crying, before she set the pony in motion once more.

'You are both good and loving girls,' Auntie Blod told them fondly, as she steered the pony out of the lane and on to the main road. 'I'm truly proud of you and I'm sure you will come back one day.'

It was now June 1946 and Daisy stood in the window of the small bedroom she shared with Petal, looking out over the endless acres of waving corn. She had had eight months to grow used to her new life but was finding it harder with each day that passed. Her bedroom faced what the Nadolskis called a back yard and the McAllisters called a garden, which was fortunate really, because the bedroom Rose and Luke shared faced the front, which overlooked the main road. What Daisy called the garage – and the other kids called the filling station – was to the left of the house, and the General Store, where Rose now worked, was to the right. Consequently, the front bedrooms were quite noisy for there was a good deal of traffic on the road and, of course, the garage was a noisy place in itself. Cars came in and out for repairs and bodywork to be done, and the mechanics shouted to one another, revved engines, hammered out dents in mudguards and fenders, and generally made a great deal of noise.

The new car showroom which Mr Nadolski had started shortly before Luke left was on the far side of the garage. Luke's brother Max had been in charge of it ever since its inception and was, Daisy thought, rather resentful than otherwise of his brother's joining the firm. Daisy knew that Luke and her mother were eager to move on, to start a business of their own which would pay them sufficiently well to rent a place of their own, too. The Nadolski house had never been intended for occupancy by so many people.

Luke's parents had been welcoming enough when the McAllisters had first arrived, had begged Daisy and Petal to call them Gran and Grandpop, as Max's children did, but Daisy knew that such tolerance could not last. The strain of having four extra bodies in a house which already contained the old couple, Max and his wife Bonnie, and their sons Dexter and Joel – stupid names – would have tried the patience of a saint, for though the house was roomy enough for the six people who had inhabited it, it was definitely cramped for ten. Upstairs, there were four bedrooms and a boxroom; one for old Mr and Mrs Nadolski, one for Max and Bonnie, one for Rose and Luke and one for Dexter and Joel. That left the boxroom for Daisy and Petal, which suited them well enough. No, the trouble came downstairs, where there was a large kitchen, a parlour which was seldom used, a small and functional bathroom and what Bonnie and Max referred to as 'our livin' room'. When Luke, Rose and the girls had first moved in, they had been told to consider the parlour as their own, but soon realised that this plan would simply never work. Mrs Nadolski had spent much time and thought on the furnishing and decorations in the parlour and the room was crowded with knick-knacks, ornaments, fancy furniture and many pictures. Because of this, Luke and Rose usually sat in the kitchen, as did everyone else in the family, for Bonnie and Max had formed the habit of letting Dexter and Joel and their schoolfriends use the living room whilst they themselves joined their parents in the kitchen. Often, the boys wandered into the kitchen as well, in search of food and a chat, or simply drawn by a need for company.

Daisy sometimes felt as if the house was pressing

in on her, as if she had no individual identity any more. Life had been so different at Ty Siriol, yet when she thought about it, the Williamses had mostly lived in the kitchen, where the farmhands had joined them at mealtimes. Thinking it over, she decided that it was the unspoken criticism from Max, Bonnie, and Gran and Grandpop which made her feel constantly unwanted. She did not blame them for this; ten people into one house simply would not go – she remembered Auntie Blod's saying about quarts into pint pots – and hard though everyone tried to give each other space, it was impossible.

Daisy sighed and sat down on the bed, getting out her pencil and the block of writing paper, and preparing to start her letters home. She wrote to Auntie Blod and Uncle Gwil once a month, and Nicky Bostock every week. In the early days, she had settled down at the kitchen table to write her letters, but the snide remarks passed by Max and his wife, and the fact that Luke's parents constantly peered over her shoulder and actually read bits of her letters aloud to one another, had speedily driven her to seek refuge in her own tiny room. There was no space for a table or a chair up here, but she preferred writing in peace to the relative comfort of the kitchen. What was more, though her letters to the Williamses were as cheerful as she could make them, she was completely frank with Nick. She told him that the lessons at school were so different that she was constantly made to look foolish, that the other pupils had formed friendships and alliances at an early age and had no interest in her, an outsider, and that to top it all she did not like the food, which was so different from the sorts of things they ate back home. She was being made to have the rest of this year in school, but even when she left, things would not be very much better since it was taken for granted that she would work in the General Store, releasing Rose either to take a job in the small town or to help her husband and brother-in-law in the new car showroom.

Auntie Blod was a good correspondent and wrote regularly – long, interesting letters, full of details about the farm, the countryside and the friends Daisy and Petal had made, but unfortunately Nick, who was so loquacious in person, hardly seemed able to string a dozen words together on paper and despite Daisy's weekly letters to him, she had only received three replies in six months.

It was a pity, of course, because Daisy longed to know every detail of Nick's life in Ruthin for, during her last months at the farm, she and Nick had grown closer and closer. Nick was eighteen now and a deep and loving friendship had grown between them. They had planned all sorts of things, had been so sure of their shared future, that Daisy had actually applied for a summer job in Ruthin, at a shop only a few doors away from Foley's.

When she had at last admitted to herself that Rose would go to America, and take her children with her, Daisy had also had to tell Nick and thought she would never forget the stricken look in his eyes, nor the way the colour had drained from his face.

'But she can't do that,' he had muttered. 'You and me, Daisy, we – we're going to be together, ain't we? I mean, when we're grown up – really grown up – we'll probably get married, won't we? If you get that job in the flower shop, we'll be able to see each other whilst we're working, as well as in the evenings. Oh, Daisy, she can't take you away from me!'

But she had, of course. Children have no rights,

Daisy told herself bitterly now, painstakingly beginning to write to the Williamses, telling them all the small events which had happened over the past month. Petal was doing well in school and had made several friends, though she missed her own place just as badly as Daisy did. But she was lucky in that Dexter was in her class at school and championed her when the others mocked her British accent, or thought her stupid because she knew nothing of American history or literature.

Daisy was still at it when she heard the thump of footsteps on the stairs and the door burst open. Daisy automatically turned her notepaper face down but she need not have worried. It was Rose, looking flushed and excited. She swooped on Daisy, giving her a big hug and half lifting her off the bed. 'It's happened at last, Daisy darling! Luke's got a job – nothing to do with car showrooms – it's the sort of job he's always wanted, and the money's awfully good; we shall be able to rent a decent place of our own. It's a fair way from here, of course, which will mean poor Petal will have to change schools, but you're almost at the end of your time in education and we'll be living pretty near a big city, so you'll have a much wider choice of jobs.'

Daisy responded to her mother with a beam and a hard hug, but said cautiously: 'Is it a flying job, Mam? I know he said that America is full of commercial airports, but I didn't know there was one near here.'

'It isn't near here; I told you, it's a hundred miles or more away,' Rose said. 'But more 'n' more towns and cities over here are taking to commercial airways and Luke's had so much experience, both as a pilot and in training others, that I was sure he'd find something – and he has. Oh, Daisy, darling, we're so happy; can you be happy for us?'

'I'm happy for me as well,' Daisy said fervently. 'And you'll be making a lot of other people happy too, Mam, because no matter how much they pretend, Max and Bonnie are dying to see the back of us.' She did not add that old Mr and Mrs Nadolski would feel the same, because it seemed unkind, though she knew it was true. Luke's parents were old, and old people don't like the even tenor of their lives disturbed. And we have disturbed them, just by being here, even though we've done our best to fit in, Daisy told herself. Of course they had done their best, particularly Mam and Luke, but the truth was, a quart into a pint pot doesn't go. 'When do we leave?'

Rose gave her another hug. 'In a fortnight,' she said exuberantly. 'Luke's already got us temporary accommodation – a flat over a greengrocer's shop – just until we find somewhere better. But oh, Daisy love, it will be all ours! We'll make our own meals and have baths whenever we want to, and come and go as we like. As I said, Luke's salary will be princely compared with . . .' she looked guilty and lowered her voice to a conspiratorial whisper, 'compared with what Max pays him now, I mean – but I'll get a job as soon as we're settled in, and you'll be in work as well, before we know it. Oh, my love, I know how hard it's been for you, how hard it's been for all of us, but that's all over now. Life is going to be so good.'

Daisy returned her mother's beaming smile. 'Have you told Petal yet?' she asked. 'She won't mind about changing school again, Mam – you know Petal, she loves change, and new people, new places. And I'll get a job just as soon as I can, because . . . well, because there are things I want to save up for, and I can't do that – save, I mean – on the money Luke's mam pays me for working at the store weekends.'

'No, I haven't told Petal yet because she's gone off somewhere with Dexter, but I thought you might tell her for me.' She pulled a face, though her eyes were still shining. 'Luke's asked me to break the news to his mum and dad – he's telling Max and Bonnie – but I wanted you to be the first to know.'

'They'll pretend to be awfully sad and complain about us leaving,' Daisy said wisely. 'They'll say you're taking their boy away before they've had a chance to get to know him again – and their grandchildren, of course. But they won't mean it; it'll be . . . what's it called . . . lip service. In their hearts, they'll be glad as glad.'

'And so they should be, because Luke isn't happy working for Max or dealing with new cars, and they both know it,' Rose said, with her hand already on the doorknob. 'You go and find Petal, darling, and by the time you get back, everyone will know.'

'Well, Rose, honey, it's all very well to say Luke hankers after flying, but he come back here willin' enough, he's settled in nicely, he and his brother is good friends . . . I guess it's kinda hard on you not having a place of your own but it's kinda hard on Father and me. You're an ambitious woman – I dare say there's nothing wrong in that – but Father and me ain't gettin' no younger and you're tekkin' our boy away after only eight months. I'm sure Father feels, same as I do, that we were just gettin' to know our Luke after all them years when he were fightin' for your country, an' now you're tekkin' him away.'

Rose suppressed a smile; Daisy was a bright kid and had anticipated exactly what old Mrs Nadolski would say, but it would never do to let her amusement show, so she said gently: 'I'm so sorry, Mother, but it's only a hundred miles away and Luke will come home often, I'm sure he will. And you know Max has said, several times, that he managed the showroom alone without any trouble during the war, so though he may miss Luke as a brother, I don't think he'll miss him in the saleroom. Luke has often told me how good Max is with customers and added that he himself simply doesn't have the same . . . knack as Max for picking out the right vehicle for each person. But he's an excellent pilot, Mother, and isn't it better that he should be in a job he loves and excels at rather than one he doesn't really enjoy?'

But Mrs Nadolski could not agree and continued to clutch her grievance to her bosom, and to blame Rose – though obliquely – for the forthcoming change, despite the bright smiles on the faces of Max and Bonnie, and her own husband's oft repeated remark that it waren't right to stand in the way of young folks, even if it did seem that their boy had changed and grown to think less of his family whilst in England.

Rose longed to point out that Luke's family now consisted of herself and her daughters, but did not do so. In a fortnight, you'll be away from them and in your own place, she reminded herself. You'll never again have to put up with Bonnie's covert jealousy and spiteful remarks, or your mother-in-law's whining, or Max's patronising air when he talks to Luke as though he were the wiser brother, when he, Max, never even went to High School. Only another fortnight and we'll be free as birds; I can put up with anything for two little weeks.

When Luke came home that evening, they took themselves off for a long walk so that Luke might tell her all about his new job and the city which the airport served. He made no pretence of being anything but jubilant over leaving his parents' house, though he admitted it had been good of them to take the family in. 'The whole thing's been my fault, in a way,' he said, as they turned for home once more. 'I meant to come home for a couple of weeks, just to see how things stood, and then I meant to get a job – any job – in another town, so that we could start our new lives as a family. But I kinda got drawn into the car business and Max was so reluctant when I wanted time off for interviews . . .' He sighed and bent his head to kiss Rose's neck, just beneath her ear. 'But it's almost over now and I guess having us at home for eight months means my parents have got to know you and the girls in a way which wouldn't have been possible if we'd only stayed a fortnight.'

Rose agreed, though she added with a chuckle that, possibly, this had not done much to improve relations between the parties concerned. 'But it doesn't matter, because when we really do have a place of our own, we can invite them over and I can cook a proper meal and serve it nicely, and show your mam that the English are just as domesticated as the Americans,' she told him. 'And there's one other good thing; even if the walls in the apartment over the greengrocer's shop are as thin as the ones in your parents' house, it won't be as – as embarrassing to have a little cuddle, as it has been these last eight months.'

Luke put both arms round her and gave her an enormous hug. 'Once we're settled, I'd like us to have at least one baby which is part of both of us,' he said, almost tentatively. 'I've never mentioned it before, because to add another soul to my parents' house would have been unthinkable, but . . . well, how do you feel, Rosie? Do you hate the thought of starting all over again with diapers and bottles and baby gear? Only the girls are growing up; Daisy wil be out in the big world before you know it. And I really like kids.'

'I like them too and I'd love to make a baby with you, darling Luke,' Rose said, carrying his hand to her lips and planting a kiss on the palm. 'As soon as we're settled, we'll make it our first priority.' She twinkled up at him. 'I'll put it in my diary when I get back tonight. One baby for Mr and Mrs Luke Nadolski; shall I order a boy or a girl?'

Laughing, and still entwined, they entered the house and shut the door behind them.

Daisy sat in the window seat of her very own bedroom, looking out at the wintry scene in the garden below. They had been in their new home for nearly two months now, for they had left the apartment over the greengrocer's shop as soon as Luke had seen the pleasant old timber house on the outskirts of the city and had managed to arrange a bank loan. It was a big, old house, and for the first time in her life, Daisy had a room of her own. She also had a job in the offices of a large department store in the city and was beginning, though cautiously, to make friends. And today she had had a letter from Nick, a proper letter with proper news, and though ill-spelt and badly written, it had brought back to Daisy's mind once more how much she longed to be back in Britain and how desperately she missed Nick.

She had always meant to go home but had never really considered how she would do so. Buses, trains, ships, planes – she guessed she would need to employ most of them to get back to Ruthin and Nick. But now that she had a job, all things were possible. She would save up, she vowed, putting away every spare cent, and perhaps by as early as the following summer she would be able to begin to plan her journey. Sitting on the window seat she could see, by craning her neck, the long, winding road which would be the first step towards home and Nicky, for she still thought of Britain as her home and America merely as a staging post.

Now, in her mind's eye, she seemed to hover above the road and to see, trudging along it, her own small figure. What was it Auntie Blod had said when she had talked to them about Rose's life? She had said that Rose had walked a long and lonely road but that in Luke she had found the perfect partner to walk with her . . . something like that, anyway. Well, she, Daisy, would soon be setting out on a long road, and maybe it would be a lonely one, but at the end of it there would be Nick. In her mind, she saw the little grey town nestling in the soft Welsh hills, as an eagle or a bird of prey would see it, and her imagination circled and dropped lower, lower, lower, until she could see St Peter's Square and Nick with his arms held out to her, and the familiar, crooked grin on his face.

Sighing, she turned back into her room once more. She thought of the miles and miles which separated her from New York, where she could perhaps get a job on a liner bound for Liverpool; then there were the miles and miles of ocean to be crossed, and more miles before she arrived at her destination. Yes, indeed, it would be a long and lonely road, but she would do it. Nick would wait.

Daisy smiled to herself and turned to go downstairs to help Rose prepare the evening meal.